INTIMATE INSTRUCTION

Emma, normally a cool, proud blonde, broke under the pressure of her fearful dread and started to beg. 'Don't, please –'

'Silence, bitch, although your whining is music to my ears.' The gym mistress remounted the wall bars.

'I didn't mean to –'

'I said silence,' Marion grunted, her face inches away in the darkness from her victim's.

Emma drew back from the warm breath of her bully.

'A gag, I think. Better to do this in silence. Don't want everyone woken up by your squeals, do we, hmm?'

INTIMATE INSTRUCTION

Arabella Knight

This book is a work of fiction.
In real life, make sure you practise safe sex.

First published in 2001 by
Nexus
Thames Wharf Studios
Rainville Road
London W6 9HA

www.nexus-books.co.uk

Typeset by TW Typesetting, Plymouth, Devon

Printed and bound by
Cox & Wyman Ltd, Reading, Berks

ISBN 0 352 33618 8

One

In the brilliant pool of light, the nude covered her breasts, her pink nipples disappearing beneath scarlet fingernails.

'No, don't squash 'em,' complained a voice from the encircling darkness.

The nude relaxed, her angled elbows slackening as she palmed her breasts gently, then cupped them tenderly, dragging her thumbnails to each firm little nipple.

'Still too cheesy. Lose the tits. Put a polo neck on. White. No. Black.'

Emma blinked as a black, stretchy polo neck pullover was tossed out of the darkness into the blaze of light. She continued to gaze steadily, her grey eyes narrowing, as the nude struggled into her pullover, tugging down the thin sheath across her trapped, swollen bosom. No, Emma suddenly realised. Not nude. The model's long, slender legs spangled as the fifteen-denier flesh-coloured tights flashed beneath the fierce spot lights.

'Ready to shoot. Hold it.'

Silence, broken only by the unbroken whirr of the SLR and soft grunts from the photographer.

'Left knee up. More.'

The girl obeyed. The camera devoured her.

'OK. Next, we'll do the – What's next on this shoot?' He snapped his fingers in the darkness. They cracked like an unseen whip. Emma shuddered.

'Pearl glaze,' a woman answered calmly.

'Pearl glaze,' he barked.

1

Emma watched the young model scamper off set, return and in less than fifty seconds in the glossy, grey tights. The model turned, peeled her tights down over her buttocks, and modestly patted her pubic bush into place. The bottom, its heavy cheeks resting on the curled elasticated waistband, wobbled as she patted her pubis.

'Need a comb?' the photographer barked sarcastically.

Emma winced. Nailing him would be a pleasure.

'Hurry up,' he snapped. 'I told the agency that you girls should come shaved.'

Emma sat perfectly still, her presence at the shoot still unobserved. The darkness gave her perfect cover and, a bonus, the psychological edge on her victim.

Getting in to the studio had been easy. Security had been nothing sterner than a work-experience kid gobbling yoghurt at the front desk. Emma, clutching her steel clipboard and mobile, had deliberately dressed for the occasion. The dizzy-blonde-something-in-the-media look. Today was a product shoot for a new range of tights and stockings so it was easy to look the bizz. With her Ray-bans pushed up into her shaggy blonde mane, silver-pink lipstick, beige silk jacket flapping open to reveal a deeply unbuttoned blouse, black pencil skirt and pink, strappy shoes, she had had no problems with gullible little Miss Yoghurt.

'Next. What's next?'

'Smoke,' the photographer's assistant replied.

The model skipped out of the inky darkness into the blaze of lights.

'Profile.'

She turned. Emma's throat constricted suddenly in response to the ripe swell of the proffered buttocks.

'Bottom out more. Better. Hold it.' The SLR went to work for twenty three seconds. 'Face me. Hold it. Turn, face away.'

Like a puppet obeying the pull of invisible strings, the beautiful girl twisted and turned. The spots on the overhead rig died. Only one remained ablaze, piercing down. It pinned the semi-nude mercilessly, like a butterfly

2

displayed for the private pleasure of some perverse collector.

More sharp commands were barked. The writhing girl responded, spreading her lithe, glossy legs and sheen-sculpted buttocks to the SLR's hungry eye.

'Seam shot. Thighs together. Tighter. Bend over. More. Come on, get it up. Like you're going to get the cane.'

The stretchy, smoke-hued nylon glistened as the bending girl's superbly rounded buttocks burgeoned. Emma's mouth dried – she swallowed softly as she glimpsed the deep shadow of the slightly parted cleft between the submissive cheeks.

'Last one. Late-night something?' he hazarded.

'Just-past-midnight,' the assistant corrected patiently.

'Whatever.'

Emma knew that she would have to judge the moment carefully. You only got one go. Like a lioness at the evening watering-hole. Timing the strike was critical. Catch them off guard – the best kills were made on unsuspecting prey. After the photo-shoot, she would approach him out of the darkness and pounce. And she would really enjoy it.

The young model, legs now bare – Emma could just make out the luxuriously thick pubic bush – didn't even bother to tug down the hem of her black polo neck sweater. Over in the far corner of the studio, silhouetted against the blue light of a blank video screen, she ate thin slices of quiche and drank ice cold milk straight from the carton.

In her pool of pure white light, a second model, a pony-tailed blonde, spread her alluringly nylon-stockinged legs wide. Emma gulped as she glimpsed the naked breasts, thrusting proudly. The pony-tailed blonde drummed her fingertips into the darker bands of her stocking tops.

The photographer lowered his SLR. Again, he punctuated his terse words with snapping fingers. 'Don't you need –' He ignored the model and barked into the darkness. 'Doesn't she have to wear a thingummy? A suspender-belt?'

'Product story-board says not. They're self-support,' the assistant replied, her voice cool and calm.

'OK. Self-support. Hands on pussy, girl. These are promo pix for wifey. Catalogue shopping, not top-shelf stuff for her bloke.'

The pony-tail swished as the model giggled and placed her hands, palms inwards, over the pubic mound.

'Get her into a bloody blouse, someone. White. And panties. Red silk.'

'Skip the blouse. Waist, hips and below,' the assistant interpreted.

'OK. Waistline shot it is. Panties, please. Red silk.'

'White. Cotton.' The voice of the assistant was stern as she over-ruled the photographer.

'Colour?' he barked resentfully, as the model wriggled into a pair of white cotton panties.

'Honey-blonde,' the assistant advised.

'Better give me an amber filter then. Ready? Show me the seams.'

Emma held her breath as the pony-tailed model turned, drew her long legs together and clamped her thighs tightly. Below, the heels kissed. Above, the soft, pantied buttocks wobbled. The SLR whirred into work.

'Next?'

'Deep Venus,' answered the omniscient assistant.

'What the hell's –'

'Dark blue.'

'OK. Dark blue. Kill those white spots and give me an Oxford.'

Emma tensed. The shoot would be over soon. Nearly finished – then she would do what she had come to do. Brief and brutal. There was no other way. She checked her watch. Twelve ten. She was already behind schedule. She undid another button and fingered her Josef Lenhik pen, twisting the gold and black veined barrel buried between the bulging curves of her cleavage. Pocketless, it was the only place for a girl to park her pen.

The spots on the overhead rig died and the neon strips flickered on. Both young models, thigh to thigh in front of the blank blue screen, shivered as they wolfed the remains of the quiche.

Wait for it. Not yet. The lioness bided her time. She was looking for a quick, clean kill. Nothing messy. And, Emma thought, she'd wait until that super-efficient assistant was off the scene.

Now. Emma slipped down silently from her leather-topped stool and strode casually towards her victim. He was fiddling with his light meter. He turned, his tired eyes flickering appraisingly, taking in the metal clipboard, the mobile, the easy stride. He grinned. Good. She had taken him in.

'You the agency? Coffee?' he asked, extending a welcoming hand.

She snapped the paperwork from her metal clipboard and thrust it at him. 'NVK Partnership. That's your third default notice. So now it's Clerkenwell Court, ten thirty, Wednesday the twelfth. Be there.'

Easy meat. A quick, clean kill.

Emma was proud of The Beast. Difficult to park, expensive to service and only a scandalous nineteen mpg – but she loved her black Jaguar Mk II. Loved the sleek lines of her waxed flanks. Loved her voluptuously rounded behind. And adored everything up front, beyond the rim of the polished steering wheel – bold, thrusting curves from which a tiny silver cat sprang, its leap fixed in freeze frame.

But The Beast was hopeless on a busy Friday afternoon, at five to one on the Embankment. She dragged the hand brake on, stuck behind a large green tourist coach with Austrian plates. Seemed to be full of schoolkids.

Emma's thoughts returned – very briefly – to the studio. It all felt a bit dodgy. The elaborate lighting rig could have served a small theatre. Video facilities and studded silver kit boxes, like a small film set. Emma suspected that the boxes were empty. And that huge display of French roses perfuming the desk of the idle receptionist. A real whiff of insolvency there. She shrugged it all off. Just another wannabe with an SLR and a nineteen thousand unpaid loan. NVK had guys like him for breakfast every day. Freshly squeezed.

Emma suddenly grinned. She was glad he had been a prick. It made it easier, more satisfying. She blinked her latest victim out of her memory. Job done.

Where the hell had he come from? Emma cursed. A taxi had just tucked itself in between The Beast and the green Austrian coach in front. Easing off the hand brake, Emma concentrated on the traffic. One more set of papers to serve. She glanced down at the metal clipboard. Canada Dock. Blackfriars would be solid so she planned to cross the river at Southwark Bridge.

Emma was bored, but didn't know it. Bored and frustrated. Working for NVK paid for The Beast and her South Ken flat. Studio, but with the coveted SW7 postcode. Emma knew, deep down, she wasn't a lioness at the water-hole. Tracking down and cornering these losers was not big game. More like a tabby taking goldfish from next door's ornamental pool.

The Thames was fat and swollen after the heavy winter rains. Under a pale February sun, the river looked brown and bloated. Crossing it, she took a sharp left into Tooley Street. The Mk II growled as it accelerated along Jamaica Road. Ahead, the dense tower blocks of Rotherhithe seemed to be shouldering each other for space. She drew up outside an eight-til-late newagents, reached over and picked up her hold-all from the back seat.

Inside the shop, she bought several unwanted magazines before pantomiming her need for a loo. The smiling Asian woman showed Emma through a coloured bead curtain into the back. There was a little golden elephant with green glass eyes in the loo. Emma quick-changed out of her 'media' togs into a Miss VAT tailored trouser suit. The Asian shopkeeper followed Emma to the door, murmuring her amazement in Urdu, and kept on staring until The Beast had disappeared down Jamaica Road, turning off into the maze of industrial units behind Canada Dock.

'Mr Hutchins? George Hutchins?'

The bloke lumbered with the warehouse full of Brazilian mahogany – and no takers – groaned. He should have bought into eco-friendly Scandinavian pine. Pale woods were in, Emma thought, deftly serving the default notice.

Mr George Hutchins cursed. Emma's trim suit, horn-rimmed specs and sensible shoes had fooled him. No one ever, ever says no to the boys or girls from the VAT. He had fallen for her ruse. Driving The Beast back into the City, Emma's thoughts briefly turned to arson. She grinned as she pictured George with his petrol-soaked rags. Another loser. And with his run of bad luck, the surplus mahogany probably wouldn't even burn.

Back at her desk, Emma felt suddenly drained. Team briefing at three. More incomprehensible management jargon to endure. She reviewed her Friday. She had been successful – if putting the financial boot into penniless corpses was success – and had met her targets.

NVK occupied three floors of an ugly seventies pile on the very edge of the City. Emma enjoyed a vista of Hackney's crazy sprawl. Her boss, a striped shirt, had a view of the Square Mile. Actionville, he called it. It was usually one-way traffic in the open plan office, with Emma going across to Striped Shirt's desk. Just before the team briefing, he came to hers. Leering.

'Supper, tonight?'

Emma was evasive. The other girls had warned her about his Pimlico lair – black satin sheets with handcuffs under the pillows. He sensed her lack of enthusiasm.

'Thought we could go through your six-monthly performance appraisal. Fine tune and tweak.'

Emma knew that it was no longer an invitation – it was now an ultimatum. She squirmed, aware of the lightly veiled threat behind the smiling eyes: eyes that did not gaze into her own but directly down at her breasts. She wriggled off the hook – a family celebration – but saw the anger in his face. Two minutes later, he was standing over Susie. Susie was so hot for promotion she'd probably do it down in the basement car park at five o'clock. Emma's eyes shone with resentment. She knew she'd just blown it. He could block her promotion into liability management and risk assessment – picking low-hanging fruit – and give Susie the plum job. Now, Emma realised, she would be stuck in credit consolidations.

The team briefing was scheduled to finish at four. It was already half past. Striped Shirt was bullish. All of Emma's contributions were pointedly rejected.

'Off topic, there,' he scorned.

Susie simpered her trite solutions to the problem-solving exercise.

'That takes us all to the bleeding edge. Good girl. Great to know you think outside the box.'

It went on like that til five thirty. Then Striped Shirt dropped his bombshell.

'Sorry, Emma.' He grinned unapologetically. 'Afraid you'll have to put that little family get-together on hold.'

Emma, mentally picturing Susie writhing in handcuffs, ankles skidding on the black satin sheets, looked up.

'A certain Rebecca Wigmore has been spanking her platinum plastic a bit too viciously –'

The team laughed dutifully at Striped Shirt's dull wit.

'– the issuing bank, our most important client, wants the matter dealt with carefully. And at once. Repossession of the card and papers served by midnight.'

Emma frowned. 'Carefully?' she countered.

'Rebecca is a Right Honourable who spends other people's money dishonourably. It's a habit with the aristos. Sort it by midnight. Tonight.'

He skimmed a thin manila envelope down the smoked glass table top towards – but not quite reaching – Emma. She blushed, humiliated, as she was forced to bend and stretch, fingers scrabbling and breasts crushed down into the table, to retrieve the package.

The M23 flowed like an open vein. Emma caned The Beast along at a steady seventy. Then the rush hour thickened to a trickle down the A23. The Beast growled, resenting being restrained on a tight leash. It started to rain. Emma flicked down the stubby switch. The twin wipers whirred, clearing the windscreen instantly, the rubber blades sweeping aside the annoying dazzle of rain drops. *Swish. Swish.* The hiss of the blades as they kissed the glass became mildly hypnotic. Emma blinked, her grey eyes narrowing as they glimpsed red tail lights stretching out in the darkness ahead. *Swish. Swish.* She felt tired. Her mind drifted. The events of the busy day returned. The beautiful models at the shoot. *Swish. Swish.* The curt command of the photographer haunted her. Bend over. Like you're going to get the cane. The image of the bending girl flashed across her brain. The lithe-legged, stockinged girl, bending obediently and presenting her nylon-sheathed peach cheeks up. As if for punishment. Emma squeezed her thighs together, suddenly aware of the moist warmth prickling her slit. Like you're going to get the cane. The bulging bottom offered up in submissive surrender. *Swish. Swish.* Emma tongued the roof of her mouth. Her slender hands gripped the wheel, the knuckles whitening.

Shit. Too late. She had just missed the turn-off for Haywards Heath. From there, she would have pointed the Mk II's nose towards Uckfield, eventually finding the Right Honourable Rebecca at Laments Hall. Well off the beaten track, according to her A–Z road atlas.

What the hell, she shrugged. She'd go straight on down to Brighton, get a decent bite to eat – seafood – and then out on the Lewes road, approaching Uckfield from the south.

Brighton was bursting with London weekenders filling the wine bars and clubs. There wasn't room to park a skateboard on The Steyne, never mind The Beast. Skipping the idea of a delicious squid risotto and Soave, Emma got on to the Lewes road and headed north east. It had stopped raining. The silent clock set in the walnut dash, to her surprise, showed 8.16 p.m.

It was approaching 9.25 p.m. when Emma eventually found the pair of wrought-iron gates. Striped Shirt had really stitched her up. Laments Hall was harder to find than a vegan in a burger bar. She parked The Beast, snatched up the manila envelope and got out. Damn. The heavy gates were locked. No sign of life in the tiny gate lodge, either. Emma peered through the gates. The darkness stretched out before her, unbroken by lights. Back in The Beast, she drove for seven minutes, following the high, red brick wall that encircled the estate. No way in. Back at the locked gates, Emma tucked the Mk II on the soft verge under a beech tree. She climbed and cleared the gates, tearing her Barbour in the struggle. Stumbling, she lost a heel in the cattle grid. Then it started to rain. Cursing Striped Shirt, Emma trudged drunkenly through the wet February night along the driveway, desperately hoping that Laments Hall would appear around the next bend.

It did. An Elizabethan pile, gaunt and grim, with a forest of sugar barley twist chimneys crowding the steep roof. The cold rain ceased and the moon came out. Emma suddenly thought how forbidding and uninviting the Hall seemed. All the leaded windows of the imposing frontage were in darkness. She would have to try around the back. Servants' entrance. Thank you, Striped Shirt.

Halfway along the terrace flanking the west wing, a chink of light at a pair of french windows caught her eye. The windows were a late Victorian improvement but Emma saw that the glass had been lozenge-leaded in keeping with the rest of the Hall. Plum-coloured curtains behind the leaded glass had been drawn together, but not completely. An inch-wide band of yellow light pierced the darkness. She peeped in through a diamond of lead.

The drawing room was brilliantly lit. The furnishings were sumptuous. A dark-haired young woman, her face stern and rather pale, was perched on the very edge of an armchair. Emma could just make out the profile of the woman's face. It was a frown of grim concentration. The young woman was wearing a beige cardigan. Emma noted that the right sleeve was drawn up to the elbow. The woman's shapely legs, brogued feet planted apart on the carpet, were sheathed in lisle stockings. Emma could see the dark seam running up over the swell of the shapely calves.

Across the young woman's lap, a bare, reddening bottom was being spanked. Emma could see – but not hear – the right hand sweeping down firmly across the punished cheeks. It was the bare, reddening bottom of a younger woman. Emma gasped softly as she glimpsed the dark, wet fig of the punished nude as, jerking in response to the fierce spanking, the slender, coltish thighs parted and the moist labia glistened.

Emma froze. Steadying herself against the weathered brickwork, she inched closer to the leaded glass. No. She shouldn't. What the hell was she doing? She knew it was wrong – peeping and prying on the privacy of absolute strangers. Sober, sensible thoughts. But Emma was enthralled. Transfixed at the narrow band of yellow light. She knew she was safe out here in the darkness. Safe enough to linger for a few delicious moments and play the voyeur.

Emma pressed her face against the glass. Her warm breath clouded the cold pane. Wiping away the blur with trembling fingertips, she peeped into the brightly lit room. The punishment had ceased. The dark-haired young woman was now smoothing and palming the hot cheeks of the naked girl across her lap. Emma watched as the spanked nude squirmed in response to the controlling palm at her buttocks, squeezing her thighs and knees together. The hand at the bottom tightened into a fist. Emma held her breath, her panties slowly absorbing the warm soak from her pouting labia. The clenched fist visited the bottom, the knuckles prodding and briefly whitening the crimsoned cheeks. Just above the carpet, the naked ankles threshed wildly. Emma gulped as she watched the single, sharp spank quell the rebellious gesture. The red cheeks wobbled in their pain as the ankles were brought together in passive submission.

The chastiser was speaking sternly. Emma glimpsed the mouth opening and closing. The silent admonishment continued. Emma shivered with raw pleasure at the tap-tapping of the punisher's dominant index finger accompanying each word, rhythmically dimpling the crimson curve of the bunched, left cheek.

11

The double doors opened into the drawing room. Emma ducked away instinctively. Two mature women entered the drawing room, arm in arm. Crouching at her vantage point in the darkness on the terrace outside, Emma watched, spellbound, as the two newcomers walked past the red bottomed girl, scarcely acknowledging either the punisher or the punished. Open mouthed in silent amazement, Emma kneeled down, wincing slightly as her knees kissed the wet flagstones, and continued to gaze through the leaded glass.

In the drawing room, the two more mature women had already settled down into comfortable armchairs, one with sherry and *The Times* crossword, the other with a note pad and pen. The young nude, a heavily breasted blonde, was now standing in front of her stern chastiser. The blonde was attempting to shield her breasts, her left hand squashing up the mounds of her swollen bosom, while her right hand modestly cupped her pubic mound. Perched on the edge of her armchair, the dark-haired woman gave a silent command. The spanked blonde bowed her flushed face down in shame, drew her hands reluctantly up to her hair and then turned around, slowly – sullenly, Emma suspected – presenting her hot bottom for inspection. The punisher leaned forward, fingering at first and then roughly thumbing both spanked cheeks, intimately perusing their scarlet blush of pain.

Who on earth could they be? It was almost a contented, domestic setting, Emma thought. A housekeeper chastising a careless maid? No, not in the drawing room. An angry aunt? Meting out a severe spanking to an errant niece? Quite possibly. Aristos, Emma supposed, lived by different rules. So who were the others? So seemingly indifferent to the drama they had just discovered there, in the comfortable drawing room. How could they withdraw into sherry, crosswords and letter writing, Emma wondered, when a beautiful young blonde was being punished?

To Emma's delight, the punished nude was ordered by her tormentress to touch her toes. Emma felt the surge of wet heat scald the inner flesh at her clamped thighs. Gazing

12

directly at the spanked buttocks, she saw the dark cleft yawn as the bending girl obediently parted her legs a fraction. The dark-haired punisher clapped her hands. The blonde rose, reached back down into the seat of the armchair and plucked up a white vest. Struggling, breasts bulging and elbows angled, she pulled the vest over her blonde mane and dragged it down over her tummy. The hem of the white vest rode her hips, keeping her pubic nest on full display. The blonde bent down and snatched up a pair of white cotton panties. But, to Emma's surprise, she did not step into them straight away. Clutching her panties, she approached each of the seated women and, turning and bending, presented her spanked bottom to them in turn. Both merely nodded, after briefly inspecting the reddened cheeks, as if approving of the severity of the recently administered punishment.

The dark-haired woman gave one final command. The blonde, head bowed, stepped into her panties and pulled them up. Emma watched the cool white cotton covering the joggling red cheeks. Thumbing the elastic waistband, the blonde unselfconsciously plucked the tight cotton from her hot cleft. She brought her hands together behind her back and gazed down at the patterned carpet, the very picture of penitence and contrition. Looking up shyly, the punished blonde opened her mouth to speak.

'Can I help you, young lady?'

Emma skidded on the slippery terrace as she twisted around, startled by the curt voice behind her. Her eyes were momentarily blinded by the blaze of a torch beam.

'Who are you, and what are you doing here?' the voice demanded.

Shielding her eyes, Emma stumbled up on to unsteady feet. Unbalanced on her broken heel, she swayed and steadied herself against the wall. The torch beam arrowed down, playing at the flagstones at her feet.

'Follow me, girl,' Emma was instructed.

They were in a spartanly furnished study. A desk, good Adam period chairs, a patterned carpet. A large blue vase of early daffodils and, incongruously, framed photographs of fifties and sixties female tennis stars, softened the hardness of the room. Orange flames flickered in an open hearth, their dancing light reflected in the polished walnut of a chest of drawers.

Emma stood before a desk. It was littered with open files and scattered sheets of papers – the only note of discord in the neat room around her. Seated at the desk, gazing at Emma steadily, was a handsome woman in her early forties. Her steel grey hair was swept back into a severe chignon. She wore a crisp blouse, pearl buttoned, with a small cameo fixed at the throat. The woman's pale blue eyes scanned Emma unblinkingly as she asked for some identification. Emma, giving her name and the purpose of her business at Laments, produced her driving licence.

The grey hair gleamed as the woman bent her head down to study the licence. Emma caught the whiff of jasmine perfume across the polished leather of the desk top.

'And what did you say your purpose at Laments was?' The pale blue eyes gazed up unblinkingly. The lipstick-free mouth was resolute, suggestive of a firm, dominant personality. The sensual lips were pursed.

Emma explained once again, producing the paperwork she had been assigned to serve and handing them across the desk.

'Ah, the Wigmore girl.'

Emma frowned. Clearly this stern woman could be no relation of the Right Honourable Rebecca. Emily's thoughts stole back out on to the terrace to the scene she had glimpsed through the leaded window. Had it been Rebecca receiving the severe spanking? Emma felt a little confused.

'You're wet, girl.'

Emma, her panties soaked after witnessing the spanking, blushed.

'Slip off your Barbour and shoes and take a chair by the fire.'

Wet. Raindrops glistened on her Barbour as she peeled it off. Suppressing a fleeting grin, Emma accepted the invitation, obediently kicking off her shoes and making herself comfortable by the blazing fire. She turned her face and hands towards the heat. Sniffing delicately, she savoured the slightly pungent aroma from the pear-wood logs crackling in the hearth.

'You shall see the Wigmore girl in a few minutes. This matter must be dealt with at once. There must be no delay, and no scandal. The girl's parents are out in Tokyo,' the silver-haired woman added, tidying up the files on her desk. 'Sir Joseph and Lady Wigmore are launching an important business deal in Japanese television.'

Those Wigmores, Emma thought, recognising the name. The family owned several theatres as well as a growing media empire.

Emma grew impatient. 'Are you Rebecca's aunt?' she asked politely, knowing that the woman at the desk certainly wasn't.

'*In loco parentis*. And you may rest assured that I will see to it that the account is settled and that the Wigmore family name is fully protected.'

Emma replied that was exactly what NVK always strived to achieve.

'I am so very glad to hear you say so, my girl.'

Brushing aside the mild annoyance of 'my girl', Emma struggled to decode an elusive clue the woman had let slip. *In loco parentis*. The phrase stirred in her brain.

'Laments,' the stern woman continued, rising from her desk, 'is an institution which takes in young ladies who, like the Wigmore girl, require guidance and training.'

A private school. A girls boarder, Emma thought. 'I see. Private, I mean public school?' Emma smiled.

'An institution,' the suave reply cut in, 'where the emphasis is placed on appropriate training. Training,' she continued, patting her chignon, 'and correction. The girls come to us the despair of their parents. Conventional methods have frequently proved profitless. They are wayward, spoiled and badly in need of discipline.'

Discipline. The nude blonde, bare bottomed, being given a hot, red bottom in the drawing room. Emma gulped.

15

'Laments, of which I am the Head,' the woman continued, approaching one of the framed photographs of tennis amazons on the wall and straightening it affectionately, 'provides such girls with a very strict regime, a bracing lifestyle along with what I deem to be the undoubted benefits of intimate instruction.'

Intimate instruction. Emma's thoughts returned swiftly once more to the bare-bottomed spanking in the drawing room. Its fascination haunted her. Just one remembered glimpse of the firm palm sweeping down across the suffering, upturned cheeks was enough to juice her prickling slit. Intimate instruction. So. Little miss hot-cheeks was a pupil here at Laments, benefiting from a little spot of one-to-one tuition.

'Felicity Flint,' the Head said, approaching Emma, extending her hand.

Emma rose, smiled and shook hands – wincing slightly at the firmness of the other's grasp.

'We'll have the Wigmore girl in now, I think.' As she strode back towards her desk to use the intercom, Emma noted the athletic, tanned legs. Powerfully thighed, tautly muscled. The Head, she observed, wore white ankle socks and white laced-up pumps. As Emma watched the Head bend down to speak, she fleetingly wondered if any of the naughty girls ever felt the fury of a supple white pump across their bare, quivering buttocks. Probably.

'Miss Watson.'

'Yes, Dr Flint?' a metallic voice replied.

'Come to my study.'

'Yes, Dr Flint.'

Moments later, there was a polite tap at the door.

'Enter.'

A slender, soberly dressed woman came into the room. Emma spotted the cruel mouth at once – and the narrowed, green eyes behind the flashing lens of horn-rimmed spectacles.

'Miss Watson, my secretary. Absolutely invaluable.'

The green eyes widened and the cruel mouth slackened to a simper.

16

'As good as a second pair of eyes and ears to me.'

The glasses flashed as Miss Watson inclined her head, bestowing a curt nod towards Emma.

'Winkle out the Wigmore girl from whatever she shouldn't be doing, will you, Watson? Bring her straight here.'

'The Wigmore girl? Early Bed, I believe. Late for French from showers. Is anything the matter, Head?' Miss Watson asked, shooting a suspicious glance at Emma.

'Nothing that cannot be settled here and now. The Wigmore girl, if you please, Watson.'

'At once, Dr Flint.' She scuttled away.

The Head fingered the cameo at her throat, then slowly undid the single pearl button at the cuff of her right sleeve.

'How many girls do you have here at Laments?' Emma asked, feeling somewhat obliged to make conversation. How do you administer their punishments, she really wanted to know. A cane? A real yellow length of bamboo whippy cane? A whippy cane that would bite into their peach-cheeks, leaving pink stripes across the proffered buttocks and stinging salt tears in their sorrowful eyes?

'Eighteen,' she heard the Head's voice say. Emma concentrated on what was being said. When Dr Felicity Flint spoke, it was wise to listen, Emma felt. 'With a staff of five. Under strength at the moment. With such a generous SSR –'

'SSR?' Emma interrupted, instantly wishing she hadn't.

'Student-to-staff ratio, my dear. It allows for the intensive tuition I mentioned earlier, and of course the girl's parents are both willing and capable of paying for this unique provision.'

Emma felt a response was appropriate. 'Your girls are very priviliged.'

'Possibly, but I fear that they do not always appreciate that fact.'

Remembering the shiny-sore red bottom in the drawing room, Emma suspected that Felicity Flint was perfectly correct in that observation.

'How old are you, girl?'

17

Emma, startled, answered at once. 'Twenty two.'

'Hmm. Five years older than our youngest, three years above our oldest girls, of which the Right Honourable Rebecca Wigmore is one.'

The door to the study opened.

'And here she is.'

Miss Watson entered, shepherding a dark-eyed nineteen year old.

'Thank you, Miss Watson.'

The secretary, eager to learn more, hesitated at the door.

'Good night,' Dr flint added, the note of finality unmistakeable.

Scowling resentfully at Emma's fleeting smile, Miss Watson withdrew, closing the door behind her. She'll listen at the door, Emma thought, recognising the prying type. Hadn't the Head mentioned something about eyes. And ears.

By the desk, the Right Honourable Rebecca Wigmore stood, head bowed, her long dark hair curtaining her pale face. But Emma saw the gleam of the dark, wary eyes. The girl shivered, scantily clad in a tight, white vest and tiny shorts. The vest, short sleeved and deeply scalloped at her bosom, rode the swell of the firm breasts with a taut stretch of cotton. The peaks of her prinking nipples were clearly defined beneath the soft fabric. Emma's tongue slowly thickened as she noted how the tiny shorts sculpted the young girl's delicious pubic mound.

'In bed, already?' the Head barked.

'Early Bed, Dr Flint. A half forfeit.'

'A half forfeit, eh?' rejoined the Head, feigning a note of surprise. 'What for?'

Rebecca stubbed the toes of her right foot into the patterned carpet. Emma, privy to the answer to the Head's question, wondered if the girl would risk a lie.

'I'm very much afraid that an Early Bed is far too lenient a punishment for such slacking. Late for –' Dr flint paused briefly '– let me see. Friday evening. Why, French conversation.'

'Yes, Dr Flint.'

'An Early Bed from Mme Puton?'

18

'Yes, Dr Flint,' Rebecca whispered, delicately tracing a fraction of the floral pattern in the carpet with her toes.

'I shall speak to her tomorrow on the subject.'

The Head turned towards the flickering fire and briskly introduced Emma and the purpose of her presence. Emma rose, eager to see the transactions completed.

'NVK work this way to spare you any –' she began.

Dr Flint broke in sharply, taking charge.

'I understand that you have been using this credit card, the existence of which I was wholly unaware, and in addition to this you actually had the temerity to exceed an agreed credit limit by some two and a half thousand pounds and,' the Head concluded, her stern voice rising in anger, 'no arrangements have been made for any repayment of the accumulated debt. Is this correct?'

Crushed by the tirade, Rebecca merely nodded and bowed her head in shame.

'You actually broke your credit agreement and failed to make any attempt at repayment?'

Rebecca's silence confirmed her guilt.

'But you know the rules perfectly well, girl. You seem to have been flouting them pretty freely. We will go carefully into the exact details of when and where you used, or rather abused, this credit card in a few moments.'

What kind of hornet's nest have I stirred up here, Emma wondered. Were the girls here at Laments gated, forbidden to visit the nearby villages and towns? If so, poor little Rebecca was really in the shit.

'May I say, Dr Flint –' Emma began.

Again, the Head curtly ignored her. Emma, hovering uncertainly by the fire, was now anxious to complete the business and get back into The Beast and on the road to London.

The Head took her seat behind the desk and spread out the NVK paperwork, smoothing it down against the polished leather desk top with her broad palms. Summoning Rebecca towards the desk with an impatient snap of her fingers, she instructed the shivering girl to read and then sign them.

'I will see to it that Miss Watson makes an immediate payment of one thousand pounds on Monday morning. These papers,' the Head continued, retrieving her fountain pen from Rebecca's nervous fingers, 'will be forwarded to the family solicitors. In the absence of Sir Charles and Lady Wigmore, I believe that to be the most prudent course of action. Epsom, Epsom, Darkling and Epsom, isn't it girl?'

'Yes, Dr Flint.' Rebecca's penitent whisper was scarcely audible.

'Well, that all seems fine,' Emma conceded. 'There's just the credit card. My instructions –'

'Ah, yes. The credit card,' the Head broke in, once again marginalising Emma. 'Where exactly is it, girl? No. Let me think. In your swimsuit?'

Rebecca glanced up, amazement battling with fear in her dark eyes. 'Yes. I hide it in my costume, Dr Flint.'

'Carefully tucked away in your locker, I presume.'

Rebecca merely nodded.

'Then we shall have to go down to the pool together after I have punished you and destroy the wretched thing.'

Punished you. Emma's tongue worked busily, trying to lubricate her dry mouth. What precisely did the stern Head mean by those delicious words. More strange forfeits? Early Beds? What if Rebecca was about to be spanked? Emma supposed that she wouldn't be around to witness it this time.

'Place that chair over there, in the centre of the carpet, Rebecca.'

The girl picked up the chair and obediently positioned it on the spot indicated by the Head's jabbing forefinger.

'Across the chair, girl. I am going to cane your bottom.'

Emma clenched her hands into tight little fists of excitement. Her nipples stirred, thickened and kissed the lace of her taut brassiere cups. A caning. It was going to be a caning.

'Hadn't I better –' Emma murmured.

'Stay where you are by that nice warm fire, girl. Much more comfortable, I'm sure, than out in the nasty rain.'

20

Stunned – but secretly thrilled – Emma slumped back down in her chair. She watched, somewhat shyly, as Rebecca bent down over the chair, planting her hands, palms down, on the polished seat. Head bowed, thighs squeezed together, she presented her rounded buttocks up for their impending pain.

'Laments,' the Head purred, approaching the gleaming walnut chest of drawers, 'dispenses all discipline immediately. Instant punishment could almost be our motto. It's the best way, I find. Sometimes, of course,' she added conversationally, 'the miscreant benefits from waiting anxiously for an hour before being beaten. Endless moments of delicious dread. Sixty minutes of sweet torment. Such waiting heightens the girl's anxiety and foreboding. Before I bare the naughty bottom, the wrongdoer has already imagined and suffered every stinging swipe, every searing slice, of the cruel cane.'

As the Head paused to open the second drawer down, Emma clenched her buttocks furtively, inching them up from the seat of her chair to ease her soaking panties clinging to her flesh.

'But in this particular case,' the Head grunted, rummaging in the deep drawer, 'prompt punishment is called for. Ah, there it is.'

She had been pawing the interior of the drawer. Emma heard the dry, eerie rattle as the Head's fingertips encountered the length of bamboo. So did Rebecca – who whimpered softly. The cane was extracted from the darkness of the drawer and brought out into the light. It sparkled beneath the electric lightbulbs above: twenty-two inches of venomously supple wood. The Head closed the drawer with her elbow. The smooth, worn wood slid home silently. Emma watched, more openly and with lively interest, as the Head shouldered her cane, stepped up to the framed photographs of the last generation of female tennis champions, smartly saluted them with the quivering stick, then turned to address the proffered buttocks of the bending girl.

'Shall we say six for actually using the credit card, such usage being, as you full well know, Rebecca, forbidden during your stay here at Laments and six,' the Head added, inspecting her cane closely for a few seconds then swishing it down to test its whippiness, 'for risking the good name of your family by flouting the credit limit and failing to make provision for repayments?'

After the flurry of words, a loud silence filled the study. Suddenly, a pearwood log settled in the embers, sending a shower of orange sparks whirling up the dark chimney. Emma, spellbound as she followed the pre-punishment preparations, almost toppled from her chair.

'But first,' Dr Flint murmured, reverently placing her cane lengthways down across the polished leather surface of the desk, 'I require you to give me full details of how, where, when and with whom you used the credit card.'

Stepping forward two paces, she reached down and placed her capable hands at the waist of the bending girl. Rebecca eased her tummy down, bent her knees a fraction and jerked her bottom up obediently to allow her tiny shorts to be dragged down slowly. The Head's slender fingers left the shorts at the lower thighs. They remained there, binding the soft flesh in a restricting band, clamping the bare-bottomed girl's legs together and rendering her exposed cheeks above perfectly poised and positioned for punishment.

Gazing at the dark cleft between the perfect peach-cheeks, Emma was struck by a sudden thought, prompted by a glint from a pearl button on the Head's bloused bosom. She has known all along, Emma realised, watching the Head roll up the unbuttoned sleeve of her blouse. She unbuttoned that cuff five minutes after I came into this room. Rebecca's fate had been sealed – and her punishment decided – even before the dark-haired girl had been dragged from her Early Bed by the eager Miss Watson.

The double echo of a blisteringly spanking hand rang around the spartan study. Emma blinked, almost angry with herself for not concentrating properly and, in consequence, missing the first two spanks. The echo had died. All that remained to attest to the fact that they had occurred were two pink blotches which deepened to a darker crimson before Emma's wide eyes. Smack. Smack. The Head stood up after delivering two more crisp spanks across the soft cheeks. Rebecca mewled in response, her buttocks reddening angrily as she squeezed them.

'Well, girl. Speak. I'm waiting.'

Under the threat of the hovering hand above her bottom, Rebecca quickly confessed to using the credit card in Brighton. Two more severe spanks elicited two shrill squeals and a full confession. Times, dates and places all spilled forth. Names were named. Less than half of it made any sense to Emma, although she was able to work out that Rebecca had taken three of her friends from Laments in a hired car to Brighton and back – before dawn – on at least a dozen memorable jaunts. Lavish meals washed down by champagne had been enjoyed. The hire car, plus waiting time and tip, must have cost at least a hundred. That, Emma realised, calculating rapidly, accounted for the earlier cash withdrawals before the hole-in-the-wall had dried up.

The Head ran her fingertips lightly over the punished rump, then briefly thumbed Rebecca's hot cleft. 'Vintage champagne? Lobsters?'

Under a staccato of five more merciless spanks, Rebecca yelped out her guilt, confessing unreservedly more details, more damning facts.

Stepping back from the spanked girl, Dr Flint rubbed her hot palm against her thigh before snatching up the bamboo cane.

'Twelve, we agreed, did we not?' she whispered, depressing the spanked cheeks under the thin whippy stick's yellow length. 'Legs straight. Up on your toes, girl.'

The Head raised the cane. Emma saw the white line its pressure into the hot flesh had left slowly fill with crimson.

'Bottom up a little more, girl. Come along. Get it up,' she rasped, tap-tapping the curved flesh mounds imperiously with the quivering tip of her cane.

Rebecca, sniffling, obeyed instantly, straining to present her smacked bottom up to her punisher's satisfaction. Dr Flint took a half pace back, levelled the bamboo in against the swell of the beautiful buttocks, swept the whippy wood up then lashed it down. Emma's soft gasp was drowned by the sound of the slicing swipe across the soft cheeks, and the loud sorrow-sob from the lips of the punished girl. A second, a third and then a blistering fourth stroke followed. Rebecca's squealing became one long howl of anguish. Emma held her breath, painfully, until the fifth cruel stroke had whipped down, bite-slicing into the striped buttocks. Criss-crossed with vivid weals, the flayed buttocks jerked and writhed. Emma glimpsed the wet fig of the thrashed, bare-bottomed girl as she twisted across the chair in an agony of torment. Emma breathed out softly, surrendering to the ache in her pent-up lungs. Her loud sigh was silenced by the brutal swish and searing swipe of the sixth stroke.

Rebecca screamed softly, wriggling and writhing as if in orgasm, bucking her hips and squeezing her cheeks as if sucking up a ribbed anal dildo into the wet warmth of her sphincter. Emma sat still. To move an inch – dragging her wet slit against her cotton panties – would, she knew, trigger a climax almost at once. Ashamed, deliciously disturbed and sexually aroused by the strict discipline being dispensed to the bare-bottomed girl across the chair, Emma was filled with the pleasurable discomfort of her new found self-knowledge: she enjoyed watching another female being punished. She found strict discipline delightful, and took pleasure in another's pain.

Rebecca wriggled frantically, her striped bottom describing erotic arabesques as her slender hips writhed.

'Stop that at once, girl,' Dr Flint snapped, trapping and taming the whipped cheeks beneath the yellow cane she had just lashed them with. 'Now get down right across the chair for the next six strokes. Hurry up, girl,' she thundered impatiently, 'you know what I want.'

Rebecca squirmed as she lowered her breasts over the far edge of the polished wooden seat and sank her belly into the shining wood. Her bottom, now horizontal, was deliciously poised, forming a tempting target for the cane. The bamboo twitched eagerly in the Head's firm grasp.

Struggling to avoid coming right then and there on her chair, Emma gazed directly on Rebecca's repositioned buttocks: longing to kiss each perfect peach-cheek then bury her hot face down between the hotter twin mounds of red-wealed flesh and tongue the deep cleft between them.

Almost swooning, Emma gripped the sides of her chair to steady herself. She felt her pulse plucking at her soft throat, sensed the hammer of her heart. Her swollen tongue seemed too thick for her mouth. She sat, her brain spinning, as the Head commenced to administer the second stage of the punishment.

Dr Flint gripped her cane firmly and angled it above the bunched buttocks directly below. The first six strokes had been swift and searing, planting scarlet stripes across the helpless cheeks in rapid succession. The concluding strokes were, Emma felt intuitively, to be slow; more deliberate and more measured.

One. Emma counted silently, surreptitiously smoothing her fingertips down over her pubis as the thin cane sliced into the rubbery spasms of punished flesh.

Two. Emma whispered it softly, her dry lips peeling slowly apart as she murmured the count. Two. Two nipples, now burning peaks of pain, aching for the fierce cupping of her crushing palms.

Three. The third stroke instantly conjured up three sounds: a shriek from the punished; a snarl from the punisher; a moan from the voyeur.

Four. The cane whistled down, kiss-lashing the upturned buttocks savagely. Rebecca slammed her hips four times into the chair in a frenzy of violent ecstasy before the Head planted her white pump firmly down on to the whipped bottom. Writhing beneath the pinioning pump of her dominant tormentress, Rebecca squirmed in agony, sobbing aloud. Emma, her slit now weeping freely, yearned to bring her fingers to her wet heat.

'Come here,' the Head instructed, shouldering her cane and summoning Emma to her side.

As if in a trance, Emma rose from her chair and approached. Dr Flint took her pump away from Rebecca's bottom and replaced it on the carpet. Emma glimpsed the chevrons of the ribbed sole working a herringbone pattern against the crimson flesh. Shrinking back slightly from the sight, at such close quarters, of the cane-striped cheeks, Emma looked up into the Head's clear gaze.

'Here. Take it.'

Emma was offered the cane.

'The girl is due a further two strokes. She has caused you a good deal of inconvenience. Her bottom is yours. Stripe her. Stripe her well.'

Two

After her A-levels, Emma had worked briefly for a local radio station, photocopying, assembling playlists and being the general go-out-and-get-one girl. A celebrity opera diva agreed to do a spell in the studio for charity. The stretch limo delivered her before noon. Within half an hour, she had swamped the station staff with her demands, tantrums and instructions. Emma was assigned by the desperate station manager to attend to the imperious diva's every whim. Spellbound by the strikingly beautiful woman who simply took the world by the balls and squeezed until it worked her way, Emma had shadowed her throughout the afternoon behind the mike. And in that shadow cast by the blazing egotist, Emma had become ensnared by the manipulative charm – and seduced by the diva's delicious beauty.

The diva had worn a silk scarf. Loosening it halfway through the broadcast, it had slipped, revealing the diva's white throat. In the heat of the studio, her unbuttoned blouse had revealed the swell of firm bosoms. Emma, peeping with shy boldness, had thrilled to the quivering bosoms – and the tempting cleavage between them – when the diva had actually deigned to sing. The scarf slithered forgotten to the floor. In the darkness of the soundproof glass cage, Emma had judged the moment carefully before reaching down and clutching the sinuous swathe of silk.

It was her trophy. Her slightly perfumed trophy of the beautiful, imperious goddess. The beautiful, impatient goddess before whom all mere mortals quailed – and whose trembling bosom made Emma's own breasts feel strangely heavy and pleasurably swollen with a sweet ache.

Thick nippled and prickling deliciously beneath her blonde pubic fringe, Emma had planned to sneak off into the toilet with the scarf and masturbate – pretending that the hands that brought the stretch of silk to her hot slit were those of the diva. Emma grew hot and trembled slightly at the notion of rasping the stolen scarf against her tender young pussy until the labial lips smiled and parted: unfurling to accept the skein into her wet heat.

No. There would be no time. She decided to smuggle it home and bring it, like a guilty secret, up to her bedroom. There, before her full-length looking-glass, she planned to use the silk on her nakedness, binding her breasts into strict bondage then, both fists tightened, punish herself between her splayed thighs until the oozing scald threatened to explode into a violent orgasm.

Emma had sat for three hours next to the diva she adored, fingering the sensual silk in the darkness, imagining again and again the shining fabric darkening as it absorbed the stain of her juices. The clock on the studio wall ticked off the seconds with agonising slowness. The planned moment came and went. Emma, trembling on the brink of doing what she most desired, had surrendered her stolen trophy – frozen in uncertainty and burning shame.

Gripping the cane and thrilling to the potent malice of the whippy wood, Emma succumbed to similar hesitation, guilt and indecision. She wanted to administer the two remaining strokes, wanted to swish the bamboo down across the already striped buttocks of the bare-bottomed, bending girl. She yearned to hear the thin whistle of the slicing strokes, and ached for the grunts from Rebecca's lips as her soft cheeks suffered. But, inexplicably, Emma found, to her frustration and confusion, that her arm could not raise the length of cane up above the shivering buttocks below.

Felicity Flint, scrutinising Emma carefully, nodded judiciously and stepped in, smartly retrieving the situation. A true dominant, she was anxious to maintain control at every stage of the discipline. Any lapse – or unscheduled pause in the proceedings – could shift the carefully orchestrated balance of power between the punisher and the punished.

'You are tired,' she murmured.

Emma, with a fleeting pang of reluctance, surrendered the cane to the Head. She nodded, avoiding the piercing gaze of Dr Flint's pale blue eyes.

Swish, crack. The remaining two strokes were delivered instantly with consummate skill, leaving Rebecca squealing and writhing in renewed anguish.

'Remain exactly as you are across the chair for two minutes, girl,' the Head instructed. 'Gin and T or sherry?'

Emma, lost in her own thoughts as she gazed down intently at the red-wealed buttocks still wriggling in pain, did not think the partly heard words were being addressed to her.

'I could get some tea or coffee rustled up, of course,' Felicity Flint continued.

'Oh,' Emma blinked. 'A G and T would be fine.'

The Head, after carefully returning the cane to its dark lair in the polished walnut drawer, fixed two gins, splashing the tonic in expertly. Emma heard the ice cubes clinking against the sides of the tumblers.

'Bottoms up.' Dr Flint arched her right eyebrow up.

Emma blushed, then drank deeply. She watched over the rim of her tumbler as the Head raised her own glass up once more in a salute to the photos on the opposite wall. Emma, shaken by recent events, found herself toying with an empty glass.

'Another?'

Coming to her senses with a determined effort, Emma shook her head. 'Driving.' She shrugged.

'Let's not even discuss your dashing back to London at this late hour,' Dr Flint countered suavely, commandeering Emma's glass and refilling it generously. 'There. You'll stay. It's settled. We have some supper when I have completed our business here.'

29

Settling down on to her chair by the fire, Emma realised that she was to remain at Laments overnight. Supremely confident in all her decisions, the Head had spoken with an air of finality without any discussion. Emma had not even agreed.

'Come along, girl,' Emma heard the Head admonish the snivelling credit card cheat, who was struggling unsuccessfully to yank up her tiny shorts over her whipped cheeks. 'Take me to your locker at once.'

Emma watched as Rebecca wiped a silver tear from her eye with the back of her hand. Snuffling as she answered, her whispered words were indistinct.

'Oh, come here, girl.'

Emma turned, alert to the new timbre in the Head's voice. It could have been one of the tennis aces framed upon the wall speaking, encouraging a colt who had just missed an ace. Felicity Flint had spoken with an unsuspected tenderness.

'Shorts down. Let me see your bottom.'

Rebecca obeyed, thumbing down her shorts obediently until the tight waistband cupped her punished cheeks – causing their swollen curves to bulge deliciously. The Head kneeled, her stern face a mere three inches from the buttocks she had just blistered with the cruel whippy wood.

Emma watched, fascinated, as the kneeling Head brought her tumbler of iced gin and tonic up against the naked bottom, pressing the cold glass into and then rolling it across the hot double domes. Rebecca gasped aloud, jerking her whipped rump back into the healing balm.

'You have been a very naughty girl,' Dr Flint murmured softly, removing the glass and, after raising it to her sensual lips, sipping slowly from it. Rebecca waggled her reddened bottom impatiently, signalling her desire for the return of the tumbler.

'Haven't you?'

'Yes, Head.'

'But you have been punished, and I note that you did not lie or attempt to deny the offence.' The Head skimmed the frosted glass teasingly across the quivering cheeks.

Rebecca whispered her penitence softly. She inched her buttocks back, seeking the touch of the cold glass against her punished flesh. The Head crushed the tumbler along the dark cleft. Rebecca whimpered happily, shuddering at and basking in the delicious aftercare.

'And you did deserve to be beaten, didn't you?'

Rebecca remained silent. It was a sulky silence.

'So,' the Head whispered, her voice returning to its tone of velvety venom, 'you resent your stripes? There will, I must warn you, girl, be more stripes for you, and your wicked accomplices.'

Emma saw Rebecca's cheeks clench in fearful anticipation of further punishment.

'But more of that tomorrow.' Dr Flint rose, finished her drink with one hand and jerked up Rebecca's tight shorts deftly with the other. 'Now take me to that wretched card and let me destroy it.'

More stripes. Sitting alone by the glowing embers in the hearth, Emma nursed her second strong gin and T. She sipped from it meditatively, relaxing as the drink warmed her. She felt drained. Exhausted. Grudgingly glad not to have to take The Beast back through the rain to London. And her slit seethed. She must, she thought, get some privacy soon and attend to the heat that was becoming increasingly more urgent between the juncture of her slippery thighs.

Emma's desire for the relief and the release of a climax clamoured loudly in her brain and at the base of her tightened belly. The roller-coaster events of the last couple of hours had left her with so much to feed her fantasies with, so much to fuel her scrabbling fingers frantic at her pussy.

One more peep at that cane. Dare she? Emma skipped across to the polished walnut chest of drawers and opened up the bamboo's resting place. Her fingers found the thin length of cane and dragged it into the light. Glancing down, Emma shivered, vividly remembering Rebecca's red stripes. Emma knew that she must hold the cane once more. It quivered in her tightly gripping fist. She swished it, thrilling to the vicious slice as the bamboo sang its cruel note of suffering. Emma's mouth dried. She sipped her iced gin and T.

The study door opened. A stern-faced woman, in the lemon vest, black short, pleated skirt and laced pumps of a gym mistress, entered the room. Her sharp, hazel eyes darted from the deserted desk to Emma.

'What are you doing in here, girl? Where is Dr Flint?' she rasped.

Emma, startled by the sudden entrance and abrupt tone, gulped – and had to wipe the gin trickling from her chin. The cane dropped silently at her feet on the carpet.

'Felicity has just gone to –'

'Felicity?' the gym mistress thundered. 'How dare you be so impertinent. All girls, without exception, address members of staff here by their correct title, understand? What were you doing with that cane?'

The svelte, athletic woman approached, her pumps treading the patterned carpet with silent menace. 'Is that gin?' She sniffed suspiciously.

'Gin and T,' Emma, struggling to explain, managed.

'Bend over this instant, girl. You may be new but there's simply no excuse for this outrageous behaviour.'

Emma, so shocked she almost giggled, stepped back. 'You don't understand –'

'I said bend over. At once,' the gym mistress hissed. 'Unless you learn to obey instantly your time here at Laments is going to be painfully unpleasant,' she grunted, wrestling Emma expertly down across a chair and pinning the struggling girl down with her right pump.

'No, don't, get off,' Emma screeched, no match for the lithe and strong gym mistress.

'Silence,' snapped the stern woman, pulling out a white hankie and forcing it into Emma's mouth – silencing her shrill protest.

Pinning Emma down by the nape of her neck with one hand, the gym mistress unfurled a coiled leather belt from her skirt pocket. As she dragged it out, a silver whistle spilled down on to the carpet. Emma spluttered into her gag and wriggled violently beneath the pinioning hand at her neck and pump on her upturned rump. But the gym mistress, snapping the length of leather ominously, was clearly adept at dealing with girls who struggled to evade the lash.

'Rule number one for new girls at Laments,' she hissed, planting her feet apart and deftly baring Emma's bottom. 'Obey all rules. Understand?'

Emma squirmed but found all struggling futile. She was bared and prepared for the bite of the leather. Helpless, she tensed, dreading the moment the hide would caress her buttocks.

'Stop struggling or I'll double your six to a dozen, girl.'

Emma's outrage collapsed into raw fear. The gym mistress was implacable – Emma knew that she was about to receive six searing strokes across her poor, defenceless little bottom. But with the knowledge came a guilty thrill.

Crack. The length of hide sliced down, bequeathing a deep pink band of pain across Emma's clenched cheeks. It stung and burned. Emma squealed.

'What on earth –' Dr Flint's voice demanded imperiously as she strode through the door into her study.

Crack. The gym mistress lashed the leather down once more, adding a second pink swathe of pain to the deepening crimson of the first stripe. 'Nothing to worry about, Head. Found this new girl in here drinking your gin –'

'No, stop –' Dr Flint commanded as the leather strap was raised aloft. 'Let her go at once.'

'Head?' came the challenging response. The leather quivered above Emma's bottom, its tip dangling teasingly across the surface of her whipped cheeks. 'Let her go?' echoed the gym mistress, lowering the strap down across the crowns of the punished buttocks.

'Not a new girl,' the Head gasped, coming to Emma's rescue at once.

'But then –' Emma's tormentress countered, baffled.

'Oh dear,' Dr Flint purred, palming Emma's bottom gently. 'Not a very good welcome to Laments, hmm?'

The gym mistress furled up her strap and pocketed it. Stooping, her lemon vest bulging as her unbrassiered breasts burgeoned, she snatched up her silver whistle.

The Head assisted Emma from the chair. 'Never mind. Time for a bite of supper.'

Deciding the incident to be closed, the Head picked up the cane from the carpet. 'How did this get there?'

Emma blushed.

'She was playing with it when I came into the study,' the gym mistress remarked.

'Was she?' the Head murmured. Giving Emma a playful tap on her bottom with the tip of the yellow bamboo, she returned the cane to its resting place in the chest of drawers. 'I am sure we shall all three of us look back one day upon this little misunderstanding and smile.'

Dr Flint and the gym mistress laughed brightly. Emma, still in shock, sore bottomed after the stinging leather and – to her discomfort and puzzlement – disturbingly aroused, did not laugh. She did not even return the Head's attempt at a winning smile.

'No sulking, now. Mistakes will happen,' Felicity Flint reasoned, her tone brisk and reasonable.

Emma attempted a political, if uneasy, smile.

'Marion, my deputy,' the Head continued, making the introductions and explaining Emma's presence at Laments.

'The Wigmore girl did that? Do we know her accomplices, Head? They too must be punished.' Marion remained unapologetic. Her manner was, Emma felt, annoyingly bracing.

A flash of anger darted across Emma's face, clouding her grey eyes. This gung-ho gym mistress had just bared her bottom and swiped it twice with a strap. No apology. Just dismissing the incident as trivial. Like Dr Flint had said, a mistake. Bloody assault and battery, Emma thought. And now all they could talk about was the institution, and the prospect of further punishments.

Felicity Flint glanced at Emma. Noting the frown beneath her visitor's blonde mane, she motioned to Marion, dismissing her.

34

'Ready for supper, I'm sure.'

Emma wanted a fuller apology. An apology for the outrage visited upon her poor little bottom. But the Head's pale blue eyes held a let's-have-no-more-nonsense challenge in their gleam. Emma decided to play safe. She smiled weakly, surreptitiously fingered her panties back into place at her cleft and followed the stern Head obediently out of the study to supper.

'Where are all your girls?'

'In bed. Bed by nine, except of course for Early Beds. Those in forfeit must be washed – spanked, if necessary – and abed by seven,' the Head replied, flapping open her starched napkin.

Smoothing out her own napkin, Emma stole another furtive glance around the dining table. She was taking supper with the staff of Laments, who had acknowledged her pleasantly – and then completely ignored her, turning their attention to the delicious salmon mousse, baskets of toast and chilled Chablis, discussing the events of their punishing day.

Emma eavesdropped.

'Spanked her bottom so hard I'm not sure which was redder, or sorer, my hand or her buttocks –'

Laughter.

'And then the wretched girl had the brazen temerity to come – actually come – after the seventh stroke –'

Disapproving tut-tutting.

Emma blushed, her fingers trembling slightly as she spread salmon mousse on to her crisp toast with a heavy silver knife. After a second glass of Chablis, and with the earlier gins kicking in, she felt her taut body slacken and relax. She suddenly felt like giggling and had to cram her mouth with the delicious food to quell her nervous laughter. Dr Flint, she sensed, would not approve of giggling at high table. Using her napkin delicately, Emma composed herself, and from behind the cover of her raised glass, studied her fellow diners.

Dr Flint, grey chignon glinting, head bowed, was in earnest conversation with her deputy. Marion received the details of Rebecca's misbehaviour with suppressed outrage. Emma suspected that one small part of the deputy's brain was kept clear – clear to calculate the severity of impending punishments.

Miss Watson, the green-eyed secretary, had ceased flashing suspicious glances from behind her rimmed spectacles at Emma and was busy chivvying Mme Puton, who responded with bored indifference.

'It is essential that you complete the registers, Mademoiselle.'

Licking her fingers with Gallic insouciance, the French mistress rubbed her palms together and surveyed the linen surface of the supper table for more toast. Effectively shrugging off Miss Watson's appeals for tighter record keeping, Mme Puton continued with her supper. Emma saw the Frenchwoman's violet eyes sparkling with amused contempt as a whine insinuated itself into the secretary's voice as she laboured her point.

'Evidence is required and must be furnished if girls are to be whipped for lateness or ducking out of lessons.'

'I know who needs the whip, *assez-bien*,' Mme Puton purred, leaving a perfect impression of her scarlet lips on her wine glass after sipping her Chablis. 'I do not read it from a book of registrations –'

'Register,' corrected the secretary sharply.

'I know when a girl needs a crisp reminder,' Mme Puton remarked, deliberately ignoring Miss Watson's interjection.

'Yes, but accurate records must –'

Emma shivered, suddenly imagining what it would be like to be bending, bare bottomed, at the mercy of the violet-eyed French mistress with the pert breasts and the chic, closely cropped auburn hair. Bending, bare bottomed, for a crisp reminder.

The two women Emma had glimpsed through the french windows from the terrace – impassive witnesses to the dark-haired younger woman spanking the blonde – were engaged in an animated discussion about the merits of the cane. Kate, the younger, dark-haired disciplinarian, was advocating spanking spiritedly.

36

Miss Monteagle, a Latinist who also taught Geography, became excited. 'It is the delicious dread, I think, that persuades me to favour the cane. The swish of whippy bamboo is so satisfying for the punisher, and so alarming for the punished. Bending, they cannot see the stroke – but can briefly hear their approaching pain. And the thin, pink stripe across the bottom. So convenient to be able to actually count the strokes and keep an accurate tally.'

Miss Rathbone, Maths and History, nodded vigorously. 'Absolutely vital to keep count. And of course, with a cane, one can achieve complete control over the bending girl. It can be judiciously used to tap her head back down or trap and tame feet when not kept perfectly still. Caning,' she added, warming to her theme and leaving the glistening triangle of toast poised at her lips unbitten, 'forces the bare-bottomed girl to assume the humiliating posture of submission. Whether across a chair, kneeling or touching her toes, it allows the chastiser to dominate the chastised both physically and, equally importantly, psychologically.'

Hell, they've thought it out like rocket science, Emma mused, watching Miss Rathbone's teeth deal with her toast efficiently.

Kate, the dark-haired spanker in the drawing room, was not to be bullied or browbeaten. She dabbed her lips with her napkin and rejoined the debate, undaunted by the experience and undoubted expertise of her maturer colleagues.

'But spanking also establishes absolute control over the bottom. Why, one becomes intimately and totally connected with the miscreant. Think of the soft warmth of her wriggling nakedness across your lap –'

They thought, 'Mm, yes,' they conceded.

'Imagine her breasts heavy against your left thigh and her hair tumbling down. A perfect picture of surrender and submission –'

They imagined. 'You do have a point, my dear,' they chorused.

'And as for domination, with one hand firmly pressing down on the neck – or gripping her wrists together – and

37

the palm of the spanking hand smoothing her sleek cheeks –'

'Yes, yes,' her listeners nodded in unison.

'And then, of course,' Kate murmured, her voice a silky whisper, 'not only does one have the exquisite pleasure of the satisfying smack-sound but one can actually both see and feel the heat of one's handiwork.'

Emma grinned as she saw Miss Monteagle plucking frantically at her napkin as, by her side, Miss Rathbone's fingertips fluttered feverishly at the double string of pearls at her throat.

'Spanking for me, absolutely,' Kate concluded.

Emma sipped her Chablis. So these were Dr Flint's staff of five. The gym mistress, Marion, hazel eyes, lithe and powerful. Dr Flint's deputy and bursar to Laments. Miss Rathbone and Miss Monteagle, the inseparable forty-somethings who preferred the cane when obliged to dispense pain. Mme Puton, chic, petite and sublimely indifferent to the administrative exactitudes insisted upon by the weasel-eyed, spiteful secretary, Miss Watson. And then there was Kate. Dark haired, slightly older than Emma herself, and with a sophisticated approach to the pleasure of punishment.

And the girls? The students, Emma supposed they were called. Eighteen in number, Felicity Flint had said, and more or less all about that age. Gazing at the other tables arranged in neat rows in the refectory – cutlery glinting in readiness for the morning – Emma found herself speculating on those consigned to Laments for intimate instruction. She had glimpsed the blonde being severely spanked, and had seen at closer quarters the ravishing effects – oops, I meant ravaging, Emma corrected herself – of Dr Flint's bamboo on the Right Honourable Rebecca Wigmore's bare bottom.

'Finished?'

Emma looked up as the Head's voice broke into her thoughts.

'I will show you to your room. Tomorrow morning, after breakfast, you will have the opportunity to see

Laments at work.' The Head's voice throbbed with pride. Emma made a mental note to play up during the Grand Tour. The Head seemed so pleased to have a visitor to conduct around her institution. 'After lunch –'

Lunch. Emma suppressed a frown. She had planned to lunch in London. A new salsa cafe to check out on the Portobello Road.

'– and of course see to it that your Barbour is mended,' the Head was saying. 'One of the girls will sew the tear, sponge clean and re-wax it.'

Despite her sinking heart, Emma replied graciously.

'Who is on dorm patrol?' the Head asked, addressing the supper table imperiously. 'It is almost eleven.'

'Mme Puton,' the efficient secretary snapped, her tone conveying a note of accusation rather than mere information.

'*C'est-moi?*' the French mistress murmured, unruffled by Miss Watson's spite. 'I do not recollect being informed –'

'You were given your typed schedule on Monday, before lunch. I remember having to look for you everywhere,' the weasel added damningly. 'You were not in your classroom although the timetable specifically –'

'Keep a sharp eye on the Middleton-Peake girl,' Dr Flint broke in, nipping the contretemps firmly in the bud. 'Though I am sure, Mademoiselle, that I have no need to remind you of how you should deal with the girl if she is not in the appropriate place at the expected time.'

Mme Puton, Emma thought, paled slightly as she inclined her chic, cropped head of auburn hair. Probably angry with the weaselly secretary, Emma supposed.

'And I'm sure we are all indebted to you, Miss Watson, for your indefatigable efficiency and sterling administrative support, my dear.'

Pays her peanuts, feeds her flattery, Emma decoded.

The secretary's green eyes flickered. Mollified, she retreated behind a simpering nod, acknowledging the tribute.

Dr Flint returned her pale blue gaze upon Emma. 'Come.'

* * *

'I'm putting you in here for tonight. Staff, naturally, enjoy more comfortable accommodation but it might be interesting for you to sample the girls' spartan life.'

Bet they don't get salmon mousse and Chablis for supper either, Emma mused, peering into the gloom of the forlorn little room.

'Go right in,' Felicity Flint instructed, opening the bedroom door wider and ushering Emma inside.

It certainly was spartan. An iron-framed bed, hard mattress and a mean, single pillow met her dismayed gaze. A plain chair, small table and ancient wardrobe completed the furniture. A single, naked bulb lit the room with a weak forty watts. The pale green linoleum floor was uncarpeted.

'I'll bring you another pillow and an extra blanket, my dear, after you have bathed.'

Emma murmured her thanks, shuddering slightly at the idea of a night in the drab, joyless room.

'This landing,' the Head gestured, 'accommodates the older girls.'

'They are here? Next door?' Emma could not conceal her surprise.

'Most certainly. The Wigmore girl I caned this evening is most probably sound asleep next door as we speak.'

'And the bathroom?' Emma ventured, eager for a hot soak and anxious for some restful sleep.

'Change in here, take that robe –' the Head indicated a white towelling wrap pegged on the back of the door '– and you'll find the bathroom at the very end of the landing.'

'Thanks.'

Emma sat down on her bed, relieved to be alone. The bed squeaked protestingly under her soft bottom's weight. Emma sighed. She should be in London now, pampered in her SW7 pad. Well, hardly pad, she conceded. And not exactly pampered. Her friends, popping in on their way down to more spacious flats in Pimlico and Deptford, teased Emma for her snobbery in sticking to her Knightsbridge broom-cupboard. Her SW7 pad, Emma concluded, was actually only a notch or two up the estate agent's slippery pole from this.

A hot bath.

She undressed, folding her clothes carefully and placing them across the back of the chair, not wishing to disturb her sleeping neighbours by clicking the wardrobe door. Naked, she padded across the cool linoleum to her window. Outside, the moon was riding high in the inky dark night sky. Gaunt, leafless elms stretched their branches up as if to snatch down the elusive moon above. A soft wind moaned, its cheerless note heralding further rain. Somewhere in the distance, a mournful owl hooted. Emma shivered, smothering a squeak as her nipples kissed the cold glass pane. Returning to her bed, she hugged her breasts, squashing their soft warmth up into a delicious bulge. Her nipples, already peaked, stiffened and engorged.

Emma's mind surged with an almost overwhelming flood of images from her eventful evening at Laments Hall. She must go and have that deliciously hot bath now, then back to her bed where, in peace and privacy, fingers flaying her slit, she would summon up the pent-up climax her body was silently screaming for.

The water was lukewarm, trickling grudgingly out of the aged brass tap. It took ages to fill the bath up to a miserable five inches. No gel, no scented oils, no astringent salt crystals. Just a dried cake of vile, yellow carbolic. And the bathroom was cold and draughty. Emma heard the low, sorrowful hoot of the owl, probably flitting above the barely sugar twist chimneys. At least the mood music is bang on, she reflected grimly, lowering her buttocks into the tepid water and missing the Thunderclap Newman tape she always took into her SW7 power-shower – brilliant music, especially that funky piano bit, to masturbate to.

Her bath took a couple of shivering minutes then, hopping out, she dried herself briskly, donned the comfort of her robe and, after using the WC to pee, returned to her bedroom.

Scampering silently down the landing in the darkness, she thought she heard a stern command. Muffled, but the terse tone was unmistakable. Pausing, she followed the landing down towards the source of the crisp command.

41

Pausing at a corner, she peeped around. It was the Head, in whispered conversation with mademoiselle. Although Emma could not hear what was being said, she sensed from Dr Flint's dominant stance that Mme Puton was being severely admonished.

They were standing in a shaft of light from a partially opened door a little further down the stretch of landing behind them. The French mistress stood, head bowed, accepting the Head's whispered scolding meekly. Suddenly, to her amazement, Emma saw Miss Watson's face appear at the open door. Remaining carefully unobserved, the secretary was spying on the two women on the darkened landing. But surely, Emma thought, the Head could plainly see Miss Watson. The horn-rimmed spectacles glinted. Emma flattened herself against the wall, unable now to escape without being spotted.

Not in the appropriate place at the appropriate time. Emma remembered the Head's words to mademoiselle after Miss Watson's venomous little betrayal at the supper table. Then Emma recalled Mme Puton's pale, anxious face.

The secretary had stitched the chic, petite French mistress up – that business about not being in her classroom last Monday morning. 'My eyes and ears,' Felicity Flint had purred.

In the dim light from the open door, the Head appeared to be holding out her hand impatiently. Into it, Mme Puton surrendered her small cane. Emma smothered a gasp as she saw the French mistress turn, bend over and drag her tight skirt up to her hips. Black suspenders appeared, stretching up black stockings and dragging up the soot black stocking-tops towards the pantied cheeks above. Miss Watson, Emma saw, was now kneeling down in the doorway, her green eyes drinking in every detail of the impending punishment. Dr Flint reached out and dragged Mme Puton's black panties down, then took a pace back. Levelling the short cane, she depressed the stretch of the black panties down, revealing the full swell of the exposed bottom proffered up for punishment.

The Head flicked her wrist up, inching the tip of the bamboo along the crease of the dark cleft between the rounded cheeks. Emma tensed, her throat tightening painfully. The cane traced the length of the shadowed cleft down, the firm finger of bamboo rasping the sensitive ribbon of flesh. Emma overhead mademoiselle hiss aloud, her feral snarl suggestive of pleasurable pain.

To Emma's surprise, Dr Felicity Flint stepped forward, her skirt brushing the bending French woman's exposed thighs. Tossing the short length of cane down – to Emma's fleeting disappointment and dismay – the Head cupped her right hand and drew it up between mademoiselle's trembling, black-stockinged thighs.

Emma's own slit seethed as she peeped into the half-lit gloom where the Head, with dominant intimacy, continued to cup and squeeze the moaning French woman's captive pussy. Emma's responsive trickle of scald seeped from her freely, the hot ooze soaking her upper thighs and seeping into the aperture of her cleft which sliced her tightly clenched buttocks. Giddy, she almost swooned, steadying herself against the wall as the low moans of the bare-bottomed mademoiselle haunted her whirling brain.

Dr Felicity Flint stepped back once more, dried her wet palm on Mme Puton's stockinged thigh, stooped to snatch up the cane – and then whipped the bamboo down four times in rapid succession across the upturned cheeks. Lowering the glinting tip of the steadied cane once more into the stretched panties, the punisher flicked the cane upwards, lightly but stingingly, into the wet heat of the punished French woman's sensitive pussy.

Mme Puton squealed softly, writhing under the cruel affection of the inquisitive cane. Dr Flint lowered the whippy wood down and, snapping the black panties back up over the caned buttocks, curtly dismissed the member of staff she had just chastised.

Emma tensed, flattening herself against the wall as Mme Puton stumbled past in the gloom. Head down, her palms pressed together as if in prayer at her pussy, the French mistress scuttled by. Emma heard the whimpering – and caught the delicious odour of the caned woman's sexual arousal mixed with the perfume of her orange water.

Back on the landing, the secretary emerged from her hiding place, remaining on her knees as she shuffled towards Dr Flint. Tearing off her horn-rimmed spectacles, Miss Watson kneeled before the stern Head. Craning her neck painfully, she stretched up to reach – and kiss – the wet tip of the cane fresh from Mme Puton's punished slit. Then, Emma shivered as she watched, the green-eyed secretary licked her lips before burying her face into Felicity Flint's pubic mound, murmuring muffled thank-yous. The Head gazed down at her devoted assistant, further rewarding her loyalty by patting and stroking the bowed head at her warmth.

Back in her bedroom, Emma slipped off her white towelling robe and eased her trembling nakedness into the cold, narrow bed. Seconds later, she was grinding her buttocks into the hard mattress, then rolling her cheeks deliberately until her splayed cleft ached sweetly. At her breasts, the fingers pinching her nipples up into painful peaks became hands that, palms cupped, squeezed her swollen bosom. Spreading her thighs wide, Emma took a deep breath and paused to linger over the delicious task of selecting an image from the evening – an image to fuel her masturbation.

There were so many – some vivid, others merely fleeting, half-remembered moments of intense excitement. The blonde being spanked across Kate's knee. Yes. Emma's fingers found her wet pubic fringe and plucked at the fronds of coiled hair. Rebecca in the Head's study, penitent and poised for her pain. Yes. Emma's fingertips spread her outer labia apart, wriggling her buttocks as the sticky flesh-lips peeled. Dr Flint plying her cane. *Swish*. Red stripes crimsoning. Rebecca's whipped cheeks writhing. Yes. Emma's fingers probed, prising her inner, tighter lips wider.

Other images flooded into Emma's brain in a riotous kaleidoscope of undisciplined pleasure. Finding her clitoral

44

bud with her thumbtip, Emma punished it rhythmically. Her belly shuddered; her climax was almost upon her. Rolling over in her narrow bed, crushing her breasts into the hard mattress, she jerked her left hand down to her bottom, her thumb extended in preparedness to probe her sphincter for an anal wank.

Hot faced, her nostrils slightly flared, Emma writhed as she punished her clitoris with her right hand – now trapped at the base of her belly – and raked her sticky cleft with the fingernails of her left hand. She brought two images into sharper focus behind her eyes: Rebecca's caned bottom and Mme Puton's exposed pussy-flesh being tormented by the dominant Dr Flint's stern cane. Emma selected the latter.

Yes. The black suspenders framing the beautiful, bare bottom of Mme Puton. The taut black straps taming the swell of her creamy ripe buttocks. Yes. The black panties stretched between poor mademoiselle's aching thighs. The glinting tip of the cane flicking up to scald the seethe above. Yes. Slipping her thumb into her pouting anus, Emma drove it ruthlessly into her muscled warmth. Her hot juices scalded her as, jabbing her thumb between her clenched buttocks – and rhythmically ravishing her clitoris – she felt the bed falling away from beneath her as her orgasms welled up like milk on the boil and spilled over in a pulsing, violent paroxysm.

No. No. Not that. Emma whimpered her denial out loud. Just as she loosened her grip on all things rational – tumbling into the mindlessness of her savage climax – Emma's mind was flooded with one dominant image: being bent over by the sterm gym mistress in the study and having her bare bottom lashed by the supple leather belt.

No. No. Not that. But the urgent image of the heavy breasts bulging in the taut bondage of the yellow vest burned brightly. Emma shook her head in denial, squeezing her eyes tightly to extinguish the overwhelming images blazing behind them. The black, short, pleated gym skirt tap-tapping against the firm, bronzed thighs as the gym mistress whipped the leather down. No.

Too late. It was into the disturbing waters mirroring her earlier humiliation, punishment and brief taste of pain that Emma drowned in as the wet heat of her first orgasm – immediately followed by a second – soaked her right hand, inner thighs and white sheet.

Eyes shut tight, mouth gaping open as she panted on the utter brink of exhaustion, Emma slowly drew both her hands up to the edges of the hard pillow at her face. Taloning it, she jerked her bottom furiously and slammed her slit into the mattress.

'And what have you been thinking of, my dear, hmm?'

Emma screamed softly in alarm. Opening her eyes wide, she saw Dr Flint standing by the side of her bed, cradling a pillow and the promised extra blanket to her bosom.

Too shocked to feel any shame, Emma merely blinked and gazed up at the dominant Head. Her grey eyes were bleary, their light dull, as if Emma had been roused from a drunken stupor.

'Tell me. I want you to tell me, Emma.'

Emma grunted an uncomprehending 'what' into her pillow.

'What were you thinking about, just then, when you were masturbating?' the Head asked gently.

Blushing furiously as she struggled up on to her elbows, Emma twisted her face away, then wriggled and shrank down under her blanket. The iron frame of her bed creaked softly. Emma felt the weight of Felicity Flint's buttocks dimpling the mattress as the Head sat down on the bed. She felt a strong, slender hand dragging down the single blanket that covered her shoulders, back and buttocks. Emma felt the chill air at her flesh as the peeled blanket came to rest at her thighs. She felt the firm palm of Dr Felicity Flint caressing and massaging her soft, naked cheeks.

'Tell me. I mean to know your secrets.'

Emma whispered into her pillow, confessing that she had started to masturbate to images of others being punished – just awake and aware enough to omit any mention of witnessing Mme Puton's sweet pain.

'Ah, but when you came, girl. Tell me.'

The silence hung between them like a heavy curtain. The Head rippled its folds with her insistence.

'Tell me,' Emma heard Dr Flint demand, the hand at her bottom pausing in its gentle massage to become a talon of firm fingers that gripped her quivering globes.

Emma swallowed, took a deep breath and admitted that it was her own two stripes bequeathed by Marion's belt that she had contemplated – celebrated – at the exact moment at her climax.

The gripping hand at her left buttock worked feverishly. Emma squirmed in her bed.

'Sleep now, girl. I believe you have more to tell me. I have been observing you, Emma, from the moment you arrived here at Laments. I sense there is a path you wish to tread but do not.'

Emma moaned as a firm forefinger lightly raked the length of her cleft. The palm pressed down against the fleshy curves of her cheeks. The slow massaging resumed.

'There is a dark pleasure you desire, but dare not acknowlege. Yet. Later, girl, when the moment is ripe, you will tell me and I will –'

The slowly massaging palm alighted from Emma's soft cheeks as Dr Felicity Flint stretched down, plucked up the blanket and drew it up to Emma's shoulders. Spreading the second blanket out in silence, the Head ensured a measure of extra warmth and comfort for the girl whose thick blonde mane lay tousled on the white pillow.

'Emma,' the normally stern voice whispered gently.

No reply came from the girl in the bed. Nothing more than a single, deep, contented moan. When Dr Flint bent down to kiss her guest good night, Emma was fast asleep.

Three

Emma opened her eyes. The whiteness of the pillow blinded her. She blinked. A soft hand, palm down, was gently stroking her hair. Face pressed into her pillow, Emma closed her eyes and swallowed silently. Her tongue thickened, feeling huge inside her dry mouth, as the hand became a single fingertip that slowly traced the line of her spine towards the swell of her buttocks. Emma squeezed her thighs together surreptitiously beneath the scant cover of her blanket. Her nipples hardened, their painful peaks kissing the taut stretch of the cotton sheet beneath. The dominant fingertip fleetingly flicked down at her anal whorl – Emma smothered her squeal of delight as the varnished nail touched her sticky sphincter – before tap-tapping the rounded swell of her left buttock. Emma squirmed, her breasts growing increasingly heavier as she crushed them firmly into the bed.

'Awake?' a soft voice whispered, softer than the whisper of the blanket being dragged down an inch at a time to reveal her utter nakedness.

Emma, recognising Kate's youthful tone, continued to pretend to sleep. The fingertip withdrew from her bottom, leaving the left cheek it had been fiercely dimpling aquiver. A slick of arousal spilled from Emma's slit-lips, staining the swathe of crisp cotton at her thighs.

Bereft of the blanket, Emma stretched in her pretence of sleep, hugging the pillow between her fists and spreading her bared cheeks wide – as if willing Kate's fingertip back;

48

back to her bottom to sweep dominantly down along the velvety ribbon of the cleft between her welcoming buttocks.

'Or only pretending, hmm?' Kate whispered.

The naked girl, smothering a giggle into her pillow, attempted an unconvincing snore as she inched her hips up a fraction from the white sheet. As she did so, a second silver bubble burst at her wet labial smile, widening the sticky stain below.

Please. Please. Touch me. Caress me. The silent shouts filled Emma's whirling brain. Suddenly hungry for pleasure, she shamelessly willed the dark-haired spanker's hand back down to visit her naked, upturned bottom. Dark-haired Kate. With those warm, brown eyes. And those slender, strong hands, one of which was now hovering deliciously above her defenceless cheeks. Strong hands. Spanking hands. Emma juiced uncontrollably as she remembered Kate's spanking hands glimpsed through the parted curtain late last night. Glimpsed from the darkness outside as in the warmth and brightness of the staff sitting room, they severely reddened the bending blonde's bare bottom.

Smack. It was a gentle spank, echoing softly in the darkened bedroom. Biting the pillow, Emma smothered her scream of delight as she ground her slit into the taut sheet beneath her. The labia spread apart, their splayed, sticky lips instantly glued to the stretched cotton. Smack. The spanked cheeks wobbled. Emma bucked, arching her spine – and painfully peeling her labial lips from the sheet. This time, her scream was piercing.

'I thought so,' Kate whispered triumphantly.

Smack. Smack. The punisher's slender, strong hand left pale pink blotches that deepened where it had briskly slapped the upturned buttocks of the naked girl on the bed.

'Pretending is a lie, and,' she hissed, 'liars must and will be punished.'

Emma moaned, writhing as the stinging warmth spread its crimson across the curves of her spanked cheeks.

'Punished,' Kate murmured, stretching her left arm out to pin Emma firmly by the nape of her neck – and delivering two sharper, distinctly sterner spanks.

Pinned down and helpless, Emma wriggled and squealed. *Spank*. The ringing blow that reddened her right cheek instantly had the naked girl twisting and threshing in response. But the spanker's pinioning grip made sure that there was no escape for her squirming victim.

'I'm awake, I'm awake,' Emma protested.

Kate forced her left hand downwards, crushing Emma's face submissively into the pillow and smothering her squeals for mercy. Emma sensed a swift movement, the shifting of weight on the bed, as Kate dropped down on to her knees. The gripping left hand was instantly replaced by Kate's right hand at the nape of Emma's neck – ensuring that full and total subjugation was maintained.

'Want to know what a real spanking feels like, hmm? Want a properly punished bottom?'

Emma shook her head into the pillow.

'Is that a no?' Kate mocked.

Emma wriggled vigorously within the vice-like grip that held her in her punisher's strict thrall.

'Or are you pretending? Again. Another little lie?' Kate insisted.

Spank. Spank. The double echo shattered the intense silence of the bedroom. Kate's hot palm fluttered down to revisit the cheeks it had just ravaged. Emma mewed aloud like a cat at its kipper as the smoothing palm circled slowly, tenderly yet dominantly across the curves of her crimsoned cheeks.

Emma's buttocks tightened, the curves hardening as she clenched them expectantly, anxiously – fearing another sharp taste of severe discipline. But the searing swipes did not explode across her naked bottom. Instead, dry, warm lips fleetingly kissed her scalded rump. Hot breath invaded the secret shadow of her dark cleft. A sticky tongue-tip flickered out. Licking. Lapping.

'Nice?' Kate whispered, mumbling the word into the satin warmth of Emma's captive cheek.

The pillow absorbed most of Emma's 'mmmm'.

'Nicer than –' *Spank*. The crisp caress of the hot palm down across the bare bottom elicited a shrill squeal from Emma.

Kate sprang up from the side of the bed, pushing her slender hands, fingers splayed wide, through the tumble of her dark hair. Elbows angled, her brown eyes sparkled as she gazed down at the reddened cheeks.

'Let me know if you ever decide –'

'Decide? Decide what?' Emma muttered sullenly, twisting over on the bed and snatching the blanket up over her breasts.

'A French poet once wrote wisely of pleasure. In pleasure,' Kate continued, still gazing down searchingly into Emma's eyes, 'there must be the kisser. And the kissed. As pleasure deepens and the joy darkens,' Kate whispered fiercely, bending now to stroke Emma's blonde mane, 'there must be the spanker. And the spanked.'

Emma's grey eyes – widening at the words – shyly avoided Kate's penetrating gaze. A blush of confusion rose, turning her cheeks as pink as those just punished.

'Which are you, Emma?' Kate demanded. Suddenly, the dark-haired girl relaxed. A wide grin spread her lips apart. 'Put you down as a don't know, hmm? Still in a state of delicious doubt?' Kate teased, adding drily, 'Pity we can't phone a friend. Bet they'd know.'

Recognising the catchphrase, Emma giggled.

'Or would they?' Kate wondered aloud.

Emma shrugged. The blanket slipped, revealing her bare bosom.

'Breakfast in six minutes,' Kate warned, her brown eyes drinking in the pointed peaks of Emma's engorged nipples. 'The Head sent me to get you. And your Barbour.'

Emma sat up in bed and nodded. 'It's on the chair. Tore it a bit getting over the gates last night. Dr Flint –'

'Will see to it that it gets cleaned up and mended. Keys?'

Emma looked up.

'You came by car?'

'Oh, yes. In the pocket. Why?'

'No doubt some girl on a forfeit'll have to wash, wax and polish it until Felicity Flint can see her own reflection –'

'But I want to be off by ten thirty. Eleven at the latest.'

51

Kate remained silent as she plucked the Barbour up from the back of the chair and patted the pockets for the keys to The Beast.

'I have to be away by eleven. I've masses to do back in London,' Emma continued, rising up from her bed, her left hand dropping down belatedly to cup and cover her exposed blonde pubic snatch.

'We'll see. Breakfast awaits. Then you'll get the Grand Tour.'

Kate's words brought a grin to Emma's face. Exactly her own words for Felicity Flint's guided tour of Laments.

'But I will be able to get away –'

Kate draped the Barbour playfully over Emma's naked shoulders. The hem of the waxed jacket skimmed the blonde's soft buttocks. Emma wriggled. Kate slowly, firmly, drew up the strong brass zip, capturing and containing Emma's swollen breasts within the tightening jacket – and causing them to bulge.

'And miss the punishments?'

Emma flushed, dropping her grey eyes down, though still acutely conscious of Kate's searching gaze.

'Punishments?'

Kate dragged the zip down. Emma's left breast appeared, the nipple nuzzling the serrated brass track opened by the zipper.

'Rebecca Wigmore. And her pals,' Kate replied softly. 'It'll be a red rubbers job. Before afternoon tea.'

Emma's fingers fluttered at the hem of her waxed jacket, pulling it open and exposing her golden nest.

Kate's knuckled fist swept up, then down the unprotected pussy.

'The Head'll be bound to invite you to tea. Afterwards.'

Emma staggered half a pace backwards – then a full step forwards, bumping her pubic mound into Kate's clenched fist.

'And then Dr Flint will probably ask you to stay on. Here at Laments. Like she did me.' The knuckles worked gently at the moist warmth.

'Stay? You mean for a day or two?'

'No. Offer you a job. She wants you. Here at Laments. I've noticed the way she looks at you, Emma. And I've seen that look before.'

Emma swayed. *She wants you. The way she looks at you.* Kate's words echoed softly in her brain.

Kate released her grip on the waxed jacket and slipped it off Emma's shoulders. 'Come on. Get dressed. Breakfast.'

Responding to the sudden chill, Emma shivered. Her swollen breasts wobbled gently. The nipples ached sweetly: their pale pink points now dark with delicious, purpling pain.

'We'll just go up to the edge of the spinney. You'll be able to see all of Laments there.'

Dr Flint strode out energetically, leaving Emma trotting obediently in her majestic wake. All of Laments. Some sixteen and a half acres, secluded from the public behind the high wall. A very private place, Emma suddenly realised. Secluded, private and undisturbed enough for wayward young privileged girls to be fiercely schooled. To be severely trained and tamed. Images of the dominance and discipline she had already briefly witnessed flooded back. She blinked, her grey eyes watering in the strong, February early morning sunlight. Laments was certainly the place to dispense the discipline these proud young beauties so sorely needed.

'Hard work is very important. I insist upon it. I take pains to ensure that rigour and vigour are at the heart of the daily regime. Hard work is –' the Head paused, surveying her realm imperiously '– one form of discipline. Self-discipline. There are, of course, many forms of discipline.

Of course, Emma echoed. The crop. The cane. Many forms of discipline. The strap. Spanking. Paddles and leather belts. All featuring in the provision for the intimate instruction Laments dispensed, Emma mused, striding out to catch up.

'And sport? Games?' she asked, slightly out of breath.

Felicity Flint turned, regarding Emma with warm approval. 'Most certainly.' She nodded vigorously. 'Very character building. Sport and games are governed by rules. Strict obedience to the rules must be observed by all my girls here. Strict obedience. Obedience is far more important than any mere skill or flair. You are quite right, Emma. Laments promotes games most earnestly. All girls must participate.'

Emma shuddered slightly, quickly picturing the coltish eighteen-year-olds sullenly lining up in tight white vests and tiny, pleated skirts for lung-bursting bouts of hockey, net ball and lacrosse. She imagined them, sulky and reluctant, hating it. Hating being braless, their heavy breasts aching after just half an hour's fast and furious play. Out in the chill winter wind, their goose-pimpled thigh flesh below the hem of tiny, pleated skirts blotched with mottled orange. Sharp, frosty mornings, their thin vests no protection against the nipple-teasing cold air. Hating it and trembling as they waited for the shrill blast from the whistle glinting between the clenched teeth of Marion Aylott-Inche.

'Excellent discipline to be found on the playing fields,' the voice of Felicity Flint gently broke the soft silence. 'All girls are encouraged to participate.'

Encouraged. Emma shivered. The unfurling leather belt. The coiled strap lengthening out instantly with a vicious snap-crack. The swish of a flickering whippy cane sparkling brightly in the sunlight as it savagely kissed plump little short-sheathed bottoms. Crisp reminders to the shivering stragglers loitering on the touchline. Harsh promises of a spanking in the changing rooms after the match for those who shrank back from the sphere of play. Obedience to the strict rules. Emma thought of eager girls colliding on the hockey pitch, fouling each other outrageously. Breasts colliding, soft buttocks writhing. Tightly laced pumps flashing out to trip and topple the opponent. And afterwards, still wet bottomed from the obligatory shower, a cruel caning across those shining peach-cheeks for those who infringed the rules. Yes, Emma mused, the girls here at Laments would certainly not be deprived of sufficient encouragement.

'Tennis,' the Headmistress continued, her voice dropping half an octave down to a sibilant whisper. 'So testing.

The eye-hand co-ordination. Split-second decision making. And the courage – to dash up to the net or race back to the line for a lob. And such scope for coaching –'

Intimate instruction, Emma decoded grimly.

'I can train a girl in the courts and within a week she'll be putty in my hands.'

Her bottom certainly will, Emma surmised. Putty. Soft. Squeezable. Yes. In the strong, taloning grip of Felicity Flint's fingers, any bare bottom bereft of its blue knickers would certainly become pliant to the touch.

Beside her, Emma saw that the Head had lapsed into the silence of blissful reverie. Feeling obliged to comment, she desperately thought of something intelligent to say. Something positive, but she wanted to avoid direct reference to the punishments, discipline, training and correction which seemed to drench the atmosphere at Laments like heavy, February rain.

'The spinney,' she ventured, as they gained the crest of the hill. 'Does it belong to Laments?'

The Head nodded. 'It was coppiced three years ago. This year it will provide us with excellent birch twigs. Birch, as you may well know, is more supple, more stinging than bamboo when applied expertly across a bare female bottom.'

God, Emma thought, they're all bloody obsessed. Everything here comes back to bottoms. Bare bottoms. Bare bottoms, bending meekly to receive the blistering strokes of stinging birch or striping bamboo.

'So – so all we can see from this vantage point is Laments?' she countered faintly.

The Head slipped her arm around Emma's slender waist, drawing the young blonde closer. Emma sensed the other's assured dominance. She felt her thigh being pressed firmly against the maturer woman's warmth.

'Tell me a little more about yourself, Emma.'

Emma looked up. In the delicate tracery of twigs and leaf buds of the beech tree above she saw the morning sunshine glint on the silver of a freshly spun spider's web. The chill wind shivered the web, drawing a small, fat spider to its trembling edge.

Emma, surrendering to the firm embrace of the older woman, spoke softly, telling the Head of her boredom and admitting to her discontentment at work. She mentioned Striped Shirt's bullying. The office politics. Her utter disillusionment.

Up in the web, a small fly struggled as it became even more entangled in the silken mesh. Felicity Flint's encircling arm tightened. An encouraging squeeze prompted Emma to continue.

At length, the Head broke her silence. 'And Laments? Do you approve?'

Up above, the spider inched towards the helpless fly.

'Approve?' Emma whispered huskily.

'Of my purpose here. Of my aims. Of my methods.'

Emma felt the arm around her waist squeeze fiercely. She glimpsed up. The spider was upon its prey. Oh God. This is it, Emma thought. I'm as helpless as that bloody fly up there. She's going to ask me to stay on. Kate was right. She took a deep breath.

But when she spoke, no one was more surprised by her words than Emma herself. 'Discipline is essential when dealing with the wilful young female.'

Dr Flint inclined her head and patted her chignon. She nodded.

'There is the self-discipline, as you said, Head, of a regime that demands hard work –'

'And the benefits of sport. Sport and games.'

'Like tennis,' Emma whispered.

For the next six minutes, Emma spoke softly of how she would use the training of a pretty young girl in the skills of lawn tennis to break down that young spirited colt's impudent demeanour and sullen, insolent ways. Felicity Flint rasped out her warm approval, nodding vigorously as she squeezed Emma's hand. Emma, who had only meant to please the Head – before graciously declining any offer to remain at Laments – found herself teasing the older woman.

'The tiny white pleated skirt. So convenient for correction of the girl. A simple flip, and her bottom is bared . . .' Emma found herself enthusing.

Hell. What am I doing? I'm turning the old trout on, Emma half-giggled, half-chided herself. Careful, or you'll stir up a bloody hornets' nest.

Dr Flint dabbed her moist brow with a lace hankie. 'I see you truly believe in my methods. My methods of correction, chastisement and the imposition of punishments.'

Emma thought it wiser to remain cautiously silent. She had no need to reply. The Head launched unchecked into a lengthy sermon on the merits of dispensing strict and severe punishments, entering into such specific detail during her discourse that Emma felt her knickers becoming wet and warm with arousal.

'You will come to learn, Emma, that the punisher and the punished enter into a very special, privileged relationship. During intimate instruction. Once that intimacy has been rigorously established, the punisher can mould the punished's will to her complete and utter satisfaction. Liars can be taught to respect the truth. A thief, hot bottomed, quickly acquires a taste for honesty. Slackers, well whipped, soon learn to quicken their step. A bad girl, once introduced to the pain of the cane, can soon be turned back on to the straight and narrow.'

As straight and narrow as the crimson weals of a bamboo's bite, Emma thought. London. Supper in London. Tonight. She held on to that comforting thought. She couldn't wait to be behind the wheel of The Beast.

Avoiding the shivering web up above, Emma followed Felicity Flint out from under the beech tree. They slowly descended the grass slope down towards Laments Hall. The talk was innocent and pleasant, with the Head discussing last season's tennis at Wimbledon. They reached a gravel path.

She didn't offer me a job. Didn't invite me to stay, Emma suddenly realised. She blushed as mixed emotions troubled her in quick succession: disappointment, resentment then relief. What could she have been thinking? Playing up to the Head like that. Pretending to be in accord with the practice of punishment. Strict, corporal punishment. The spanking, slippering, strapping and caning of young girls' bare bottoms. Stay on here, in this hell-hole? No fear. She'd be back in London before poor Rebecca Wigmore's whipped buttocks had cooled.

'Let's just pop along to the gym,' the Head suggested.

Their feet trod in unison, crunching softly along the gravel path that skirted the neatly manicured lawns. A fresh wave swept over Emma. An intense feeling of anti-climax replaced the confused struggle she was experiencing. A struggle to identify her feelings between the opposing poles of relief and rejection. No job. Relief. Phew. No sticky awkwardness having to find the polite formula to say no. But rejection, too. Kate had said a job would be forthcoming. Why no job offer? Did the Head sense a weakness, a character flaw in Emma? And then there was that haunting phrase Kate had used. Red rubbers. The Wigmore whipping was to be a red rubber affair. Emma grew intensely curious despite herself.

They paused at the clear perspex doors that formed the inner entrance to the gym. Emma glimpsed the harsh neon strip lights burning within. A harsh, relentless light beneath which everything glinted and gleamed.

'Saturday morning workout for slackers,' Felicity Flint announced. 'I trust Marion is teaching them the error of their lazy little ways.'

Emma gulped. Marion Aylott-Inche. Lean, lithe and strap-happy. Emma had experienced the raw kiss of that strap. Briefly, but indelibly.

They passed into the gym. The perspex doors slapped loudly behind them. The sound of squeaking pumps on polished wood greeted Emma's ears. She froze, rooted to the spot. There were no girls in the gym. No nubile delinquents in cropped vests and buttock-sculpting shorts. Beneath the blaze of the bright neon above, she saw Marion, strap in hand, whistle poised at her pursed lips; and Miss Monteagle, Latin and Geography; together with Miss Rathbone, Maths and History. A shrill whistle blast brought the two panting teachers to an abrupt halt. They had both been running vigorously on the spot when Emma

58

had entered the gym behind Felicity Flint. Emma, blushing shyly, hung back in the shadows as the Head strode into the pool of light. Emma saw that both the teachers being disciplined were pink and perspiring. Each wore a pale green track suit.

'Caught slacking on Thursday afternoon. Chepstow. Watching the racing instead of their tutorial groups. Very lax.'

Sneaked on by the prying weasel Watson, Emma supposed, recovering somewhat from her initial shock.

'Good morning, Marion,' Felicity Flint bellowed good-humouredly. 'Putting these two slackers through their paces, I trust?'

The gym mistress nodded, gave her whistle a short blast and clapped her hands together sharply. Emma watched as both teachers sank down to the polished wooden floor to commence press-ups.

'Thirty,' the Head announced, treading the polished wood with menacing steps as she approached the two tutors. 'Followed by an ice cold shower.'

Miss Monteagle, jabbing her elbows out as her breasts squashed down into the hard wooden surface beneath, groaned. The Head's winking brogues inched closer to the prostrate teacher as Felicity Flint took up a dominant stance alongside. Emma thought she saw Miss Monteagle shrink back a little. The polished toe-caps came together and touched as the Head glared down. Miss Monteagle whimpered; a shudder quivered down her outstretched body. Felicity Flint raised her left shoe. The brogue hovered six inches above the buttocks of the Latin and Geography mistress.

'Naughty,' the Head hissed.

'I'm so sorry –' came the whimpered response.

The sole of the polished brogue kissed the swell of the upturned buttocks.

'Naughty,' the Head murmured, treading the curved cheeks down vehemently.

Emma, still loitering in the shadows of the outer gym, gasped softly as she watched the Head of Laments viciously treading the pinioned tutor down into the shining surface of the floor.

'Another whimper? Not complaining, I trust, Monteagle?'

'N-No, Head.'

'But then you are familiar with the rules. And the penalty that must be paid for breaking them. You know my insistance upon strict observance. Break the rules, Monteagle, and be prepared to suffer.'

'Yes, Head.'

'Intelligence reached me that you were slacking on Thursday afternoon. Slacking must not and indeed will not be tolerated, Monteagle. Track suit bottoms down, if you please.'

'Please, Head –'

'At once.'

Emma instinctively stepped back shyly as she saw the elasticated waistband peeling back over the swell of the teacher's upturned cheeks. Grinding her breasts into the wooden floor of the gym, the Latin and Geography mistress wriggled her buttocks as she bared them obediently.

The Head stubbed the toe of her brogue into the polished wood. 'Marion,' she purred, gazing down at the naked cheeks below. 'Five strokes, if you would be so kind.'

Emma blushed furiously yet stared hungrily at the bottom that was about to be beaten. Her nipples rose up stiffly, as if saluting the length of leather being unfurled by the gym mistress.

'Marion Aylott-Inche is superb with the strap. Watch. Watch and learn, my dear,' Felicity Flint whispered, joining Emma and linking arms. Firmly.

'Discipline must be maintained,' she remarked, gently propelling Emma forwards into the arena of impending pain. 'All here at Laments must obey. The privilege of punishment must not apply to the girls alone.'

Emma gasped softly as she found herself gazing down directly at the plump cheeks of Miss Monteagle. Firm, swollen. Pliant. So deliciously curved. And the tantalising dark shadow of the cleft-crease dividing each flesh-hillock with mathematical exactitude. Superb cheeks, perfect specimens of the female form, quivering slightly as they shivered in anxious suspense for the kiss of the cruel strap's hide.

'Commence,' the Head barked.

The leather barked louder. Four blistering snap-cracks echoed around the cavernous gym, each raising a broad red weal across the ivory domes. The third slicing stroke elicited a low grunt from Miss Monteagle – the fourth, a smothered groan.

'One more, I think.'

Marion turned, nodded her agreement to the Head, then addressed the whipped cheeks once more. *Swish, crack.* Her leather lashed down viciously. Latin and Geography writhed, jerking her crimson buttocks up in a frenzy. Emma saw the cleft yawn obscenely. Saw the wet slit winking in the harsh neon light. Saw the taloning fingers of the whipped mistress scrabbling uselessly into the polished wooden floor.

The Head tightened her grip on Emma's arm. Emma felt her panties growing heavy with her wet arousal. Her soak stuck to the fabric just as if an egg had been cracked against her pubic mound.

'That'll teach you to watch the racing at Chepstow instead of conducting tutorials,' Felicity Flint hissed, treading down the strap-seared buttocks with her dominant brogue. 'Agreed?'

'Yes, Head.'

'Rathbone,' Dr Flint rasped.

Emma, who had been avidly watching Miss Monteagle's fingers snatching her track suit bottoms up over her striped cheeks, looked across to where the Maths and History mistress gazed up in dread at the Head. Twisting awkwardly, the tutor's perspiring face turned pale. Felicity Flint angled her elbows as she rested her hands on her hips and planted her feet apart. The tutor's eyes widened. The pale blue suddenly darkened with fearful expectation.

'Your horse was running at Chepstow, wasn't it?'

'Yes, Dr Flint.'

'A tenner on the nose, I gather.'

Miss Rathbone flushed and lowered her head in shame. 'Yes, Head.'

Watson again, Emma shuddered. Worse than bloody MI5.

'Then I think ten on the backside a most fitting punishment. Marion,' the Head commanded, 'ten strokes, if you will.'

Emma looked on, spellbound, as the gym mistress strode across, strap in hand, and straddled the bare-bottomed Maths and History tutor. *Swish, crack.* The leather was plied and planted judiciously down, expertly striping the creamy cheeks with a livid line of scarlet. Miss Rathbone hissed like a scalded cobra. The whipping continued, filling the echoing gym with the eerie swish-swipes of the cracking leather and the choking sorrow-sobs from the writhing, red-buttocked teacher.

Miss Rathbone squealed piercingly after the seventh, jerked in agony after the bite of the eighth – and strove to protect her bottom with fluttering hands before the tenth and final stroke. Emma held her breath as she studied the pathetic pink palms quivering to protect the crimson cheeks from the leather.

'Rathbone,' the Head growled, her harsh voice breaking the intense silence. 'Hands away this instant. You know the rules here at Laments. Break them, and you will suffer. The rules stipulate that no movement of the hands is permitted during punishment. As you very well know.'

The hands, palms facing outwards, knuckles in against the punished cheeks, remained in their defensive position. Emma tensed, wondering how either the Head or the cruel gym mistress would deal with this disobedience. This disobedience to the rule. The leather belt snapped twice in vicious succession. Emma exhaled silently, sensing the relief in her tightening lungs as she breathed out, when the trembling hands turned palm-inwards then slid down the swell of each whipped cheek to the polished wooden floor.

'Disgraceful,' the Head barked – causing Miss Rathbone's hands to tighten up into frightened little fists.

'You broke the rules, Rathbone,' Marion snarled, thumbing her length of supple hide eagerly and looking to the Head for further instructions.

'You know perfectly well, Rathbone,' Dr Flint murmured suavely, 'that all punishments on the bare must be received and accepted without any interruption or show of defiance. Defiance or resistance. Marion, repeat the punishment from the beginning. Ten strokes. Commence.'

Emma averted her gaze, avoiding the mute appeal of anguish in Miss Rathbone's frightened eyes. Already slightly uncomfortable – but not unwilling – at being an intruder into this very private circle, Emma simply could not meet the Maths and History tutor's troubled eyes.

Crack. Crack. This time Marion really made the leather sing. Sharp notes in praise of pain. The leather snapped down across the defenceless cheeks, the cruel hide blistering their crimsoning globes. Emma saw both buttocks clench in an agonised spasm then suddenly loosen, joggling deliciously. Emma concentrated her gaze on the cleft between them, her throat tightening in response as the dark shadow narrowed to a fierce crease as the superb cheeks spasmed and hardened again under the third and fourth strokes.

Crack. Crack. The fifth and sixth. Marion, astride the outstretched tutor, paused, dangling the tip of her leather strap down for a delicious, spellbinding moment or two, allowing the snout of the leather to caress the peaches it had just punished. The dark cleft narrowed once more into a severe crease as Miss Rathbone, fists clenched and drumming the polished wooden floor, squeezed her whipped buttocks tightly.

Emma felt the light touch of the Head's outstretched hand alight on her shoulder, then sensed the gentle tug as Felicity Flint drew her closer to witness the conclusion of the punishment.

'Punishment is my policy and pain is my philosophy here at Laments, Emma,' came the excited whisper. 'Observe.'

Crack. Crack. Crack. A searing triple echo rang out as Marion, responding to the Head's vigorous nod, brutally applied the lash. Miss Rathbone suppressed her whimpering moan, just. Emma saw the tutor's face pressed fiercely into the hard wooden floor as her hips and whipped cheeks jerked and bucked up in the air behind her. Half-sprawled, half-kneeling, it seemed to Emma as if the tutor was raising her buttocks willingly for the whip. No. Surely not.

Felicity Flint's hand found Emma's and squeezed it hard. A single stroke snapped aloud, leaving a livid line of pale blue pain that quickly deepened to a purplish weal.

Punishment is my policy, pain is my philosophy. The Head's words haunted and troubled Emma more than the firm hand clasping hers. As she gazed down with shy eagerness at the bare bottom being brutally whipped by the gym mistress, she suddenly remembered her own brief but blistering experience under Marion's belt.

But other words spoken by Felicity Flint swam up into her consciousness. Words Emma had not understood – or had refused to countenance. What had she said? *The privilege of punishment.* Yes. What the hell did that mean?

Crack. The final stroke. As it sliced down witheringly across Miss Rathbone's bunched cheeks – perfectly poised in the air for their pain – Emma blinked. The Maths and History teacher was moaning softly now, lips stretched wide apart, she was kissing the polished wooden floor feverishly. Even as Emma stared, wide eyed, the wet tongue protruded, licking the veneer's sheen fervently. Emma shivered as the glistening pink tongue lapped the wood hungrily. God, Emma murmured, barely audibly, she's coming. She's coming right there on the bloody floor. Emma shuddered and closed her eyes, burning with acute embarrassment.

Felicity Flint's grip tightened dominantly. Emma's grey eyes opened reluctantly, obediently, in response. As she gazed down at the whipped tutor writhing in an ecstasy of anguish on the gym floor, the opaque meaning of the Head's words crystallised into a sharp mosaic of meaning. *The privilege of punishment.* The sure and certain perverse pleasure that comes swiftly on the heels of sharp pain. A sweet suffering. A sugared sorrow. And it was not the sole preserve of the girls here under stern tutelage at Laments. Emma bubbled freely at her slit. Her outer labia pulsed as they smiled widely into her wet panties. The inner labia plucked and throbbed, a delicious tingle flamed deep into her wet heat. Emma squeezed her thighs together and staggered back two paces – causing the silvery bubble to burst silently, soaking anew her blonde pubic snatch. Emma positively dripped sweet honey from the depths of her hot hive.

'A cold shower apiece before lunch,' the Head instructed, satisfied with the results of Marion's dexterity with the leather on the bare bottom she had just finished inspecting. 'Four minutes under the water, at least.'

Marion, furling up her leather belt, nodded briskly. Miss Rathbone rose up from the gym floor, drawing her track suit bottoms up to her thighs. All strength seemed to have drained out of her trembling fingers. Useless, they left the elasticated waistband halfway up across her freshly whipped cheeks. The waistband bit fiercely into their pliant softness. Emma's nipples ached and her pussy became molten as she saw the upper curves of the squashed, punished buttocks bulge above the restricting elastic.

The Head steered Emma as they followed Marion Aylott-Inche and the two tutors into the showers at the far side of the gym. Quickly stripped out of their track suits, the two nudes shivered and shrieked as they stood penitently under the icy deluge.

'Four minutes, minimum,' Felicity Flint warned.

And where is the weasel, Emma suddenly wondered. Surely Miss Watson would have been given some reward for squealing on these two red-bottomed miscreants wailing under their cold shower. Hadn't she been allowed to secretly witness poor Mme Puton's harsh punishment from the shadows? Emma tore her eyes away from the shower under which, buttock to crimson buttock, the two tutors shivered and yelped. She glanced around, surreptitiously. Yes. There. The third changing cubicle on the left. Behind the plastic curtain. More than a shadow, surely. Yes. The silhouette of a crouching, concealed form. Now the figure was standing up, pressing into the plastic curtain. Emma saw the dull cloud where the moist heat of a mouth gasped into the opaque plastic.

Emma looked down. A grim smile of satisfaction flickered across her mouth, vanishing before Felicity Flint noticed it. Two toe-caps of two highly polished black shoes, pressed firmly together like the thighs of the hidden voyeur above, peeped out below the plastic curtain. Miss Watson's reward. To overhear each and every stroke of the whipping being administered out in the gym; every crack-snap of the leather and every shriek it elicited, then to spy on the torments of the two whipped teachers as they shivered, naked and ashamed, together under their cold shower.

Shit. The sooner I'm behind the wheel of The Beast and back on the road to London, Emma thought.

'Lunch,' Felicity Flint announced, having ostentatiously consulted her wristwatch to count out the four, long, miserable minutes for the shivering teachers squirming in their torment. After thanking Marion warmly for carrying out the punishments so superbly, she piloted Emma out of the gym.

Back outside in the crisp, bright February sunlight, Emma struggled to regain her poise. She ached for normality. To be far away from Laments. To be distanced from all it had shown her, especially her own inner turmoil. Emma strove to reject all of those delicious, dark desires welling up within her. Dormant desires that had remained both undisturbed and unsuspected until Laments. Laments, where the swish of the cane was smothered by the hiss of sorrow – and satisfaction – from both the whipper and the whipped.

To be in The Beast and speeding away from Laments. To be miles away from the predatory menace of Felicity Flint whose easy dominance threatened to overwhelm. To be removed from this claustrophobic realm of pain and punishment. And the perversely pleasurable feelings they kindled and ignited.

As they entered Laments Hall, Emma found herself answering questions she had both anticipated and dreaded. The Head grilled her intimately on her reactions to what had just been witnessed in the gym. Emma blushed as she parried, unskilfully, unsuccessfully and increasingly unconvincingly. She struggled to avoid admitting to Felicity Flint the scale and depth of her intense curiosity and arousal. She almost managed to openly deny that which she secretly desired. That which thrilled and erotically electrified her. The Head listened impassively. Probably convinced her, Emma hoped. Probably. But in her innermost heart Emma knew that the wily old vixen had no doubt picked up on her scent. The whiff of her feral arousal that silvered from her tingling slit-lips.

Emma hid behind bland logic to mask her feelings. She admitted only to the need for rules and discipline. Logic dictated that punishments secured rules, obedience to them and strict codes of conduct.

'Pain is a stern tutor,' Emma heard herself confess.

Felicity Flint paused, turned and narrowed her eyes. Nodding slowly, she continued to gaze directly into Emma's wide, grey eyes.

'And out of obedience comes harmony. Without which,' she added, her tone warm and confiding, as if sharing an important secret, 'a small, tightly knit community such as Laments cannot possibly hope to function.'

Emma conceded the point. 'I see the need for your absolute authority when dealing with the wayward, wilful girls here, Head.'

'And staff, too, my dear. My staff need to be managed just as vehemently. Now run along and change your knickers. I'm sure after all that excitement in the gym you must be absolutely soaking.'

The Head turned on her brogues and strode away. Emma watched her, her face growing scarlet beneath her golden mane.

She met Kate on the stairs.

'Done the Grand Tour?'

Emma poked her tongue out in response.

'Take you to the gym?' Kate teased.

Emma grinned and nodded.

'Did Tweedledum and Tweedledee get it hot and hard?'

Emma blushed, then giggled. Kate's cheeky description of the two tutors was as apt as it was unkind.

'And was the weasel Watson there, peeping?' Kate whispered, stepping closer to Emma and touching her nose playfully.

Emma did not shrink back, but allowed Kate's hand to remain against her cheek. Kate saw Emma's silent, though eloquent, expression of surprise.

'I knew she'd squeal on them for slacking last Thursday. And –' Kate frowned fleetingly '– be allowed to watch. She's seen me being whipped.'

'I'm sure I saw her. Hiding behind a shower curtain,' Emma whispered.

'Knew it,' Kate crowed. 'She's always rewarded for her spying. So, who beat them? The Head, or Marion?'

'Marion.'

'Cane? Or that leather belt of hers?'

Emma replied, finding herself briefly launching into a vivid description of the whipping. She faltered, then fell silent.

Kate grinned. 'Cold shower afterwards? They'll be at it like bloody rabbits by now,' she remarked.

Emma's slightly raised eyebrows silently voiced her unspoken question. Kate nodded vigorously.

'Like bloody rabbits. Bunny and Cunny.'

Emma's mind flashed back to the gym. Not in memory but in her imagination. Across the polished gym floor in the darkness. Into the changing rooms at the far side. The showers. There, framed against the gleaming harshness of the wet, white tiles. Two naked, red-bottomed forty-something-year-old women teachers. Whimpering and shivering. Drying each other in silence, perhaps. A silence broken perhaps by occasional snivels. But surely nothing more?

Kate saw the doubt cloud Emma's grey eyes.

'Oh, but it's true. Inseparable, those two. Have been since the year dot, or whenever they graduated together. Tweedledum and Tweedledee. Offer you a job yet?'

Emma grinned, struggling to catch up with Kate's quicksilver mind.

'A job?' She shook her head. 'Nope.'

'She will. And will you take it?' Kate pressed eagerly.

'No way,' Emma gasped, surprised at her own sudden rising note of protest.

'You will,' Kate replied simply.

Unsettled by Kate's calm assurance, Emma tossed her head back in unspoken challenge.

Kate raised her left eyebrow, slightly. Ironically.

'Shan't,' Emma snapped, instantly regretting her silly, schoolgirl retort.

'You'd have been out of here like a shot at the first bare bottom if you didn't like what you saw,' Kate replied, her tone assured as it was maddeningly complacent.

Emma crimsoned, hating the truth being made so obvious.

'I betcha –' Kate laughed, easing the tension '– I betcha she'll offer you a temporary post here. A job. On trial. And I betcha you'll go for it.'

Emma released her hold on Kate's hand. 'What do you bet?' she bantered, suddenly enjoying the flirting.

'Hmm,' Kate mused aloud, exaggerating her consideration. 'Let's see. I know. A spanking. Tonight. Yes. I'll spank you in my bed, tonight –'

'But I'll be in –' Emma protested hotly.

'My bed. Tonight.'

Emma instinctively clenched her cheeks, despite her sure and certain knowledge that she would be miles away before sunset.

'You'll enjoy it,' Kate promised, laughing, as she skipped down the stairs and disappeared before Emma could reply.

At it like rabbits. Emma found herself fascinated by Kate's words. Fascinated by the thought of the two recently whipped teachers in the gym. No. Kate was only teasing. Surely? Kate was just being a little malicious. Mischievous. Tweedledum and Tweedledee. Two matronly tutors. Emma's mind refused to accept the idea, but her feet drew her hurriedly back along the gravel pathway between the manicured lawns towards the gym.

En route, in the crisp, cold sunlight, three girls were busy at The Beast, bending into their task of washing, waxing and polishing the car's sleek contours. Emma supressed her smug smile of satisfaction as she walked past and headed quickly for the gym. Pushing through the slapping plastic doors, she held them apart gently before closing them silently behind her. Inside, all was quiet and in darkness. Emma's nostrils caught the reek of female perspiration mixed with rank arousal haunting the darkness after the morning's punishments. She tiptoed across the polished wooden floor towards the changing rooms and showers at the far side of the gym. Halfway across, her toe scuffed the gym floor. She froze as the sharp squeak split the brooding silence. Listening intently, she heard nothing but the excited hammering of her heartbeat.

Stealthily inching towards the entrance to the changing area, she saw the dim light within. A single light bulb cast a soft light down on the white tiles below. Then she saw them. Latin and Geography, naked and kneeling, her face pressed up into the whipped buttocks of Maths and History who was spreadeagled face inwards against the shower wall.

Tweedledum and Tweedledee. It was a harsh, somewhat spiteful tag, Emma thought. The two tutors were, she discovered, quite beautiful women. Stripped of their dowdy cardigans and pleated skirts – the frumpish uniform of the sensible schoolmistress – they looked shapely, supple and sensual. Miss Rathbone's wet hair streamed down over her gleaming shoulders. It was much longer than Emma had suspected. It hung in loose abandon. In wet wantoness. The Maths and History teacher who had suffered so severely under Marion's strap faced the wet shine of the white tiles, crushing her heavy breasts into their hard shine. Her arms were stretched and splayed out wide up above her head, fingers star-fished out in ecstasy. She was kissing the white tiles as feverishly as she had earlier kissed the polished wooden floor during her punishment. Emma's grey eyes narrowed as they followed the sinuous furrow of the nude's spine down to where Miss Monteagle, kneeling, buried her upturned face deep into the whipped cheeks above.

Tweedledum and Tweedledee – a cruel term. Here were no staff room twitters, fussing over crosswords and cups of Earl Grey tea. Emma saw two superb specimens of naked womanhood drowning slowly in the velvet pool of intimate after-care. Two nudes entranced in their cameo of tenderness and devotion. Emma held her breath as she gazed at Miss Monteagle's tongue silvering the crimson of the other's belt-punished buttocks. Latin and Geography, kneeling in rapt adoration, had her hair still disciplined in a tight bun. Emma noted the broader, slightly fleshier shoulders and waist. The shorter spine, plumper hips. And the gorgeous swell of the ripe buttocks, accentuated by the kneeling nude's posture. Emma gasped as the heavy buttocks wobbled when Miss Monteagle shuffled slightly, parting her knees wider to nestle her face closer into the punished cheeks at her lips.

Miss Rathbone jerked her bottom out and groaned deeply as she felt the firm tongue raking her cleft. Her fingers scrabbled helplessly into the wet tiles. She screamed softly, then turned, guiding her pubis into the kneeling nude's mouth. Emma gulped as she watched Miss Monteagle cover the wet fig with her willing lips, and shuddered on seeing the ripple of Miss Monteagle's spasming buttocks as she sucked savagely at her partner's slit.

Grinding her whipped cheeks into the wet, hard tiles behind her, Maths and History thrust her pubis down on to the welcoming mouth of Latin and Geography. The kneeling nude drew her hands up to the other's hips to tame and steady her partner against the tiled wall. Emma saw Miss Monteagle's buttocks tense and tighten. She's tonguing her, Emma realised, gazing with fascination as the bare bottom softened then tightened rhythmically. She's tonguing her, Emma knew, decoding the spasmodic clenches that signalled each renewed tongue-thrust into the slit above.

Four

The refectory remained silent until Felicity Flint raised the little silver bell by her napkin and shook it briskly. It was the signal for lunch to be served. Two girls brought the baked potatoes, bowls of salad and delicious selection of cold meats to the top table. Kate forked both turkey and baked ham on to her plate. Emma took a snow white chicken breast. Marion, Emma noticed, prefered to pile her plate high with dark, thigh meat.

A low buzz of chatter rose up from the two long wooden tables seating the rest of the girls. Emma noticed that they consoled their appetites with baked potatoes sprinkled with grated cheese. A meagre, typical boarding school Saturday lunch. As she drizzled golden dressing on to her salad, she stole a glance along the top table to where Marion was firmly quartering her baked potato. It all seemed so civilised. So perfectly normal. As the escaping steam from her baked potato clouded Marion's silver knife, the gym mistress turned her pale, hazel eyes unblinkingly towards Miss Rathbone. The teacher she had, less than an hour since, whipped into orgasm with her leather belt.

'Are you doing Cromwell this term?'

Maths and History nodded.

'There's an excellent radio series coming up. Shall I ask Miss Watson to record them for you?'

Emma noticed that Dr Felicity Flint's eyes widened as an alertness quickened the Head's features.

Miss Rathbone glanced briefly at the Head then replied, thanking the gym mistress. 'Do, please. My girls will enjoy that.'

'They are not here to enjoy themselves,' the Head pronounced.

'No, Head,' Maths and History murmured, returning to the safety of her lunch.

Emma saw the Head fix the gym mistress with a challenging stare, but Marion pretended to busy herself with the salad dressing.

'I did not know you had an interest in the history curriculum, Marion,' Felicity Flint remarked. 'I would have thought it quite outside your province.'

Marion rejoined smoothly that surely each member of staff should have an interest in what was best for Laments.

Love all, Emma scored. They seemed evenly matched.

'And does your concern extend to Maths, Latin and French as well?'

Wow. What a volley; forty–thirty.

'I pride myself in being equal to all curriculum domains, Head,' came the sharp return.

Deuce. This was becoming a bloody grudge match, Emma thought, suppressing her sudden urge to giggle.

'An excellent strategy, my dear, and one which suggests ambition. No harm in it at all,' the Head conceded, adding the lethal lob, 'as long as you do not neglect that which is your right and proper concern.'

Hot shot. Game, set and match, Emma adjudged. Marion's cold stare met Emma's innocent grey gaze. Emma blushed and stared down at her chicken breast. Snow white and soft. As pale and seductively soft as the bare bottom of the Maths and History teacher. Beside it, the oil-drizzled halves of a tomato glistened. Bright red. Red and shiny. Just like the whipped bottom glimpsed in the cold shower after the blistering punishment with the leather belt. Emma jabbed her fork into the succulent flesh and raised it up to her lips. Just as the leather-lashed cheeks of the naked tutor had been offered up to be kissed slowly by her kneeling lover. Emma's throat tightened. She found it impossible to swallow.

'Wholemeal or –' the Head's voice broke into her reverie.

Felicity Flint was holding out the bread basket towards Emma.

'Thank you,' Emma whispered huskily, selecting a crusty, poppy-seeded cob and nibbled at the delicious, freshly baked bread.

'I have come to a decision. The wretched Wigmore brat and her confederates will not be beaten.'

A sudden silence swept over the entire room.

'This afternoon. Punishment postponed.'

Somewhere in the refectory, a knife clattered noisily down on to the polished surface of the dining table.

'Punishment postponed,' the Head repeated, thumbing open a soft bap.

Across the table, Marion Aylott-Inche frowned, openly signalling her dismay at the Head's pronouncement. Emma tensed. The hush pervading the refectory grew into a loud silence. An alert, uneasy silence.

'I really think –' Marion began, the note of protest in her voice unmistakable.

As if conscious of the dramatic effect of her words, the Head carefully inspected her baked ham.

'Delicious meat,' she announced to nobody in particular, crushing the gym mistress into a sullen silence. 'Marinated in marmalade, rum and French mustard before bringing it to the oven, I believe. Do try some, my dear.'

Swallowing awkwardly, Emma consented meekly to a thick slice of the moist meat.

'We'll have 'em all caned tomorrow afternoon. Before tea.'

The avidly listening girls suddenly became noisily busy with their knives and forks, digesting the prospect of this punishment postponed along with the melting cheddar inside their baked potatoes. Emma, now addressing her lunch with more concentration than was strictly required, tuned into the babble of their voices. The talk seemed prattling, typical schoolgirl stuff; teasing and boasting, clothes, the charts. No mention of pain, punishments or the strict regime here at Laments; no incautious asides or

74

injudicious whisperings. Just like any gaggle of rich and privileged boarding school girls loud at their Saturday lunch. Only one difference, Emma suddenly thought, dabbing a little American mustard on her ham. Instead of going out clubbing tonight on a weekend 'free' like their counterparts across the Shires, these eighteen- and nineteen-year-old young lovelies would remain gated here at Laments tonight: gated and under the constant threat of that intimate instruction which was both the policy and the philosophy of the stern Head.

Pudding – apple crumble and cream – was presented to the top table only. Emma saw that along the two tables, the girls made do with a yoghurt each.

'No, thanks.'

Emma and Kate skipped pudding, making straight to the cheese board. Felicity Flint glanced across just in time to see both their hands collide intimately over a wedge of ripe Brie.

'Ah,' the Head bantered, 'I see you share the same tastes. And appetites, I trust?'

Kate smiled. Emma blushed. Kate won the cheese knife and expertly cut a portion of the Brie for Emma's plate.

'Yes, Head,' she murmured, licking her fingertips delicately. 'Same tastes. Same appetites. Your judgement is sound.'

Felicity Flint patted her silver grey chignon complacently. Her pale blue eyes widened imperceptibly as she beamed across at Kate. 'Thank you, my dear. I find your comment considerably helpful in a matter I am hoping to resolve.'

Across the table, Marion Aylott-Inche champed a stalk of celery with unnecessary vigour. Kate winked at Emma across the bowl of fruit. Emma, crushing down the urge to giggle, bit into her Brie.

'Headstrong. And quite spoiled, of course. Pampered, no doubt, but I often find that there is a price to be paid for privilege. A very painful price.'

Emma's coffee had grown cold. For forty-five minutes she had sat toying with her *demi-tasse* in the Head's study listening as Felicity Flint, under the stern gaze of the tennis amazons arrayed up along the wall, expounded her principles on the strict tutelage of the wayward young daughters of the rich.

'Rehabilitation, training and correction through intensive, intimate instruction.'

Accessing wilful minds through the chastisement of nubile bodies. The battle for the spirit through the pains of the flesh. Lingering in delicious detail, the Head had lovingly explored every possible aspect of discipline and punishment at the disposal of her staff at Laments. The intensive teaching and coaching methods, the vigorous regime of hard work and games, obedience to the rules – and punishments. As Emma dragged her spoon through the dredge of congealed sugar at the bottom of her exquisite little coffee cup, she fervently wished she had changed her knickers before lunch as Felicity Flint had instructed. They were now quite soaked and stuck to her uncomfortably. The moist warmth spread back to her cleft. Sitting perched upon the edge of the leather club chair, she ached to pluck the crease of her wet panties from the divide between her swollen cheeks. Pluck the wet satin away from her buttocks and then prise it from her tingling pussy. Then, in privacy, deal with the molten seethe at her slit.

'Vigilance must be constant,' the Head continued.

She's bloody unquenchable, Emma mourned.

'Constant. Relax the rule for an instant and order crumbles into chaos,' Felicity Flint continued warmly.

Constant vigilance. Cue weasel-eyes Watson, Emma thought. An ever-vigilant second pair of eyes. And ears.

'I'll take you along with me on dorm patrol, tonight. You'd be surprised what the girls get up to after lights out. It never ceases to amaze me. Despite the severity of the penalties, some girls will risk flouting my rules.'

Dorm patrol. Tonight. Emma gently placed her coffee cup down.

'I really think that I must be –' she started, a little falteringly.

'My rules,' the Head broke in brusquely, ignoring Emma's attempt to speak. 'It has taken me almost six years

76

to get Laments this far, and there is still some considerable distance to go. And I still have my doubters, Emma. Oh, yes. There are enemies within the gates of Laments poised to replace me the moment I drop my guard.'

Emma's face rose, her sudden concern evident in her frown.

'It's true, I'm afraid.' Felicity Flint nodded. 'I cannot quite fully trust some of my own staff, would you believe. That is why I have to be so relentlessly firm with them.'

Emma, refusing to be sidetracked by the Head's sense of insecurity, doggedly returned to the question of her departure.

The Head dismissed the issue summarily. 'We will discuss that after the Wigmore girl has been properly punished tomorrow afternoon.'

The finality in Dr Flint's tone closed the matter firmly. Emma was confused. Confused and confounded. The Head was implacable. Try as she did, Emma could not reopen the subject of her departure.

Sod it. What's another day, she comforted herself. Stay. Stay and see what Kate meant by red rubbers. Stay and see the Wigmore girl get thrashed.

Emma suddenly relaxed. At least the sticky moment Kate had predicted had not materialised. The Head had not asked Emma to stay. There was no job on offer. That danger had, at least, passed safely by. She was, she realised, just a weekend guest. Relax, she told herself. Relax and enjoy it.

'Do some of your staff disagree with your methods, Head?' Emma asked, partly out of politeness and partly out of curiosity. Which of them could it be, she suddenly wondered. Tweedledum and Tweedledee were certainly under her thumb – and ever eager to please Felicity Flint.

'Disagree?' the Head echoed. 'No.' She laughed harshly. 'By no means, my dear girl. No. They do not disagree with me. They wish to replace me.'

Marion Aylott-Inche. Emma knew at once. Of course. It would have to be the forceful gym mistress. So, a potential coup, Emma mused. And what would become of Kate and

Mme Puton under the lash of the strap-happy gym mistress waiting in the wings to become the new Head of Laments.

Felicity Flint studied Emma carefully. 'Yes, Emma,' she whispered, 'the danger is very real. And very close.'

But with Watson as her watchdog, surely the Head was in no real danger. It all seemed too familiar to Emma, who remembered Striped Shirt back in London. Office politics and power games.

'Your deputy head –' Emma murmured, instantly wishing she hadn't.

'Marion?' Felicity Flint's head rose up sharply.

'She is the bursar here at Laments, isn't she?' Emma asked, somewhat lamely.

The Head nodded.

'A very –' Emma paused, uncertain of how to continue. 'A very sensitive position.'

'How right you are, Emma. And how shrewd. Yes, it is a strategic position to occupy.'

Their eyes met. Emma's grey gaze returned the Head's unblinkingly. Nothing more was actually said. But, tacitly, each felt they understood the other. The brief spell of silence that ensued was broken by a polite knock at the study door.

'Come in, Watson,' Felicity Flint commanded.

Emma found herself unsurprised to see the efficient secretary, spectacles flashing, enter. Everything in this place goes like clockwork, she thought. They're all like well-oiled cogs in a smoothly running machine. Everything's planned and prearranged to perfection.

Watson struggled into the study with a flip-chart. Having erected and positioned it to the Head's satisfaction, she departed in silence. The Head approached her desk and, stretching her slender hand down, selected a red-tipped felt pen. Back at the flip chart, Felicity Flint revealed the timetable for the coming week. The tip of the felt tip tapped the slot for Monday morning. Emma glanced up at the grid, making little of it, and caring less.

'I'm placing you here, with Mme Puton, for Monday morning. Nine sharp. Classroom six. I'd better initial it in.'

Open-mouthed, Emma stared up in stunned silence as she watched the Head's red felt tip initial her into the slot.

'There we are. E.W. Are you a Wiltshire Wyndlesham?' the Head asked.

Dumbfounded, Emma merely nodded.

'Then I dare say I know your people. Vaguely. Now, let me see,' she continued, studying the flip-chart and ignoring Emma's struggle to find her voice. 'Monday afternoon, you can watch Miss Monteagle at work, and I think a free on Tuesday morning. My plan is,' Dr Flint said, turning around to address Emma directly, 'to put you in with each of the tutors. Shadow them. Watch and observe their methods closely. Each has a different technique but all aspire to one goal. Discipline and punishment. You will, in time, come to devise and develop your own methods for instilling order and maintaining strict discipline. But remember this, my girl. However you choose to do it, however harshly it is done, strict discipline must be maintained. Understand?'

'But –' Emma quavered.

'I'm taking you on as a teaching assistant, initially. You will be upgraded in due course. When you've won your spurs. The financial rewards cannot, of course, hope to meet or match those you currently enjoy but,' the Head continued, barely pausing for breath, 'there are many, many pleasures to be enjoyed here at Laments.'

Pleasures and privileges, Emma thought. The privilege of punishment. She closed her eyes and pictured the naked, whipped buttocks of the punished mistress orgasming on the gym floor.

'Pleasures which I am sure you will come to discover will more than compensate for any mere loss of earnings.'

'Yes, but you see I don't –'

'The following week, you will deliver a programme of money management to the girls. Personal financial planning. That sort of thing. They need that practical sort of guidance. I think the Wigmore girl's behaviour proves my point. This can develop into sensible saving strategies followed by the management of investment portfolios. I leave the detail to you, my dear. You will give me a syllabus by the end of the month, I trust?'

'But I'm not sure that –' Emma replied haltingly.

God. This was it. The moment she had thought safely passed had suddenly arrived, catching her completely unawares. She was being offered a post here at Laments. More than that, she was being added to the timetable. Monday morning, with Mme Puton at nine sharp. It was just as Kate had threatened. No, promised. Emma felt confused.

'Well?' The red felt tip remained poised above the white paper. Poised like a cane hovering above pale buttocks. The Head slowly turned to the flip chart and underlined Emma's initials. A thin, scarlet weal. Just like a cane stroke bequeathed by the biting bamboo.

'I really wasn't expecting –'

'Oh, come now, surely Kate has already teased you about the possibility of your remaining here at Laments? Hm?'

Emma blushed. The Head's omniscience discomforted her.

'You do fully understand and appreciate the task we have before us here at Laments? Training and taming these wild and wilful young girls?'

'Oh, yes, of course. It is admirable.'

'Admirable it may be, Emma, but vital it most certainly is. And you approve of my strict regime –'

Emma nodded.

'And have no objection to the policy of punishment?'

And the philosophy of pain, Emma added silently. Again, she nodded.

'So what possible objection could you have to leaving your desk where you are harassed, unappreciated and undervalued and joining me here. You will neither be bored or unfulfilled as you presently are, and the girls will adore you.'

Emma's nipples stirred within the cups of their brassiered bondage.

'The work here is as remarkable as it is richly rewarding. You do not have any rooted objection to dispensing discipline, do you?'

Emma reddened. Her nipples peaked painfully.

'You are fully prepared to apply the cane to a naughty girl's bare bottom, aren't you?'

'I don't know. I've never –'

'You have observed our methods here at Laments. And responded positively. Tomorrow afternoon, you will witness the public punishment of Rebecca Wigmore. And her partners in crime. Soon, very soon, you will be obliged to apply the crop and the cane. Or strap, as Marion favours. You will, I hope, be equal to that task.'

'Yes. I will try –' Emma heard herself – to her amazement – respond.

'Spanking is a very acceptable form of chastisement. No doubt Kate, our resident expert, will instruct you in the finer points of that particular mode of discipline. Tonight, if I'm not mistaken –'

Emma gasped aloud.

'She won the bet, didn't she?' the Head countered.

Emma grinned, despite herself.

'She has brought to perfection the art of warming a bare bottom across her knee. Yes –' Felicity Flint nodded judiciously '– you will learn much from her – as you will when shadowing the rest of the staff. Good,' she concluded, covering the flip chart. 'It is settled, then. Please feel free to explore your new surroundings. I have already seen to it that you will be comfortably accommodated in new quarters. I've billeted you next door to Mme Puton. Hmm, that should prove both interesting and instructive. But take care, Emma. Look, listen and learn. I shall be watching you very carefully in the coming weeks. Do not disappoint me.'

'I'm going to teach you once and for all. It's either me or her,' Emma heard the voice of Marion Aylott-Inche hiss furiously. 'Once and for all, understand?'

Emma paused, holding her breath. She was upstairs on a landing forbidden to the girls. So who was behind the closed door, no doubt shivering in dread before the cruel gym mistress? Who was about to taste the lash of the unfurled leather?

There was no keyhole to peep through, and Emma certainly did not want to be discovered loitering outside the door. Especially not by Marion.

'Hands together. No, bitch, up above your head. Do it,' came the stern instruction. It brought a tingle of dark delight to Emma's labia. The moist lips parted slightly, kissing the fresh cotton panties she had just changed into.

'Legs open. Come on, wider. Wider, I said, or your breasts will suffer my strap again.' Marion's voice held a brutal tone of bullying.

Emma grew obsessed. She had to find out what was going on behind that closed door. Whatever the risk – or painful cost – she simply had to know. She glanced along the shadowed landing. The next door – leading into Miss Rathbone's quarters – was slightly ajar. Emma scuttled to the open door and peered in. Deserted. Of course, she had left Tweedledum and Tweedledee watching the last race from Wetherby down in the staff sitting room. She slipped inside and dashed across to the bay window. At the glass, she craned desperately, trying to look into the neighbouring room. Useless. The curtains next door had not been drawn fully across but the restricted angle did not give her a clear sight line.

Shit. No. Wait. On the far wall next door there was a mirror. An oval Queen Anne period looking glass suspended from a looped silver chain. In the glass, Emma glimpsed the image of Marion Aylott-Inche, fully clothed, tying a trembling pair of upraised hands together by the wrists. Lashing them fiercely and binding them tightly with a bronze nylon stocking.

Emma's outer labia kissed the cotton at her pubis hungrily. Her tiny clitoral thorn raked the stretch of wet fabric, causing her to squeeze her buttocks in delight.

The wrists struggled briefly in their bondage – a last futile gesture of defiance. Marion stepped back. Seconds later, Emma saw the tip of the strap flick across the Queen Anne glass. It had, she knew, just lashed the breasts of the bondaged nude.

To her increasing fury, Emma could not identify the punished nude in Marion's strict thrall. But she watched as

Marion stepped back once more, after fully satisfying herself that her victim was securely bound. Emma could partially see what was happening next door – but now she could not hear.

How utterly defenceless and helpless that victim must feel. Naked, squirming and bound before the lithe, powerfully muscled strap-wielding gym mistress. Emma had just had a taste of mesmeric helplessness in the Head's study – seated in the leather club chair, silent and astounded – as the Head had confidently scribbled in the initials E.W. into Monday morning's timetable slot alongside Mme Puton. She had been powerless to argue, resist or interrupt. And yet, sharpened by her experience working under Striped Shirt, Emma had a clever brain and subtle tongue. But the Head had rendered her helpless. How much more helpless and vulnerable, Emma realised, must Marion's naked, bound victim be right now.

Emma peeped through the bay window into the adjoining room. In Marion's clenched fist, reflected by the clouded looking glass, she saw the cruel length of a cream dildo. Oh, God, no. Not that, Emma whispered aloud.Arabella Knight But from the angle of Marion's elbow, Emma suddenly realised that the gym mistress was inserting the phallic shaft into her naked victim's mouth. To silence her. Emma shuddered.

Marion's image in the mirror shifted slightly as the gym mistress appeared to take two paces back. Emma saw the strap flicker and snap and then saw the tip arc up and away from the nude. Where had it kissed the naked flesh? Breasts, belly or below? From the brief glimpse of the gleaming leather, Emma knew with a cold horror that the lash had just savagely caressed the bound nude's slit.

Just visible over Marion's shoulder was the fleeting image of a jerking brunette. No face, just the writhing head of gleaming hair. Whose? Emma calculated rapidly. It could be Kate. Or one of the wretched girls. The tip of Marion's leather strap flashed up and backwards once more. Another fierce, upward swipe into the exposed pussy of the suffering nude. Emma strained up on painful tiptoe, but the Queen Anne glass stubbornly refused to reveal more than a tantalising glimpse of the dominance and discipline unfolding next door.

Should she sneak back outside and listen at the door? Bend, breathless and alert, to catch some overheard clue? Emma paused. To be caught doing so could ensure that Emma herself tasted the leather before supper.

Then, unexpectedly, in the mirror suspended by the silver chain, Emma saw Marion Aylott-Inche bend down, apparently kneeling. Emma dragged a chair across to the bay window and mounted it, precariously, her hot face pressed against the cold glass pane. All was now visible. The gym mistress could now be seen, in sharp detail, kneeling down to kiss the pussy she had so ruthlessly whipped with her leather belt. As the gym mistress buried her face up between the thighs of her jerking victim, Emma swore softly as she glimpsed the contorted features of the school secretary, Miss Watson, in the mirror. The distorted features of Watson, her spectacles still flashing despite being wildly askew. The thin, mean mouth was filled with the dildo – smothering her squeals of anguish and delight.

All staff were requested, by invitation of the Head, to attend supper in the refectory that night. Saturday supper was usually optional, Emma discovered. But not tonight. All were required, by instruction. Emma was quickly discovering that Dr Felicity Flint dressed all her steely imperatives in the velvet glove of politeness.

All staff – with the exception of Mme Puton – arrived punctually and took their places at the top table. The Head picked up the little bell and shook it impatiently. The Middleton-Peake girl, a smiling little busty blonde, appeared at the door.

'So –' the Head grimaced, lips pursed '– another forfeit, eh, girl?'

'Yes, Head, I'm runner tonight.'

'I'm sure a good hiding would have been a more fitting punishment.'

The Middleton-Peake girl's bosom bounced as she instinctively cupped her buttocks protectively with both hands.

'No matter,' the Head continued, 'I want you to inform Mme Puton that we await her presence here in the refectory.

'Yes, Head.' The young blonde's breasts, burgeoning within the straining stretch of her tight white vest, bounced again as she turned and scampered off to retrieve the missing French mistress.

Felicity Flint's pale blue eyes grew icier by the minute. Emma watched the slender fingers of the Head's right hand rhythmically drumming the polished surface of the refectory table. The tension was palpable as the silence grew ominously loud. The sound of running feet announced the return of the busty little blonde.

A pink face, framed by golden curls, above a heaving bosom, appeared at the refectory door.

The slender, strong fingers ceased their imperious drumming. 'Well, girl?' the Head demanded.

'Please accept Mme Puton's apologies,' the Middleton-Peake girl recited, struggling to remain word perfect with her message, 'but she has an awful lot of marking to catch up –'

'Nonsense,' the Head roared. 'Is our French mistress actually marking or is she having another of her interminable beauty treatments?'

Emma just caught the suppressed twittering of Tweedledum and Tweedledee.

The Middleton-Peake girl panicked. 'She's got cucumber on her eyes, Head,' she admitted slowly. 'And,' she continued, gathering pace, 'lots of cream all over her face and –'

The fingers recommenced their troubled drumming. 'Silence,' thundered the Head. 'You are to return to Mme Puton's quarters this instant and inform her that if she isn't present in this refectory, with or without her blasted cucumber, the consequences will be so dire that they will make the storming of the Bastille seem like a vicar's tea party. Do you understand me, girl?'

The Middleton-Peake girl paled. Committing the essence of the message to her fragile memory, she dashed off.

'Marking to catch up on,' the Head snorted. 'Cucumber slices. What's wrong with a bar of soap and a decent flannel, hmm?'

Maths and History, echoed by Latin and Geography, eagerly voiced their agreement. Emma fiddled with her napkin, avoiding Kate's ironic eye-brow play.

'At last,' the Head fumed, offering a less than enthusiastic greeting to the French mistress who strode into the refectory in a black silk kimono vividly decorated with red dragons.

Emma judged that, from the sinuous show of thigh and buttocks beneath the flowing silk, Mme Puton was naked underneath. Traces of face cream still adorned the latecomer's chin. Kate came to her rescue, miming with her napkin. Mme Puton dabbed at her chin insouciantly. Too late, Emma realised.

'Thank you,' the Head barked, 'for giving up your marking to be with us. Eventually. Be so good as to come to my study directly after supper, if you will. There are a few little matters relating to habits of punctuality and courtesy I feel we might fruitfully examine together.'

A whipping, Emma decoded. A searing appointment with the cane.

Mme Puton paled. Underneath the sarcasm, the promise of punishment and pain was implicit. Coated in exquisite politeness, but brutal when laid bare. Stripped of the velvet glove of politeness, Emma realised, the Head's steely menace glinted brightly.

'We have several issues to discuss this evening, now that we are all eventually assembled,' Felicity Flint announced. 'I therefore propose that we tackle the agenda and supper together,' she concluded, snapping open her folded napkin and tucking into her supper of sandwiches and chilled Soave.

All around the table agreed. Some merely nodding and biting into their sandwiches; Tweedledum and Tweedledee crowing a chorus of approval. Across the table, Kate

86

pulled a lightning-quick monkey face at Emma. Emma snorted, instantly earning a censorius glance from the Head. As Emma choked, red faced, into her smoked duck breast on rye, the pale blue gaze of Felicity Flint burned into her icily.

'First of all, my plans to develop the lower meadow into a full-size tennis court. I have decided to go ahead. Are we all in agreement?'

The question the Head had posed was clearly rhetorical. Dr Flint clearly envisaged no opposition to her plan. A murmur of approval came from Miss Monteagle and Miss Rathbone. Kate sipped her Soave then nodded her assent. Mme Puton, preoccupied with her appointment with the Head in the study after supper, said, 'Oui,' in a small voice.

It was Miss Watson, to Emma's surprise, who ventured the first note of dissent. 'But can we afford it at this juncture, Head? The drainage costs alone for such a venture will be prohibitive.'

Felicity Flint's eyes narrowed then widened. The moist crabmeat sandwich at her parted lips returned to her plate unbitten. 'Drainage costs?' she echoed coldly. 'What do you know of drainage costs?' the Head demanded, crushing the weasel-eyed secretary with a withering glance.

Emma froze, suddenly alert to a tension looming over the supper table. Clearly, she thought, the Head had expected to get full backing from her staff. Miss Watson, clearing her throat primly – and encouraged by a swift nod from Marion Aylott-Inche – returned to the fray.

'And such an expenditure for so few participants,' the secretary whined, her tone almost accusing. 'Even with such elaborate facilities, tennis will only be taken up by a mere handful –'

'All the girls here at Laments will be required to play,' the Head rejoined brusquely. 'Tennis is a splendid game. Character building –'

All the girls here at Laments will play, Emma repeated silently to herself. And in those tiny, white pleated skirts, white ankle socks and pumps topped by tight white cotton vests, won't they look delicious, Emma thought.

'All playing tennis?' the gym mistress interposed.

'Staff too,' the Head countered firmly.

'But we urgently need to upgrade our computing facilities, Dr Flint. You yourself stressed that only a week ago. And the gym needs some new equipment –'

The Head turned, like a lioness beset by snapping jackals. 'You and your precious gym. Get the girls outdoors. Fill their lungs with fresh air. Kate?'

Kate gazed over the rim of her wine glass.

'Your thoughts, please.'

Kate sipped her wine. After dabbing her napkin to her wet lips, she replied. 'I'm with you, Head,' she said.

Felicity Flint paused, heartened by the sincerity of the brown-eyed girl's positive response but dismayed by the lack of any actual argument.

'What does Emma think?' Kate murmured. 'As an outsider, what does she feel would be the best way to resolve this?'

Emma sensed all the faces around the table turning towards her. The Head repeated Kate's words, inviting Emma's opinion.

Emma considered her response very carefully. There definitely was something in the air. An ill-defined sense of unease, tension. It was even getting to Tweedledum and Tweedledee. Emma saw their fingers fluttering nervously at their untasted supper. Not open rebellion against the Head. No. But certainly an implicit challenge to her authority.

Or was Emma just very tired. Tired and confused after the roller-coaster ride of the last thirty hours. She had no intension of letting the Head down, but she certainly didn't want to annoy either Marion or the weasel Watson. No wait, she chided herself. She wasn't working for Striped Shirt any more. No more juggling integrity with fear. She'd been chosen to remain here at Laments by the Head and by God she'd back her to the hilt. Tough if she annoyed Marion and the weasel. Kate'd look out for me, she suddenly realised. Marion couldn't get her revenge with that bloody strap.

'An excellent idea,' Emma announced emphatically, instantly launching into a short sermon on the enormous potential for discipline, training and punishment opportunities that left Tweedledum and Tweedledee in silent rapture and the Head goggling with delight.

Shit. I've overdone it wee bit there, perhaps. Reining in a fraction, she became a little more sober. More the financially shrewd city whizz-kid.

'So I suggest a feasibility study followed by a cost-benefit analysis,' she concluded, adding that the medium- and long-term advantages must be considered. 'A huge selling point to future parents and guardians.'

'Excellent,' Felicity Flint pronounced, adopting Emma's contribution as a ringing endorsement. 'That's settled then.'

'But with respect, Dr Flint –' Marion butted in.

'I said that's settled,' the Head rejoined swiftly and suavely, a flash of steel shining in her voice.

'Not with the trustees,' the gym mistress muttered.

'And now, my second announcement. Please raise your glasses to welcome Emma, our new member of staff.'

Emma saw that the glasses of both Marion and Miss Watson were obediently raised – but not sipped from. Both abstained from the welcoming toast. The Head was quick to spot the gesture. Her silver chignon flounced as she turned swiftly towards them.

'Not drinking?' she challenged angrily, resenting the snub.

'This is all highly irregular, Head. I was not aware that interviewing for a post here at Laments had taken place –'

'Emma more than adequately meets our current curriculum needs –'

'I really do need an assistant in the gym –'

'Our current curriculum needs,' the Head reaffirmed. 'Emma is my choice. That is all that –'

'Have you consulted the trustees, Head? The staff budget is very tight, and then there is the matter of appropriate experience, references,' Miss Watson, taking her cue from Marion, objected.

The Head swept all such considerations aside. 'Miss Wyndlesham has joined Laments to teach money management and personal financial planning on a trial basis, naturally. The costs to Laments will be minimal.'

Bloody hell, Emma thought. I'm not doing this for a pittance. Bed and board and bare bottoms to beat. I want a proper salary.

'My decision is final. Please make Emma welcome. I trust you will all see to it that she settles into Laments and our ways as quickly and as smoothly as possible. She is a novice to the arts of discipline and will benefit from the instruction and guidance of you all,' the Head concluded. She tossed her napkin aside. 'Mme Puton. The study, if you will.'

Emma inspected her new quarters more closely, now she had the leisure to do so. They met with her instant approval. More than that, they met with her delight. It was a vast bedroom-cum-study. A large bed, fashioned in the French style from fruitwood, dominated the centre of the capacious room. A fitted gold carpet of Chinese silk softened her footfall – and prickled her pussy when she sprawled belly down and naked into its smooth pile. Soothing jade green and orange wallpaper graced the room with a touch of opulence. The furniture was sparse but exquisite: Dutch colonial cane pieces. Emma especially liked the small dressing table and mirror made from clouded silver bamboo. She fingered the shiny wood, thinking of other uses for the cane. Bare-bottomed uses. Studying the clouded sheen, her nipples thickened as she suddenly saw the opaque silver as pain trapped for eternity within the supple cane.

She turned, guiding her bare cheeks in against the raised curve of the desk top. Her buttocks parted as her cleft kissed the cool wood. Pressing her bottom more firmly, she shuddered as her cheeks splayed, allowing her hot anal whorl to pucker and plant a sticky kiss.

Dutch colonial bamboo. Before being bent to the craftsman's will to be fashioned into furniture, the individual canes would have been used to beat bronzed-buttocked slave girls. The silvery wands of woe would have whistled down, lashing their dusky cheeks and striping them with the crueler hue of crimson. Their shrieks, Emma imagined, raking her hot cleft down over the smooth curved wood, would have been absorbed by the bamboo that beat them – clouding its silver just as their tears of suffering softened their big, bright eyes.

She spun round, up on tiptoe, her pussy at the edge of the desk. Just as her buttocks had enfolded over the smooth cane, so did her labial flesh-folds. She felt the sticky lips of her outer labia dragging against the smooth cane. Shivering in her nakedness and increasing excitement, she flexed her knees and rode the bamboo rhythmically, her wetness lubricating the glide of secret flesh upon stern cane.

Her climax was imminent, its unseen fist about to clench within the trembling walls of her tight belly and punch downwards in violent ecstasy. Peeling her pubis away from the cane, she teetered tipsily across to the huge bed. Sprawled face down into her duvet, she ground her wet heat into its exquisite softness.

The image of Mme Puton flooded her brain. Behind tightly closed eyes, Emma conjured up feverish pictures of the punishment downstairs in the Head's study. Mme Puton would have been disciplined by now. Supper had been concluded abruptly forty minutes ago. Emma concentrated hard. Her squashed breasts felt full and swollen as she pictured the chic French mistress standing, her cropped auburn hair gleaming, head bowed in contrition. The Head would have delivered a stinging sermon, harshly castigating Mme Puton's vanity. Then the ominous silence, soon to be broken softly by the whispering threat of impending pain as the Head opened the drawer – *squeak*, Emma tensed, remembering that squeak of the opening drawer in the study below – followed by the rattle of the whippy cane being extracted.

Emma rasped her breasts savagely, dragging her stubby nipples up into tantalising torment. Down below in the

Head's study, behind the firmly closed door, the French mistress would have been curtly ordered to disrobe. Disrobe, and bend over to receive her punishment. To receive her cane strokes bare bottomed and bending before the ruthless Felicity Flint.

Emma juiced rapidly, soaking the duvet. The slightest rasp of the satin duvet at her nipples threatened to spill her headlong and helpless into orgasm.

Up on her elbows, inching her breasts away as she took deep, slow calming breaths, Emma squeezed her thighs together to capture and contain her wet heat. Shit. She'd never experienced anything quite like this. What the hell was happening to her?

Bowed down under the implacable weight of her seething desire to come, Emma sank back into the duvet's satin sheen. Instantly, as she screwed her eyes shut, the silent film started to flicker, flooding her once more with images of the punishment in the study below. Mme Puton being ordered to undress for the cane. The black silk, red-dragoned kimono being plucked open by trembling fingers before slithering down to form a puddle at the feet of the naked French mistress.

So intense, so vividly intense, were Emma's imaginings that she could almost smell the apple tree logs perfuming the study as they flickered in the open hearth. The Head, she knew, would have tap-tapped the desk, signalling with her cane tip that the moment had come. The moment for Mme Puton to bend over and offer her bare buttocks up submissively. The Head would then jerk up her bamboo, saluting the tennis amazons frozen behind the glint of their photo frames. Stepping forwards, the French mistress would obey – meekly bending and spreading her arms out across the desk as she nuzzled her face into its leather surface.

Emma loosened her thighs a fraction, allowing the slippery scald to ooze from her pussy. The hot trickle maddened her as it soaked her blonde nest and seeped between her thighs. Suddenly, she bubbled massively as she pictured the penitent's violet eyes, now wide with fearful expectation as the Head lightly skimmed the proffered buttocks with the quivering cane. Emma saw it all as if she was there, in the study. She saw the chic auburn hair become enchantingly disarrayed as Mme Puton bowed her head submissively; saw the bare bottom wobble imperceptibly as she tightened her cheeks in delicious dread of the bamboo's bite.

Would the Head have dispensed the discipline briskly and blisteringly? Eight cruel cane cuts in vicious succession? No. Emma thought not. Her fingers stole down below her belly to peel her labia even wider apart. So wide, it really hurt. Despite the sweet pain, Emma's fingers persisted, finger-nailing the more sensitive, inner labial lips until her spine arched and the cleft yawned between her jerking buttocks. Buttocks now thrust upwards like those of the French mistress would have been as the Head's cane lashed down. Slowly, savagely. Yes, Emma hissed aloud, biting into her pillow and worrying like a jackal with a bone. It would have been a slow, strict caning. Pacing the pain, prolonging the punishment. Adding red weal to each reddening stripe with measured majesty. The Head, queen of pain. The French mistress, her subject in suffering.

Swish. Emma almost heard the whistle of the slicing stroke. Emma knew that Mme Puton's heavy breasts would have been painfully squashed into the desk as the whipped nude jerked her whipped cheeks in agony. *Swish*. Remorseless. *Swish*. Relentless. *Swish*. Ruthless.

Emma forced three fingers frantically up her juicing hole, while striving to thumb her clitoral thorn for maximum pleasure. Struggling, almost choking into her pillow, she managed to arch her spine up, raising her belly and hips clear of the satin duvet to do full justice to her wet seethe. Rolling slightly now from hip to hip, she cried out aloud at each imagined cane stroke across Mme Puton's beautiful, bare bottom. Emma's slippery fingertips scrabbled hungrily inside her tightly muscled warmth. She had never been so wet. So drippingly hot and horny. God, she'd die soon if she didn't climax.

Face crushed once more down into her pillow, her shoulders burned. The hot sensation spread down her spine. Her supporting arms grew heavy and rigid. She grew increasingly frustrated. Frantic. The sizzling images of the imagined punishment below in the study still burned behind her tightly shut eyes, but her thumbtip slipped away from her clitoris and in her frenzy she could not reconnect. She groaned. God, not now. Not now. With a massive effort of will, she eased herself up further from the duvet. Her right hand felt the wet flesh of her upper labia, seeking then securing within a vicious little pincer of finger and thumbtip her clitoris. Yes. Pincering the tiny little thorn of tingling tissue, she began to pinch and squeeze. Pinch and squeeze. As if she were milking a mink. Her belly tightened.

Swish. God, yes. She pictured the violet eyes of Mme Puton opening wide in anguished reaction to the searing stroke. She saw their colour cloud then deepen to an indigo of pain. Yes. *Swish*. The eyes at the leather closed, squeezing out a tear. The teardrop splashed down, dulling the polished hide below. Then the red lips. A firm line suddenly flowering, opening up like a rose, the lips forming a wide circle as they parted for the thin scream. *Swish*. Yes. Emma started to come. God, yes. And then the darkest desire of all suddenly exploded in her brain. Just as she clenched her buttocks before loosening them in savage orgasm, Emma saw herself beneath the stern Head's cane.

That did it. In a crimson flash of sudden light, and equally startling self-knowledge, Emma came. Massively. Loudly. And as she shuddered and screamed only one image blazed behind her eyes. The image of herself bending bare bottomed beneath the glint of Felicity Flint's raised bamboo.

'Enjoying yourself?'

It was Kate. She had appeared at Emma's bedside, her ironic voice instantly shattering the spell.

Emma groaned, slumping down in exhaustion. She ached sweetly all over. Her slit was hot and slippery, like a freshly fried egg. But already a cold thought, a thought that grew into a fear, gripped her. Gripped her and congealed in her brain. Her sudden understanding began to blaze with a clear, frozen flame. She could not stay. She could not stay here at Laments. She had no right to be here. She was not a natural dominant. And never could be. She was a submissive, desiring only to be disciplined.

'Stay exactly where you are,' Kate purred.

'Mm?' Emma murmured, almost forgetting the other girl's presence at her bedside. 'What?'

'I've come to collect my debt. A spanking, we said.'

Emma moaned softly into the pillow and started to tingle once more.

Five

'Smells like a dorm in here,' Kate sniffed loudly, gazing down at the bare bottom she was about to blister – and then narrowing her dark brown eyes to focus on Emma's gleaming wet fig.

Emma's brow wrinkled uncomprehendingly.

Kate jerked her thumb over her shoulder to the door – and the dorms beyond. 'After a punishment the night before,' Kate explained, gently fingering Emma's sticky cleft. 'Next morning, it stinks. After all the girls have been rubbing pussy all night. Same sweet reek.'

Emma blushed and wriggled on her bed. Her bare buttocks joggled. Kate's throat tightened. A soft snarl escaped her lips.

Bending down, Kate dominantly tap-tapped Emma's naked cheeks with her straightened finger, emphasising her words. 'We made our bet. I won. A spanking, we said. Pay up, or should I say,' Kate whispered silkily, 'bottom up.'

With a shrill excited squeal, Emma made a bid to escape, diving down from her bed to the silk carpet. Kate pounced, kneeling astride Emma's upturned buttocks, straddling the proffered cheeks to pinion her naked captive between her scissoring thighs.

'Relax,' Kate murmured, stretching down to stroke Emma's blonde mane. 'You won't be sorry you lost the bet. You'll consider yourself the winner. Not at first. No,' she dropped her voice to a husky thrill, 'not at first. But when the suffering becomes sweet and the pain melts into liquid pleasure. When the fierce heat spreads. When the fire takes hold within. Deep within you. Then you'll think yourself the winner. Come on,' she commanded, her voice bright and brisk, 'I want you back on the bed. Up. Where do you want this?'

Emma twisted her face up away from the silk carpet and saw that Kate was holding her Barbour in her left hand. She nodded towards the chair by the dressing table. Kate sauntered unhurriedly across to the chair and draped the waxed jacket carefully over the bamboo frame.

'Do you wear stockings or tights?'

Emma, surprised by the unexpected question, rested her chin on her hands as she kneeled against the bed. 'Stockings, why?'

'Doesn't matter. They'll do.' Kate shrugged.

'There should be a pair of nylons in my bag. Haven't unpacked properly. Why do you –'

'To tie you up.'

'Tie me up?' Emma squealed.

'Found 'em,' Kate replied over her shoulder as she plucked out the packet of nylons and thumbed open the cellophane wrapping. 'Yes,' she continued, turning to face Emma who was now standing by the bed. 'To tie you up.'

Emma's bare bosom bounced gently as she slowly backed away.

'B-but that's b-bondage, isn't it?' Emma faltered.

'B-bondage?' Kate teased. 'If you want b-bondage, my girl, just you slip along and watch old Ma Aylott-Inche at work in her precious gym. Leather hoods, harnesses, ropes. The works. Now shut up and come over here back by the bed –'

'I don't think –'

'Be quiet. Or I'll gag you.'

'Oh, no don't, please –'

'OK. No gag. But I don't want you yelling the place down, or waking everyone up when you come,' Kate warned sternly.

'When I come?' Emma echoed.

'When you come,' Kate repeated matter-of-factly. 'I want you here. No. Kneeling.'

With reluctant obedience, Emma's feet brought her back to the bed. She kneeled down slowly before Kate, steadying her descent with one hand on the bed. Kate moved swiftly behind the kneeling nude and sank her knees down into the soft silk of the carpet. The bronzed stockings clenched in Kate's right hand dangled down, annoyingly tickling Emma's bare bottom. The soft cheeks clenched. Kate spotted the reflexive spasm and danced the stockings, skimming their tormenting sheen across the quivering cheeks of the kneeling nude. Emma moaned.

'Silence, I said,' Kate hissed.

Emma crossed her arms, hugging and crushing her squashed breasts.

'Hands together, please.' The 'please' was a superfluous irony. Kate was rapidly gaining control And they both knew it.

Emma joined her palms together just above the blonde nest below.

'No. Behind your back.'

'But –'

'At once.' The command was crisp. The tone increasingly terse.

Emma's buttocks dimpled as her elbows angled, but her hands merely rose up uncertainly to cup her breasts.

'I said behind your back,' Kate insisted softly. 'Remember,' she added, her voice now honied with sweet reason, 'your bare bottom will be all mine in a few minutes. All mine. Best not to annoy me, hmm?'

Slowly, Emma's trembling hands appeared over her bare hips, seemingly caressing their curves. The fingertips collided gently, then both palms kissed just above the point where the furrow of her spine melted into the invisible crease at the start of her cleft.

'That's better,' Kate encouraged. 'You'll learn.' She rewarded Emma with a brief kiss on the nape of her bowed neck. Then a sterner kiss, sucking slightly, below each shoulder blade as, down below, above the swell of the naked cheeks, her fingers busily bound the nylon stocking around the passive wrists.

'Knees and feet together.'

Emma, flexing and testing her tightly bound wrists, obeyed. Her bare bottom wobbled as she jammed her knees and ankles firmly together. Kate threaded the second nylon stocking around then between her victim's submissive feet. The tight knot welded them seamlessly in strict surrender. The tiny toes scrabbled helplessly into the soft silk.

Kate rose, maddeningly slowly and unhurriedly, then gazed down dominantly to peruse the nude she had just prepared for punishment. The naked blonde she had just bound before beating. 'Up.'

Emma struggled, her breasts spilling as she finally lurched clumsily face down into the bed.

'Quite the little novice, aren't you?' Kate murmured gently, taloning Emma's blonde mane and forcing the wide, grey eyes to gaze up into her own. Reaching down swiftly, she nipped at a tuft of Emma's damp pubic fuzz.

'Up. Further across the bed.'

She tugged the golden coils. Emma shrieked and barrelled across the bed, her nipples raking the duvet's shiny satin.

'Hips up.'

The bare bottom rose up obediently as Emma, face down and helplessly bound, inched up her hips. Down in the silk of the carpet below, her toes whitened as her bound feet skidded beneath her. Kate snatched at the pillow and dragged it down, forcing it under Emma's belly then easing it down more gently until Emma's pussy was nestling into its cool cotton.

'One more touch and you should be ready for that spanking.'

'No gag,' Emma whimpered. 'You promised.'

'No gag,' Kate whispered. 'I keep all my promises. Including my promise that you'll come.' She fished out a length of dark velvet from her skirt pocket and snapped it softly.

Emma's head rose inquisitively, puzzled by the whispering velvet.

'No gag, tonight. Later, perhaps. But I am going to use a blindfold.'

Emma shivered. Not a frisson of raw fear, more a tremor of delicious dread. She mewed aloud – but her chin jutted out as she offered her face up to the swathe of soft velvet. It covered her eyes, pitching her instantly into a darkness she had never known.

A sudden chill thrilled Emma's kneeling nakedness. A draught from an opening door. Someone had stepped silently into the bedroom. Emma shrank, cringing into the bed. Hating the unseen, unknown eyes that were drinking in her naked humiliation. Her bare bottom. Hating it, yet writhing in exquisite torment as she wondered if the newcomer could see her breasts squashed into the bed, see her cleft between her cheeks, see the glint of her wet fig below.

'No need to stay up –' the voice of Felicity Flint began, then Emma heard the sharp, appreciative gasp.

'Good evening, Head,' Kate said, completely unabashed.

'I was going to tell Emma that there was no need for her to stay up tonight to accompany me on dorm patrol.'

Emma shivered as she heard the approaching tread of brogue on silk. The Head's warm breath played on her bare shoulder blade as the Head's voice sounded unbearably close.

'But I see she is otherwise engaged and –' the Head paused, chuckling '– I see you have won your bet, Kate. I trust you will make this spanking as instructive as no doubt it will be memorable.'

'Won't you stay? It's a virgin bottom, I believe. The results should be interesting,' Kate countered, her voice cool and detached.

'Thank you, but no. Other bottoms await me in the dorm. But take care, Kate. Do not hurry the punishment, though she needs to learn and learn quickly. Teach her well, Kate. Goodnight.'

Kate replied politely.

'Goodnight, Emma,' the warm breath whispered against her nakedness.

Emma, blazing in shame, murmured a quiet response. The footsteps faded across the silk carpet towards the bedroom door.

'Oh, and girls,' the fainter voice added as the Head paused, turning back into the room. 'Thank you both for your support today. I knew I could rely on you. You did not fail me. Nor will you, I trust, should I need to count upon you again.'

The door clicked shut behind her. Emma, nestling into the bed, her slit pressed into the pillow, flexed her bound wrists and ankles. To her surprise, and pleasant alarm, the sensation of being tightly tied and helpless, of being naked, bound and bare bottomed, grew disturbingly delicious. Although her mind struggled to both acknowledge yet deny this burning thrill, her pussy showed no such coy reserve. Already, the tight stretch of white cotton so close, so very close to her pouting labial folds was sticky.

In a supremely controlling, dominant gesture, Kate kneeled in alongside Emma, positioning herself so that her left hand gripped and pinned Emma's neck down. Kate's bosom, now burgeoning in its brassiere, squashed into Emma's left buttock. The hard nipples, piercing the cups and the silk of Kate's blouse, dimpled the cheek's soft swell. And all the time, from the moment of the Head's departure, the right hand – Kate's spanking hand – rested lightly across the smoothness of Emma's right buttock.

Emma mewed aloud like a kitten impatient for cream, tensing and clenching her cheeks, her slit spilling hot silver in response to the thrust of the brassiered breasts into her left cheek and the controlling, punishing hand caressing her right cheek. To signal for silence, Kate swiftly raked her thumbtip down the warmth of the cleft. Her thumbnail scraped across the hot little anal whorl. Emma shrieked, bucking and jerking her bottom.

'Be quiet,' Kate soothed. 'You will enjoy this, Emma. But try to learn. Experience is a great teacher. Try to remember how I prepared you. How I took pains to ensure that yours would be so pleasing. By binding you with the

101

nylon stockings, how I took absolute control over you. Over your naked helplessness.'

Emma wriggled, moaning softly.

'Made your bottom mine. Utterly and entirely,' Kate whispered, dabbling her fingertips into Emma's pliant cheeks dominantly.

'It's yours –' Emma began, her voice a husky grunt.

'No, Emma. It is not yours to give to me. It is mine to take. Do you understand me? Mine, to take, own and control. To punish as I please.'

'Yes,' Emma hissed fiercely, nodding vigorously. She shivered in her restricting bondage, a frisson of exquisite anticipation jerking her nakedness with a fresh spasm.

'I want you to try to focus hard. On all your thoughts and feelings. Try to understand their true, deeper meaning. Learn.'

'I will,' the bound nude whimpered.

'Concentrate not just on your painful pleasure but on how I actually administer the spanking. How hard, how slow or indeed how fast does my hand visit your cheeks. Am I using the palm of my hand. Although you are blindfolded, you must try to picture the punishment. Are my fingers splayed, or tightly closed? Is my palm flattened or cruelly curved?' Kate's right hand slowly enfolded the captive buttock, squeezing it with a sudden viciousness.

'Please –' hissed Emma, uttering the words she never thought she would ever hear herself saying. 'Spank me. Please spank me. Spank my bare bottom very hard until it is red and shiny and –'

'Be silent,' Kate warned, squeezing even harder.

Emma bowed her head and kissed the soft duvet in obedient silence. Satisfied, Kate relaxed her grip and smoothed the blotched cheeks with her circling flattened palm.

'Afterwards, we will discuss all aspects of your discipline in detail. In very intimate detail. From this, I can learn how much you have been taught,' Kate continued suavely.

Emma lost control, grinding her slit into the pillow.

'Please –' she whined. 'Please do it. Now. Spank me.' She jiggled her buttocks impatiently. 'Spank me. Hurt me. Make my bottom blaze.'

Kate deliberately ignored this, remaining cool and detached as she calmly surveyed the naked cheeks offered up in eagerness below. 'You will tell me everything, Emma. All your thoughts and all your feelings. You will tell me frankly, concealing nothing, how your pleasurable pain evolves into something even more disturbingly delicious. And,' Kate murmured, thumbing Emma's left cheek, 'I will attempt to answer all of your questions. Honestly. Avoiding nothing. But now, be quiet and give me your bottom.'

Outside the bedroom door, in the darkened corridor, Felicity Flint crouched in the chilly silence. Steadying herself against the door with her left hand, she pressed her ear into the wood. The stern murmuring had finished. Kate was about to beat Emma's bare bottom. Felicity Flint held her breath – as her right hand squeezed a tennis ball. Taloning it fiercely, her hand guided the ball upwards between her splayed thighs to her pantyless pussy.

The angry bark of a spanking hand cracked out aloud, instantly followed by a smothered squeal. Again. And again. *Crack. Crack.* The Head knew that inside the bedroom, beyond the door at which she crouched, Kate was blisteringly chastising Emma's bottom. Three more sharp spanks rang out. This time, the ensuing squeals were more subdued. More like smothered moans. The Head imagined Emma biting the duvet. The image brought her hand up in a sudden jerk, rasping the furry surface of the tennis ball along the damson-dark labial folds. The ball raked the slit three times in rapid succession, bringing a wide smile to the ravished lips. Thick, moistening lips. Lips that soon dribbled their drool, juicing the ball and staining it darkly. *Spank, spank, spank.* Each searing swipe echoing inside the room jerked the taloning hand upwards – bringing the ball back into play.

Felicity Flint closed her eyes. Closed her eyes and remembered. Remembered her own virgin bottom being punished, crimsoned and blistered for the very first time. Shutting out the sounds of Kate's soft grunts, Emma's choking squeals and the relentless crack, crack, crack of the spanking hand across the suffering cheeks, Felicity Flint punished her pussy with the tennis ball and was instantly back in her seventeenth summer. At the tennis club.

Her seventeenth summer. A cloudless canopy of azure sky held up by stretching alders. Down on the grass court, neatly lined out in white lime, two lithe young women, ten years her senior, battled it out in the burning heat for a county medal.

A sparse crowd of spectators sprinkled the shade under the glistening alders, their sandwiches and dark Thermos tea neglected as match point was called and the game drew to a climactic finish. Even the engines of Humbers, Fords and Austins burning in the sunshine seemed to cease their ticking as everyone held their breath.

The final serve. Felicity Flint remembered it all vividly. The local vet, a leggy beauty, strained up on white-pumped tiptoe to serve – Felicity Flint recalled peeping shyly but eagerly at the tight-pantied buttocks beneath the white, pleated skirt – then the sudden cry splitting the silence. A wasp had stung the young Felicity Flint's thigh. The vet, serving, stumbled, faulting the ball into the net. Minutes later, her rhythm broken, the young goddess lost the match – and her medal.

Kate tightened her spanking hand into a fist and slowly knuckled Emma's expertly reddened cheeks. Kneading the hot, soft crimson domes, she dimpled each cheek to see if white showed beneath the punished curves. But the heat of the blistering chastisement had burned deep. Both buttocks, knuckled searchingly, remained uniformly red.

Emma squeezed her cheeks tightly until her sticky cleft became a severe crease. At her pussy, the pillow was stained and soaking. The heat was spreading now, just as Kate had promised. Draining into her, first tickling and now bubbling in her puckering rosebud sphincter, the tight little petals of which were now fully unfurled for the first time in her life. Emma sensed that her hole was almost as wide and as wet as her split at the pillow – and knew it to be just as hot. And hungry. And the heat from the spanking. God! The sweet ache spread until even her belly burned.

Kate slowly lowered her face down into Emma's spanked buttocks. Emma hissed out fiercely. Below her stocking-bound wrists, her fingers starfished. Kate gently nosed the dark cleft, licked its length twice and rested her face against Emma's crimson bottom. Soon, both punisher and punished were united, moaning cheek to cheek.

Outside in the corridor, the wet fur of the tennis ball scalded Felicity Flint's raw pussy. Locked into her trance-like reverie, the sounds of sugared sorrow from beyond the bedroom door receded – to be replaced by the distant buzz of excited congratulations.

It had been a very hot day. Tearful after her wasp sting, the seventeen-year-old Felicity Flint had sought refuge between the rows of parked cars. Rubbing her sore thigh, she sank down on to the sedge in the shade of a Hillman Sunbeam. Beside it was the young vet's sporty little Triumph Herald. It had brash, whitewall tyres – the only ones in the neighbourhood – and the hood was down. The red leather seats reeked of polished hide. Felicity Flint's eyes flickered as she remembered. Her knuckles whitened. The tennis ball ground up into her slit.

The defeated amazon, trim, lithe and graceful, swooped down along the grass between the line of parked cars. She spotted the young Felicity Flint and pounced. Her language would have made a docker blush.

Protesting hotly, Felicity Flint had tried to excuse her shout that lost the young vet the match. But the wasp sting was brutally ignored – and the squealing young girl hauled across the hot bonnet of the adjacent Hillman. Pinned and helpless, the strong young vet had flipped up Felicity Flint's summer skirt and yanked down her blue knickers. The memory of those strong, slender hands. The tanned skin. The white tennis outfit. White pumps smudged with the green of the court. The smell of perspiration. Then, belly and breasts squashed into the hot metal bonnet, the spanking. Helpless across the fat car, Felicity Flint had been spanked severely by the angry tennis-playing vet. The loud crack across her hot bottom. The howling. The tears of pain and shame.

Felicity Flint slumped softly down on to her knees against the bedroom door. She swallowed, lubricating the thickening tongue in her tight, dry throat as she remembered. The tennis ball at her slit was a blur as it savaged her ruthlessly. Her memories of her first spanking spilled out in a frenzied stream. The pain and the pleasure. The dread delight. Memories as hot and scalding as the climax that had smeared the shining bonnet of the Hillman and that now drenched the tennis ball in her grip.

Inside the bedroom, Kate whispered to Emma, ordering the sniffling, red-bottomed nude to remain absolutely still. Emma obeyed, allowing only fitful sorrow-sobs to escape into the satin duvet at her lips.

Kate rose up, strode across to the Dutch colonial dressing table and picked up the square, cane-framed looking glass. Snatching up a hand-held oval mirror, she returned to the bed.

Emma's blindfolded face rose up, following the soft sounds inquisitively.

'Stay still. Absolutely still and silent until I say you can move. Understand?' Kate said sternly.

Emma whimpered. Out of sight, down on the carpet, her bound feet struggled futilely in the severe bondage of the nylon stocking's bite.

Kate carefully positioned the square, cane-framed looking glass eight inches in front of Emma's face, balancing it on the slippery duvet after pulling the glass forward from the vertical axis. Resting her chin briefly in the cleft between Emma's crimson cheeks, she glanced up along the nude's body, checking the angle of the glass. Perfect.

'Don't move,' Kate warned again.

Emma shivered pleasurably at the stern command.

Kate sat down gingerly on the bed, alongside Emma. Gripping the wooden handle firmly, she guided the mirror face down until the cold glass kissed the spanked cheeks. Emma writhed and squealed in both alarm and delight. Her jerking response to the glass as it kissed – and clouded – at her seethe threatened to topple the square looking glass balanced on the duvet. Kate reached out in alarm, staying and steadying it.

'Keep still,' she hissed.

Emma froze obediently.

Stretching her hand up along Emma's spine, Kate fingered the velvet blindfold loose. The blonde's head jerked up. In the glass, her widening grey eyes glimpsed the oval mirror Kate had repositioned at her buttocks. Emma gasped as she stared directly up at the captured image of her spanked bottom.

Kate's controlling hand gripped into the soft neck, pinning Emma face down into the duvet. Angling her wrist, she slid the hand-held mirror beneath Emma's jerking hips, bringing the upturned cold glass face to the weeping slit. Gently massaging the splayed, dragging labia with the glass, Kate paused, collecting juices, before withdrawing the mirror and inverting it back down into the spasming, reddened cheeks.

Emma squealed as her hot bottom felt the sticky surface of the cool glass. Squealed in delight at the icy touch of the dominant glass. Squealed in torment at the loss of the mirror at her slit. Squealed excitedly. And then again, as she came.

Tap. Tap. Tap.

Three soft, reticient taps. Loud enough to stir Emma in her stupor of exhausted sleep.

Tap. Tap. Tap. The gentle knuckles at her bedroom door became more insistent. Emma's left eye peeled open. She saw that it was almost an hour after midnight. God, she felt wrung out. Utterly spent. And who the hell was this?

The door inched open then yawned wide. Emma, yawning wider, murmured indistinctly.

'*C'est moi,*' a velvety voice whispered.

Mme Puton. Emma struggled to sit up in bed and peered into the darkness.

'I have come to see you, *ma petite*. I heard. Yes, I heard it all. The spanking. And so I have brought for your poor little bottom this.'

A soft click at the wall flooded the bedroom in light. Mme Puton looked superb in a simple white lawn negligee. Tiny pearls sparkled at her bosom, coyly concealing her dark nipples. A girdle of pearls glinted at the swell of her hips. Emma could just make out the pubic delta. She gripped the duvet tightly as she saw that the French mistress had clean shaved her nest. In her right hand, her nocturnal visitor held an onyx jar of expensive cosmetic cream.

'Your bottom, it is sore? Very sore, yes?' Mme Puton murmured solicitously, sitting down on the edge of Emma's bed.

Emma nodded, wriggling her spanked buttocks beneath the duvet. The French mistress leaned forward. The lawn negligee strained, revealing a voluptuous cleavage. Emma's pussy prickled with interest.

'Let me see. Come, *ma petite*. Do not have the shyness with me. I will make it better.'

Emma's throat tightened even at the thought of turning over face down into her bed and baring her sore bottom for the perusal of those intensely violet eyes.

'It's – it's not that sore –' she shrugged, blushing.

'Ah, *oui*, but it is, little one. Let me see,' Mme Puton purred, her sweet breath now warm on Emma's face.

Spellbound, Emma shyly twisted down into her bed, shrinking as she felt the duvet being inched down. The French mistress gasped with frank pleasure as Emma's bare bottom was slowly uncovered. Emma shivered, burying her face into her pillow, instantly wrinkling her nose as it met the feral tang from the soak of her earlier orgasm. Squirming deliciously at the thought of those violet eyes gazing down to intimately inspect her spanked buttocks, Emma froze, suddenly ashamed at her own perverse responses. Despite the burning shame that flushed her buried face, Emma was already imagining the weight of Mme Puton's thick-nippled breasts at her bottom, already willing those moist, scarlet lips to press fiercely into her punished rump. What a little whore you are, she thought, squeezing her eyes shut. Your Kate's, aren't you?

'Kate has done the thorough job,' the silky voice behind her observed. 'That one, with her passionate eyes, is becoming the expert with the bottom, no?'

Emma tensed, then quivered, as a cream-laden fingertip stroked down along the length of her cleft. She clenched her cheeks. Mme Puton laughed gently.

'She has spanked you very, very severely, I think.' Mme Puton seemed to be talking to herself. Her voice had a remote, dreamy tone.

Again, the cooling balm of the creamed fingertip firmly followed the tightened crease of Emma's cleft, pausing this time at her anal whorl. The slippery fingernail scratched at the shrivelled petals. Emma bucked her hips and drove her sphincter on to the finger.

'No, not yet,' Mme Puton whispered. 'First, I must soothe your poor, sore little bottom. Spread your legs for me. Open up your thighs a little wider.'

Forcing down any guilty thoughts of betraying Kate, Emma promptly obeyed – her cheeks were still scalding and were eager for the healing touch. At her slit, a silver bubble of arousal burgeoned. Swollen at once by the sudden thought of what Kate would say, and no doubt do, if she walked in now and caught Emma in the very act of betrayal. The bubble burst, soaking Emma's blonde fringe. Another grew in its place, trembling and shining at her outer lips. Emma snuggled down, blissfully surrendering her buttocks.

Mme Puton proved to be as expert in the tender art of aftercare as Kate had been in bringing about its need and necessity. Where the cruelly curved hand of the spanker had earlier crimsoned both buttocks beneath a rain of pain, now the more mature French woman's touch brought soothing relief. Adroitly daubing, smearing then gently palming each cheek, Mme Puton spread the cold cream across the ravaged domes. Inching her bottom up to meet the slow sweep of the circling palm at her cheeks, Emma mewed happily into her slit-soaked pillow.

'You enjoy, *n'est-ce pas*?' the purring voice insinuated.

Emma nodded into her pillow. Her buttocks jiggled, signalling her delight.

'*C'est bon.*' The French mistress withdrew her hand, tenderly knuckling the swell of Emma's left buttock as she did so. Seconds later, the cream-drenched forefinger's tip probed a little lower down beneath and between Emma's parted thighs. Pop. It burst the tiny shimmering bubble of lust peeping out from the pouting labia of Emma's glistening fig. Shivering as her blonde fringe received the sudden soak, Emma moaned aloud.

A freshly creamed fingertip traced the contours of each spanked cheek then boldly pierced Emma's tightened anus. Emma clenched her cheeks savagely, trapping it.

'I too was punished tonight,' Mme Puton said simply, twisting her finger inside Emma's muscled warmth and causing the blonde to grunt.

Emma, remembering the appointment the French mistress had kept with the Head in the study after supper, jerked her bottom back excitedly – driving the creamed forefinger deeper in between her tingling cheeks.

'Did – did it hurt?' she asked, twisting her face up from the pillow.

'It is a special kind of pain, punishment. Have you not found this to be so?' Mme Puton countered. 'One hates it; one adores it. One comes to reluctantly love the brutal bamboo.' She lapsed into silence for a moment before adding, 'Would you like to see?'

Emma felt the finger sliding out. It made a soft plopping sound. She ground her slit into the bed to compensate its going.

'You would, I think, like to see my stripes, *n'est-ce pas*?'

Seconds later, Emma was kneeling on her bed and gazing directly into the caned cheeks of the French mistress. Thighs apart, her negligee dragged up above her hips, Mme Puton offered her punished bottom up for inspection. The buttocks, Emma thought, were superb. Slightly larger than she suspected, rubbery, firm and so deliciously swollen at the curves. The French mistress

110

inched her thighs together and coquettishly thrust her bottom backwards and upwards. The cheeks bulged, their pale ivory flesh clearly scored by eight lines, eight pale blue cane-kisses which had lashed down to lick with fire the beautiful buttocks. Each stroke, Emma noticed, planting its stripe exactly an eighth of an inch from the last.

'Beautiful,' Emma whispered, holding out her trembling fingertips but not quite touching the punished cheeks. She inched her face closer, suddenly compelled to kiss the bare, bamboo-whipped buttocks before her. Her tongue-tip flickered out, hungrily – greedily – straining in its aching desire.

The velvet voice broke into her trance. 'Use this. Please,' Mme Puton begged urgently, passing back the pot of cream.

It was a very expensive brand. Emma fingered out a generous scoop and applied it tentatively to the cruel cane cuts, smearing it with doubled fingertips horizontally across each severe welt. The French mistress moaned loudly in response, jerking her bottom closer, then closer still. Swaying sensually, her cleft widened and narrowed as she clenched her cheeks reflexively, responding instantly to Emma's fingers as they scored the cream across each darkening weal.

'Do not tell Kate,' Mme Puton whispered. 'She can be so fiercely jealous.'

Emma's fingers fell away from the swollen cheeks in guilty shame.

'Let this be our little secret, *ma petite*,' Mme Puton whispered. 'And when we are punished, we will take care of each other's poor little sore bottoms, no?'

Emma's hands returned to the buttocks before them. Nodding silently – so thrilled she could not speak – Emma continued to caress the punished flesh. Mme Puton's bottom wobbled as she trod the carpet silently, inching back towards Emma on the bed. As her thighs collided against the mattress, she parted them. Her elbows rose up. The negligee swept up over her chic auburn hair and landed in a puddle at her feet.

'My breasts, they hurt so much. It is a sweet pain. They need your hands and lips, *ma petite*.'

Emma hissed softly and knuckled her pussy savagely.

'But first, finish my bottom.'

Emma shuffled forwards, dimpling the duvet with her knees. Framing and capturing the proffered cheeks within her cream-smeared palms, she jerked her belly and hips forward. Their naked flesh met in soft, mutual surrender, Emma's proud pubis melting into Mme Puton's rubbery-buttocked swell. Grinding her bottom then raking her cheeks from side to side, the French mistress opened up the lips at Emma's juicing slit. The perfumed cream's haunting fragrance soon yielded to stronger, fiercer odours – the feral arousal of the two nudes who were now weeping freely as one buried her bottom into the other's hot slit.

It rained all day. Real February rain – sleet, almost – that silvered the windows of Laments Hall and shivered the wisteria. But, Emma realised as she gazed out into the murk, it wasn't the depressing Sunday rain that brought the loud silence that had hung heavily inside Laments since breakfast. It was the prospect of the impending punishments before tea.

'Always goes quiet before a public thrashing,' Kate explained as they took coffee together after the traditional Sunday roast lunch.

The brooding silence stretched out deep into the afternoon, broken only by the ominous tick-tock of the clock, slowly measuring out the minutes, then the hours, before Rebecca Wigmore and her unhappy accomplices were to be beaten. In the sitting room, the staff settled into various tasks. Work was marked, further lessons planned. The girls were all up in their respective dorms. Outside, a handful of rooks called noisily up in the dripping elms.

Emma felt the tension building. She went out into the grounds but the driving sleet soon forced her back inside. At the rear porch, shaking her Barbour, she paused, sniffing. Rising up from the Aga in the basement kitchens, the delicious smell of scones greeted her nostrils. How normal. How comforting. Scones baking in the oven for the tea table. Probably cake as well. A perfectly ordinary country house smell on a wet Sunday afternoon. Except, Emma remembered, that before tea, young women were going to be publicly whipped. Bared, scolded, humiliated and chastised. Once again, Kate's haunting phrase sprang to mind. Red rubbers. What could that mean? Red rubbers. Emma instantly forgot about the scones rising up in the hot belly of the Aga in the basement kitchen below.

A shrill bell broke the silence at four fifteen precisely. Before the last echo of the clanging summons had subsided, softly padding swift feet had brought all the Laments pupils down to the main hall, and from there, in neat single file, into the refectory where the staff were already assembled.

Emma watched as the eighteen girls entered, their heads bowed, their eyes averted. She was already able to name or identify several of them. Bubble and Squeak, the twins. So called by Kate because, Emma had been advised, under strict punishment one would bubble while the other twin squeaked.

Felicity Flint looked magnificent, Emma thought, in her black, ermine-trimmed gown topped with a silver tassled mortar board. Both Tweedledum and Tweedledee sported black, though slightly shabbier, gowns, and carried their black tassled mortar boards under their arms. Marion, track-suited and sharp eyed, marshalled the girls into neat rows of six along the refectory walls. Kate stood next to Emma, her reassuring hand frequently stroking Emma's bottom.

Emma glanced around the refectory. Mme Puton, chic and insouciant, was inspecting her recently varnished crimson nails. Miss Rathbone and Miss Monteagle fluttered in their dark gowns excitedly. Miss Watson, Emma noticed, peered into the refectory from the doorway.

All were assembled. Absolute silence reigned. The Head stepped forward, gathering her gown around her. A sudden squall battered the window panes. Emma looked up, startled. The gust whipped the wisteria into a frenzy at the spangled glass. It grew dark suddenly, adding to the sense of drama.

'Lights,' the Head commanded.

Two girls immediately broke ranks, peeling away to the right and the left of their line. One, hopping up and stretching, managed at last to draw the heavy, plum-coloured curtains together. The other switched on the lights.

In a tone of sharp severity, the Head ordered the four miscreants to step forward, calling them forth one by one. 'Rebecca Wigmore. Olympia Scott-Hammerton. Ann Cordery. Charlotte Bicknell.'

Reluctantly but obediently, each stepped forward, heads penitently lowered in fearful shame, hands contritely folded together behind their backs. Emma watched, fascinated. A glint of light from the doorway caught her eye. Weasel-eyes Watson. What had she seen? Then Emma spotted a slight movement in the ranks of silent girls. It was the twins. Bubble and Squeak. They had inched furtively together, hands fleetingly touching. And Emma knew. The twins were frightened. Had Rebecca Wigmore brought them back some forbidden little treat? Were they shivering anxiously in case they too were to be subjected to the dreadful red rubbers. And, even more importantly Emma thought, had Watson seen their nervous display of guilt?

The Head called for the punishment book. It was as big as a bible and covered in red velvet. Two girls brought it to her, open, upon a lectern. In a leisurely manner that only increased the tension in the silent refectory, the Head carefully inscribed each girl's name, the nature of her misconduct and the punishment to be awarded. Clicking her pen shut, the Head invited each girl up to the lectern. After reading what had been inscribed, each penitent borrowed the Head's pen and signed – sealing their doom in black ink. When the Bicknell girl, who had whimpered slightly on reading her punishment, had signed and returned to her place, the Head looked up from the lectern.

'The actual offences these girls committed are of no concern to the rest of you. It is sufficient to say that scandal has been averted and the matter fully resolved. Only their punishment remains; to be dispensed and witnessed by you as a clear reminder that disobedience and delinquency will not be tolerated at Laments. You are all here for training and correction and it is both my privilege and my duty to see to it that appropriate punishment is meted out by myself and my loyal staff in full measure.'

Loyal staff. Emma briefly thought of the simmering rancour at the supper table.

'On this occasion, these four girls are to be beaten and beaten soundly. A dozen strokes. The paddle, I think,' the Head added judiciously. 'Yes, the paddle. Not the cane.'

Emma sensed the slight easing of tension, almost an anticlimax, sweep through the refectory. But she caught the challenge in the stare Marion Aylott-Inche flashed at the Head. *My loyal staff.* God, she won't query the Head here and now. In front of all the girls. Emma tensed. The gym mistress continued to glare. Clearly, a dozen strokes were deemed to be insufficient.

Dr Flint thumbed the edge of the lectern and carried on imperturbably. She's seen Marion and is pointedly ignoring her, Emma thought.

'One singular feature of this escapade is the fact that these wretched girls had the audacity to repeat their offence on numerous opportunities. And furthermore, each are as guilty as the other, for not once did any one girl caution or counsel the others. I deem it fit and proper, therefore,' the Head continued, lowering her voice to a stern whisper, 'that they will not be punished by my members of staff nor indeed by myself.'

'Really, Head,' Marion snorted, unable to control or conceal her anger any more.

Marion's response was just audible above the soft gasp that greeted the Head's pronouncement. Dr Flint held up her hand for silence.

'Each must punish the other.'

Oh, shit, Emma thought. Calculating rapidly, she worked it out that each girl was about to receive thirty-six strokes of the paddle. Marion got there a few seconds later, Emma observed, and blushed with both anger and embarrassment. The Head had wrong-footed her deputy. Nice one, Flint.

Emma struggled to suppress her grin. The Head had teased Marion up the garden path only to publicly slam the gate shut in the face of the spluttering gym mistress. A dozen apiece, to each other. Thirty-six of the paddle. Shit. Felicity Flint was a twisted genius, Emma thought. Marion was now openly bowing in deferential agreement with the Head's decision. Tweedledum and Tweedledee were almost dancing with delight.

Savouring her moment of triumph, the Head paused. All looked towards the lectern in intense expectation.

'Strip,' Felicity Flint barked.

The four accused – and condemned – struggled inelegantly out of their penitential uniform of white cotton vests and tight little shorts. Soon, they huddled in shivering nakedness before the collective gaze. Emma's grey eyes greedily drank in their delicious nudity, darting from Ann Cordery's swollen breasts bunched behind her protective right arm to the dark, glossy pubic snatch of Charlotte Bicknell, a pert little brunette.

'Bring me the red rubbers,' the Head commanded.

Here it comes, Emma thought. At last. The red rubbers.

'And the punishment stool.'

Miss Watson seemed more than eager to oblige, stumbling into the refectory, her left hand pressing a bundle of what looked to Emma like red rubber knickers to her breast – and dragging a four-legged high stool behind her. The legs of the stool scuffed and squeaked as they skimmed the polished wooden floor.

'Thank you, Miss Watson,' Felicity Flint said, accepting the red rubberwear and tossing a pair of panties to each naked miscreant. 'Put those on.'

But it won't hurt them so much if they wear those, Emma caught herself thinking. Chiding herself for such callousness, she blinked away her brief shame and watched intently as the Head positioned and arranged the high stool in a pool of space between the refectory tables.

Glancing back at the four nudes, she gasped softly. Ann Cordery, her delicious breasts squashed between her straightened arms, was yanking up the red, stretchy panties. They snapped into place, hugging her hips and moulding themselves at the pubic mound. Ann Cordery. Emma's eyes lingered, then switched to the left where Rebecca, similarly pantied, cupped her breasts protectively. It was when the petite Bicknell brunette turned that Emma saw and fully understood the purpose of the red rubber panties. The fabric had been cut away where it would normally have gripped and squeezed the wearer's cheeks – leaving both buttocks totally bare. Bare, vulnerable and exposed.

Rebecca Wigmore knew that she would be punished first. She had already taken two faltering steps when the Head instructed her to approach the stool.

Emma's pulse quickened. She felt her breasts grow heavy and her nipples harden as the ringleader of the credit card outrage obediently stepped up to the punishment stool.

'Bend over,' barked the Head.

Slowly, with her fingertips trembling at the edge of the square wooden seat, Rebecca Wigmore eased her naked bosom down. Emma saw the stubby nipples of the bending penitent kiss the seat's polished sheen.

'Further, girl,' came the curt command.

Soon, the bending, red-rubber-pantied girl was belly down across the punishment stool, her exposed cheeks bulging within the taut rubberwear offered up in absolute submission.

'Perfect,' commented the Head. 'You three girls. A paddle apiece. At once.'

The three girls charged with the task of punishing their ringleader padded self-consciously across to a huge, empty fireplace. Emma noted that their exposed cheeks bunched enticingly within the red rubber's squeezing grip. The paddles were resting on a mantlepiece above the empty hearth. Above, a seventeenth-century darkened oil painting of a squire, posing with fowling pieces and assorted dead game, gazed down haughtily. Emma noticed that the red-rubbered girls' exposed clefts darkened as each reached up in turn to secure their paddle.

The paddles were twenty inches long, with fourteen-inch handles. The edges of the elongated curves were stitched, the white cotton weaving in and out as it zig-zagged along the pale leather sheath. Emma imagined the weight of them, balanced in the spanker's hand. Imagined the sharp crack as they struck smartly down across naked, upturned cheeks. Imagined the searing pain as the leathered wood kissed and burned bare buttocks.

Lining up behind Rebecca's bare buttocks, Ann, Olympia and Charlotte shuffled anxiously, paddles upraised.

'Remember the rules of paddle-punishment when conducted in red rubbers, girls. You must ensure that her punished bottom is left as red as the rubber around it. Understand? I'll be looking for a perfect match. And if I am not perfectly satisfied, in every aspect, and with every bottom,' the Head added softly, 'your punishment will commence all over again. Doubled.'

It was a savage punishment. The harsh crack-cracking of the paddles rang out relentlessly for a full twenty minutes, each sharp swipe splitting the silence of the refectory. Rebecca Wigmore squealed, waggled her crimsoning buttocks then sobbed and writhed under the concluding dozen strokes. A proud beauty, Emma thought, broken under the paddle's harsh bark.

Emma didn't miss a single stroke, blinking deliberately as the punishers drew away from the stool to give way to the next paddle-wielding chastiser. Her pussy prickled at the thought of the red rubber biting up into the wet slits of the red-bottomed sufferers, but juiced furiously when Ann Cordery stepped up – this time to paddle the bottom of the pert little Bicknell girl. Imagining herself across the punishment stool, Emma's belly tightened.

Kate's reassuring squeeze brought Emma to her senses. What the hell am I thinking? I'm here to beat these girls – not to be beaten by them. It is to me they will come for a sharp reminder. For their intimate instruction.

Managing to dispel the delicious idea of being spanked with a paddle across the bare bottom by the delightful Ann Cordery, Emma gazed at the Bicknell girl's reddening cheeks. The game little brunette only began to howl – really yell – after her nineteenth.

By thirteen minutes past five, the punishments were over. All four girls came away from the high stool sobbing aloud. Emma shuddered as she saw the glitter of tears behind Ann Cordery's tumbling fringe.

'She'll need lots of aftercare,' Kate whispered into Emma's ear.

Emma blushed.

'They all will. Wouldn't mind being Mme Puton tonight.'

Emma attempted an inquiring look. Kate seemed to accept it at face value.

'She's very good at aftercare. As you well know.'

Emma's blush became a blaze.

Six

'What happens to the girls now?' Emma sighed, exhausted yet exhilarated by the group punishment she had just witnessed.

'Early bed for everyone. No TV or reading in the dorms allowed,' Kate replied. 'Marion has got the unlucky foursome over in the gym –'

'More punishment?' Emma broke in.

'No. Not official ones, though she does like to get her victims up against those bloody wall bars. No,' Kate added, 'they'll wash their red rubbers out in the sluice then take a shower before bed.'

'Watson kept the twins back. Bubble and Squeak.'

'I saw that,' Kate nodded. 'She's on to something. I wonder where they are now.'

Kate, who was punishing Emma for enjoying aftercare with the French mistress, dug her fingers into Emma's buttocks and dragged the soft cheeks painfully apart. As Emma opened her mouth to protest, Kate covered it with her own, sucking and tonguing Emma fiercely before capturing the tip of Emma's quivering tongue between her teeth. Emma stopped struggling and surrendered. Keeping her captive by trapping Emma's tongue tip, Kate slid her hand around to seek out and secure the slippery little clitoral bud. Tormenting it, she brought Emma up on to scrabbling tiptoe.

Twenty minutes later, after Emma had abjectly promised to bring her bottom to Kate and only Kate for future aftercare, they lay in each other's fierce embrace.

'Bubble and Squeak,' Emma murmured.

'What about them?'

'Nothing, really. Just wonder where they were.'

'If Watson has her claws in them, they'll be in trouble.'

Marion undertook the task of supervising the four publicly punished girls as they took their compulsory showers, tearfully towelled themselves dry and scampered out of the gym up to their dorms.

As the gym doors slapped shut behind them, Miss Watson emerged from the shadows, steering Bubble and Squeak into the pool of light bathing the large vaulting horse. Her spectacles flashed as she nodded conspiratorially to the gym mistress.

'Thank you. I will take over from here,' Marion murmured, exchanging the soiled red rubbers discarded by the punished girls for the trembling twins.

Watson, richly rewarded, shrank back into the shadows. There, kneeling on the polished gym floor, thighs splayed, she carefully thumbed the sticky rubber panties open. Exposing them at full stretch, she inspected them intimately before burying her nose into their sheen and snuffing up the slit-smears. Inhaling deeply, she soon became lost in her heady rapture. Instead of taking them to the sluice to rinse them clean, she would lick them out at her leisure.

In the strong shaft of light, wriggling and blinking, Bubble and Squeak lay side by side, thigh to thigh, belly down and bare bottomed across the vaulting horse.

Marion, standing behind them, flexed her leather strap, examined its stitching appreciatively then captured its suppleness between a finger and thumbtip pincer. Dragging the hide upwards to her bosom, she sensually thumbed the leather. Across the horse, the bare bottoms dimpled with dread. Marion's sharp eye caught the slight movement. She smiled grimly. She cracked her strap. The tiny toes scrabbling in the empty air flexed with fear. Marion studied them pleasurably. Suspended above the polished floor, the naked feet of the twins arrowed down, revealing slightly grubby soles. So poignant. So full of pathos. So perfectly symbolic of submissive surrender. Marion cracked the strap once more. Its vicious bark made the four feeet dance in exquisite anguish. The gym mistress stepped closer to the horse, playing the tip of her leather to stay and steady the feet into obedient stillness.

'I'm waiting,' she whispered. 'I know you both have something to tell me. Something to confess.'

The only response from the bare-bottomed twins face down across the vaulting horse was a frightened whimper.

'Something to do with Rebecca's little escapade. Yes. You are in some way involved in the Wigmore girl's misdeeds. I'm certain of it. Speak. Come along. Own up.'

The two clefts became tight creases as the twins clenched their cheeks in terror of the lash.

'Perhaps this will help.' She carefully arranged the length of leather across their proffered buttocks. Their poised peaches shivered beneath the cool caress of the hide, shivered beneath its light but lethal weight. Marion let a full, agonising two minutes elapse before gathering up her strap.

'No?' she murmured. 'Speak up,' she barked suddenly, 'or suffer.'

The twins whimpered as their beautiful little bottoms tightened.

Good old Watson, Marion thought, thumbing her leather strap. Never misses a trick. Spotted their brief show of guilt back there in the refectory.

'Speak, girls, or my leather will loosen your tongues.'

Across the dull hide of the horse, both bare bottoms tensed until the light from above shone on their tightened curves, sculpting and shadowing the fear-frozen flesh.

Crack. Crack. Two searing swipes, two crimsoning weals – but only one shrill squeak.

Crack. Crack. The belt flickered out, jagging and straightening as the leather lashed down, biting savagely into the bouncing buttocks. Again, two sharp barks, two reddening stripes – but, again, only one anguished squeak.

'You were on to her. Knew what she was up to, weren't you? Rebecca bought you little presents to buy your

122

silence, didn't she?' Marion demanded. It was shrewd insight more than inspiration. A shot in the dark, but well calculated.

Bubble and Squeak answered in unison, almost relieved to admit their crime. Their small voices barely reached the corners of the gym as they eagerly spilled out their confession under the threat of the hovering strap.

'I thought so.'

Crack. Crack. As their bottoms blazed, Bubble bubbled into the scuffed hide while Squeak squeaked her response.

Marion palmed her leather, fingering its increasing warmth. 'I would be perfectly within my rights and indeed only doing my duty to report this matter to Dr Flint. It would mean, of course –' Marion paused for maximum effect '– a red rubber tomorrow before the whole of Laments and weeks of miserable forfeits for you both.'

Crack. Crack. Marion stepped right up to the vaulting horse, pressing her wet slit against the hide. Bending down, she closely inspected the results of her strap on the naked cheeks she had just whipped.

'But,' she whispered, palming the bare bottoms firmly but tenderly, 'I could just as well punish you both right here and now. I have a new riding crop that needs breaking in.'

Marion paused. Bubble furtively ground her slit into the horse at her belly. Squeak tongued the hide at her lips.

'There is a possible solution, though. Perhaps. I want you to do something for me, twins. But it must remain strictly our secret and nobody must ever know. Do I make myself clear?'

The twins responded readily, their heads rising up eagerly as one.

'The new mistress. She needs to be put through her paces. Needs to be tested. Entirely for her own good, of course, and for the good of Laments.'

'Yes, Miss Aylott-Inche,' Bubble and Squeak rejoined.

'Needs to win her spurs, as it were. So –' Marion drew her forefinger down the length of both tightened clefts '– I want you to test her. When she is on dorm patrol tomorrow night. Just be as naughty, as disobedient and disruptive –'

'But, Miss Aylott-Inche –' they protested.

Crack. Crack. The sleeping leather woke and spoke.

Crack. Crack. Bubble silvered the dark hide as Squeak's shrill squeal split the silence.

'It is decided then. Excellent. Remember, you have my authority to be as naughty tomorrow night as you can be. It is my wish, twins. No. It is my instruction.'

'Yes, Miss Aylott-Inche.'

'But not one word of this to anyone. And, girls –'

'Yes, Miss Aylott-Inche?'

'Fail me in this matter and you will be back across that horse.'

Crack. Crack.

Monday morning brought even more miserable February rain. In accordance with Felicity Flint's timetabled programme of induction, Emma joined Mme Puton and her class immediately after breakfast. Memories came flooding back as Emma saw the neat little desks and chairs, the books and pens, and sniffed the faint smell of chalkdust.

It was supposed to be French literature, Molière, but the dog-eared paperback copies of *Le Misanthrope* remained unopened all morning as the chic French mistress treated her class of nine to a detailed lecture on infamous courtesans, followed by a vivid account of erotic art treasures kept locked away in the cellars of the Louvre.

Emma, sitting alongside Mme Puton at her desk – it was a tight, thigh-squashing squeeze – surveyed the class speculatively. Mme Puton, to her credit, frequently lapsed into her native tongue, but Emma noticed that this caused most of the assembled girls to wrinkle their brows uncomprehendingly. As the short but graphic lecture on the erotic adventures of eighteenth-century Hanoverian courtesans – who supplied bondage and whipping to satisfy their aristocratic lovers – unfolded, Emma glanced down at the register. Matching names to faces was already becoming easier for her now.

Ann Cordery, her dark fringe now sleekly parted, sat slightly pale faced at the back of the class. Emma noticed that, from time to time, the girl who had worn the red rubbers yesterday edged from cheek to sore cheek throughout the morning. Rebecca, Olympia and Charlotte were in Kate's class, but Emma recognised the blonde, heavily breasted Middleton-Peake girl. And sitting together, heads bowed and eyes averted, were the twins, Bubble and Squeak. They seemed to avoid Emma's gaze – or was it just her imagination?

No need for harsh discipline here, Emma mused. Mme Puton taught her class enthusiastically if somewhat eclectically, missing the syllabus by miles, and the girls seemed to lap it up.

Emma was suddenly conscious of the twins. They were staring at her. She glanced down the row of desks. The twins averted their gaze, turned towards one another and smiled fleetingly and enigmatically. Emma shivered slightly.

Mme Puton was launching breathlessly into some obscure detail of Hanoverian flagellation. Prince Wilhelm, a minor, now forgotten Bavarian royal, enjoyed – Mme Puton assured her enthralled class – having his ankles bound together and being hauled up, naked and inverted, so that his exposed buttocks could be flogged by two Neopolitan courtesans adept in the dark art of whipping. They were expelled from the Bavarian court after being caught catching his ejaculation in a silver goblet and sipping from it in triumph while their bound, punished victim sobbed. Beats plodding through those polished but dull passages of the more edifying Molière, Emma thought.

And how well behaved the girls were. Bright eyed, attentive and keeping a respectful silence. No need for harsh discipline here, Emma mused once more. Not a cane or crop in sight.

But the tranquil surface was soon rippled by the promise of pain when Mme Puton suddenly decided to test the girls in French vocabulary. It started amiably enough with the days of the week.

'Le weekdays,' as the French mistress said in her own peculiar English.

The Middleton-Peake girl got both Tuesday and Saturday wrong. Mme Puton pressed on, unruffled by the lapse. She tackled the nine pupils one by one, requiring them to name the months of the year. All answered correctly until, once more, the blonde, heavily breasted Middleton-Peake girl fluffed on both April and August.

'Susie,' Mme Puton purred, 'you know very well that I asked you to learn these for today's testing. But you do not know them yet. You have not tried very hard, I think. Come up here, *s'il vous plait.*'

A ripple of expectation fluttered through the row of desks as Susie Middleton-Peake was instructed to approach the blackboard. Emma sensed it instantly. Here it comes, she thought. At last. Intimate instruction in action.

Susie's chair scraped noisily as she rose up from her desk. Mme Puton stepped up to the blackboard and quickly scribbled – perfectly illegibly – the seven days of the week. In French. The white chalk squeaked as her supple wrist scribbled.

'*Ici, ma petite.* Stand here.'

Strap or cane, Emma wondered. Or does Mme Puton haul each miscreant across her warm, nylon-stockinged knee and spank their bare bottoms?

Emma juiced suddenly at the thought of being spanked across Mme Puton's knee. Juiced viciously and scalded her slit at the thought of being pinned down, bare bottomed, wriggling and helpless, as the beautifully manicured, scarlet-nailed hand cracked down. Mme Puton, her violet eyes deepening to a shade of wild heliotrope, her moist, crimson lips slightly parted, grunting softly, carnally, as she smacked Emma's helpless cheeks. The soak at Emma's panties spread. She squirmed. Squirmed deliciously as she imagined herself, her heels kicking frantically in the tightly restricting panties around her feet, jerking across the nylon-stockinged thighs of her chic punisher – rasping her labia into their sheen as the slender hand spanked her pink bottom.

126

Emma took a deep breath and squeezed her buttocks. Concentrate. Pay attention. In a day or two, that'll be you, up there, with the Middleton-Peake blonde. Her bottom will be yours to deal with. The thought sobered Emma up instantly – as did the thought of the severe punishment Kate would dispense if she ever discovered Emma enjoying a taste of chastisement à la Puton.

'*Dimanche, lundi, mardi –*' Susie Middleton-Peake recited, her fluting voice filling the classroom.

'*Bon,*' the French mistress murmured. '*Assez bien.* Now, *ma petite,*' she instructed, reaching for the board rubber, '*repetez, s'il vous plait.*'

Before Susie could rattle off the weekdays from the board, Mme Puton, breasts straining within her silk blouse, had erased them. Susie gazed up at the pale white smear, perplexed.

'*Dimanche,*' she faltered, drying before Monday dawned.

For a full stubborn minute's silence, the French mistress waited, patting the board rubber against her upturned palm.

Strap or cane, Emma speculated, her anticipation mounting. Or a spanking.

Mme Puton spoke. Her tone was slightly waspish. 'Take your skirt up, Susie. Up above the hips. No, higher. You know how I want to see your bottom.'

The pert blonde's bosom bounced softly as she stepped back from the blackboard and, elbows angled, dragged up her uniform pleated skirt until it rode her hips. Emma gazed at the plump little rump within the navy knickers. Tight little knickers that bit into the tempting cleft.

'I will give to you the second chance. The last go, *n'est-ce pas?*'

But Susie did not break the ensuing silence. Emma saw the clenched buttocks wobble then tighten again as the blonde struggled to remember.

'*Non? Quelle domage.* Skirt up a little more, I think.'

She's going to spank her, Emma decided. She grew impatient. Hungry for the punishment to commence. Thumb those knickers down, she silently urged the French mistress. Thumb those pants dominantly down and smack those firm little cheeks until they crimson and bounce.

Emma watched, fascinated, as Mme Puton kneeled down directly behind Susie. Raising her hands up to her pupil's hips, the French mistress lowered them slowly, palms inwards, dragging the blue knickers with them. The navy serge rolled up into a thickening band and slid down beneath the bulge of the exposed buttocks above. Down, from thighs to knees. Down, from knees to ankles. Emma swallowed. Her mouth was dry. At the shadowed juncture of the clamped thighs, directly below the vanishing point of Susie's cleft, Emma could just discern the tuft of her blonde snatch. Emma's tongue thickened. She juiced her mouth to lubricate her tongue. Around her, the rest of the class gazed up in spellbound silence.

Mme Puton rose up gracefully from her knees and adjusted her skirt. Wiping her hands free of chalk dust, she stood alongside her quivering blonde pupil.

'You must try to learn these words, Susie. The fierce Dr Flint says so. It is important. One day soon she herself will test you. And you will not know these words and so, *ma petite*, she will use the bamboo cane on your bottom. That is not *tres jolie*, that little whippy cane. So, *ma petite*, if you will not learn, I must teach you.'

Emma held her breath – but the expected sharp crack of a spanking hand did not ring out. Only a soft moan. A soft moan of sweet suffering as Mme Puton slid her hand down from where it had been caressing Susie's firm belly to the pubic mound below – where it started to pluck and tease, tease and tug, at the blonde pubic nest.

Emma gasped as the Middleton-Peake girl rose up on her toes. The French mistress had enclosed her fist over the full bush now and was scrunching it ruthlessly – really pleasure-punishing her lazy little pupil. Susie clenched and unclenched her buttocks as if she was drawing up an anal dildo into her tight little sphincter. Emma thought it quite beautiful. Beautifully obscene. Susie's thighs quivered as the French mistress worked her fist busily. As Susie squealed aloud, Emma swallowed hard.

'Ah, *mais non, ma petite*. Not the noise, *s'il vous plait*. I do not want to hear the noise. Only the months of the year. *En Francais, d'accord*.'

The punishment of the blonde's pussy seemed to quicken her memory. Suddenly, Susie Middleton-Peake was able to faultlessly recite 'le weekdays' followed by the twelve months of the year, in perfect, sonorous French.

'*Pas mal*,' Mme Puton purred, gently patting the blonde pubic coils. 'Now, *ma petite*, just to be sure. The months. *Repetez, s'il vous plait*.'

Susie, stunned by her recent success, paused uncertainly. A warning thumb at her clitoris was all the prompting she needed. Emma grinned, willing the pert little blonde on as Susie almost sang her way through the calendar, stumbling only once over the tricky vowels of *Août* until a scarlet thumbnail raking her love-thorn spurred her on.

'*Formidable, ma petite*,' Mme Puton cried. 'And now, after the punishment, the reward.'

Placing her flattened palm in against the blonde's pubic plum, bending down to do so, Mme Puton gently masturbated Susie Middleton-Peake until the pert little pupil buckled at her knees and, hobbled by the navy serge knickers binding her ankles, staggered into the blackboard, coming loudly.

Just before lunch, Mme Puton produced a rose pink Max Factor lipstick. The golden, bullet-shaped shaft glinted as she palmed it, presenting it to the rapt attention of her pupils. Denied, under the strict rules and stern regime of Laments, the possession still less the usage of cosmetics, the sudden appearance of the delicious pink lipstick on a bleak February morning caused quite a stir.

'*Et maintenant*,' the French mistress whispered, 'before the disgusting lunch of liver and onions that awaits us –'

Mme Puton's Gallic grimace was enthusiastically returned by the entire class.

'I have for you one final little lesson. *Regardez*, the correct application of the lipstick.'

Desks were deserted in seconds as the pupils pressed eagerly around their mistress in an excited scrummage.

'*Eh bien*, who shall I choose?' she teased, twisting the base of the golden bullet to allow the soft, pink shaft to emerge, gleamingly erect.

'Me, me, me, please, Madamoiselle, me,' they crowed.

'*Moi, moi*,' a clever few chorused.

Mme Puton beckoned Ann Cordery to her side. 'After the wearing of the rubber that is *rouge* yesterday, today the little treat, no?'

Disappointed not to be chosen, still none of the girls begrudged the choice. Ann smiled, offering her pale face up eagerly. Emma saw the lips being wetted in anticipation by a flickering tongue-tip.

Mme Puton gave a brisk demonstration, explaining that normally, tissues, ice cubes and a soft-haired cosmetic brush would be used. Applying the pink shaft deftly to Ann's lower lip, she depressed the flesh down dominantly before smearing it carefully from side to side.

'Do not close the eyes and think of it as the man's penis, girls,' she warned.

The huddled girls giggled.

'Ah, *non*. Keep your eyes wide open. And do not touch it with the tongue.'

Again, the classroom echoed to their smothered laughter.

'Now, *regardez-moi*,' she instructed.

Mme Puton pressed her lips together. Ann Cordery imitated her tutor's action, spreading the lipstick from her lower to her upper lips.

The assembled girls squealed their delight. Ann basked in the centre of their attention, yesterday's suffering now just a memory almost as sweet as the Max Factor smudging her lips.

'Of course, the sophisticated young woman takes full advantage of her assets,' Mme Puton purred. '*Par example*, the breasts. Give to me your bosom, *ma petite*.'

The class giggled and squealed delightedly as Ann Cordery, blushing gently, unbuttoned her white cotton blouse and let her brassiereless breasts spill free.

Bloody hell, Emma thought, if Old Ma Flint comes in now the solids will really hit the fan.

But the Head did not interrupt the ad hoc cosmetic lesson. Cupping and gently squeezing Ann Cordery's left breast, the French mistress thumbed the tiny pink nipple up until it was swollen and hard.

'*Regardez*. Can everyone see?'

The excited girls pressed closer still, crushing their bare thighs together tightly. They giggled and gasped aloud as Mme Puton plied the soft snout of the pink lipstick first to the nipple and then to the dark skin surrounding its proud peak.

'This time, girls, you can close your eyes and think it is the penis of the ardent male in adoration.'

A frisson of dark delight ravished the squealing pupils.

'And now, who would like to do the other breast, hmm?'

All the girls begged loudly but it was to Emma that the French mistress proffered the golden bullet.

'Mademoiselle Wyndlesham, would you like to?'

'*Oui*,' Emma replied instantly. She took the lipstick. It weighed quite heavily in her prinked fingers. Her grey eyes met Ann Cordery's steady gaze. There was no reluctance or defiance there, merely a silent invitation.

Emma reached out, delicately cupping and squeezing the pliant flesh up into a submissive bulge. Her slit tingled. She loosened her grip slightly, careful not to hurt or bruise the pretty little breast. Ann responded with a shudder and a smothered moan.

'Ooh, you have the touch, Mademoiselle Wyndlesham. *Mais oui*, but you have,' remarked the French mistress appreciatively.

Emma weighed the warmth of the captive breast in her palm, then cupped and squeezed it tenderly again. Ann hunched her shoulders then arched her spine, thrusting her breast fully forward. Emma worked her thumbtip back and forth across the nipple, rubbing and worrying it with increasing ferocity. It felt delicious. As it grew increasingly firm, it did not lose that pliant, rubbery feel that juiced Emma's cotton panties with a fresh scald. The nipple rose and thickened under Emma's thumb. Thickened and peaked. Emma tamed it slowly, deliberately with the pink, waxy lipstick, applying the soft snout into and then around the nipple dominantly. Their eyes met again. This time, Emma glimpsed both arousal and surrender in those of the bare-breasted, lipstick-nippled Ann Cordery.

'*Vites, vites*,' Mme Puton cried in alarm as the lunch bell rang out, splitting the spellbound silence. 'Button your blouse and wipe your lips.'

And your tits, Emma thought, taking out a lace hankie and carefully wiping Ann Cordery's nipples and lips clean.

'And what have you been studying this morning, girls? In case La Watson asks?'

The class giggled. 'Molière,' they replied loyally.

'*Très bien*, but La Watson, she is the clever one, no? What book of M. Molière did you read?'

They dutifully chorused that they had been studying *Le Misanthrope*.

'*Bon*. Now go and do not be late for your disgusting liver and onions.'

The classroom was deserted.

'But you did not punish her. The Middleton-Peake girl. No cane or strap,' Emma replied. They had been discussing the lesson.

Mme Puton smiled and took Emma's hand. 'The cane, the strap. I leave those to the fierce Dr Flint and Marion, the mistress of the gym. For me, I have other methods. Pain, *ma petite*, is not the only persuader.'

Emma wanted to linger. She burned to hear, and learn, much more.

'I think you do not like too much to use the strap or cane, *n'est-ce pas?*'

Emma deflected the unexpected question with an enigmatic smile.

'But you are not displeased to receive these punishments, no?'

This time, Emma's smile failed her. She blushed, hating yet loving the idea that Mme Puton knew what Emma herself was still struggling to understand.

'You are the complex little one. And yet I think you will soon acquire the taste for punishment. Yes. Soon, you will

132

enjoy the punishment of naughty girls' bare bottoms. Sooner than you acquire the taste for the disgusting liver and onions, I hope.'

Emma grinned.

'But come now. Come along with me up to my room. I have a *poussin*, a little how you say of the cold chicken and some wine waiting for me. And we can discuss punishment and its many pleasures at our ease.'

But halfway up the sweeping staircase, Emma bumped into Kate.

'Don't be late for lunch,' Kate warned, her passionate eyes darting back to the sensual sway of Mme Puton's retreating bottom.

Reluctantly, Emma turned and descended the stairs, following Kate down to the refectory and her liver and onion lunch, leaving the French mistress to dine alone.

It wasn't liver and onions. It was for the girls – and it looked to Emma as gruesome as it no doubt tasted. The staff, assembled at the top table, lunched on delicately poached sea bass followed by a black grape and Brie tart.

Escorting Emma into coffee, Felicity Flint steered her aside into an alcove. Emma felt the controlling grip of the Head's hand at her elbow.

'Instructive morning with Mme Puton, I trust?'

'Oh, yes, Dr Flint. I feel more confident now. She has a – a way with the girls.'

'Spends far too much on damn cosmetics. Cold cream for their bottoms and expensive lipsticks.'

'I – that is –' Emma flushed in her confusion, amazed at the Head's omniscience.

'No harm in it, I grant you. Girls seem to love it. No, I do not perceive Mme Puton to be subversive or any threat to the work we do here at Laments. Bit of an exotic, perhaps, but she's French, isn't she?'

Emma grinned.

'Now before you join Miss Monteagle for Geography, I think you should have a quiet word with the Cordery girl. Her nipples appear to be extraordinarily prominent today.

133

Quite pink and peaked. For goodness sake, get her to wipe that lipstick off properly before our sharp-eyed gym mistress threatens to do it for her.'

Emma, blushing, lowered her head. Was nothing secret from Felicity Flint?

The Head returned, moments later. 'There's your coffee, my dear. Mocha. Drink up. Geography awaits. And you don't want to be late for Tweedledee. Or is it Tweedledum? Kate has yet to disclose to me exactly which is which.'

The Head departed to speak with Miss Watson, leaving Emma twirling her little silver coffee spoon in the empty air.

Miss Monteagle took her group of six girls on a relentless tour along the Pan American Highway, dispensing copious amounts of tedious data concerning demographic trends, climatology and primary industries. Time congealed for the class. As the clock on the wall struggled towards three, chins were being propped up and yawns stifled. Emma chose to sit alongside the pupils, between Rebecca and Olympia, and was finding the going very heavy indeed. By three fifteen, she too had her hand under her chin and was smothering her desire to yawn.

Miss Monteagle, a mature beauty with strangely compelling eyes, appeared stronger, meaner and tougher when divorced from her ever-present companion, Miss Rathbone. Together, they seemed to dilute each other's energy and verve. Alone, Emma suspected that Miss Monteagle – suddenly Kate's 'Tweedledee' tag didn't fit – could be a force to be reckoned with. Yes. Cane in hand, or crop aquiver, a stern disciplinarian.

Emma concentrated hard. Not on the Pan American Highway but on the teacher. She did it all by eye contact, Emma decided. And the voice. Sitting in the confines of her desk, Emma followed Miss Monteagle's darting eyes. Eyes that missed nothing. And what a clever questioner, Emma suddenly realised. All questions were directed at a named individual, forbidding the girls to hide within the safety of the group. Searching questions, always requiring more than a mere yes or no answer.

But Emma sensed the boredom building up and knew that soon the class would be up to mischief, rebelling against the irksome deluge of dry statistics.

'Most of the peoples living along the Pan American Highway speak Spanish,' the class was informed.

'Ribbit,' a naughty voice frogged.

Miss Monteagle paused. It was a dangerous moment. Emma, remembering how Miss Monteagle had earlier extolled the use of the cane, felt the hairs on the nape of her neck prickle.

'Although in Brazil, the population are chiefly Portuguese speaking –'

'Ribbit,' another frog-voice called out impudently as Miss Monteagle turned to the overhead projector.

The class collapsed in laughter. Miss Monteagle turned instantly, crushing the girls down into silence with a glare.

Emma tensed. Any minute now, she sensed, bare bottoms would suffer.

'The Spanish for frog,' the teacher remarked, smiling thinly, 'is *rana*, and the Portuguese, I seem to recollect, is –'

'Ribbit.'

Shit, that's done it, Emma thought. They've pushed too hard.

After turning the overhead projector off, Miss Monteagle calmly strode across to a locked cupboard. Unpocketing a chained key, she opened the cupboard and extracted an evil-looking thin, cane-like wand. Returning slowly to her desk, she placed the supple length of wood lengthways across her desktop before turning towards the class.

'One of you, or possibly more than one of you, has had the temerity to interrupt my lesson this afternoon. The silly girl, or girls, will now stand up and apologise.'

Miss Monteagle had spoken in such a soft tone Emma had to strain to hear her. How lethally effective to whisper, Emma considered. If Miss Monteagle had shouted or ranted angrily, her credibility would have collapsed.

'At once,' she insisted, jutting her chin out aggressively.

And at that moment Emma sensed the teacher's true forcefulness.

'Very well, I shall beat you all.'

'No –'

'But, Miss –'

'That's not fair –'

Miss Monteagle reached back across to her desk and snatched up the whippy rod. She swished it vehemently, thrumming the air. The thin wood whistled as it sliced down. The class fell silent instantly.

'All of you,' she barked. 'Stand up by your desks.'

Emma, spellbound by the forcefulness of the curt command, almost stood up with the rest of the girls.

'Miss Wyndlesham, I think you will learn more if you come beside me to observe. You may find this part of the lesson a little more instructive than my little excursion into South America.'

Emma, conscious of this gentle rebuke – God, had she seen me yawn? – joined Miss Monteagle at the front of the class. Turning, she met the frightened eyes of the six shivering pupils.

'Draw the desks together in a straight line.'

Her instructions were obeyed at once.

'Turn, facing your desk.'

Six soft bottoms wobbled as the girls shuffled up to the edge of the desks, bumping their pubic mounds into the wood.

'Shorts down.'

Emma was treated to the delicious display of six bottoms being bared as the beautiful young girls wriggled out of the tight white shorts.

'Bend over. Across the desks. Bottoms up.'

Olympia and Rebecca displayed bottoms still pink from their previous red rubber punishments.

Miss Monteagle strode along the line of upturned buttocks, tap-tapping all six bare bottoms lightly with the tip of her whippy wood. Emma saw the cheeks dimple anxiously as the rod caressed them in turn.

'Our visit to Central and South America this afternoon introduced us to the climate and vegetation there,' Miss Monteagle commenced, her tone suave but grim. 'And now you have given me the perfect opportunity for a practical demonstration of both. This –' she trailed the quivering tip of her wand across the upturned bottoms '– as you are to painfully appreciate when I whip you in a little while, is not bambusa, or bamboo cane. Bamboo, Olympia, comes from?'

Mumbling sorrowfully into her desktop, the Scott-Hammerton girl accurately named the geographical locations where the bambusa species thrived.

'Correct. This –' she thrummed the stick down viciously, causing the bare cheeks to flinch with fear '– is a species of subtropical fern. *El helecho*. It grows in the undergrowth, or *la maleza*, beneath the canopy of the Amazonian rain forests. This particular fern much prefers the darkened shade. It thrives, I am given to understand, where conditions are warm, moist and *muy sombrio*.'

The bare-bottomed girls bending across their desks shivered as Miss Monteagle's lecture on the properties of *el helecho* narrowed from the general to the very, very specific. She launched into how supple and springy the gathered, dried fern stem proved to be. 'Far superior to the supposed whippiness of the Indonesian yellow bambusa.'

Miss Monteagle explained how the length of the thin, pliant frond was covered in tiny hairs.

'Touch your pubic hairs with your thumbtips,' she ordered.

Emma watched enthralled as the six bare bottoms swayed in response to the thumbtips stroking the pubic nests.

'Sleek and silky, no doubt. Except,' the teacher whispered, 'these tiny little hairs have a peculiar property. They secrete a sticky bead of resin that stings. It deters creatures from inhabiting the tall fern parasitically. Butterflies, ants. Even larger species, like *la rana*, or frog.'

The irony of this remark was not wasted on the girls bending over and awaiting their pain. Emma saw their peach-cheeks dimple with dread.

'This particular specimen,' Miss Monteagle murmured, again tap-tapping each bare bottom in turn, 'is the female

137

of the species. How appropriate that it is shortly to be used to punish female bottoms. The female of the species, or, as they say along the Pan American Highway, *la hembra de la especie –*'

God, Emma thought, she's really making them suffer. Not a single stroke yet and already they were writhing in an agony of fearful expectation. This is discipline, pure and raw discipline. Miss Monteagle had achieved a measured mastery over the girls she was about to punish. Without crimsoning a single cheek, she held them all in her absolute thrall.

'It is plucked in the late autumn when it is ripe, swollen even, with resinous sap. A very luxuriant species. *Muy frondoso*. My word,' the teacher gushed suddenly, almost lapsing into Tweedledee mode, 'this lesson is certainly going well. Botany, Spanish and, as you girls are about to learn, the most important part of our curriculum here at Laments, obedience.'

Emma knew that the moment was rapidly approaching when the lecture would cease and only the whippy wood would speak. Eloquently. Again, and again, singing out its cruel notes in praise of suffering and pain.

'It is, admittedly, somewhat thinner than bamboo, but being more resinous it is more supple. More biting. It is said by those who use it to discipline disobedient young female buttocks that the squeal of pain it can elicit from the lips of the whipped carries further than the screech of the Dobson's macaw. Much further.'

Miss Monteagle strode forward and planted her feet slightly apart. Settling into the appropriate stance, she raised the quivering *el helecho*.

'I propose to give you three strokes apiece.'

An even crueller touch, Emma conceded, sensing that Miss Monteagle was going to administer the girls' stripes singly, allowing them to suffer the anticipation of the impending strokes in exquisite anguish.

Across each desk, the bare buttocks were perfectly poised and positioned for punishment. More so, Emma considered, than if the girls had been ordered to bend over and touch their toes. With their bellies and hips pressed down into the wooden desktops, their cheeks seemed to almost rise up to greet their impending pain eagerly.

Swish, swipe. Olympia squealed and squirmed as the pliant frond lashed down. Miss Monteagle leisurely caressed the bouncing buttocks with the length of her fern, drawing it across the clenched cheeks as if drawing a bow across a fat cello. Emma understood at once the cruel intention: as the tiny hairs rasped the punished flesh, spilling sticky beads of stinging resin, Olympia howled aloud, clenching her buttocks in renewed anguish.

Swish, swipe. Miss Monteagle was a consummate disciplinarian. Pacing sedately down along the line of proffered bottoms, she administered a stinging single stroke to each. Following each ruthless slice-swipe with a flesh-tormenting caress of the stinging frond. Such an adroit punisher, Emma marvelled. Such poise, pace and prowess. As the last girl in line – Rebecca Wigmore – received her opening stroke, down along the desks Olympia was still snivelling from hers.

Miss Monteagle repeated her slow, measured tread down along the line of punished rumps, each now bearing a single crimson weal together with the spreading pink scald where the frond had stung like a nettle.

Swish, swipe. In addressing each bare bottom, the teacher levelled her whippy fern stem inwards against the cheeks, jerked it up and then, flicking her supple wrist with an economy of effort, swished it down. Each pupil was left smothering their squeals as, bottoms jiggling in agony, they each suffered their second stripe.

Swish, swipe.

The punishment continued towards its inexorable conclusion.

God, they must be in agony, Emma thought, beginning to juice in response to the sight of bottom after bottom jerking lewdly in a blaze of pain.

Unhurriedly, efficiently and in supreme control of her weeping penitents, Miss Monteagle administered the third stroke to each bending pupil's bare bottom.

'Legs apart,' the teacher whispered softly.

Emma frowned, caught out unawares by this unexpected development. She had not thought Miss Monteagle tender enough to dispense aftercare to the buttocks she had just beaten. But what else did this command mean?

'Further apart, girls,' Miss Monteagle instructed them, her tone even softer, more sweeter than before.

She's going to kiss them better, Emma concluded, suddenly remembering the scene in the showers. The thought of the mature, cosmetic-free stern face bending down to bury itself in the six whipped bottoms of the beautiful young girls sluiced Emma's cotton panties with a warm soak from her slit.

'Tummies flat against the desk,' Miss Monteagle's treacling tones ordered. 'Legs as wide apart as you can, please.'

Their naked cheeks, each blistered with three reddening stripes, wobbled as the bending girls splayed their thighs obediently.

'Miss Wyndlesham, did you think my little talk on the Pan American Highway instructive, or not?'

'Oh, very much so,' Emma replied quickly, snapping out of her daydream.

'So did I,' replied the teacher, her voice as soft as silk. 'But I was mistaken,' she snarled, her anger ripping the silken tones in shreds. 'Mistaken.'

Emma's throat tightened. God. She's about to lose it. She's really furious beneath that mask of deliberate calm. Furious and dangerous.

Emma almost closed her eyes – the thought of that cruel frond whipping down once more was too much to bear. Almost. She blinked, keeping her grey eyes open wide.

Cringing in abject misery, the six bare-bottomed girls crushed their breasts into the desktops. But the expected strokes did not slice down. Overmastering her rage, Miss Monteagle sank down to her knees. Shuffling along from bare buttocks to bare buttocks, she gently fingered each yawning cleft then briskly dragged the stinging fern's stem down their shadowed warmth – as she would play a delicate bow at a violin: leaving all six pupils squealing pitch perfect A sharps of agony.

Dr Flint handed the powerful torch and the dark leather strap to Emma.

'Dorm patrol, my dear. And I think you should conduct it on your own. Already, there are whisperings in the staff room questioning my wisdom in your appointment. A growing anxiety, voiced in certain quarters, that you have neither the spirit nor the soul of a sound disciplinarian.'

Marion Aylott-Inche, Emma decoded.

'What nonsense.'

Emma clicked the torch, checking the battery.

All the girls in the first, more senior dorm, were asleep. Or at least pretending to be. Rebecca and her unfortunate friends were keeping a very low profile, Emma sensed. No trouble from them, she thought, switching her torch beam from pillow to pillow.

The girls' faces looked carefree and seraphic in sleep, their combed-out hair tumbling wantonly in sweet disorder on the white pillows.

But what if it was a subtle ruse? She certainly didn't want to give either Marion or the weasel Watson any ammunition. She snapped off her torch and gently opened, then quickly closed, the door – without actually leaving the dorm. An old trick of her own dorm prefect several years ago. Holding her breath, Emma counted to twenty. Then she heard it. A faint rustling. Or was it a mouse-like scratching? Directing her torch towards the faint sound, she snapped the beam on. It illuminated the smiling face of Charlotte Bicknell – a smile instantly frozen in the sudden shaft of light. Playing the beam down over the swell of Charlotte's blanketed breasts, Emma saw the spider-like movement of the hidden fingers at the wet slit. The girl was masturbating. Little minx. Sighing with relief, Emma killed the torch and left the dorm.

When Emma entered, the junior dorm was in complete disarray. The younger girls, some naked, others scantily

141

clad in either vests or tight panties, were engaged in a silently uproarious pillow fight. The Middleton-Peake girl was straddling one of the twins, probably Squeak, and buffeting her opponent's bare bosom. Emma strode in to suppressed squeals of glee and a snowstorm of duck feathers.

Emma clapped her hands. The dorm fell silent, a silence filled with wide-eyed, frightened girls. Emma stamped her foot. The imps scrambled delightedly into their beds, sensing that their bottoms would escape the dark leather strap dangling from Emma's left hand.

But the twins, Bubble and Squeak, snatched up a pillow and lobbed it over Emma's head, tossing to each other just out of her reach. Emma ordered them to stop and get into bed, snapping her strap dangerously. The pillow caught her by surprise, knocking both her torch and strap down on to the feather-strewn linoleum.

The dorm erupted in laughter as Bubble and Squeak scampered, bare bottomed, for safety – leaping over then under the occupied beds. Girls screamed as soft, stamping feet trod them down – and screamed again as Emma, red faced and furious, flew after them in hot pursuit.

The dorm echoed to a ragged cheer as Emma caught but then lost Squeak. The twins were as nimble as quicksilver trout in a mill race and just as elusive to catch. Emboldened, they paused, panting, to check Emma's attempts to capture and punish them.

'That's enough,' Kate's voice hissed from the open dorm door. 'Into bed, everyone. This instant.'

Bubble and Squeak scrambled into their beds, pulling their blankets up to their chins.

Kate snapped the lights out and ushered Emma through the door. On the landing, she turned and stroked Emma's face gently.

'You've done really well. They can be such little stinkers.'

Emma knew that she had failed. Failed, and let Laments down.

'Why don't you go and run a bath?' Kate suggested.

Emma did not respond.

'Our bath,' Kate whispered. 'I'll join you in a few minutes.'

At breakfast the following morning, Emma sensed the whispering cease abruptly between Marion and Miss Watson as she approached the top table. Dr Flint sat down moments later and, picking up the small bell, shook it vigorously, signalling to the assembled girls that breakfast could commence.

Just as the crisp bacon, plump sausages speckled with herbs and fluffy scrambled eggs were presented to the staff table, Miss Watson flicked out her napkin and remarked that there seemed to be a lot of noise coming from one of the dorms last night.

'Mm,' Miss Rathbone, forking a second sausage on to her plate, agreed. 'The junior dorm. Yes. Quite a din. Who was on dorm patrol?' she inquired pleasantly, scanning the table.

'Miss Wyndlesham,' Watson replied readily, managing an insinuating tone.

'Did you deal with the culprits?' Marion broke in, rudely interrupting Miss Rathbone.

'Deal with them severely?' chimed in Miss Rathbone, refusing to be upstaged.

Emma swallowed slowly before nodding.

'But there's nothing written down in the punishment book,' Watson weaseled.

'I'm sure that Emma dealt with the situation quite satisfactorily, didn't you, my dear?' Felicity Flint interposed.

Emma, buttering her toast, nodded briskly.

'Spank them?' Miss Rathbone pressed eagerly.

Felicity Flint, remembering the strap she had entrusted to Emma along with the torch, watched Emma's face closely.

'Well?' Marion challenged bullishly. 'Just how many did you punish? And how exactly did you punish them?'

Dr Flint, about to sip from her cup of aromatic Gunpowder tea, hesitated. Her eyes widened imperceptibly then narrowed as they gazed unblinkingly at Emma over the brim of her tea cup.

'Emma punished them all,' Kate said quickly. 'She simply forgot to enter it into the punishment book before breakfast,' she added, turning to Miss Watson.

Marion snorted dismissively, plated her knife and fork then tossed her napkin down. Like a gauntlet in a challenge.

'I think not. I have it on good authority that Miss Wyndlesham did not, in fact, punish anyone in the junior dorm last night. In fact, one could say that she actually lost control up there.'

The silence that settled over the staff table quickly spread to the rest of the refectory.

Kate repeated her statement in a calm, steady voice.

'We'll soon see about that,' Marion barked. 'You, girl. Yes, you. And you. You three also. Come up here at once.'

The five junior dorm girls rose up from the milky tea and toast and slowly approached the top table.

'If Miss Wyndlesham punished the junior dorm last night, then I expect to see five red bottoms.'

Miss Watson nodded vigorously. Emma paled, her toast suddenly difficult to swallow.

'Turn around, shorts down.'

The five girls, perplexed but obedient, turned and yanked down their tight little white shorts. Five recently punished, red bottoms were offered up submissively to the staff table.

'Capital,' Felicity Flint boomed. 'Did you use a strap?' she quizzed.

Emma gazed in disbelief at the reddened buttocks. A novice disciplinarian, she knew that no strap had caused the bottoms to blush so uniformly with that particular shade of unblemished crimson.

'You borrowed my table tennis bat,' Kate prompted.

'Welcome to Laments.' Dr Flint laughed, toasting Emma in Gunpowder tea.

Seven

The detour around Uckfield to avoid the rising floodwaters
– it had rained almost every day since Christmas – seemed
to make Kate edgy. She cursed every diversion sign softly.
The clock of the dash showed 7.20 p.m. in the dark. Emma
nursed The Beast along at a steady fifty-five as they headed
west, planning to get on to the fast-track M25 south of
Crawley.

'You're sure this is OK? We won't be missed?' Emma
asked for the third time.

'Course. We're not doing a bloody Rebecca Wigmore,
are we? Trust me.'

Emma grinned. 'So what's this treat you've laid on for me?'

Kate had persuaded Emma to take The Beast up to
London shortly after nightfall. Nosing the Mark II down
past Home Farm, and using the gates on the far side of the
spinney, they had slipped out of Laments unobserved.

'Think of it as therapy,' Kate murmured.

'Late night shopping?' Emma squealed. High Street Ken
was ablaze til midnight these days.

'Not exactly.'

The clock told them that it was 8.50 p.m. as The Beast
slewed into the car park of New Cross Hospital.

'We're going to pay Striped Shirt a little visit,' Kate
announced.

Emma swore.

'No. Listen. You've told me all about him. It's time he
was taught a lesson. A very painful lesson.'

145

'But –'

'Phoned him this afternoon. Nicked the number out of your purse,' Kate confessed. 'Told him you were sorry –'

'Sorry?'

'Sorry for ducking out last Friday night and that you had thought it over –'

'I did, did I? And?'

'You were prepared to party. Big time. And could I come along too? Cosy little threesome.'

Emma laughed. Nervously. 'Painful lesson. You said painful lesson.'

'You'll see. Let's go. I said 9.30 for ten.'

Emma found it difficult to concentrate as she drove The Beast along the Old Kent Road. Memories of small frustrations and gross humiliations working under Striped Shirt flooded back. Tears spangled her eyes as she approached the Elephant and Castle.

'Here,' Kate whispered, passing her a tissue in the darkness. 'It'll be his turn to cry before the night is over.'

Emma peeled left for Pimlico.

It was a high rise. Thrown up in the seventies, abandoned in the eighties and gentrified – or at least reclaimed by brute financial force – a decade later. Striped Shirt liked to impress Blackheath dinner tables with his Brixton address. He was on the ninth floor.

Emma felt uneasy about leaving The Beast parked in the open. A trio of bored dudes in silver jackets and black peaked caps eyed the sleek Mark II appreciatively – and its emerging occupants even more so. The lurid neon of a burger bar warmed the cold, dark night across the street.

'Fancy a coffee?' Emma asked, nodding to the lights.

The dudes looked hard. Proud and scornful. Emma produced a tenner. They grinned.

'Window seat. Watch her for me.' She took out a twenty and carefully tore it in half. 'You get the other half in two hours.' She looked at Kate.

'Two hours.' Kate nodded.

The lift had a beige carpet, no graffiti and was no longer used as a loo. It whispered them up to the ninth floor.

Striped Shirt met them at his open door, glasses of bubbly at the ready.

He grinned triumphantly, leering from Emma's breasts to Kate's thighs. He didn't say much. His cock said it all. It throbbed up against his belly, tenting his green boxer shorts.

He boasted them around the flat. Hi-tech, low taste and very expensive. Kate vamped it up unashamedly, actually leading them all into the bedroom. It was all there. Just as the office grapevine had warned. The mirrored ceiling. The black satin sheets. The cuffs – two sets – clinking softly under the pillows. Emma checked.

Finishing their champagne, they stripped his shorts off playfully, carefully teasing his erection up to bursting point, then pushed him down on to the bed. Kate used her bottom in his face. Playfully. He spanked then gently bit her. She laughed.

Sticking carefully to the plan they had devised at the Elephant and Castle – and had finalised in the lift coming up – they entered into a slow, sensual double strip-tease. Striped Shirt's veined shaft threatened to explode as it quivered in its salute to them as they stood at the foot of the black-sheeted bed, delicious in their brassieres and silk panties. Kate twirled her nylon stockings in her hand, then, leaning over him, trailed them down over his face – then over his swollen, angry glans. He writhed.

'Close your eyes –'

'Let me see your tits,' he barked.

'You can take my bra off with your teeth and play with them in a minute,' she whispered. 'Come all over them and rub it in,' she promised. 'Just close your eyes. I've a special surprise for you.'

Strip Shirt closed his eyes. Pinning him into the pillows was easy. Whipping out the cuffs and securing his wrists and ankles was even easier. His eyes flashed open. Wide with sudden fear. He started to shout. Kate's nylons, bunched and stuffed into his mouth, silenced him. His eyes bulged wildly above swollen cheeks.

'Red rubbers, I think,' Kate murmured, producing two pairs.

Emma clapped her hands excitedly.

'Get these on his head. I'll undo these –' she fingered the cuffs binding his ankles '– and cover his cock.'

Cuffed securely at the wrists and gagged, the office wolf went to his humiliation and bondage like a lamb. Emma rasped her brassiere into his back as she stretched the red rubber panties down over his head, smothering his mouth but leaving his nostrils free. His black, expensively coiffed hair sprouted up where the cheeks of the rubber panties had been cut away. The hair allowed Emma extra dominant control. She managed him easily with her taloned hand.

Kate undid the cuffs, slipped the red rubber panties up to his knees, then clicked the cuffs tightly shut. His toes whitened as they curled in fear. He grunted softly into the nylon-stocking gag – the soft moans rendered almost inaudible by the red rubber stretched across his mouth – and drew his knees up protectively. His exposed balls shone within the sheen of his tightened sac. Kate tapped his knees imperiously. They clamped together defensively. She reached down and flicked his balls sharply. The knees dropped obediently. Capturing his fat cock in her encircling fist, she squeezed, instantly bringing him to heel. The rubber panties slid up over his knees and snapped snugly into place. His erection strained against the stretchy red rubber. They turned him over, face down into the black satin. His pale cheeks, slightly cupped and bunched by the rubber, bulged invitingly, bare and very vulnerable. Kate fingered the cleft then slapped the left buttock savagely.

Leaving him writhing face down in the satin, they sat down at either side of the wide bed.

'Can he hear us?' Emma wondered.

'Doubt it.' Kate shrugged. 'He's deaf, dumb and blind. Quite helpless.'

'What now?'

'Your decision entirely. Thought you'd like to whip him.'

'Me?'

'It's you he's bullied, not me.'

Emma nodded. 'Yes, but –'

'Look. You've quit your job there, right. You'll never see him or his kind again. You're at Laments now. But there's a block, isn't there? You want to punish but something holds you back.'

'A block?'

'Nothing to worry about. Nothing that can't be over-come.'

'You mean –'

'Punishment. It attracts you. You desire it. You enjoy it. But,' Kate dropped her voice to a whisper, 'think about it, Emma. You haven't spanked, cropped or caned a girl since coming to Laments.'

Emma lowered her eyes, as if afraid to face the truth.

'So,' Kate continued, leaning over to spank-swipe her hand harshly down across Striped Shirt's quivering cheeks, 'I fixed up a little therapy session for you. Punish him and you'll be a discipline-virgin no more. His red bottom is your lost cherry.'

Emma giggled.

'And when we get back to Laments, you'll soon get into your punishing stride.'

Emma's eyes sparkled.

'Ann Cordery. Just think of having her bare bottom all to yourself.'

Emma blushed. She had been thinking exactly the same.

'Really? This therapy thing. Will it really work?'

'Sure of it,' Kate replied. 'Come on. Get cracking.'

On Kate's instruction, Emma ransacked the wardrobe. Her rummaging unearthed two leather belts, a pair of kingfisher blue yuppie braces, a brace of whippy wire hangers and a single, soft-soled slipper.

Emma fingered the find curiously, tentatively, as Kate bent down to adjust the red rubbered panty-mask at Striped Shirt's face.

She glanced down at Emma's little arsenal. 'Stuck for choice, eh? Wottcha fancy, ducks?'

'I don't know,' Emma replied softly, gently palming the sole of the supple slipper. She looked up anxiously. 'Shouldn't I say something. Give him a stern lecture?'

'No need for that,' Kate said firmly. 'A few choice words of reproach when the bottom has been bared and prepared for punishment are a good idea, normally. Builds up the sense of delicious dread and causes tormented imaginings to haunt the miscreant's mind. Back at Laments,' Kate added conversationally, 'the girls get quite juicy across my knee as I deliberately delay their discipline. But him?' Kate jerked her thumb at the bound man on the bed behind her. 'He knows what's coming to him and he knows why. Just relax. This is your first time. Take it slowly and enjoy it. He's utterly helpless, believe me. His bare bottom is all yours, Emma. All yours.'

They approached the black-satin-sheeted bed from both sides. Kate's plump cheeks dimpled the rippling sheen as she sat. Emma chose to kneel, steadying herself quickly by pressing her splayed right hand down across Striped Shirt's bottom. The buttocks clenched defensively. Emma giggled. Just above the red rubber waistband, his cuffed hands writhed.

'Teach me,' she whispered. 'Teach me the secrets of chastisement. Make me a punisher you will be proud of.'

'The correct approach to correction?' Kate bantered. 'Sure, OK. But don't rush into it. First of all, look.'

'Look?' Emma queried, surprised.

Kate tossed her dark hair back before running both her hands through it slowly. Her proud bosom heaved in its brassiered bondage. She thumbed the strap at her shoulder to ease the swollen weight straining in the white cotton cups. 'Gaze down at his bottom. No,' she added quickly, 'don't touch. Just look. Look at it. Contemplate it. Begin to picture the buttocks as you would like to see them after the punishment. Reddened by a spanking. Striped by a cane. Writhing in torment, bucking and jerking in agony. The cleft severe crease between the whipped, clenched cheeks. That's it. Look, Emma. Look at the bottom you are about to blister. And try to visualise in your mind's eye what your hands – or your strap, paddle or cane – hope to accomplish. And that is?'

'A punished bottom. A thoroughly punished bottom,' Emma replied.

'And, tonight, a howling, snivelling man. His pain will fuel your pleasure. Deny yourself nothing, Emma. Feast on the sticky sweetmeats fashioned from his suffering.'

Emma licked her lips. 'Sticky sweetmeats,' she whispered.

'Take your bra off, Emma.' Kate's tone became matter-of-fact.

Emma looked up, puzzled.

'It might be too tight and restricting. You need to feel free. Absolutely free. Only he must remain fettered. Besides,' she dropped her voice to a warm curdle, 'you might like to whip him with it later. A little personal touch. Make him wish he'd never hoped you'd take your bra off for him, eh?'

Emma laughed. Drawing her hands up beneath her hunched shoulder blades, she unclasped her brassiere. Shrugging it off, she jiggled her breasts, relishing their freedom from its tight restraint. Kate bent over the bare bottom between them and fleetingly tonguetip-kissed each of Emma's berry-red and firm nipples. Emma absently gathered up her white brassiere from the rippling black silk and wound it around her left hand.

Obeying Kate's instructions, she gazed down at Striped Shirt's vulnerable buttocks. Kate's sharp spanks had left two mild, pink blotches. Emma, concentrating hard, envisaged the bare cheeks deepening from crimson to a shiny cherry red as her punishing strokes spread a more severe pain. And would the leather belt leave thin, bluish weals, she speculated. And the whippy wire hangers. What shade of sorrow would they bequeath?

'Good. Well done,' Kate murmured, breaking the spell of silence. 'Now, before you use any – or all – of these,' she continued, gesturing down to the instruments of punishment arrayed on the carpet, 'you must first of all take him across your knee and spank him. It is the most intimate, the most absolute method of owning and controlling a bare bottom. Belts, slippers and coathangers may, in his case most definitely should, be used as the punishment progresses. Yes,' Kate whispered, tenderly

151

tracing the quivering curves of his left cheek with a dominant forefinger, 'in his case, the leather must bite. And bite hard. But to begin with, a severe spanking.'

Emma's grey eyes flickered up from the anxiously clenched cheeks and gazed directly into Kate's passionate eyes.

'Now?' she whispered.

'Now.' Kate nodded decisively.

Emma unwound her brassiere from her left hand and tossed it down on to the carpet. Turning on the bed, skidding slightly on the slippery black satin sheet, she positioned herself alongside Striped Shirt's prone body – her right hand raised.

'It's not quite the same if the bottom you spank isn't actually across your knee,' Kate advised. 'Intimacy is a necessary part of absolute domination.'

'I don't understand. How can that be?'

'The dominatrix must of course be severe and aloof at all times during discipline. But just imagine the effect of her stern fingertip fleetingly caressing the cheeks she has just chastised. Or, should she choose to do so, crush her breasts into the blazing buttocks of the whipped.'

Emma shuddered. 'But I don't want to have him so close to me. His flesh touching mine. His belly. And his thing –'

'His thing?' Kate grinned. 'Don't worry about his thing, as you call it. We've tucked that well away for the night. You might feel it twitch and throb. Just ignore it. If he comes –'

'Comes?' Emma echoed in a horrified squeal.

'If he comes,' Kate persisted placidly, 'it won't stain you. The red rubbers will collect the soak.'

Emma shivered. 'I'd rather just smack –'

'Spank. Severely spank,' Kate corrected sharply.

'Spank him,' Emma confessed. 'On the bed.'

'No. Try it my way. Try spanking his as he is bent helplessly across your lap. Just taste the power, the supreme authority, of pinioning him bare bottomed across your knee.'

'OK,' Emma said simply, willing to be persuaded.

She hauled Striped Shirt by his shoulders off the bed, forcing him to kneel down alongside it. The cuffs at his ankles made the maneouvre difficult for Emma – and painful for her captive – but she taloned his exposed hair and managed him adroitly. Sitting squarely on the edge of the bed, feet planted firmly apart, she dragged him over her lap. She gasped as his bulging cock, sheathed by the shiny red rubber, raked her thighs. With his scrunched toes digging into the carpet, his straining legs took most of his weight. Emma removed his elbow from her tummy, forcing the cuffed hands a little further down his back. Sensing her prowess – her sovereignty over his bound nakedness – Striped Shirt flexed his fingers in fear.

'See?' Kate whispered. 'He's utterly helpless. And he knows it. Now pin his neck down. No, not by his hair, by the nape. Yes, that's right,' she encouraged. 'Keep your left hand there. No. Keep the thumb securely over the nape. If he wriggles, just squeeze. Excellent.'

Gently guided by Kate's experience, Emma positioned Striped Shirt in the classic position for a bare-bottomed spanking. Cupping her right palm, she fleetingly swept it down across the proffered cheeks, thrilling as they clenched and dimpled in dread.

'Place your hand down over his outer cheek. Yes, that's it,' Kate instructed.

Emma flinched slightly at the soft warmth of his flesh.

'Now mould your palm in against the curve of the cheek. A flattened palm makes for uneconomical spanking. And if the hand is curved too much, it won't fully connect on impact. What you must try to achieve is a clean, sharp spank. The sound – and the jerk of the punished across your lap – will tell you all you need to know. Don't judge it by the redness alone. A good disciplinarian should be able to beat a bottom with her eyes closed.'

Emma smiled, savouring these pre-punishment instructions.

A sharp, ringing spank. With maximum contact between the palm and the punished cheek.

Emma could not resist quickly squeezing the cheek she was moulding her spanking hand against. As she did so, and Striped Shirt writhed across her lap in a spasm of response, a delicious sense of dominant control and power lit up inside her. The warmth imploded in her belly, trickling down to her slit. Her breasts grew swollen and heavy, the nipples aching sweetly in their peaked pride.

'Play with him,' Kate urged. 'Go on. Before you spank it, play with his bottom. Thumb it, pinch it, caress it. If you treat it with utter contempt, you'll find it easier to punish.'

Emma prised the cleft open. Striped Shirt immediately squeezed his buttocks together tightly – but Emma won the unequal struggle. The dark little anal whorl glinted. Emma giggled. Striped Shirt shuddered, suddenly barrelling across her lap in a last ditch desperate bid to escape.

'No,' Emma warned – as if he were a puppy frisking on a lead.

His struggles increased.

'Balls,' Kate prompted. 'Knuckle him.'

Emma obeyed. Striped Shirt grunted and froze into submissive stillness the instant Emma's fist dimpled the stretchy red rubber between his thighs.

'See? Utterly yours, now. Back at Laments, with a bare-bottomed girl, I make them admit that their buttocks are mine. It perfectly balances the power equation between the punisher and the punished. Tonight, you must take control more directly.'

'Yes, I see.' Emma nodded.

Tightening her grip at the nape of his neck, she nipped up the flesh of his left cheek between a fierce finger and thumbtip pincer. Dragging the buttock-flesh up, she twisted it viciously.

'Excellent,' Kate enthused as Striped Shirt collapsed across his tormenter's lap – slumped in abject submission.

'Is he ready?' Emma asked anxiously.

'He's definitely yours, now, girl. All yours.'

Spank. Spank. Spank. Emma swept her hand down three times in rapid succession, her breasts bouncing as her curved palm cracked out loud against the swell of the upturned cheeks. She paused, placed her hot hand down below his bottom across his thighs and peered closely at the spanked cheeks. Her spanking hand had landed on the same spot each time. The upper, outer curve of his right buttock. It was already pink. Playfully, with a delicate dominance reflecting her inexperience, Emma thumbed the punished flesh, dimpling it with increasing severity until a white patch showed – releasing the rubbery buttock and watching it flush as the pink pain flooded back.

'It's best not to interrupt the punishment,' Kate warned. 'Try to avoid any delay. Get a momentum going. A rhythmically paced punishment is much more satisfactory. And satisfying.'

Emma looked up and grinned. 'OK.'

In a blistering staccato, she slapped his bare bottom seven, eight, nine times in less than six seconds – reddening the right cheek so ruthlessly that the crimson flesh merged seamlessly into the red rubber cupping it.

'No, no.' Kate laughed, interposing. Leaning across the punished buttocks, she reached up to stay Emma's raised hand. 'Not so fast. Not so fast. That way your hand will start to hurt and it'll just be a blur of pain for him. He'll just experience a stinging numbness. No. Pace the punishment so that each and every spank stings. Build up his pain, spank by sharp spank. And give him just enough time to dread the next one. But make every spank count. And try,' Kate urged, 'to redden every exposed inch of flesh.'

'Lots to remember.' Emma grimaced.

'You're learning.'

The spanking recommenced. Soon, Striped Shirt was jerking and writhing across Emma's lap, his buttocks bouncing under her steadily administered rain of pain. Emma sensed his thickened, trapped cock straining behind the stretchy red rubber – sensed it raking into her supporting thighs. Enraged, she dealt him six stinging swipes. So vicious, so severe, her palm actually flattened his hot cheeks' swell.

'Perfect,' Kate cried out. 'Now pause, for a moment, and inspect your handiwork. Inspecting a spanked bottom is all part of the punishment. His humiliation is assured as you peruse the reddened cheeks. And his humiliation feeds your pleasure, remember.'

'May I touch?' Emma asked.

'You may touch. It is, after all, entirely yours to do with what you please.'

This time, Emma conducted her examination by smoothing the curved cheeks down beneath her spanking hand, depressing the right buttock suddenly to expose the dark cleft. Emboldened, she fingered his cleft, rasping her fingernail along its soft helplessness, but fastidiously avoiding his sticky anal crater. Less fastidiously, she plucked out a shiny black pubic hair. Settling into her perusal of his suffering flesh, she started to knead and knuckle the buttocks.

'How do you feel?' Kate asked, watching.

'OK,' Emma admitted, engrossed in tormenting him.

'And? Nothing more?' Kate pressed, her voice soft and husky.

'A bit – you know, a bit aroused.'

'Yes? Nipples?'

'Like bloody thimbles,' Emma confessed.

'Wet yet?'

'Soaking. Pussy's positively dripping.'

'Good. A natural dominant and disciplinarian. Now just relax. You've only warmed him up, remember. Not a bad job, though,' Kate observed, judging the bottom to be satisfactorily spanked. 'Not bad at all.'

After spanking Striped Shirt relentlessly for another seven and a half minutes, Emma taloned his sprout of dark hair and guided him down on to the carpet. Instinctively, she poised her prinked, right foot over his shining cheeks then trod them down dominantly, grinding her heel into his suffering flesh.

'You're learning fast,' Kate remarked appreciatively.

Emma, after a refreshing half glass of chilled champagne, selected the wire coat hangers. Picking them up, she gripped them tightly, swishing them down into the black satin sheet.

The practice stroke brought a glint to her sparkling grey eyes.

'Shit,' she whispered. 'I bet that hurts.'

'Let's hope so,' Kate replied.

They hauled him, kneeling, against the bed, positioning his reddened buttocks up to receive the whippy wire. He was probably begging for mercy by now, Emma mused. But the gag effectively silenced any such pleading.

Swish, swipe. Swish, swipe. It wasn't very satisfactory.

'Try using just the one. And angle it inwards instead of down.'

Emma followed Kate's advice. *Swish, swipe. Swish, swipe.* But Emma wasn't a big fan of the whippy wire coat hanger. It wasn't easy to control, despite her fierce grip, and it seemed to bounce off the buttocks it was supposed to bite. Striped Shirt, jerking his hips into the black satin sheet, wasn't a big fan of it either. The fifth swiping stroke made him come, though. Emma stared down, fascinated, as he orgasmed. She saw his thick shaft twitch and spasm, saw the stretched red rubber retain every single drop of his squirted seed.

'Did you see that?' Emma shrilled in outrage. 'He's just come. I certainly didn't –'

'What, Emma? Didn't what? Give him permission?' Kate prompted.

'Exactly. I'm in charge here. I control him. I tell him what he may or may not do.'

'That's perfectly correct, Emma. You're in charge. And you control his every move. Even his whimpering. But don't worry. This is your first time. Relax. You'll learn. Quickly. And it wasn't exactly pleasurable for him. Let's just say it was a necessary release. Exquisitely painful, I'm sure. Exquisitely.'

'Good.'

'But the important thing is,' Kate added quickly, 'you knew that his coming like that, without your permission, was wrong. You knew it instinctively, didn't you?'

'Yes. I want absolute control –'

'Now you're speaking with the voice of a true dominatrix, Emma. A natural chastiser. A proven punisher. Whip him hard for that orgasm. Whip him for any reason you can think of. Whip him, Emma, because he is yours to punish as you please.'

157

Emma looked up, her grey eyes losing their puzzled expression – and gaining one of slow understanding.

The leather belt made an excellent strap. Doubling it before wrapping it tightly around her right hand, Emma straddled her victim and cracked it down across his upraised cheeks. It made a very satisfying 'snap' as it whistled down to bark across his buttocks. And it left a very satisfactory weal: a thin, bluish welt that rapidly deepened to pale purple as the pain intensified.

Snap. Snap. The leather cracked out loud. Emma administered eight strokes from her standing, straddling, position before forcing him face down across the bed and, standing back, lashed the leather inwards four more withering times. Snarling softly, Emma tossed the belt aside. Mounting the bed, and Striped Shirts whipped cheeks, she peeled her soaking panties down to enable her to rake her slit-lips savagely across his hot flesh. Reaching down to grapple and grip his shoulders, she rode him frenziedly then slipped back a fraction to trap and squeeze his rubber-cupped buttocks between her pinioning thighs.

'Bloody hell,' Kate marvelled, goggle-eyed.

Kneeling, Emma arched her spine and screamed softly, forcing her pussy into his buttocks and spilling the quicksilver of her scald into his gaping cleft. Striped Shirt threshed in response to this ultimate humiliation. As her wet heat splashed his velvety cleft, his cuffed hands writhed and his tethered feet twisted in torment.

'God,' Kate muttered, slightly taken aback, 'if there was a degree in discipline, you'd get a First. With Honours.'

Sliding away from her slit-slippery, red-bottomed mount, Emma groaned and collapsed on to the black satin sheet.

'Shit,' Kate whispered. 'Almost feel for the poor sod.'

'Don't,' Emma said, suddenly stern. 'Bastard's been begging for that for at least a year.'

'Everything comes to those who wait,' Kate murmured philosophically.

* * *

They raided the fridge. Striped Shirt did himself well.

'How long have we got?' Emma, naked and perspiring, asked – licking her fingers after gouging caviar out of its stone jar with a wedge of lemon.

'We said two hours,' Kate mouthed through her lobster. 'Half an hour left. Why?'

'Bet he has a web cam.' Emma suddenly giggled.

'You wouldn't.' Kate laughed.

'Wanna bet?'

'Think he has?'

'Bet he has lots of things,' Kate replied, biting into her lobster.

They explored the flat. The computer, a real boy's toy, was on wheels. They guided the trolley into the bedroom.

'Take off his mask. Those panties,' Emma urged, taking control.

'Gag on?'

'Yeh. He's got more howling to do. But no blindfold. Just the gag.'

'You got it.' As Kate obliged, peeling off the red rubber panties, Emma linked up the web cam to the office home page. Aligning it carefully, she checked that it captured the black satin sheet and the cuffed, red pantied figure sprawled across it.

'Is it on?'

'Not until we go,' Emma replied. 'I've linked it up. Tomorrow, at nine, they'll all get him on screen.'

Kate laughed. On the bed, Striped Shirt groaned into his gag.

'Want to see his stickies,' Kate enquired politely. 'Your trophy.'

'No – yes,' Emma replied, undecided.

'First scalp,' Kate countered.

'OK. Go on.'

Kate peeled the red rubbers down. Striped Shirt hated them with his eyes as they peeped down at the semen-soaked stretch of rubber.

'Ugh,' she gasped. 'Did I really do that?'" But the creeping pride in her tone was stronger than her pretence of disgust.

Kate laughed. 'Yep,' she added, snapping the panties back into place and forcing him face down into the pillow. 'And that.' She stroked the ravished cheeks. 'You've passed in flying colours.'

'Red. Blue. Yellowish purple.' Emma giggled, fingering the result of her spanking hand, wire coat hanger and snapping leather belt.

'Satisfied?' Kate murmured.

'Let's cut his hair,' Emma said suddenly. 'The creep always spends too much on it. Always at the mirror, patting it.'

Kate swallowed. 'That's a bit –'

'Necessary,' Emma retorted crisply. 'Get me some scissors.'

She butchered the hundred-pound haircut, leaving him with a grim stubble. Like something from a Gulag the permafrost had spared.

'Big boy here can't keep it going all night for the likes of Susie,' Emma announced, sweeping the snipped hair away from the black satin sheet.

'Susie? Oh, yes. You told me.'

'Sad bitch,' Emma snarled. 'Too eager to bite the pillow for this creep –'

'Do I detect a touch of jealousy?' Kate teased.

'Bet he's got a dildo in here. Let's look.'

'Only ten minutes left,' Kate warned. 'And we've got to get dressed –'

'Long enough.'

They looked at each other. At each other in their utter nakedness. During the discipline, both had shed their bras and panties. Emma's grey eyes swept over Kate, drinking in the dark-haired girl's naked beauty. Kate's eyes glinted with passion, deepening from brown to sloe black as they sparkled with frank lust.

Ignoring the bound man on the bed they had just punished so fiercely, both nudes stared at each other – transfixed for a timeless moment.

'Later,' Kate whispered.

'Promise?' Emma pleaded.

160

'Promise. Back at Laments. In my bed. Tonight.'

Nothing more was said. Not a single word was spoken. Each treasured the moment, holding it in their heart as they worked busily.

'Got it,' Emma cried, unearthing an extravagant, ribbed ivory dildo. 'Help me.'

They teased Striped Shirt's puckering anus with the cruel tip for several minutes before plugging him brutally – burying the dildo deep between his clenched cheeks.

'Ten – no, five minutes. Shit, we're late,' Kate warned.

'Grab that slipper.'

'No time,' Kate shouted, frantically pulling her bra-cups over her breasts.

'I've got its twin,' Emma grunted, fishing the second supple slipper out from under the bed.

Kate succumbed. For a full, furious two and a half minutes, facing each other across the dildo-dominated buttocks, they repeatedly cracked the supple soled slippers down. The swiping leather barked loud across his helpless cheeks. Unfingering the tightly bound nylon stocking from Striped Shirt's mouth – 'I'd love to hear him howl' – Emma quickly replaced the gag to stem her victim's stream of obscenities and curses. Curses that crumbled into whimpering sobs as the slippers brought a fresh red shine to his ravaged bottom. And the dildo dug deeper into his burning shame.

'Check the web cam,' Kate urged, panting from exertion, making a final inspection of their victim's cuffed wrists, ankles and the cruel shaft up his arse.

'Web cam on.'

'Let's go.'

Plundering bottles of gin, brandy and champagne after gathering up their underwear, they scampered out to the lift. Inside, as it whispered them down, they struggled into their coats and shoes.

The dudes were waiting by The Beast.

'Some party,' one laconically remarked as Kate, breasts peeping out through her gaping coat, scrambled into the leather seat in the back of the Mark II. Bottles chinked.

161

Emma, obviously naked beneath her coat, slipped behind the wheel, dropping her brassiere on to the wet asphalt.

'Proper,' a dude exulted.

Emma slammed the door and struggled to fish out the other half of the torn twenty. She thrust it out into eager hands.

'Can I keep the bra?' the dude asked excitedly.

Emma laughed. 'Keep it. Take it home and into bed with you tonight.'

'Result.' The dude swaggered.

'Promise me one thing,' Emma whispered.

The dudes crowded down at the open window.

'Kiss the cups then cover your prick. Wank like hell until you come. See if you can manage to fill a cupful before dawn, OK?'

The torn twenty fluttered down forgotten as the dudes ignored their prize. Open mouthed, they stared in stunned silence as The Beast growled softly and stole away into the night.

It was long past midnight and Laments Hall was still an hour away. Unable to contain their lust for each other a minute longer, they pulled off after Wych Cross into the fringes of Ashdown Forest. Despite the dense cover from the trees crowding above, the rain drummed relentlessly down on The Beast, quickening their already racing heartbeats.

Scrambling over on to the back seat, Emma embraced Kate, hugging and kissing fiercely. The humiliation and punishment had inflamed them. Their slits bubbled like boiling milk rising on the seethe. Warm, sweet mouths opened hungrily. Flickering tongues fenced playfully then probed, Kate's thrusting deeply into Emma's submission. Excited fingers fanned out, roaming and caressing to seek and find soft limbs, softer flesh. Shrugging off their coats, they surrendered their nakedness to each other. The Beast was filled with excited moans as each nude cupped and squeezed the other's breasts.

Kate, a natural dominant and more expert through experience, struggled to mount and control Emma – but

162

the blonde, fired up by her recent conquest of Striped Shirt's bottom, battled boldly back. The tension in the darkness of the back seat of The Beast increased. The rain rattled furiously on the roof. Kate's dark eyes glinted with fury. Emma's grey gaze sparkled with frustration. They wrestled, grinding their breasts into each other – and their buttocks into the polished leather seat. But the wriggling and squirming proved futile. Locked in their naked impasse, they stopped struggling for supremacy. Suddenly giggling, they released each other and slumped apart, Kate's knee nuzzling Emma's slit between her splayed thighs.

'Me first,' Kate whispered thickly, 'please.'

'Only if I can have you in bed tonight,' Emma countered, mumbling her words in a mock-sulky tone.

Kate drew Emma's face towards her own, then kissed the blonde's surrendered mouth slowly. Capturing Emma's lower lip gently between her predatory teeth, Kate bit into the soft flesh tenderly – only releasing it to turn the blonde over and crush her face down into the pungent leather. Fiercely palming the blonde's hips up, Kate drew Emma's bottom to her mouth.

Emma squealed, lapping the leather at her lips, as Kate's tongue raked up and down her aching cleft. Spreading the captive buttocks wide, Kate taloned them dominantly before burying her face in their passive warmth. Back at the cleft's feral warmth, she nuzzled it intimately, using both her nose and her tongue at the sensitive flesh. Despite the taloning hands that gripped them, Emma squeezed her cheeks, jerking them rhythmically into Kate's face.

The flickering tongue-tip lapped lower down, tasting the sweet-sour silvery juices dribbling freely from the pouting labia. Her desire to finger-fuck overwhelmed her, but she didn't dare release the squirming blonde from her thrall. Kate knew instinctively that unless she kept her firm control of Emma's bottom maintained, the tempting slit at her tongue would be wriggled away.

Spank. Briefly relinquishing her dominant hold, she smacked Emma into stillness. The blonde mewed happily,

163

butting her bottom up submissively in abject surrender. *Spank. Spank.* Kate made sure – before gripping each cheek savagely again, dimpling the satin curves beneath her thumbtips. She lowered her face into the spanked buttocks, dragging her chin down between them. It slid along the sticky length of their divide.

Tongue-tip flickering, she lapped at the golden down fluffing Emma's pubic mound. It crackled in the darkness – a silent darkness since the rain had ceased. Somewhere in the distance of the forest night, an owl hooted mournfully. In the back of The Beast, Emma echoed with a moan.

Lapping noisily, Kate's tongue played at the hot slit with an increasingly hungry fervour that matched her sharpened appetite. Unable to suck or bite because of the constraints of their cramped space, she suddenly snarled into Emma's flesh – tongue-punishing the slit viciously in the violence of her frustration. The delicious little clitoris was beyond her tonguetip's reach. Both girls knew it. Both girls grunted fiercely.

Thrusting her tongue out at painful stretch, Kate failed to achieve her desire. She spanked the inner lips with the back of her tongue until it grew heavy with pain – but still failed to bring Emma up to full boil.

It was almost a gesture of despair when she dragged her right knee up. The flexed knee kissed the hot slit reverentially. Emma rocked gently, rolling her splayed labia over the increasingly slippery shine pushing up into her. Grinding herself deliberately down, she managed what Kate's tongue could not – a gathering climax that clenched and unclenched its knotted fist deep in her belly.

Kate, steadying her knee at Emma's slit, crushed her face back down into the blonde's sinuously swaying bottom, snuffing up the exciting whiff of the slit-spilled scald. At her face, she sensed the soft buttocks spasming as they tightened severely, signalling Emma's orgasm. Licking deeply into the cleft's crease, she impulsively sought out the anal crater's heat and drove her tongue deep into the blonde's muscled warmth. As Emma's sphincter stretched to take the thick tongue, she came loudly, crying out repeatedly in her brutal delight. Savagely riding the knee at her slit, she screamed again – drowning out the screech of the startled owl as it soared above them.

Tip-toeing got them almost to the safety of Kate's bedroom. The landing light snapped on as her fingers found the door. They spun round, startled by the sudden light. Marion's hand still remained at the switch.

'Where have you two been? We were about to raise the alarm. Your unauthorised absence has been of great concern,' she rasped.

Emma hastily gathered her coat across her nakedness, trying not to clink the cold bottles at her bosom.

'Just out for a little stroll,' Kate volunteered. 'Some fresh air, after the rain.'

'A very long stroll,' Marion replied waspishly. 'You were missed at supper.'

'Not hungry,' Kate countered, reaching down to open her bedroom door.

'One moment. I have not finished with you. It is almost two thirty. You have been missing for some seven hours. At least. I am far from satisfied. You offer neither explanation nor excuse.' She craned to glimpse the bottles Emma was unsuccessfully attempting to conceal. The trophies they had secured from Striped Shirt's flat.

'You two have been for more than a walk and I intend to find out where. Are those bottles you are trying to hide? So, you have left the grounds. Left the grounds of Laments without permission –'

'Without permission?' Emma echoed, accidently clinking the bottles.

'The rules are perfectly plain for both staff and pupils.'

'I didn't realise –' Emma shrugged.

'Kate did. Come along with me.'

'But –'

'Both of you. Now. Down to the gym.'

'No way,' Kate said sharply. 'I'm not –'

'Of course, we can wait to settle this in the morning. With Dr Flint. And I'm sure after the recent Wigmore

165

fiasco, she simply will not be able to overlook your deliberate absence from Laments. An absence without permission sought or granted. Probably have to make a very painful example of you both.'

She had them. Cold. And they knew it.

'To the gym. At once.'

Under the bleak light of a single bulb in a far corner of the cold gym, Kate and Emma shivered. Tired and cold, both longed for the soft warmth of bed and each other. They remained sullenly silent as Marion Aylott-Inche waited with maddening patience for a full explanation.

'Put those bottles down,' she instructed Emma. 'And take your coats and shoes off. Both of you.'

One by one, Emma obediently deposited the bottles down on to the polished wooden floor.

'I said coats and shoes off. Both of you. At once. I may be obliged to punish you. It depends,' Marion added tantalisingly, 'upon the veracity of the account you give me for your unpardonable behaviour.'

Acutely aware of their nakedness, both girls pretended to shiver in need of their coats.

'At once,' Marion barked, fingering the leather belt at her waist. 'I won't tell you again.'

Shrugging off their coats and kicking off their shoes, Emma and Kate stood naked before the amazement of the gym mistress.

'Monstrous behaviour,' she thundered, staring wide eyed at the bare breasts the girls unsuccessfully attempted to shield. 'What possible explanation can you give me? Well?'

Their stubborn silence continued. Emma scrunched her toes into the polished wood. Her soft buttocks rippled as she clenched them, clenched and unclenched them anxiously as Marion unbuckled her belt.

'You have clearly been behaving in a manner likely to bring both notoriety and disgrace upon Laments. And we so dearly prize our privacy here. A privacy we cherish in order to pursue our strict regime of punishment.' Marion snapped her leather belt twice. The golden buckle sparkled.

166

'The nearest shop must be at least nine miles away. Did you take the car, Emma?' she snapped suddenly.

'We walked,' Kate cut in.

'No,' Emma lied, loyally echoing her pal.

'Little liar,' the gym mistress raged. 'You think you can, on top of all this, treat me like a fool?' She doubled the leather and fingered it firmly. 'I'll get the truth out of you with this soon enough.'

They heard the gym doors slap as someone entered. Oh, God, Emma thought. Not Felicity Flint. She could not bear to face the displeasure of the Head. So soon after being appointed. Anything but that.

But it was only the weasel Watson.

'The engine is still warm. And by the increased mileage,' she added, ignoring the nudes and reporting directly to Marion, 'I should say they've been to London and back.'

'As far as that? Are you sure?'

'I make a careful note of these things,' Miss Watson purred complacently. 'That is my job, after all. Working with figures – to a demanding degree of exactitude. Too much on the clock for Brighton, like the Wigmore bitch. No. They've been to London tonight. Stopped in a muddy forest en route. The tyres are covered in oak and ash leaves. An owl has messed on the bonnet. Ashdown Forest, I'd say.' Miss Watson's spectacles glinted as she turned to face the nudes.

Emma shivered – not with cold but from dread. Bugger Watson, she was as deadly and as remorseless as Sherlock Holmes himself.

'Thank you, I am indebted. Please take those bottles as a token of my gratitude for your unfailing assistance.'

Watson scuttled across the polished wooden floor of the gym to scoop up her reward.

'Already a picture of the truth is forming and you have yet to answer to my leather,' Marion whispered, savagely snapping her belt. 'You, Kate. Touch your toes.'

Emma whimpered softly as Kate backed away out of the pool of light into the fragile cover of darkness.

'Come back here where I can see you to beat you.'

'No –'

'Miss Watson.'

'Yes, Miss Aylott-Inche?'

'Be kind enough to go up and rouse Dr Flint –'

'No,' Kate muttered. 'Not that.'

'Bend over. Come along. Touch your toes and give me your bottom.'

'May I stay?' Miss Watson whispered excitedly.

'No. I want to do this all alone.'

The bottles clinked, the doors slapped and they were all alone in the gym. Marion, thumbing her leather excitedly, Kate, bare bottomed and bending for her stripes – and Emma, tears clouding her sorrowful grey eyes.

The gym mistress motioned Emma away. 'Face the wall. No, don't look round,' she warned as Emma risked a peep.

Emma's throat tightened. As the belt whistled and cracked down across Kate's beautifully bunched cheeks, eliciting smothered gasps of suffering, she shut her eyes tight. But the unseen, overheard punishment haunted her. Haunted her and grew large in her imagination. Marion had crisply announced 'twelve strokes' before plying the leather belt. Emma found herself counting each cruel stroke. As each lashed down, she fought – but lost – the battle not to picture the dark hide biting into Kate's pink cheeks. Whipping sharply across the swollen curves of her obediently bent buttocks. Emma struggled not to imagine the licking leather leaving a cruel weal each time it savagely caressed the proffered softness of the submissive cheeks. Try as she could, she failed to block out the squeals and grunt of Kate's anguish as they echoed around the darkened gym.

Nine. Ten. Two Judas-swipes, planted in quick succession, eliciting a thin scream. Emma swallowed painfully, wiping her sweating palms down across the wobble of her soft buttocks.

Eleven. As her sorrow for Kate eased with the approach of the twelfth and final lash her fear for herself increased. Me next. Bending, bare bottomed. For a hot dozen. Oh, God. No. Please.

Twelve. Emma heard the soft patter of Kate's feet as the whipped nude stumbled forward slightly under the final withering stroke.

'Now get out,' Marion snarled.

Kate shuffled out of the gym in silence. Emma, a frisson of fear rippling her naked buttocks, remained facing the wall.

It's coming. She couldn't swallow, her throat betrayed her. Any second now. Her mouth was dry. Her tongue useless. She's going to call me out into the pool of light and order me to bend over.

But Marion's stern voice did not bark out the expected – dreaded – command. Out of the deafening silence came the sudden whistle of the leather belt. It lashed upwards, between Emma's softly parted thighs, the tip scalding her defenceless pussy-plum. She gasped – swallowing her scream – and shrieked aloud as the tongue of the belt burned up along her cleft's dark gape.

'Mount,' the gym mistress commanded, snapping her belt down at Emma's ankles. The leather flickered upwards and across, whipping her clenched cheeks. 'I want you up those wall bars. Move.'

Emma staggered forward in panic and disbelief, her bare breasts squashed painfully as they bunched into the horizontal bars. As her toes scrabbled up the first slippery rung, the snap-crack of Marion's belt barked across her buttocks, compelling her to climb.

Eight

Bubble and Squeak. Did little Bubble really soak your stockinged thighs as you palmed her hot cheeks after spanking her hot and hard? And did the pert minx Squeak, wriggling and rasping her slit against your warm nylon's sheen, really toss her head back and 'squeak' during severe chastisement? Kate had said so. Kate had promised they did – and would, for Emma. And Emma was filled with a burning desire to find out. To feel the wet slit bubble and hear the shrill squeak for herself.

Susie Middleton-Peake. Those heavy breasts swaying enticingly as she bent over, proffering her ripe peaches up for punishment. The fuller-buttocked Olympia Scott-Hammerton. Did the leather strap really make a scorching thwack as it lashed down, bite-striping those deliciously swollen orbs. How they bounced when beaten! And Charlotte Bicknell, whose rubbery cheeks jerked so perfectly in response to the cruel cut of the cane. Plump, gently quivering pear-shaped buttocks that nature designed to demand bamboo discipline. Not forgetting Ann Cordery. Emma never forgot beautiful Ann Cordery. It would be a slow, searching punishment for her. Tender dominance followed by velvet violence. Ann was the ideal pupil to practise intimate instruction upon. She had the ideal bottom. That tumbling fringe of dark hair spilling to curtain those large, sorrowful eyes. Those eyes – brimming with liquid penitence – from which silver pearls of anguish would spill under the crop.

Nosing The Beast along the narrow lanes back to Laments, Emma had been obliged to squeeze her thighs tightly together to prevent the ooze of her wet heat from soiling the leather at her buttocks. It had started to rain again. She had flicked the wipers on. *Swish. Swish.* They had whispered across the screen. Back to Laments. *Swish. Swish.* Kate had slept on in the back seat. The rain silvered the windscreen. The wipers scraped it clear. Mesmerically, like a sparkling cane slicing down to deliver a slow, searching stinging six. *Swish. Swish.* Back to Laments.

Kate had been correct in her diagnosis of Emma's initial reluctance to punish. There had been a block. Then there had been Striped Shirt – bare bottomed and pleasurably beaten. Now, Emma found herself back on the road to Laments, wondering with whose bottom she would soon celebrate her newly awakened appetite for punishment. Whose cheeks would she redden as she acknowledged and exercised her desire to discipline.

The block was gone. Her reticence had been removed. Dispelled by the discipline and humiliation of Striped Shirt. Emma was eager to commence. When would it be? A late, late night dorm patrol? The clock on the dash had shown a little after two. A very late dorm patrol. Slipper in hand, would she catch some miscreant out of bed? Or tomorrow. After breakfast. An opportunity to spank some unlucky girl discovered committing a petty misdemeanour. However petty, Emma had vowed to pounce.

In the dark warmth of The Beast, Emma had considered every dark, delicious detail. The soft scratching of the pen as it entered in the details of both the offence and the proposed chastisement in the punishment book. The intimate moments of being alone together. The punisher and the girl about to be punished. Dominant eye contact. Meek averted gaze. The touch under the chin, bringing the frightened face back up to greet the stern chastiser's gaze. The deliberate silence, broken at last by the terse instruction to undress. To peel down the shorts, the knickers and present a bare bottom. Those soft cheeks dimpling in delicious dread. The crisp command to the miscreant to bend over. The instant presentation of the plump rump. The swell of the proffered cheeks straining up in obedient submission. The surrendering up of skin to a spanking hand, of buttocks to a supple bamboo. The dark line of the dividing cleft, clenched tight in fear. A flickering shadow across the bare bottom – that of the hovering cane or quivering crop. Emma had considered every delicious detail of all that awaited her pleasure back at Laments.

But now, instead of the late night dorm patrol and the baptism of her first bare bottom – now, just when she desired to dominate and discipline a naughty girl's bare bottom – her own nakedness was being subjected to Marion's dominance and wrath.

Crack. The leather belt lashed up, searing Emma's defenceless cheeks as they swayed, jutting out from the bars. She inched up frantically to escape the stinging hide. *Crack*. Not fast enough – another lash drove her scrambling up the wall bars.

'That's high enough. Stay exactly where you are,' the gym mistress hissed.

In the darkness, Emma trembled against the wall. Her feet trod the bar beneath them, scrabbling for a grip. Her chin rested awkwardly on the bar above the one that tormented her squashed bosom. Stretched out painfully at either side, her fingers flexed and unflexed in their struggle to hold on tight. She was six and a half feet clear of the polished floor below.

A soft creak signalled Marion's ascent of the wall bars. The creaking in the darkness paralysed Emma's mind. Each muted protest of wood under the weight of warm flesh whispered her approaching pain.

'Remain still while I secure you,' Marion's voice suddenly warned her.

Emma smothered her squeal of protest as leather was lashed to her right wrist, binding it tightly to the bar. The impromptu bondage was expertly applied. Emma squirmed, tugging to be free. Her hand remained immobile within its leather restraint. Marion, level now with her victim, edged sideways along the bars, covering Emma's soft nakedness closely. Emma shivered as her skin shrank from Marion's tickling skirt and cool silk blouse. Emma flinched from the dominant pressure of the firm bosom pressing into her back: recognising and resenting the hardness of the aroused nipples. Marion, grunting softly, crushed even closer into Emma's naked body. Emma flattened herself painfully into the wall bars to evade the pubic mound of the gym mistress nestling up into her bottom as Marion reached out to subject the left hand to the leather and bind it tightly to the bar.

'Nice and tight,' Marion remarked, testing both tethers again. 'Legs apart, bitch.'

'No –' Emma's show of defiance was utterly futile.

Crack. Crack. Swinging out free from the bars, balancing nimbly on one foot and holding on with her left hand, Marion leisurely lashed Emma's bare buttocks twice with her supple leather belt. The strokes bit deeply as they snapped across Emma's naked cheeks, both slice-swipes jerking the whipped nude into the wooden bar at her slit.

'I said legs apart, bitch. Do it,' the gym mistress snarled, dangling the leather belt down to teasingly tap-tap it against her victim's ankles.

Emma obediently, though with sullen reluctance, inched her thighs apart. Down below, her feet spread outwards along the shining wooden bar.

'You would do well to obey me, bitch. Remember,' she whispered, gently stroking the strap across Emma's clenched cheeks, 'your bottom is bare and it is completely and utterly at my mercy. Just remember that before you think of disobeying me. Your bottom is bare,' she flicked the leather against Emma's buttocks, 'and at my mercy. Mine to punish as I please. And believe me it pleases me very, very much to have it so.'

Crack. Crack. Emma squealed as the hide scorched her satin cheeks.

'Defy me, bitch, and you will undoubtedly suffer tonight – more so than I had intended.'

Emma, normally a cool, proud blonde, broke under the pressure of her fearful dread and suddenly started to beg. 'Don't, please –'

'Silence, bitch, although your whining is music to my ears.' The gym mistress, who was back on the floor, remounted the wall bars.

'I didn't mean to –'

'I said silence, bitch,' Marion grunted, her face inches away in the darkness from her victim's.

Emma drew back from the warm breath of her bullier.

'A gag, I think. Better to do this in silence. Don't want everyone woken up by your squeals, do we, hmm?'

Emma resisted the gag, first with her clenched teeth and then, in a desperate effort to deny the suffocating cloth, with her tongue. *Crack. Crack.* The belt whistled down, lashing her upper thighs. Emma screamed, opening her mouth wide for the gag.

'Just to make sure,' Marion whispered, dragging an eyeless rubber hood firmly over Emma's blonde mane and yanking it brutally over the startled face below.

Smothered by the rubber, sightless, choking on her gag, Emma was tumbling headlong into her first experience of utter helplessness. Tiny holes at her nostrils allowed her, grudgingly, to breathe – but her fear-fuelled panting filled the inner face of the rubber mask with moist heat, making it sticky and clammy at her pinched cheeks. Oh, God, Emma shuddered. Get me out of this. Get me out of –

The hand taloning her labia, squeezing them before dragging the lips out, stopped Emma's silent prayer even as she uttered it. She screamed, filling only her own ears with the shrill shriek of anguish.

Back at her ear, very close – lips pressed at the rubber hood – Marion whispered her cruel intentions. And explained her venom.

'You've played right into my hands, bitch. There's no place for you here at Laments. Flint made a grave mistake in appointing you. You're utterly useless. I've been watching you. And other eyes have monitored your lack of progress, your inability to be strict with the pupils. You have proved unreliable in the most important part of our work here – dispensing discipline.'

But you're wrong, Emma gasped uselessly into her gag. So wrong. I'm ready to ply the lash now. Ready and eager. Just offer me a bare bottom and I'll show you.

'All that sucking up to Flint and backing her wretched tennis court won't help you now. She'll be out of here soon and then Laments will be mine. All mine.'

Shit. Felicity Flint had been right. Her treacherous deputy had designs on the Headship.

'You thought you'd been so clever, wriggling out of that disaster in the dorm, didn't you? But it was Kate who punished those pupils with the bat. Not you, bitch. Kate. I know –'

Yes. Your spies will have squealed, Emma thought.

'I know everything that happens here at Laments. Everything. My knowledge is my strength, and will help to make Laments mine.'

Got to get through this. Got to get through this and warn Kate, Emma determined. And warn Dr Flint.

'You'll be gone. Tomorrow. I'm informing all the staff how you flouted the rules – broke them flagrantly – and that, of course, I have had to punish you for the offence. What a very poor example to set for these girls we are trying to train and discipline. A very poor example. Even if Flint objects, the trustees will back me.'

The whispered words – and the warm breath that carried them – withdrew from Emma's rubber-flattened ear. Where has she gone to? What is she doing? Will she lengthen out her strap and is she even now taking aim? Or, Emma suddenly panicked in the helplessness of her hooded bondage, is the leather to remain silent and will those cruel fingers return to torment my poor pussy? Emma tried to clench her cheeks defensively. Within the dark, sweaty silence of her rubber-hooded world, she tensed expectantly. The slow, agonising seconds ticked inaudibly as the hands on the clock of her terror inched inexorably on towards her impending pain.

Where the hell was she? Was it over? Was that it? A half dozen very painful stripes of the belt followed by strict bondage within which she received the stern, boastful lecture. Emma relaxed, slumping as far as her leather tethers would allow. That's it. All over. Marion Aylott-Inche was merely a bullying megalomaniac. Her sights were set on higher things than Emma's bare bottom. In her struggle to secure the bigger prize – Headship of Laments – a bare-bottomed blonde bound to the bars was merely a –

Splatt. Splatt. Splatt. Seduced by her logical optimism, Emma had almost reasoned her way safely out of the threat of further punishment and pain. Sure and certain that the gym mistress had dealt – and done – with her for the night, the sudden triple echo in her brain caught her completely by surprise. Was that a slipper? A paddle? What was it that had just cracked down, exploding across her bunched buttocks. Her gag silenced her shrill squeals of torment as the swiping, searing pain blazed in crimson blotches at her cheeks and in crimson flashes behind her eyes.

Splatt. Splatt. Splatt. It was a thick-soled trainer. Yes. Emma remembered spotting them earlier in the gym. White, with royal blue piping and an expensive designer logo. The gym mistress had trod them down into the polished wooden floor in her confident stride as she had approached Kate and ordered her to bend, bare bottomed, for the kiss of the punishing leather belt earlier on.

Marion rubbed the ribbed sole into the cheek she had just viciously crimsoned. Emma felt the chevroned sole dragging at her ravished buttocks, further punishing their blistered curves. Again, she tried to squeeze her bottom to defy the torment, forgetting then instantly remembering that Marion had cunningly rendered such a gesture useless. In splaying the blonde's thighs wide before consigning her victim's feet to their leathered bondage, the gym mistress had made sure that the bunched cheeks remained immobile, helplessly exposed to every blistering blow.

Forcing the toe of the fiercely gripped trainer into Emma's cleft, Marion intimately humiliated her bound, naked victim. The burning torment at her cleft continued until the sphincter was a molten crater.

Out of the silence, warm breath at the side of the rubber hood brought cruel words back to Emma's ears.

'I've only got tonight. And it's past three already. Almost four. So I'll have to make every delicious second count. I've got you here, naked, at my mercy, til dawn, bitch. Til dawn. Tomorrow, you'll be gone. Kicked out in disgrace. But tonight,' Marion hissed in a rising note of frenzy, 'your bare bottom is mine.'

Splatt. Splatt. Splatt.

She's mad. This isn't punishment – it's something darker. Something more disturbed. Kate warned me, Emma thought, that the gym mistress used bondage on the pupils. To terrorise them. Not intimate instruction, the Laments way. But intimidation and brutal bullying, the Aylott-Inche way. She shouldn't be here. She's no right to –

Splatt. Splatt. Splatt.

Three more severe swipes blazed across Emma's blistering buttocks, inflaming her flesh with fresh flames of flickering fury. Their leaping tongues lapped up along the crease of her exposed, gaping cleft and down to the seethe of her tormented slit. But it was a cruel flame – a flame the spun sugar of liquid lust spindling down from her pouting labia could not douse.

Marion rubbed the trainer's ribbed sole ruthlessly up and down across the crimsoned cheeks – dominating the domes she had just disciplined. Emma jerked in agony, punishing her pussy against the polished wooden wall bar.

Silence.

No, wait. Soft creaks of the stressed wood as Marion adjusted her weight. Oh, God. She's getting closer. Emma could feel the tweed skirt's rasping kiss at her scalded buttocks. What? What was that? That sinuous slithering of prickly material down against her thighs. Shit. That's her skirt coming off, Emma realised. She's just taken her tweed skirt off. What the hell?

Marion, easing away from the red-bottomed blonde balanced in bondage at the wall bars, shrugged off her skirt and let it drop down into a soft pile on the floor below. Knickerless, her pubic bush stood proud. Gripping on to

177

the bars above Emma's head, she crushed her crisp nest into the whipped cheeks.

Emma – fully aware of the outrage being perpetrated upon her hot bottom – instantly flinched and spasmed her cheeks, but the devilish tickle of her punisher's pubic coils maddened her buttocks. They jerked back uncontrollably in a frenzied response. Hating her helplessness, Emma ground her rump into the slit of her cruel tormentress.

A harsh laugh came through the rubber hood at her ear. 'You're like a puppet. A mindless marionette. Marion's little marionette. And I pull the strings.' The gym mistress raked her labia savagely into the cushioning warm satin of her victim's punished peaches.

Silence. More long soundless moments. What next? The dominator's flesh had ceased to torment that of the dominated. But what the hell now, Emma shuddered. Unable to bear the tantalising silence a second longer, she screamed a stream of obscenities. The gag stemmed her outburst. The lurid curses echoed mockingly in her spinning brain.

What was that? Emma tensed in her naked bondage. Something was happening. But she could not quite work out what. The gym mistress seemed to be taking ages. Doing what? Undressing? Retrieving her dropped trainer up from the floor below? Scooping up the abandoned leather belt? Her mind became a whirlpool of agony as successive images of further pain and degradation flooded and tormented her. Not knowing was as dreadful a punishment for Emma as actually experiencing the lash. What further brutal excesses was she to be subjected to by the cruel gym mistress? But even as her worst imaginings haunted her – burning deep into her brain – one thought managed to remain sharp and clear. After this, Emma swore to make sure that Marion Aylott-Inche was ousted from Laments.

Balancing her feet a few inches from Emma's bound right ankle, the gym mistress eased her leather sheathed belly, pubis and upper thighs in against Emma's punished buttocks. The black corselette she had quickly donned gleamed softly in the lack of light. Emma grunted into her gag as her soft bottom flattened under the fierce thrust. Emma panicked, still unable to comprehend what was happening to her. Marion's cold leather harness – the tightly strapped girdle with the socket fashioned at her slit – squashed up dominantly against the crimson cheeks once more.

Marion kissed the punished rump then jerked her bottom out, withdrawing her right hand from the wall bar above Emma's hooded head. after plucking out the dildo from her clenched teeth, she deftly inserted it into the socket at her pubic mound and, with a quick twist of her supple wrist, secured the dildo firmly into its seat.

Emma, suffering the smothering of her tight rubber hood, cried out into the tight gag at her lips as the snout of the cruel shaft raked along the length of her sticky, aching cleft.

Oh God. No. No. Not that.

Marion inched up on her toes, resting her heels securely on the bar below. She trod the wood blindly in the darkness. Poised and balanced, her feet drawn together, she guided the dildo down the hot cleft then further down, nuzzling the tip into Emma's wet plum.

No! Emma tried to resist the tickling tip of the dildo at her labia, but with her feet bound far apart she was incapable of denying the cruel shaft. Marion swayed her hips. The dildo nodded in the dark between Emma's thighs, jerking up obediently to worry and juice the thick, outer lips. Teasing them for a full four minutes of utter humiliation, the dildo probed their velvety slipperiness and sought out the more sensitive, inner petals.

Marion's buttocks clenched rhythmically within the tightly bound, criss-crossed straps of her black leather harness. Her fat cheeks dimpled within their constraints as she renewed her pelvic thrusts, supremely dominating the pussy of the bound and beaten blonde in her thrall.

Emma braced herself against the wall bars, denying herself the delicious drift into sleep she so achingly desired. Marion had gone, after whipping out the dildo and forcing

Emma, her rubber hood briefly pushed up and her gag momentarily removed, to lick it clean. Marion had gone. But Emma's waking nightmare remained. The dildo had gone too – the thrusting, burning shame that had possessed and filled her. Filled her with its hateful firmness. Its length of stiff domination the ultimate humiliation.

Emma, gagged and hooded, hung alone in her bondage. The gym was cold and deserted. It must be the dead of night now. Way past three. Possibly later still. Naked in her bondage at the wall bars, she shivered, jiggling her sore nipples into the stern wood. Then she shuddered, remembering just how brutal Marion had been. The dildo had been driven hard.

Emma flexed her wrists and ankles. It would be dawn soon. An hour or so. Three at the most. Then she would tell Felicity Flint everything. Everything? Emma blushed hotly in the darkness, knowing that it would be difficult to put some of her night's suffering into words. Images of her recent subjugation welled up, as did the tears in her clouded grey eyes. Her throat tightened, her tongue thickened. After probing her pussy, the blunt snout of the dildo had been withdrawn to instantly pierce the sphincter deep between her punished cheeks. Emma burned as she relived those ruthless, punishing thrusts of the frenzied gym mistress. Marion's firm thighs had powered into Emma's helplessness, driving the dildo painfully deeper. Then deeper still. Probing, piercing and possessing. Then, to her horror, the acrid taste in her mouth as her gag was moved to one side and the curved shaft was forced down on to her tongue. Emma had truly tasted her shame.

Just before Christmas, Emma had dived into an 8-til-late in Deptford and grabbed a bottle of dodgy Chianti, an industrial wedge of Cheddar and a video. Back in her broom-cupboard flat, the Chianti uncorked and the sweating cheese left untasted, she played the tape. Not the *Wallace & Grommit* she had expected. Some under-the-counter cock-up presented her widening eyes with images of sadism. Brutal anal punishment. Pseudo-German officers appeared in monocled menace. Low-budget production values had chewed up the continuity but soon Emma watched the Huns interrogating a blonde Belgian agent. Jump-cuts took the monocled Prussians into another sequence of underlit scenes. The writhing blonde was gagged and bound. At her bare buttocks, her interrogators grew busy with their crops. Then, in a brutal flourish, one of the cruel Huns had unbuttoned himself before taking the brave little Belgian from behind.

How long had she watched it? Eight, ten minutes at the most. Emma remembered her finger pausing over the remote button unable to switch it off as leathered boots gleamed and grey breeches jerked. Jerked inwards against the bound helplessness of the straddled blonde.

Emma shuddered. That was exactly what had happened to her. Here. Tonight. In the gym. Just as that supposed Belgian blonde had suffered the humiliation of her Prussian bulliers in the Deptford video, so Emma had been subjugated to the brutal attentions of the gym mistress.

But now it was all over. Now she was safe. Cold, naked and still bound to the wall bars. But safe.

A soft slapping sound at the doors announced the arrival of a nocturnal visitor to the gym. Emma, still rubber hooded, twisted at the bars as the sudden draught of cold air played across her nakedness. She stiffened in her bondage, tense and alert. Who? Kate? Felicity Flint? Or Marion returning for more? Who had just stolen softly into the gym? Whose feet were now silently treading the polished wood? A rescuer, or a stern tormentress? Saviour or sadistic predator? Emma held her breath. Her heart pounded, sending her blood singing in her ears.

Emma sensed the approaching presence. The nearness of shadowless stealth. Rubber-hooded, Emma remained suspended in an agony of uncertainty. Then she felt it. The inverted knuckles of a tentative hand grazing the smoothness of her lower thigh. A gentle, hesitant touch. Kate's? A face inched closer to her bottom as the unknown climber took another rung of the wall bars silently. Emma tingled in suspense, but the two cold discs kissing the swell of her cheeks told Emma all. Spectacles. It was Watson. Emma groaned into her gag. The weasel had crept back into the gym to claim another furtive award. And Emma knew that she, naked and helpless, was the delicious morsel.

Emma became rigid with repulsion. Watson's face – the spectacles now removed – was pressing fiercely up into Emma's cheeks. A sharp nose dug into the anal rosebud deep between the cheeks as the weasel's tongue lapped at the slippery slit below. Soon, small hands grew confident, cupping and squeezing Emma's bare bottom. Emma shivered and groaned, hating and detesting the perverted attentions her nakedness was receiving: the perverted attentions of the weasel-spy Watson.

Emma's rubber-hooded head tossed back as Watson buried her face deeply into the divide between the captive cheeks in her thrall. Nuzzling the feral heat of the cleft, she teased then tormented the taloned cheeks with increasing ferocity. The satin soft peaches of swollen flesh dimpled as the weasel's fingers dug deep. A thick tongue rasped the length of the cleft, heralding the sucking lips that visited the sphincter, dragging up the puckering whorl and opening it for the tongue-tip. The tongue-tip flickered before it probed. Emma sobbed into the rubber stretched across her mouth.

Now Watson, twisting in an arabesque of dark ecstasy, forced her face up between Emma's thighs. With her neck resting on a wall bar, she sucked at then softly bit the exposed labia, chewing their rubberiness between tiny white teeth. Emma's scream bubbled the rubber at her lips briefly but remained inaudible beyond the shrill echo in her brain. Watson was eating her slit now. Flattening the back of her tongue against the exposed inner labia. Forcing her thick tongue up to tip-tease the tingling clitoris. Emma, helpless, felt her belly implode as the weasel between her straining thighs began to bite and tug at the soaked pubic nest.

A shrill cry broke the intense silence. Emma just caught the shriek despite her rubber hood. The face at her slit withdrew. Had her tormentress slipped from the bars and crashed to the floor below? No. Emma sensed the weasel scrambling down the wall bars, sensed the awkward, jerking retreat – like that of a crab scurrying from a poking stick.

Muffled voices locked in sharp conflict reached her through the rubber at her ears. Angry exchanges rose up from the gym floor in a kaleidoscope of confused sound.

Silence. Then, out of the silence, tenderness, the tenderness of a careful hand peeling away the rubber hood from her head. In her sudden freedom, Emma tossed her golden mane, relishing the cool on her hot face. The gym was in darkness. Only a soft light from the entrance challenged its absoluteness. Twisting her face, Emma's grey eyes met those of Mme Puton. The French mistress smiled and returned to her task of unbinding Emma from her leathered bondage at the bars.

'Thank you –' Emma whispered hoarsely, the words difficult through her dry lips.

'*Ma petite. Ma pauvre petite*,' Mme Puton murmured, guiding Emma carefully down the wall bars to the gym floor.

'But how did you know?' Emma whispered, licking her lips to lubricate them.

'Your bed. She remains empty. The midnight comes and still the bed she is empty. I say nothing of this to anybody but I am worried, no?' Mme Puton stroked Emma's face gently, then patted the blonde's bare bottom. She continued, whispering, 'Yes, I am greatly worried. Soon it is two o'clock. Then, three o'clock comes. I get up. I get dressed –'

Emma suppressed a grin. Mme Puton had 'dressed' in a simple transparent silk nightgown. Her dark mulberry nipples prinked the taut stretch at her bosom. Below, the darker pubic nest rustled against the silk.

'And so I am determined to seek you. From my window, I see the dreadful Miss Watson going across the gardens to the gym. I watch. That one, I tell myself, moves like one with a secret. Perhaps *ma petite* is in trouble, I think. So I came here and I was right. I find her at your helplessness, feeding her mouth between your legs like the dog at his bone –'

183

Emma shuddered at the memory of Watson's guzzling. She drew her thighs together and squeezed hard, as if squeezing out the disturbing memory from her ravished flesh.

'But now you are safe with me. I deal with that one. She has gone. Let me see your bottom. I think I have something special for it up in my room.'

Emma, still shivering after her double-ordeal, allowed her nakedness to be turned between the controlling palms of the French mistress. Allowing Mme Puton to kneel and closely examine the ravages brought to her bottom by the blistering punishment dispensed by Marion's cruel trainer.

Mme Puton gently kissed the swell of both buttocks. after rising, she cradled Emma gently to her breasts. 'Come. Let me take you up to my bed. There, you will be warm, and I can take care of your poor, sore bottom.'

They left the gym quickly. Out in the rain, they scampered across the wet gravel. Emma squealed, but was silenced by a warning sign from her rescuer. Mme Puton placed her finger at Emma's lips then pointed it up at the darkened windows of Laments' grim façade.

Inside the shelter of the porch, Emma paused.

'How did you get rid of Watson?' she asked. 'What did you say? Or do?'

'Never mind,' the French mistress whispered, adding darkly, 'She is gone to lick her wound –'

Instead of mine, Emma thought grimly.

'I have a new tube of almond oil. I shall squeeze it on to your poor bottom and rub it in. Slowly.'

Emma snuggled into the protective warmth beneath the taut silk nightdress. The soft warmth, slightly perfumed, that cradled her as it steered her away from her recent misery towards the promise of delicious, almond-oiled aftercare.

Kate pounced out of the shadows on the upstairs landing.

'So there you are. I should have known. And I've been worried sick,' she snapped accusingly.

'No, you don't understand,' Emma, recovering from her shock, protested. 'Marion was dreadful.' Catching the jealous flash in Kate's dark eyes, Emma disengaged herself from Mme Puton's encircling arm.

'That was over an hour ago. Two –'

'No,' Emma squeaked. 'She tied me up. On the wall bars. It was horrid.'

'Tied you up?' Kate echoed, advancing.

The French mistress calmly reclaimed her prize, threading her sinuous arm around Emma's naked hips. '*Mais oui*. What the little one says is true. And there was the ugly rubber over her face. The mask. And her hands and feet all tied in how do you say – ah, yes – the bondage.'

'And after, Watson came into the gym and she . . . and she –'

Kate took another step forward, speaking in a gentler tone. 'That's all right,' she soothed, taking Emma out of Mme Puton's protective embrace and hugging the nude to her own bosom. 'It's all over now. My God, those bitches will pay for this. But how did you get involved?' Kate demanded, turning to the French mistress.

They faced each other like two vixens over a fresh kill in the henhouse.

'I was worried for *ma petite*.'

Ma petite. Emma felt Kate's embrace tighten.

'I see Watson running in the darkness to the gym. I follow. I find Watson tormenting *ma petite*. I deal with that one. Easy. Then I take care of *ma petite* –'

'Thank you,' Kate replied coldly. 'And now, "*ma petite*" is coming back to my room. I will look after her –'

Emma sensed a dangerous moment descend. The tension crackled like static.

Mme Puton broke the silence with a soft sigh. '*Mais oui*, of course. The little one must go with you, Kate. I have almond oil. Would you like to have it for her bottom?'

Kate released Emma and impulsively kissed the French mistress full on her mouth. 'Thank you for rescuing Emma. I'll take her now –'

A torch beam shattered the shadows, making them blink. Emma raised her hand from her bosom to protect her startled eyes. The torch beam played from Mme Puton's shiny negligee to Emma's naked breasts.

185

A voice barked out from behind the powerful light. 'Emma is going nowhere,' Dr Flint's stern voice hissed, 'until I know exactly what is going on here.'

Mme Puton shrank back in dismay. Instinctively, she clutched her tight silk sheath around herself. Straining at her bosom, the silk caused her breasts to bulge. Emma, naked and trembling, slipped behind Kate.

'I'm waiting,' the Head barked impatiently. 'Mme Puton. Please explain your presence here at once.'

The French mistress, skirting a wealth of detail, responded.

The torch twitched in Felicity Flint's dismissive gesture.

'In the gym, you say. Kate? Why were you and Emma being punished in the gym at such a late hour by Marion? What reason did you give her to ply her strap, hmm?'

Kate took a deep breath. And confessed everything. Her concern for Emma's inability to punish the girls at Laments. Striped Shirt. The therapeutic little trip to Pimlico. Their late return. Marion and Watson. The gym. The bare-bottomed punishment.

After a long pause, the torch beam began to quiver. Soon it danced, danced as Dr Flint shook with mirth. The length of the entire landing echoed to her fruity laughter.

'Priceless,' she grunted, unable to still the torch beam. 'And she caught you out. And punished you. As if you were the Middleton-Peake brat caught raiding the mid-night larder for milk and cake, eh? And you, Emma? Did you also get a taste of that leather belt, hmm?'

Emma remained silent. Dr Flint repeated her question, her tone filling with concern. A sudden suspicion coloured her voice.

'Or did she,' the Head demanded, 'deal with you more harshly?'

Emma remained silent. The silence of deep shame.

Kate, speaking softly, explained Emma's fate under Marion's cruel dominance. Mme Puton, nodding vigorously, attested to Emma's suffering.

'That is why I am taking Emma with me to my room –' Kate began.

186

'Emma remains with me tonight,' the Head murmured. 'In my bed.'

The bed was huge. The pillows soft. As soft and white as snowdrifts. The crisp cotton sheets were cool and soothing at her punished cheeks. Emma ground her punished rump into them contentedly. The large bed was deliciously soft. Emma scrunched her toes like a child in new shoes, then stretched her limbs out luxuriously into the far corners of the bed.

The Head undressed quickly. Naked, she dragged down the duvet and spent over eleven minutes intimately inspecting Emma's bottom. Acutely conscious of Felicity Flint's steady gaze devouring her buttocks, Emma suddenly yearned for a gentle caress – that tender sweep of knuckles across rippling satin curves.

'Mm,' the voice at her bottom murmured at last, the tone crisply professional and detatched. 'She certainly wielded that trainer viciously.'

Emma sank her face disappointedly into the pillow.

'My poor little thing,' Dr Flint suddenly whispered, palming then kissing both cheeks before covering them up tenderly beneath the duvet.

Emma furtively bumped her slit into the cotton sheet in response.

The weight on the bed eased as the Head rose and turned to undress and – to Emma's surprise – dress for bed.

Turning over on to her back, and clutching the duvet at her chin, Emma peeped over its fat softness. Standing naked before a long cheval mirror, the Head displayed her ripe nakedness in all its splendour. The powerful, tanned thighs golden, even in the depths of an English winter. Tanned, athletic thighs. Supple and graceful. The sweeping line rose up to the heavy, mature buttocks above. Emma's throat tightened. Her pussy tickled as she peeped at the beautiful nude before the reflecting glass – a lithe, powerful beauty made strong by summer after summer of tennis.

Turning slightly to her right, the Head bent over, offering Emma a superb glimpse of the burgeoning buttocks. Bulging ripeness divided by a deep, dark cleft. Peeping from her bed, Emma blushed slightly as her pussy prickled with her increasing inquisitiveness.

Felicity Flint, naked, was dressing for bed. Bending, the Head fingered out a pair of white panties from the second drawer of her fumed oak dresser. On the polished surface of the venerable wood, five miniature silver statuettes celebrated the athleticism of lawn tennis amazons. Emma's eyes darted back over the duvet to the cleft between Felicity Flint's wobbling buttocks. She saw the Head prinking her left foot before stepping into the stretched panties. Two seconds later, the cotton snapped softly around her bulging bottom, its tightness snuggling into both pubis and cleft.

Next, a white sports bra. A white sports bra with shoulder straps a little wider than usual, to take the strain of the ripe breasts – to ensure firm support and strict control of the heavy breasts when at play – in either the bedroom or on the green grass court. Emma noticed the supporting bands that hooked together at the back, crossed below the shoulders. Emma gazed wide eyed into the cheval's bright glass. In the sheen of light, she watched as each cup obediently bulged to accept its burden of ripe breast. As Felicity Flint slowly fingered the wide white strap at each shoulder, the cups in the reflection seemed to brim with trembling flesh, causing a slow trickle to ooze from Emma's ignited slit.

Snapping sweat bands on to each wrist, and white ankle socks over her feet, the Head selected a sleeveless tennis shirt and matching cream, short, pleated skirt.

Emma looked on in increasing bewilderment as, dressed smartly and bewitchingly for the grass court, Dr Felicity Flint opened up a canewood box, taloned out a tennis ball and turned towards the bed.

Emma closed her eyes, feigning sleep. She felt the Head peel back the duvet and enter the bed alongside her. A touch of the tennis ball at her belly failed to open Emma's eyes. But the sweep of the tightly clenched ball at her slit instantly opened them: drawing their startled gaze up to meet Felicity Flint's amused gaze.

'Not asleep? I thought so. Sleep could not be possible after such a hectic night. Not yet.'

The tennis ball was bounced, twice, from a height of four and a half inches, on to Emma's pubic mound. An expert hand held the ball on its return. Emma swallowed silently – as if waiting for a powerful serve from the amazon ace beyond the rippling net.

The hand that had snatched the ball above her belly held it aloft. Emma squirmed. The cream, pleated skirt was tickling her thigh. Emma wanted to scratch down at her flesh but dared not move. She remained spellbound under the hand that held the ball.

Dr Flint leaned down into her naked captive. Her firm breasts bulged beneath the stretch of the tennis shirt, the warm weight of her brassiered bosom in its firm-control cups dominating Emma's squashed breasts.

'Tell me,' Felicity Flint murmured, tenderly dragging Emma's lower lip down with the curve of the tennis ball, 'what did it really feel like? Punishing your first bottom?'

Emma kissed the ball submissively before it was whisked away.

'Beautiful,' she whispered. 'There are no words for it. The sense of power, the sense of control. Owning the bare bottom, and knowing it is yours. Absolutely yours.'

Teasingly silencing Emma with the tennis ball pressed down against her lips, Dr Flint nodded.

'I came –' Emma confessed, mumbling the words into the softness at her mouth.

The ball was whipped away.

'No, not yet. Tell me slowly. Everything. From the very beginning. From your first glimpse of his bare, bending buttocks.'

Emma edged her face away slightly, rolling her head in the pillow. Gazing across at the glinting statuettes, frozen in silver as they pranced and served, volleyed and rallied, she heard herself whispering softly. Whispering softly as she spoke frankly, revealing to herself and to the Head just how delicious it had been to bare and carefully prepare – then beat – the naked bottom before her. The bare bottom, so quickly reddened, jerking under the spanking hand, the wire hanger and the snapping leather belt. Jerking and spasming in its suffering. In its utter helplessness. Emma fully admitted the thrill.

'A man's bottom. I've had so many of them. Quite satisfactory. Yes, a bare-bottomed man will give you a great game. Straight sets victory, perhaps. But a good game. But wait til your up against a female bottom. No contest, my dear. Beating a man is simple. And they're often unseeded – or quickly become so –'

Suddenly relaxing, Emma giggled.

'Wait til you experience the subtleness, the guile, the challenge of bare, female buttocks –'

'Yes,' Emma broke in excitedly. 'I want that. I want to spank – to spank and punish the girls here. I really do. Now that I've discovered the pleasure, the delight. I want to be like Kate and punish the girls here at Laments properly. But –'

'But?'

'Not like Marion.'

'No,' the Head whispered, 'not like Marion.'

'But like you,' Emma confessed uninhibitedly. Adding, 'And Kate and Mme Puton. I want to make Bubble squeak and little red-bottomed Squeak bubble across my lap.'

'I'm sure you do, my dear,' Felicity Flint murmured drily. 'You have not disappointed me, Emma. I knew my instincts and my judgement to be sound. Yes. When I first saw you. How your eyes sparkled in the darkness.'

Emma remembered the encounter – she had just witnessed Kate spanking a broad-bottomed blonde through the window.

'Remember?'

Emma nodded.

'I caught you peeping through a gap in the curtains. How your eyes sparkled. As if you'd just won your first championship shield. Then, a little later in my study, as I caned Rebecca Wigmore's naughty little bottom, you watched, spellbound, from your chair by the fire. From that moment, I knew you were a natural. I knew there had to be a place for you on my team here at Laments. I wanted you right there and then –'

The tennis ball bounced down from a slightly increased height. Emma squeezed her buttocks tightly in response.

'But Marion said that I'd have to leave –'

'My gym mistress overstepped the mark tonight. Double fault, there. Clearly out of play. I've had my concerns for some time now about her exceeding the limits but it has been difficult for me to prove. I suspect she has been bullying the girls in a similar fashion – and bullying them into silence as well. No. Marion Aylott-Inche has clearly exceeded the limits in her methods of discipline. At Laments, each tutor is encouraged to develop their expertise. But within boundaries. Kate, for example, has perfected the art of spanking –'

'Mm,' Emma murmured readily.

'And each derives pleasure from the punishments they dispense. Mme Puton,' the Head confided in a conspiratorial whisper, 'has to change her panties at least three times a day.'

Emma giggled.

'And this man you punished in London. Did he come?'

'Yes, several times.'

'Men. Hopeless, except for mixed doubles. Even in their pain, they respond with perverse pleasure. Pleasure is, strictly speaking, the punisher's portion. Here at Laments, I relax the rules. As I say, Mme Puton has to change her panties several times a day – as do the pupils she has punished.'

Rolling Emma over on to her side, facing away, Dr Flint eased her knees in between Emma's parted legs then, interlocking and trapping them, spread her captive's thighs apart. Flipping up her cream, pleated skirt, she pressed her pantied pubis into Emma's bare bottom.

Game on, Emma thought, melting happily.

Helpless within the Head's controlling embrace – and jerking herself back into both the brassiered bosom and cotton panties behind – Emma returned the volley.

The tennis ball visited her slit, guided by the strong, tanned hand. It swept upwards, repeatedly raking her wet lips. Crushing down into them harshly, it splayed her labia apart. Poised at her pussy, the ball yielded to the Head's circling palm.

Voices from long hot summers listening to the radio filtered into Emma's head. Warm, firm voices from aces in the commentary box. Amazons serving up into the mike, thrilling schoolgirls everywhere.

As Felicity Flint's ripe breasts bulged into Emma's back, and the cotton panties rasped her tightening buttocks, Emma closed her eyes and succumbed to the snatches of commentary echoing in her brain.

'And she's really taking control now. Dominating . . .'

The tennis ball was being swept in tight circles at her flesh now. With an increasing vigour.

'Supple wrist action is certainly giving her the edge . . .' the voice in her brain remarked.

Emma felt the tennis ball settle at her clitoris.

'This could be it . . .' the Amazon whispered into the mike. 'The big serve . . .'

The furry surface of the ball – sticky from Emma's weeping slit – teased the clitoral thorn with savage tenderness.

'Oh, what superb pinpoint positioning and placement of the ball . . .' the excited commentary observed.

Emma shuddered, overwhelmed by the seethe at the juncture of her splayed thighs. The ball was skimming the tip of her erect little bud. Her belly tightened. Her slit shone as it wept gently.

Grunting as she served the ball into Emma's wet heat, Dr Flint rode Emma's bare bottom ruthlessly – masturbating herself as she brought her trembling captive to climax.

Both tensed, quivered and lay motionless for a timeless moment. Both moaned long and loud in unison as, hammering into each other, they came with a sweet savagery.

Screaming out loud as the Head's hot soak rekindled the soreness of her punished cheeks, Emma threshed as her own scald began to burn.

'Deuce . . .' the Amazon gasped into Emma's brain.

'Juice,' she slurred drunkenly, correcting the understandable mistake.

Nine

The girls began to fidget at their tables, squirming from
cheek to plump cheek on the polished wooden seats of
their chairs. Heads bowed in silence, they watched their
meagre ration of toast growing colder.

At the top table, Marion glanced from the two empty
chairs back to her watch. Jerking her head back, she
reached across the table, fingers stretching for the little bell.
Kate deftly removed it from her grasp.

'Give it to me,' the gym mistress hissed, snapping her
fingers impatiently.

'Dr Flint –' Kate began.

'– Is late. I will ring the bell.'

Before Kate could prevent her, Watson had scooped up
the silver bell and passed it over to Marion. Smiling her
triumph, she rattled it with unnecessary vehemence, signalling that breakfast was to commence.

Unaware of the small drama at the top table, the pupils
sighed audibly as they tucked into their weak tea and toast.
Watson tackled her grilled kidneys, mushrooms and bacon
eagerly. Kate, her napkin unfurled, remained motionless at
the breakfast table. Mme Puton also left her scrambled
eggs and smoked salmon untasted.

Emma glanced down the gleaming white tablecloth.
Tweedledum and Tweedledee were hesitating uncertainly,
fingering their cutlery tentatively as their bacon and
sausages awaited them.

'Not eating?' Marion purred dangerously.

Tweedledum and Tweedledee twittered, wondering aloud where Dr Flint was, and what could have possibly delayed her.

'Rathbone, Monteagle.' The gym mistress addressed them curtly. 'Is there anything amiss with your breakfasts?'

Anxious eyes met her stern gaze. 'No, nothing at all,' they whispered in unison.

'I have, have I not, given the signal for breakfast to commence?' She spoke to them as she would to a sullen pupil she was about to beat.

They nodded, fear suddenly clouding their eyes.

'Then please do me the courtesy of –'

'But,' they chorused, 'Dr Flint always –'

'Eat,' Marion snapped.

Emma's heart sank as she watched Tweedledum and Tweedledee tuck in. Her own breakfast, along with Kate's and that of Mme Puton, remained untasted.

'Miss Wyndlesham. You have tasted my wrath only recently. If you defy me I will take my strap to you right here and now.'

Emma reddened. The sudden silence in the refectory told her that all the girls were agog, their pink ears straining.

'Why has breakfast begun? Who gave the signal?' Dr Flint demanded, swooping down on the table imperiously in full gown and mortar board.

'You were late, Flint,' Marion retorted rudely. 'I decided –'

'You decided?' the Head echoed sarcastically. 'May I remind you of your position here at Laments is to function merely as my deputy, Marion. I take the decisions here. Your task is to see that my wishes are carried out. That is all.'

'You were late, Flint,' Marion persisted. 'I saw fit to take charge.'

'You saw fit, Aylott-Inche –'

'Like I saw fit to punish Miss Wyndlesham for her flagrant breach of the rules last night.'

Emma blushed. The girls, all pretence of eating toast now abandoned, strained to follow the drama unfolding at the top table.

'We will discuss the matter of Kate and Emma's absence from Laments without leave after breakfast,' Dr Flint broke in abruptly. Snapping out her napkin, she nodded to Kate, Emma and Mme Puton to tuck in.

In the oppressive silence that followed the brusque exchange, Emma had little appetite for her fried breakfast – and no desire to meet the gaze of her punisher or her subsequent tormentress as Marion and Watson finished their breakfast across the table.

Dismissed after prayers by Felicity Flint, the girls filed out of the refectory in silence.

Then the simmering row broke out in a storm at the top table. 'How dare you' and 'I saw fit' streaked across the silverware like tracer fire. Tweedledum and Tweedledee cowered under the cross-fire, petrified as Felicity Flint and the gym mistress waged battle royal. God, Emma thought. This is it. Not a cat-fight or a spat – this is the open rebellion. The *coup d'etat*.

Suddenly, Marion stood up violently, scraping her chair away from the table in a shrill squeak. Knuckling her fists down into the table linen, she dropped her voice to a lethal whisper.

'Very well, Flint. You cannot see, or you deliberately refuse to acknowledge, that many of your recent decisions are proving disastrous to the well being of Laments. Your plans for a tennis court – expensive nonsense –'

'How dare you –'

'The appointment of Miss Wyndlesham, taken, I might add,' Marion spat, 'without either my knowledge or consent, even more so. She has failed to dispense discipline and has already treated the rules here with contempt, dragging Kate down with her.'

'I said that I will deal with that matter –'

'No need,' the gym mistress countered. 'She must go. And go today. Do you at least agree with that?'

'I neither agree nor disagree with your impertinence, Aylott-Inche. I abhor it. And I refuse to be spoken to by you in this insubordinate –'

'Then I shall put it to the staff,' Marion snapped.

'Laments simply cannot continue to have such a weak link in its chain of command. All those in favour of letting Miss Wyndlesham go, forthwith, please –'

Shit, Emma thought. She's bringing it to a vote. I'm done for.

'There shall be no vote taken now or at any other juncture regarding Emma's continuing position here at Laments,' the Head barked. 'On what grounds do you dare to challenge me in this matter, Aylott-Inche?'

'If there is to be no vote allowed,' the gym mistress hissed, bunching the table cloth savagely and making the plates rattle, 'then I must insist upon calling a vote of no confidence in your headship, Flint. I call for a vote to secure the future of Laments,' she cried, 'and your removal. All those in favour of Flint as Head –'

Felicity Flint paled in anger, tossing her chignon as she surveyed the silent breakfast table. Kate, Emma and Mme Puton instantly raised their hands.

'Put your hand down, Wyndlesham. You've no vote. You have no right to be here.'

Tweedledum and Tweedledee, Emma noticed, seemed to be caught in an agony of indecision. Their hands hovered inches above the remains of their unfinished breakfasts.

'Two,' Marion said slowly, her tone of contempt, and her sense of victory, unmistakable. 'All those against Flint remaining as Head of Laments –'

Watson's hand shot up. Marion raised her own right hand, leaving her left at her waist to finger the leather of her belt. She glared down dominantly at Miss Rathbone and Miss Monteagle. Their arms rose up, their rabbit eyes fixed upon the supple leather tight at Marion's waist.

'Four,' she whispered triumphantly.

To Emma's surprise, the gym mistress did not linger to savour her victory but strode abruptly out of the refectory, the weasel Watson scuttling in her wake.

At the silent breakfast table, Felicity Flint calmly sipped her coffee.

'This means nothing. Absolutely nothing at all, you understand. Stuff and nonsense. But I am afraid I am going to have to have a very serious talk with my gym mistress. She is taking far too much upon herself of late.'

Miss Rathbone, reddening, fiddled with her teacup. It rattled noisily. Miss Monteagle's fork crashed to the polished floor from her nervous fingers.

'Loyalty,' Dr Flint murmured, smoothing her napkin firmly before sliding it back into its silver ring. 'Loyalty must be earned. I do hope I have always acted in the best interests of Laments. And its staff.'

Tweedledum and Tweedledee coughed and fidgeted.

'It must also be pledged willingly, and not –' the Head paused, glancing at them significantly '– under the threat of the whip. The bully will not reward such loyalty; she will merely insist upon absolute obedience. I have always given you both your autonomy, have I not? Tell me, where and when did I cease to enjoy your confidence in my headship?'

Tweedledum and Tweedledee mumbled indistinct apologies, instantly silenced by Dr Flint's raised hand.

'You had your moment. Both of you. You have made your choice, your feelings in the matter quite plain.'

'But, Head, we –' they whined.

The Head was on the brink of challenging their craven behaviour when Marion, shadowed by Watson, rejoined the breakfast table. Emma saw the flash of triumph in her hard eyes.

'I have just spoken with the trustees,' she crowed. 'I can confirm that Miss Wyndlesham is no longer a tutor here at Laments. The trustees are in accord with me. She is to be out of here within the hour.'

'That is monstrous. Petty and monstrous,' Dr Flint exploded. 'And to betray me like that by speaking with the trustees –'

'On the second matter, Flint,' Marion snapped brusquely, 'the trustees again concur with me.'

'What do you mean?' the Head whispered softly.

'Following the vote of no confidence in your headship of Laments, they have instructed me to inform you that you must step down.'

'Step down?' Felicity Flint gasped.

197

'With immediate effect. The trustees are convening an emergency meeting here at the end of the month. Until then, you are relieved of your duties, Flint. Laments is now under my absolute control.'

Emma looked up. Beside the gym mistress, Watson was rubbing her hands in a paroxysm of delight. Emma shuddered.

'Laments is mine, from now on, to manage as I see fit.'

Emma blinked. Her eyes were becoming a little tired after four hours at the screen. The snarl of the gridlock rose up from the surrounding streets. Coffee would be good. She left her desk to get a plastic beaker of indifferent instant. Back before the ice blue screen, she sipped, pulling a face at the acrid aftertaste.

Laughter. She looked up. Across the open plan office, Susie and the boys were gathering around their new boss. Another Striped Shirt. Wise-cracking, predatory and ruthless. More sycophantic laughter. Emma sighed. Her recent time off, explained away as a virus, had attracted little comment and less sympathy. She had not been missed. But the images fed back from the web cam at Striped Shirt's bed had caused a riot throughout the office the morning after the little visit to Pimlico. Striped Shirt had been shunted down to consolidations in Croydon – and had been replaced by a clone. *Plus ça change*, as Mme Puton would undoubtedly say.

Mme Puton. Sweetly perfumed and superbly buttocked. Emma was instantly miles away from the computer terminals, the treacherous office politics, the over-heated, air-conditioned limbo perched on the edge of the Square Mile. She heard the stiff breeze rustling the dancing elms, saw the driving rain silvering the bay windows down at Laments Hall.

Mme Puton. Chic, severe and so very, very tender when palming cream into a sore bottom. Aftercare. Emma closed her eyes, shutting out the vivid computer screen and the brightly neon lit office, and imagined herself back in the secret shadows of the landings down at Laments. Landings along which naughty girls scampered, running from or

198

towards some mischief which was bound to bring the bamboo's bite to their bare bottoms.

Laments. And Kate. Being with Kate. Dark-eyed, possessive and passionate Kate. To be wanted, so fiercely. In the bath. Kate so firm with the flannel. In bed. Kate, so deliciously brutal at the bosom, so skilful at the slit.

Emma squeezed her thighs together beneath her desk, containing in her silk panties the hot trickle of oozing arousal memories of Laments had conjured from her pussy. On the desk, her right hand clenched the plastic beaker. It crackled within her grip. Hot black coffee scalded her fingers. Emma opened her grey eyes wide in fleeting pain. She looked at her curled fingers around the leaking cup. They reddened under the slight scald. Reddening flesh. Hot pain. Emma moaned gently as she thought of the pleasures of pain. Of soft bottoms crimsoning under a severe spanking hand. God, yes. That delicious crack, crack, crack of the dominant spanking hand. The jerk and wobble of the punished cheeks. Under her desk, Emma's pussy prickled. The labia smiled, pouting its lips to kiss the silk stretched tight across her weeping slit.

And what of Felicity Flint? Brief, guarded phone calls to Kate since being banished into exile from Laments had told her little. The Head had been consigned to her room. Relieved of all duties, Kate had said. Fretting, Emma supposed, like a vixen driven deep into her den by snapping hounds. Watson. Watson and Marion Aylott-Inche. Would the trustees listen to Dr Flint at the emergency meeting next week? No, of course not. Marion was the bursar, perfectly placed to paint a financial picture that would damage Felicity Flint's future at Laments. And her few loyal supporters. A financial picture. The phrase trickled over the top of Emma's brain and slid down beyond conscious reach.

She gazed around the open-plan office, her reddened fingers wrapped in a tissue. They throbbed. Cold water. Emma rose up and made for the loo. Inside, the cool tiles reminded her immediately of a cold dorm at midnight. She closed her eyes, steadying herself at a wash basin.

Midnight. Kate on dorm patrol. The girls, caught red handed at some naughtiness, about to be red bottomed.

Emma slipped inside a cubicle. Skirt up around her hips, she yanked her oyster silk panties down. A spun-sugar slick of slit juice stretched and spindled, following the silk panties down to her knees. The wet thread snapped silently, slightly soaking her inner thigh. Emma groaned.

Kate on dorm patrol. Kate, the dark-eyed, predatory punisher. Leisurely, with a soft footfall and menacingly measured tread, approaching the first bed. Susie Middleton-Peake, like the rest of her dorm, standing by the bed. Naked, except for the tight white vest. Susie Middleton-Peake, nervously plucking down the hem of her vest, tugging it down to cover her blonde nest – and baring her rounded cheeks as she did so. And causing her ripe breasts to bulge within the tight cotton's stretch.

Emma slowly thumbed her outer labia, spreading them easily. Her thumbtip, soon shiny, slipped between their wet velvet, her nail gently raking the sensitive inner lips. Emma squealed as she rose up on tiptoe, crushing her bare buttocks up into the cold tiled wall. The heat from her squashed cheeks clouded their cold sheen. The thumbtip flayed her wet flesh. Emma grunted, bumping her bottom rhythmically as she shut her eyes tight.

Kate. Sitting on the bed. Cool and in control. Carefully and unhurriedly arranging the Middleton-Peake girl across her lap for a spanking. Deliberately prolonging the anxious blonde's delicious dread. Gazing down to inspect the bare bottom she was about to beat. Pausing, briefly, to flick away a soft golden pubic curl from the dark, tempting cleft. The spasm of the sensitive cheeks jerking as the fingertip flicks away the tiny curl.

Oh God, yes. Emma slid a finger up her wetness, imagining Kate's left hand pinning the wriggling blonde firmly down into the punishment position. Imagining Kate's right hand, palm flattened, poised above the proffered cheeks below.

Spank. Spank. Spank. A second firm finger joined the first, pumping slowly, as Emma pictured the spanking in

200

the midnight dorm at Laments. Pictured, vividly, the blonde's cheeks bouncing and deepening in colour from pink to crimson as Kate's harsh hand cracked down. Charlotte Bicknell would be next. Bigger bottomed; a louder, ringing spank as Kate expertly reddened the bulging buttocks across her lap. A third finger joined the other two as Emma celebrated the punishment. Interlocked and slippery, they flew at her pussy, filling and stretching her wet warmth.

Crack. Crack. Crack. As the imagined spanks rang out, each accompanied by a shriek from the Bicknell girl's parted lips, Emma ground her bare bottom up into the hard tiles. Her cleft ached, her climax gathered, her belly tensed.

Ann Cordery next. Oh God. In her surge of frenzied imaginings, Emma took over. Replaced Kate at the next bed to punish the beautiful brunette. Emma was now in Laments. In the midnight dorm. At the bed of Ann Cordery. Bending the delicious girl over her knee. Catching her breath as the beautiful bottom obediently rose up in meek surrender for its sweet pain. Ann Cordery. Emma strummed her clitoris savagely. As she pictured herself spanking Ann Cordery's bare bottom, a hot stickiness bubbled from her anal whorl. Dragging her soft cheeks in a sudden frenzy against the hard tiles, Emma tried to kiss their cold surface with her sphincter but her cheeks were too swollen, the cleft between them too deep.

Thumbing herself, she slumped helplessly under the savage climax triggered by her wank. A riot of confused images flooded her brain. Kate. Cool and in control of so many hot, writhing bottoms. Tightly vested girls standing by their beds as their punishment approached. The sharp, ringing spanks of the punisher. The shrill squeals of the punished. Red buttocks nestling back on to white sheets. Ann Cordery, her dark fringe curtaining her tear-spangled eyes, writhing as Emma spanked.

Coming almost drunkenly, Emma buckled under the combined delight of the seethe at her slit and the blaze deep between her buttocks. Filling the cubicle with an echoing squeal, Emma came a second time, jerking her thumb out from her anus and hammering her soft buttocks into the hard tiled wall.

Lunchtime. Susie and the lads were down at the wine bar buying Chablis for Striped Shirt's clone. The open-plan office looked twice the size when empty. Emma, alone, fiddled with her mouse. Random images flickered up on her ice blue screen. She felt spent. Rinsed out and exhausted. A cold longing filled her emptiness after the savage masturbation. A yearning to be back at Laments. Small icons grew on her screen, loomed large and disappeared. Little electronic pictures. Investment options. The financial picture. The phrase swam back into Emma's dull brain. She wanted to be back at Laments. Impossible. But to be able to help Dr Felicity Flint? And Kate? Perhaps. She wanted to do something to hurt Marion. And Watson. Definitely.

Most of all, I want to be back at Laments.

Once the words had been softly spoken – cautiously, but out loud – Emma knew that she must do anything and everything she could to quit her desk and non-job to fulfil her true vocation. To practise the art of intimate instruction at Laments.

Picking up a pencil, she scribbled some random figures down. Number of pupils. Planned growth. Monthly expenditure, times twelve. A five-year plan. A picture began to form. Careful expansion was the key. Emma found herself doodling with the zeros. They became two rounded cheeks. She shaded them delicately to enhance their voluptuousness then striped them as if with a cane with the sharp tip of her pencil.

Then it came to her. Financial gearing. She could do it. She was trained and talented in spotting investment and matching it to opportunity. Emma looked around. The office was still deserted. She was at Striped Shirt's former desk in seconds. His replacement clone had not cleared it yet. Emma found the disks. Juggling them, she raced back to her desk and fed them into her computer.

All the more sensitive disks were password protected. No problem. Emma fished out from her bag the ribbon of paper she had purloined and pocketed down in Pimlico. Passwords. She had no difficulty prising Striped Shirt's secrets out on to her pale blue screen. Details of ripe plums – potential investors, capital-rich, dripping with funds. Striped Shirt had kept them all to himself. Now they were hers for the picking.

Head down, concentrating hard, one hand controlling the mouse, her other hand jotting down names and contact numbers, Emma worked busily until she heard the approaching hiss of the lift. In less than a minute, the office would be buzzing with noisy late lunchers. Soon, inquisitive faces would be rubber-necking her screen, checking the markets since late morning. What was the FTSI saying? Had the NASDAQ edged up? Was the euro sexy in Bonn?

Emma rejected all the male names, scanning the data base for female monied 'angels'. Women financial backers prepared to invest, long term, for a return of two per cent above the base rate.

But Emma knew she had to be careful. She had to cover her tracks. Approaching the single, rich women could lead her straight back to a vengeful Striped Shirt. And where were they? How could she pick them out – these specific needles buried deep inside Striped Shirt's hi-tech haystack?

Ping. The lift had stopped at the floor below. Sappho's. That club in Mayfair. Sappho's – for rich, single, more mature women. Emma keyed it in – yes. Sixteen names came up. Emma keyed in a further search refinement: a financial base line, with liquid assets of at least half a million plus to play with. The list of names now on screen was reduced to nine.

Before the returning late lunchers had started to mill around her desk for updates, Emma had pocketed the print-out and was virtuously scanning the derivatives bulletin.

'I can't talk. Watson's being unbearable. She's everywhere. Marion's unleased her completely.'

'I can guess. Look,' Emma whispered urgently. 'What are the chances of my coming down? This Saturday night?'

'No. Let things cool off. Too risky –'

'With a team,' Emma continued.

'A team? What the hell do you mean? Are you mad?'

'Nope. Need to shoot a promo video.'

'You are mad.'

'Trouble is, I'll need a couple of hours, say ten to midnight, undisturbed. A completely free hand.'

'Impossible,' Kate hissed.

'If only you could keep Marion and Watson occupied.'

'No way. Absolutely out of the question.'

'I know you'll think of something. Better go now. Love to pussy.'

'Love to pussy,' Kate echoed. Bewildered.

Emma had to make a big sacrifice.

'Very greedy, a bus like that. Very thirsty lady.'

'She's not an alcoholic,' Emma countered. Prepared to make the painful sacrifice, she was not going to be ripped off.

She named her figure. He sucked his breath in as if over a sore tooth.

'Sweet runner. So reliable. Log book's like a health certificate. Regular check-ups,' Emma persuaded, coming down five hundred.

'With BUPA, are you?' He chuckled laconically, coming down another five.

Emma bit her lip. Already a thousand less than she had hoped for. With tears in her eyes, after being thumped hard during an ill-judged attempt at haggling, she settled for two thousand less than expected. Handing over her keys, she patted the sleek rump. But selling The Beast gave her the money. Up front.

'Cash. Up front,' the Australian girl warned, naming her price. 'Is that a problem?'

Emma shook her head and showed her roll of fifties.

'Great. That's the shoot, the editing – twelve minutes – voice over and a portfolio of stills. And we're to go in under cover?'

Emma nodded.

'Animal lib? Free the beagle stuff, eh?'

Emma shook her head. 'Girls' boarding school. Night shoot. Punishments in the dorm.'

'Jeez, no shit,' the Australian girl whispered. 'You mean, like we go in there and shoot these rich young sheilas gettin' it hot and strong?'

Emma nodded. 'That's why I need an all-girl team.'

'You betcha.'

'And no identities. The girls mustn't be identified.'

'No sweat. We can pixie out their mugs post-production.'

Emma handed over the cash. 'Then we've got a deal. I'll be here with transport at six thirty, Saturday.'

'What was all that about?' the MD asked, nodding after Emma's exit and spotting the bundle of fifties.

Shit, the Australian girl thought.

'Interesting little project. Giving a talk on dentistry in Tudor England Saturday night. In Milton Keynes. Wants the seminar on video. Interested? We need a sound man.'

'I'd rather pull my own,' he muttered, crying off.

'You usually do,' she grinned to herself, fingering the fat roll of fifties.

The Sherpa was sluggish after The Beast, but Emma got the van – and the three-girl video team – down to Laments a little after dark.

They chatted as they played cards til eight-fifty, then drank lukewarm mushroom soup and ate cheese and crackers. At ten to ten, Emma went through the final briefing.

In the back of the Sherpa, the video team checked their equipment. Camera. Light. Sound.

'Ready?' Emma whispered.

'Why are you whispering?' Sound asked, puzzled. 'They can't hear us here.'

'We'll keep it down from the moment we leave the van,' Emma cautioned. 'So, are you ready?'

'You bet,' they chorused eagerly.

Emma led them over the wall and through the rain-soaked bushes, keeping under cover until they had reached the stern, brooding Hall. The February moon was huge and unusually bright in the cloudless night.

Camera Girl paused, shouldered the video and panned across the glinting gables in a sweeping long shot. Emma joined her.

'Establishing shots,' she whispered.

'Forget it.' Emma shook her head. 'Too Hammer House of Horror.'

Unshouldering her equipment, Camera Girl giggled. 'OK.'

Emma peered into the inky shadows skirting the Hall. She bit her lower lip. Kate had promised. Something must have –

Mme Puton, lurking in the laurel bushes, terrified the video crew as she emerged. They relaxed immediately as the French mistress greeted Emma in a firm embrace, and a slow, searching kiss.

'Do I get that on tape?' Camera Girl whispered, her eyes taking in Mme Puton's gripping, cupping hands at Emma's bottom.

'Skip it.' Sound shrugged. 'Save your tape for the fillies getting it upstairs in the dorm. Don't shoot til you see the pinks of their cheeks.'

Guided by Mme Puton, the crew tiptoed into the stately gloom of the deserted refectory. There, Camera Girl recorded the neat rows of chairs tucked under the soft gleam of polished wooden tables. A red-velvet-cushioned punishment stool was produced, as was the lectern and Punishment Book. All the ritual and necessary trappings for dispensing discipline and imposing intimate instruction. Camera Girl called softly for more light for some big close-ups.

They trod the darkened corridors down towards the classrooms, entering each one in turn stealthily, leaving Emma on guard at the door. Inside each classroom, the French mistress (fully briefed by Emma through Kate) drew the attention of the lens to the chalk board, allowing it to capture calculus, maps of Eritrea, snatches of Ovid in translation and the scribble of French verbs in the past imperfect.

Sliding open a drawer at the teacher's desk, Mme Puton extracted a yellow length of bamboo cane. It glinted, potent with the promise of pain, as she presented it to the camera. Swishing it twice, she sliced it down, thrumming the chalk dust in the moonbeams. It whispered viciously, raising the nipples of Sound Girl who was checking her flickering needle for level.

At the chalk board, pointing out the verbs, Mme Puton tap-tapped the tip of the quivering cane, softly whispering the tricky conjugations. Turning to face the camera directly, she grasped the end of the whippy cane, bending it almost double.

Camera Girl, her right eye buried in the rubber view-finder, reached down blindly with her left hand to pluck her cotton panties from her moistening plum. Sound Girl knuckled her nipples as they all silently left the classroom to its haunting stillness.

Upstairs in the senior dorm, the girls crowded around Emma, squeaking excitedly. Emma was moved by the warmth of their greeting. Tears softened her wide, grey eyes.

'It's all right, Kate's told us what to do,' they whispered eagerly. 'You want to get some shots of dorm discipline.'

Emma laughed. 'So who wants to be spanked by Mme Puton?'

Sound Girl stepped forward – to be instantly pulled back into line by her colleagues.

'Me, me, me,' peppered the dorm.

Emma raised her hand, placing her finger at her lips for silence.

'Rebecca, I think.'

Camera Girl and her lighting assistant kneeled down for the set-piece shots. Sound Girl, deliciously disturbed by her fiercely peaked nipples at her heavy, aching breasts, stood out of shot, directing the fluffy boom mike down at the bare botton.

'Spank her, for level.'

Mme Puton looked up, appalled. 'It is not possible, just to spank the girl's bare bottom. No, no. That would be *inutile. On ne peut jamais –*'

Emma giggled. 'It's OK. Just clap your hands together. *Comme ça.*'

Mme Puton, her lecture on the etiquette of punishment neatly stemmed, nodded and obliged.

Sound Girl ducked as the ringing crack of hands echoed like a pistol shot. 'Strewth, will it be as loud as that across her arse?'

'*Mais oui, d'accord.*'

Sound girl repositioned herself. 'Better hold it up above the bed,' she explained, edging closer and stretching her arm high. 'I want to capture the exact sound. Get it as clear as a bell. Spanks probably echo unless recorded from above.'

Some tiny adjustments were made to the light source, allowing the strong beam to play across the bare, upturned cheeks.

'OK, silence please,' Emma whispered. 'Go.'

Mme Puton spanked Rebecca Wigmore. It was a classic example of intimate, feminine discipline. Tenderly cruel, sweetly savage and delicately dominant.

'The spanking, it must be the sugared sorrow, no?' the French mistress whispered directly to camera.

Rebecca, spread and pinned down across Mme Puton's dark chocolate-brown nylon-stockinged sheen, nestled her soft nakedness into the lap of her stern chastiser. The Wigmore girl writhed, wobbling her buttocks and showing a glimpse of the shiny fig below her slightly gaping cleft. Mme Puton, ignoring the camera now, gazed dominantly down at her pinioned victim. Her left hand, grasping the nude's neck, suddenly tightened at the nape. Rebecca's buttocks bunched in fearful expectation, and the slight gape of the cleft between the cheeks narrowed to a firm crease.

The dorm fell silent. Across the dark brown stockings, the creamy buttocks tensed. The French mistress, inverting her right, spanking hand, swept her knuckles down across the proffered domes. The delicious cheeks dimpled – inching up their tight satin curves to kiss the knuckles fleetingly.

It was the signal – flesh speaking to flesh – between the punisher and the pinioned nude about to be punished. Then the spanking commenced.

The rest of the senior dorm kneeled in a silent circle out of camera shot as the video team captured every nuance, every intimate detail of the bare bottomed punishment. The steadying palm placed down across the soft, tightly squeezed thighs after the fifth harsh spank. Rebecca's tumble of hair spilling down as she jerked after the seventh. The tightening grip at the nape of the subjugated neck at the eleventh. The cunning pause after the fourteenth spank, allowing the punisher to sweep her hot palm across the reddening cheeks of the wriggling nude.

Camera Girl, kneeling at her task, her thighs parted as her knees whitened into the linoleum, inched her hand down to rub her pussy. Echoing the gesture, her lighting assistant furtively thumbed herself through her denims.

The French mistress administered a four-minute, twenty-six-stroke spanking, leaving Rebecca, the video team, and all the silent, wide-eyed schoolgirls soaking wet. Bending down, tenderly dominant, Mme Puton gently kissed each ravished cheek, burying her face in both blazing buttocks.

'We'll edit that last bit out,' Emma whispered.

Like hell we will, Camera Girl thought, glad she had it all on zoom.

'What now?' Olympia Scott-Hammerton hissed excitedly, her lust sparkling in her large eyes. 'Would you like to video me being caned? Across the bare bottom? Me, bending and touching my toes, being caned across my naughty bum?'

The video crew agreed readily.

'No, me,' big-bottomed Charlotte Bicknell squealed.

'Me, please, me.'

All the dorm seemed to want to be caned by Mme Puton.

Emma, smiling, made a snap decision. 'Tonight,' she announced, 'Olympia will bare her bottom for a straight six.'

The disappointed losers glared at the lucky winner. Mme Puton produced the cane with a flourish. A lethal twenty-one inches of silvery white bambusa.

In the gym, all but one of the lights were out. Frozen in the single beam, across the back of the vaulting horse, naked and bound at her feet and ankles, Kate grunted into her gag. Marion snarled as she rummaged in the long cricket bag of instruments unzipped at her feet, muttering her satisfaction as she fished out and lovingly gripped a leather-backed paddle.

Swipe. She cracked the paddle down into the hide of the plump horse. Kate winced, tensed then dissolved into a trembling shudder. The ripples from the swiping paddle's impact, the savage caress of leather upon leather, reached Kate's belly tight across the hide. As her flesh sensed and soaked up the tiny tremors and the promise of imminent pain, her bound wrists writhed helplessly in their bondage.

Marion lowered the leather face of the spanking paddle down gently and flattened Kate's bare buttocks.

'In a moment, a moment I and only I shall choose, this will crack down across your helpless buttocks. I want you to imagine it, bitch. Take the thought inwards. Savour it, as it dwells within. Let the fear taste sour in your mouth. Let the fear drag its icy finger down along the length of your spine. Let the fear,' she hissed venomously, crushing the leathered bat down into Kate's soft bottom, 'grow slowly behind your tightly shut eyes.'

Seven feet away, in the darkness, Watson writhed naked upon a four-metre-square coconut mat. Squeezing and cupping her breasts, she raked her naked buttocks into the fierce fabric. Dragging her hands down between her clamped thighs, she drew them together, palms inwards, before punishing her wet pussy. Masturbating for the third time, Watson raked her naked cheeks across the harsh prickle of the matting, drinking in every dominant snarl from the tormentress at the horse, and every smothered moan from the nude bound across the fat horse's hide.

A two-hour diversion. That's what Emma pleaded for. Shit. Marion's had me for less than an hour, Kate calculated. Another seventy minutes of this nightmare to endure. It had better be worth it, Emma. It had better be –

Splatt. Kate's train of thought smashed into the buffers as Marion plied the paddle down, searing the helpless buttocks below.

Up in the senior dorm, Mme Puton flicked the pale bambusa up, controlling the whippy wood adroitly as she brought it up into Olympia's nipples. Depressing the wand of woe into the bulging breasts, the French mistress tamed and controlled them with sweet severity.

'Feet together for the first two strokes,' she murmured, withdrawing her cane back against her chocolate-brown stocking. The thin shaft of silver wood rasped softly at the sheen.

Olympia, hands arrowing down obediently, fingers splayed out across her toes, trod the linoleum as she scrunched her naked ankles together. Under the imperious gaze of the French mistress, the bare bottom bulged as it submitted to the cane.

'Jeez, this is great,' Camera Girl whispered. 'Are you getting all this?'

Sound Girl, spellbound, twisted her face around and nodded.

'*Le premier coup. La deuxieme.*' Mme Puton announced the first two strokes in delicious French, raising the supple cane up above the buttocks before whipping it down at an angle of 45 degrees into the proffered cheeks.

Olympia squealed twice as pinkish weals appeared where the slicing cane had kissed her soft curves.

'Feet a little further apart.'

The cleft darkened and deepened as Olympia obeyed, slowly inching her thighs apart. Unhurriedly, Mme Puton

211

tap-tapped the end of the cane down on to her naked, bending victim's soft neck, dominatingly depressing the caned girl's head into abject submission.

'*La troisieme. La quatrieme.*' The third and fourth slicing strokes swiped down at a less acute angle, adding two fresh angry weals a little below the first two. As the former strokes darkened from pale blue to a livid indigo, the latter burned a deeper shade of scarlet.

'And now, feet wide apart, *s'il vous plait.*'

A soft sob escaped Olympia's lips. The French mistress instantly brought the tip of her cane up to silence the sniffling. Olympia kissed the quivering bamboo that had just kissed her buttocks.

'A little wider, *ma petite.*'

All assembled watched in utter silence as Olympia jerked her buttocks up, spreading her thighs even wider apart. Both cheeks were tightly curved now. Their striped satin skin stretched painfully across the straining buttocks.

'*Tres bon.*' Mme Puton levelled her cane an inch away from the swollen cheeks. The clouded bamboo sparkled as it bisected the dark cleft. Under the strong beam of light directed by Camera Girl's assistant, Olympia's tiny little sphincter winked with wet, pink impudence down between her bulging buttocks.

'*La cinquieme,*' the French mistress whispered, jerking the cane away then swishing it savagely inwards. '*Et la sixieme. Voila,*' she cried, lashing the bare buttocks then turning to address the camera. '*Voila,*' she inclined her head, saluting the lens by shouldering her clouded cane.

Olympia remained bending. Across her bare bottom, six searing weals darkened in their purpling pain.

'I don't think you'd better tape the next bit,' Emma warned, knowing that Olympia's caned bottom was about to receive and enjoy some delicious aftercare.

'I won't,' Camera Girl lied, leaving the record button depressed.

Kneeling down before the bottom she had just beaten, Mme Puton lowered her face down into its cane-striped curves. Tongue-tip flickering, she began to trace the fiery,

212

horizontal stripes, steadying the nude between her controlling hands as Olympia threatened to buckle at the knees in ecstasy.

Down in the gym, Marion Aylott-Inche fingered out the golf-ball-size rubber-spiked sphere from Kate's ravished slit. Palming the wet, prickly rubber sea urchin, she enclosed it within her fist. Opening her hand, she gazed down at it for several minutes before almost reluctantly switching her gaze to Kate's juicy sphincter.

Bending down across the vaulting horse, she crushed her breasts dominantly into Kate's punished bottom. She grunted as her nipples kissed the hot cheeks. Easing her bosom up a fraction, she reached down between Kate's splayed thighs to check the wedge between them that kept the thighs forced wide apart, stretching the bare buttocks above and the glinting sphincter between them.

Marion brought the prickly spined sphere to the wet anal crater, teasing the puckering flesh as she dragged the torment down along the velvet valley of the cleft. Kate squealed long and loud as her hot anal rosebud suffered. And squealed even louder in her dread of what was about to occur.

Positioning the sphere between the whipped cheeks, the gym mistress suddenly fisted her knuckles tightly and pushed – driving the softly spined ball deep into Kate's muscled heat. Kate, helpless in her bondage at both wrists and ankles, jerked and bucked as her sphincter stretched and burned. She barrelled her belly across the smooth hide of the vaulting horse, grinding her seething slit into its hardness as the rubbery spikes raked her rectal softness. Despite the tight gag, Kate's thin moan of dark delight echoed around the gym.

Marion, slightly detached, ignored her victim's anguish for seven long merciless minutes then returned to the writhing cheeks to talon and squeeze their ripeness. To talon and squeeze ruthlessly, bunching their rubbery flesh viciously to contain the torment within.

Six and a half minutes later, the gym mistress rested the crop she had been lashing down across the suffering

213

buttocks. Thumbing open Kate's wet anal hole, she fingered out the softly spined sphere. As Kate sobbed brokenly into the scuffed hide at her face, Marion strode out into the darkness, pausing when her feet met the stubble of the coconut matting.

'Up,' she whispered. 'Open your mouth. I have a little treat for you.'

Like a seal, Watson craned her neck up, mouth stretched wide.

'Good.' Marion dropped the sticky spined sphere down. Watson snapped at it, caught it between her teeth, then closed her eyes and lips, sucking and chewing hungrily.

'Well done,' Marion muttered, absently patting Watson's head. 'I told you I would reward you well.'

Like a seal at its fish treat, Watson writhed sinuously on the prickling coconut matting.

'What time is it? Emma asked.

'Who cares?' Camera Girl murmured, back from the loo after a three-way wank with her crew.

'Eleven-seventeen,' Rebecca Wigmore announced, still basking in the glow of her spanking and Mme Puton's tender aftercare.

'I'd like to punish Ann Cordery,' Emma remarked.

'Who wouldn't?' Camera Girl muttered.

'As a demonstration of Laments' intimate instruction. But time's tight.'

Behind her curtaining fringe, Ann Cordery's dark eyes danced.

'I've got to squeeze in a quick interview with Dr Flint. Come on.'

The French mistress, after tucking all the girls into their beds and kissing them all lingeringly goodnight, accompanied Emma and the video crew down along the darkness of the landing.

'Where's Kate?' Emma suddenly demanded.

Mme Puton seemed not to hear the question. Emma persisted.

'She is – how are you saying it? Ah, *oui* – she is playing the diversion. Tonight, she keeps the gym mistress occupied. And the creature Watson. She too is busy with Kate. Until midnight.'

'And Watson?' Emma murmured, wondering.

'And the creature Watson,' Mme Puton whispered.

'I wish I knew what she was up to. Whatever it is,' Emma mused, 'it's working. This way.'

Dr Flint refused to respond to the deferential tap at her door.

Emma knocked again. Louder.

The door was wrenched open. The Head, eyes flashing angrily, stood in total astonishment at the group gathered on the landing in the darkness.

'What the hell?'

'Nice to see you, too,' Emma giggled, kissing Felicity Flint. 'Quick, now,' she bustled. 'I want to take you at your desk –'

'Just what is going on here, Emma? And how did you –'

'No time. Trust me. Mme Puton will explain everything later.'

'She most certainly will,' Dr Flint muttered grimly. 'Is that a video camera? Here? In Laments?'

'Yep,' Emma replied happily. 'We've been shooting punishments in the dorm.'

'You've been what?' the Head gurgled.

Emma giggled. 'Shush. It's OK, honestly. No identities revealed. Just trust me.'

'I do. But –'

'Then sit at your desk. And try to look as severe as you can. Really stern headmistressy stuff.'

'Don't I always?' the Head challenged, bridling.

'Not really. You're quite sweet, actually,' Emma murmured, propelling the astounded Felicity Flint backwards and down into the chair at her desk. 'Kate's keeping Aylott-Inche and Watson busy.'

'Don't mention that treacherous woman's name to me,' Dr Flint thundered. 'And as for that snake Watson –'

'Yes, yes,' Emma soothed. 'But we won't be disturbed for the next ten minutes or so. That just about gives us enough time.'

Emma briefly explained.

Addressing the video camera with remarkable aplomb – and betraying an unsuspected knowledge of lighting technique, medium close-ups and the use of the tracking pan shot – the Head spoke unblinkingly into the lens, delivering a faultless four-minute sermon extolling the work, method and results of Laments. Warming to her theme, Dr Flint's voice acquired a rich resonance as she concluded with a ringing endorsement of the merits of pain, punishment and strict discipline.

'Hey,' Sound Girl cried as the video crew wrapped it all up. 'Isn't that –'

'Probably.' Emma grinned. 'She knows them all.'

She dragged Sound Girl away from the picture of a bronzed Aussie tennis star gazing sternly down from the wall.

after kissing and hugging Dr Flint reassuringly, Emma hurried the video crew out into the darkness of midnight.

'See you with the trustees,' Emma promised, leaving the Head open-mouthed at her study door.

'I've an idea,' Sound Girl murmured.

'What?'

'Facilities. Sports. Have you got a pool here? We could just squeeze a shot in. Or a gym.'

'*Mais non*,' Mme Puton, fluttering anxiously, dismissed the idea instantly. Tapping her watch, she urged Emma to depart.

Or a gym. Emma froze. Shit. Kate was in there. Right now. Tasting Aylott-Inche's cruel appetite for brutal bullying. Kate's diversion – sacrifice – to ensure Emma's success.

Tears scalded her grey eyes. 'She's in there. With them? Isn't she?'

Mme Puton embraced Emma, comforting her. '*Ma petite*, there was no other way. But her suffering is nearly over now. You must not spoil everything. Not now.'

But Emma, hot faced and blinded by her tears, forced her way past the French mistress. Four minutes later, they were all shivering in a huddle outside the gym.

'I knew it.'

Peeping through the window, Emma had glimpsed all her worst fears in the flesh. The naked flesh.

'They're both in there. Kate's tied up across that wretched vaulting horse.' Emma could not bring herself to actually utter the words to describe the dildo-torture she had briefly witnessed.

The Australians inched up to the window.

'Strewth,' Sound girl murmured, 'that's some heavy duty shit going on in there.'

'Don't,' Mme Puton pleaded, restraining Emma's instinctive urge to dash inside and free Kate. 'If you go in now, all is lost. All her sacrifice will be wasted. I will go in, I promise, and put an end to it once you have safely made the departure.'

After a brief but bitter battle with herself, Emma reluctantly agreed.

'OK. But point that camera through the window. No lights or sound. Just see what you can get.'

Ten

Tucked behind the unassuming stucco of the white Mayfair Georgian façade was the most exclusive club in the land. It took Emma several phone calls, a working lunch, two personal visits and a final tug on the 'lavender line' (the Old School Tie network equivalent for City women) to secure the private conference facility for lunch and a seminar on the 26th.

Emma knew she was cutting it fine. Very fine. The trustees were converging at Laments to decide Dr Flint's future the following day. The Australian girls edited the video sharply, exactly as Emma had requested. She spent the remaining days checking tax opportunities, trustee law and the financial health of comparable institutions.

Sappho's. The most exclusive club in the land. It was not notorious, its all-female membership preferring discretion. Nor was it sumptuously opulent, its patronesses opting for elegant comfort. But it still overwhelmed Emma. Even the receptionist, tricked out like an opera diva, seemed to have a PhD in attitude. Emma was double checked before being escorted up to the third floor.

She had planned lunch as a simple affair. Quails' eggs in saffron aspic, authentic sushi, Tiger prawns served with diced swordfish all washed down with either chilled rosé or jasmine tea. Easy grazing for busy businesswomen. She inspected the buffet anxiously. Impeccable. And not too clever. Emma had to be careful. Cleverness was so easily mistaken for contempt. They wouldn't eat much. 'Clittylickers' – Emma knew the men'sroom term for successful women city-slickers – usually fed on raw adrenalin and Splitzers. The rosé was chilled to perfection, ready to drink at exactly the right temperature of 4.7 degrees.

Emma had RSVP'd nine potential clients. All had confirmed through e-mail or their personal assistants. Nibbling on a quail's egg, Emma checked the time – 12.54 p.m. Eight minutes later, all nine chairs in the reception were occupied by women.

Emma surveyed them covertly. Mostly dressed in dark grey, with a silver or gold pinstripe. Designer blouses from Milan. Expensive shoes. Little make-up, no jewellery. Plenty of hey-look-I-must-be-important hi-tech toys.

All her clients were ignoring the buffet, saving their appetite for the red meat of Emma's financial pitch. At her suggestion, they sat, arms defensively folded, mentally steeling themselves to repel either hard sell or seductive persuasion. It was going to be tougher than she thought, Emma suddenly realised. Thank goodness I'm not pushing yet another dot-com window to jump headfirst through.

Briefly introducing herself, boosting her marketing and financial management CV more than was strictly truthful, Emma dimmed the lights and played the video. The audience of nine impeccably dressed businesswomen oozed self-assurance and poise. Within minutes, they were enthralled, gazing wide eyed and open mouthed as the images from the cleverly edited, sharply cut video filled the wide screen.

Three sequences in particular would get them, Emma calculated. One was coming up. Now. Mme Puton, pinning Rebecca's neck firmly down then spanking her bunched cheeks in a brisk, ringing staccato. Emma heard several pleasurable gasps break out in the darkness. Good. Next bit. Coming up. Now. The French mistress inspecting the Wigmore girl's reddened bottom. That gentle pinching up of the punished flesh. So pliant. So rubbery. And that thumbtip sweeping along the hot cleft. Emma was rewarded by the sound of dry throats trying to swallow. Shit, it's steaming. One more big close-up. What was it? Yes, of course. Here it comes. A real panty soaker. The cane quelling the writhing buttocks of Olympia. Three strokes in and Mme Puton had dominated the bottom she was whipping by depressing the clouded cane down firmly to trap and tame the delicious cheeks. In the ambient blue light from the screen, Emma could have sworn she saw expensively manicured nails inch inwards to scratch at erect, tormenting nipples straining at the taut stretch of designer silk. Eight minutes into the tape, precisely, Emma pressed pause. Turning up the lights, she suggested lunch.

They raided the rosé, swallowing it down greedily to lubricate their dry mouths. Loosen their tightened throats. Encouraging them informally to nibble, Emma returned to her desk and, after selecting a portfolio of blown-up stills from the video – the spanking hand frozen at the heat of Rebecca's punished cheeks, the cane Judas-kissing Olympia's bruised peaches – distributed them casually among her clients. Carefully and expensively groomed heads bowed down, enraptured by the graphic stills. Tiger prawns remained unbitten as mouths drooled over plumper flesh – the punished fruits of Eve.

Her audience returned to their seats. After explaining why Laments needed inward investment, and the financial projections to be gained from prudent expansion, Emma launched directly into the financial package. She was managing the sale of £100,000 options. Each had a minimum five-year term tie-in. The return was two per cent over base rate. Options, she warned, were limited. After five years, preference would be accorded to those already on board wishing to extend or increase their stakehold.

Several technical questions were asked. Emma responded fully and frankly, thankful that she had done the ground work on tax spread-overs, trusteeships, 'Lien law' and charitable status rules regarding capitalisation. She saved her clincher for the last questioner.

'Inward investment, as you are well aware, into an educational foundation attracts generous tax discounts.'

They stiffened to attention. She had earned their grudging respect, and now had them on the edge of their seats:

sexually and financially aroused. Judging the psychological moment exactly, Emma turned, dimmed the lights and played the tape. Dr Flint addressed them with a direct sincerity that gripped. Her stern voice, august demeanour and imperious grandeur did Emma's campaign little harm. Dr Flint's eloquence on the vital role of corporal punishment in the rehabilitation of delinquent young ladies had them all nodding vigorously in agreement. As the Head briefly but graphically expounded the policy, principles and practice of intimate instruction, three or four actually stood up and applauded.

The video closed with a lingering close-up of Olympia Scott-Hammerton's freshly caned bottom. Emma fingered the freeze frame. Standing by the wide screen, she caressed the image of the whipped cheeks lingeringly.

'One can almost feel the heat.' She smiled. Changing gear after the tease, she grew stern. 'The spoiled and privileged young ladies consigned to Laments for intimate instruction are swiftly brought to heel. Sadly, some have to suffer the strict regime and severe punishments for over a year before finally coming to their senses.' Emma paused. 'But that merely ensures the pleasure of profit for all financial backers.'

Eager questions were asked. Emma countered them by ensuring that every potential investor was given both a copy of the video and a portfolio of disturbingly delicious stills.

'There is absolutely no need to rush into any decision. This investment opportunity remains open to you all for at least another two, perhaps three months,' Emma lied. 'Get your people to run over the figures. In all matters of finance, even when there is no element of risk, it pays to be cautious.'

The ultimate tease. She was talking to risk-takers. Big players. Get your people to look over the figures. As if they were dizzy debs buying their first SW3 flat. These women disregarded actuarial tables, odds-on wagers and cautious gilts – that was why they were rich. That was why they were here.

221

Emma was right in her judgement. It was no longer a matter of finance. Their questioning took a more intimate turn. Tell me more about Laments. How many strokes of the cane does a girl get for swearing? Is the paddle used? On the bare? Do the forfeits include undertaking menial tasks? Naked? Why don't the young ladies wear uniforms – opaque tights, cropped vests?

Emma encouraged the excited women to lunch. The authentic sushi, Tiger prawns and swordfish yielded the fresh tang of a salt sea breeze. Emma sniffed the air, immediately detecting the feral whiff of the elegantly dressed women's sexual seethe.

Two of the shrewdest, most hard-boiled started to probe Emma on technical points of tax set-aside discounting. Emma did not want to lose the advantage she had gained to dry detail. She played the tape again. Deep into the caning of Olympia's swollen cheeks, Emma noticed that the two shrewd operators were pretending to tap calculations into their laptops, but were actually drumming their pubic mounds. This time, she played the tape straight through. When it was over, she nailed them.

'Of course, those of you who eventually decide to take up an investment option will gain the entitlement to spend three weekends each academic year as a guest down at Laments. Almost like honorary school governors. But no paperwork, or tedious committees.' SDhe laughed.

They laughed.

'And of course, you will not have to suffer the spartan, boarding school fare. Dr Flint will entertain you royally. No duff or stodge.' She laughed.

They laughed again. Putty in her hands.

'You will have a chance to see Laments first hand. And as every bare bottom you witness being punished will affirm, your investment will be as sound as it proves profitable.'

The questions came thick and fast. They could have been ball-girls down on the Centre Court mobbing an ace for an autograph.

'Three weekends?'

'Actually shadowing a mistress?'

'And allowed to witness punishments?'

'May one go on dorm patrol?'

Emma raised a calming hand. 'During your weekend sojourns at Laments, you will enjoy a hands-on opportunity to track your investment.'

The nailer. Deliciously ambiguous. Teasingly explicit.

'A hands-on opportunity to participate in the regime at Laments, the strict regime of intimate instruction.'

Emma's voice was drowned out as contracts and cheques were eagerly signed and dated.

Down at reception, the opera diva behind the desk fawned on each departing client and pointedly ignored Emma. Fuck it, Emma blazed. I've just done a million-pound deal and she treats me like shit. I'd like to get her across my knee!

Emma suddenly giggled. She wanted to be down at Laments. Away from the brittle glass jungle of Mayfair and the concrete thickets of the Square Mile. Everything here was twisted, distorted. Down at Laments, all were equal when naked. True worth became apparent under the lash. Emma leaned across the reception desk and stared directly into the bored eyes of the snotty receptionist.

'If my schedule wasn't so tight I'd bare your backside and cane it until one of us came.'

Emma banked the £1,000,000 at her Brompton Road branch. She didn't feel triumphant. Just curiously tired. Not unsurprisingly, she was dealt with by the manageress.

'Coffee?'

'I could use a phone.'

The manageress pushed the phone across her desk.

Watson answered. Emma disguised her voice, raising an interested eyebrow in the chair opposite. Emma asked for Kate. Insurance.

'That will not be possible,' Watson replied primly. 'I'm afraid she is indisposed and unable to receive any calls, or callers.'

Out in the busy Brompton Road, Emma saw the conga line of black taxis through tear-filled eyes. Oh Kate. Dear

Kate. What have they done to you? How you must have suffered.

Her success at Sappho's an hour since was instantly forgotten as Emma, who had just banked the million, sat down on the steps of her Brompton Road branch and furrowed her brow in concern for her beloved.

The trustees of Laments, a rural dean, three tweedy matrons of the Shires and a sharp-nosed solicitor called Bentham were shepherded into a classroom and directed behind uncomfortable desks. Watson served milky tea and damp digestives, simperingly assisted by Tweedledum and Tweedledee. Emma, seasoned in the City, felt she was at the AGM of a failing textiles firm. All bullshit and bluster. But the atmosphere was tense – as if the MD was about to be arrested on the steps outside. Emma returned Marion's glare and sat at the back, mechanically breaking a digestive into a pyramid of crumbs. She looked up, flashing a grin, as Dr Flint, Kate and Mme Puton entered quietly and sat alongside her behind the slightly balding rural dean.

Marion steam-rollered them, like an MD bluffing through a massive trading loss to ordinary shareholders up for the day. Twice she managed to crush the assiduous Bentham. She was arrogant in her presentation, weak in actual financial strategy, grandiloquent in her own prospective headship of Laments. The trustees tried to pin her down on specifics, but the gym mistress was dismissive.

'I demand full governance of Laments. Under my iron rod, a stricter regime will be imposed. Costs will be cut. Savings will be made.'

It went on like that until the milky tea in the china cups turned cold. The trustees, bridling, stirred restlessly in the strictures of their cramped wooden desks. Marion Aylott-Inche, in full megalomanic flow, ignored both their questions and their evident discomfort.

'Laments will survive,' she promised, 'with me at the helm. Appoint me as Head and there will be no more slipshod decision making –'

Emma rose. 'If I may now ask you all to accompany me to the refectory –'

'How dare you?' the gym mistress thundered.

'That will do, Aylott-Inche. You have had quite enough to say,' Dr Flint barked.

Grateful to escape their desks, the trustees rose up and followed Emma into the refectory. There, Kate and Mme Puton treated them to moist little fingers of madeira cake and a sound port. Settling comfortably into their seats and refreshments, they were more than willing to give audience to Emma.

She took a glass of port from Mme Puton, toasted their health and sipped. She nursed her glass to her bosom. 'I have been privileged to spend a little time here at Laments as the guest of Dr Flint.'

'No, that's a lie,' Marion cried. 'She was going to employ you. Give you a position here.'

The rural dean quivered at the accusatory epithet 'lie'. The solicitor, Bentham, urged moderation.

'She is a liar.'

Bentham rebuked the gym mistress. Nodding benignly to Emma to continue, he sipped deeply from his port.

'Dr Flint did extend to me the opportunity to conduct some cost-analysis and undertake certain financial feasibility studies.'

Watson's catlike green eyes narrowed viciously. Her spectacles flashed as she tossed her head back. 'Marion is the bursar at Laments. Dr Flint –'

'Appears to have lost confidence in her sometime deputy,' Emma countered suavely. 'Cutting the young ladies' diet down to the bone can only alienate those paying for their upkeep while securing minimal savings within the overall budget.'

The tweedy matrons from the Shires agreed. Growing girls needed feeding. False economy, cutting back at table, they opined in unison.

'But Marion –' Watson whined.

'Be quiet, woman,' the rural dean roared. Adding in a stage whispered aside to Bentham, 'Dammed woman. Who the hell is she, anyway?'

Emma avoided grinning by sipping her port as Watson reddened and squirmed.

'Here are my recommendations which I believe Dr Flint has initially endorsed, subject, of course, to your approval.'

The trustees, mollified by Emma's subtle psychology, nodded gently. Bentham and the rural dean beamed.

'The number of pupils, currently eighteen, could be quite easily increased to twenty-four.'

'Preposterous. As bursar I have absolutely –'

'Neglected to ensure the conditions for controlled growth and reasonable expansion in the core area of your revenue source.' Emma, gloves off, was jabbing sharply. That punch winded the gym mistress, leaving her gasping on the ropes.

'Your fees,' Emma murmured, 'are too low. Your illustrious clients are having their problems sorted out for them at a huge discount. After all, it costs over eight hundred pounds a week to keep a young lady in Holloway Prison. Laments could quite easily demand a comparable fee.'

The rural dean choked quietly on his moist finger of sponge. Bentham the solicitor on his mirth.

'A random survey of past and present parents and guardians confirms this. The Wigmores are willing to go up to a thousand to keep Rebecca out of the courts and the tabloid headlines.'

Marion, red faced and blustering, made a last ditch attempt to sabotage Emma. The trustees silenced her instantly.

Emma changed gear. 'I have secured the management of an investment portfolio of one million pounds. I am prepared to plough that investment into Laments on three conditions. Dr Flint remains as Head of Laments, enjoying your full support. The sports curriculum is to be changed with immediate effect to tennis, and Marion Aylott-Inche is to be removed because of this.'

Emma simply had to press the button. The monitor and tape were put in place earlier. The screen showed the two and a quarter minutes of footage shot through the gym window. It was of poor quality and lacked a sound track. But the images were vivid, depicting Marion and Watson, both naked, using both a crop and a dildo on a bound, naked but unidentifiable victim. The trustees had individually and collectively made up their minds before the tape had run for ninety seconds.

'Outrageous,' the tweedy matrons crowed.

'Woman's an absolute bounder,' the rural dean roared, crossing his legs to conceal his erection.

'What we have just witnessed, fellow trustees, could readily merit a custodial sentence for the bursar and strict censure from the bench for us.'

Aylott-Inche sagged at the knees under Emma's knock-out blow.

The girls had been confined to their dorms all day. They were becoming increasingly restive. Mme Puton popped upstairs from time to time to spank the more obviously boisterous who had dared to step out of line. But the girls soon got wind of the turmoil breaking out below.

By teatime, they had the essential facts.

'Miss Rathbone's retiring.'

'She'll take Monteagle with her. Inseparable, those two.'

'Watson's for the chop.'

'Hurray.'

By five thirty, Mme Puton could not detain the girls any longer. Watson, struggling with her hastily packed cases, was spotted scuttling down the drive. Mme Puton unleashed the girls, urging them with Gallic insouciance to be sure to give the good secretary a very warm sending-off.

In the Head's study, Emma, Kate and Felicity Flint were deep in detailed discussion. The trustees had gone. Tweedledum and Tweedledee were to depart forthwith, their future secured by a generous pension. Marion would be dealt with at their leisure. Dr Flint was eager to discuss the new curriculum proposal the trustees had endorsed. Total tennis.

The sudden outburst in the drive brought all three to the study window's leaded panes.

227

'It's Watson, decamping. Look,' Kate squeaked, 'the girls are hounding her down to the gates.'

'Outrageous.' Dr Flint chuckled heartily.

'Shouldn't worry,' Kate remarked. 'Mme Puton's on duty this evening. I'm sure she knows what she's doing.'

Unperturbed, they watched as the girls tossed Watson's cases over the wrought iron gates then turned their attention to their shivering captive. Watson shivered even more when partially stripped of her coat, skirt and stockings. The girls frog-marched the shrieking secretary back up the drive, dumping her down on the front stone steps of Laments Hall. The weasel, source of so much of their torment and suffering, squirmed as her bare buttocks kissed the cold stone.

Mme Puton supervised the girls. Leather belts, rubber-soled pumps and supple leather slippers were distributed into eager, outstretched hands. The French mistress graciously supplied a couple of whippy bamboo canes, ensuring that all eighteen girls gripped an instrument of punishment.

Watson was dragged to her feet. Rebecca Wigmore began to intone the charges, but the rest of the impatient girls cried out a loud guilty. They gagged her and bound her hands together at her belly. The secretary's eyes were wild above her gag but seemed to glint in anticipation, too.

Lining up to form a guard of dishonour, the girls trotted down the drive in the gathering dusk, whipping Watson's bare buttocks with their belts and canes, and crimsoning her naked cheeks with slippers, pumps and leathered paddles. Impelled by belt, bat and bamboo, the secretary, howling into her gag, stumbled twice. Rising in her misery, she offered her whipped cheeks up invitingly for a renewed onslaught. The rain of pain lashed down unmercifully. Soon her buttocks were blisteringly ablaze.

At the wrought iron gates, they loosened the bonds at her wrists. After forcing her to bend, each girl plied her instrument of punishment one more time.

She scrambled inelegantly up and over the wrought iron gates, desperate to escape the pupils' contemptuous wrath.

'The girls are a little frisky this evening,' Dr Flint murmured, nodding approvingly at the muted screams of the former secretary down at the wrought iron gates.

Kate, at the window, could just make out the image of Watson being beaten into banishment. 'Do them good to let off a little steam, Head. They've been cooped up all day.'

'And Mme Puton is there, overseeing things,' Emma grinned. There would be no tender aftercare for the weasel, she thought. Emma had seen Mme Puton clutching the vinegar, salt and pepper to her bosom. To be applied to the ravaged cheeks of the whipped secretary any moment now. French dressing. Emma hugged her breasts tightly, shivering with delight at the thought of the French mistress drizzling pure pain on to the weasel's whipped cheeks.

'Mme Puton will see that justice is done,' Kate remarked.

'No doubt she will,' Dr Flint agreed, chuckling. 'I'm sure our French mistress has everything in hand.'

Joining Kate at the window, threading her arm around the dark-eyed girl's waist, Emma peered out into the azure twilight that threatened to darken to violet within minutes. They could just make out events down at the wrought iron gate. Emma's hand found Kate's and squeezed it gently. They watched as Watson scrambled, bare buttocked, over the top. Behind her, dominantly in control, Mme Puton used the paddle viciously on the cheeks she had just drenched with the stinging sear of her French dressing.

That night, they slept in Kate's bed. Emma undressed quickly and scrambled under the duvet, her soft bottom dimpling the pillows as she slid down into the dark warmth.

Kate stripped slowly, lingeringly, forcing Emma to emerge from the duvet flushed and impatient.

'Quickly,' Emma squeaked, aching to embrace.

Kate, shrugging off her unbuttoned blouse, was down to her silk scanties. Her breasts filled the cups of her brassiere with their swollen warmth. As she bent down to thumb away her panties, her bosom spilled forward and wobbled deliciously, the cleavage dark and tempting between the bulging breasts. Emma taloned the duvet's satin in sharp appreciation, and anticipation. Rising, kicking away her panties that had become entangled at her toes, Kate drew her hands up below her hunched shoulder blades, exposing her dark nest to Emma's feasting eyes.

'Please,' the blonde on the bed whimpered, her own pussy pulsing juice as it purred.

Kate unhooked her brassiere, flipped it away into the shadows and gently palmed her swollen breasts. Bluish bruises showed where Marion had been brutal. Emma cried out.

'You can kiss them better in a moment,' Kate teasingly promised.

As Emma watched, enthralled, Kate tenderly cupped her breasts so that her fingertips just touched within their cleavage. She spread her fingers wide, almost squeezing the bulging breasts with dimpling fingertips before raking her thumbtips down over her dark, engorged nipples.

The gesture drew a carnal whimper from Emma's parted lips, and a silvery trickle from her pouting labia below. 'Please,' she whined, bunching the satin between her knees. Slumping on to all fours, her bare buttocks straining up behind her, Emma craned her face towards the pleasurably punished nipples. Stretching her tongue out painfully, the blonde begged aloud for the bare bosom.

Kate paced softly towards the bed.

'She hurt you,' Emma mumbled. 'Emma kiss it better.'

Like lovers the world over, they lapsed into baby-talk, their feverish whisperings muffled as the warm flesh of Kate's breast filled Emma's wet mouth.

At the bed, bending, her legs astride, Kate eased back a fraction and used her nipples across Emma's mouth like a lipstick. On the bed, kneeling, her soft thighs splayed, Emma bowed her head down before offering her face up submissively to the swollen orbs above.

The thick, stubby nipples dragged across her upper lip. Emma moaned. The thick, rubbery little buds raked her slippery lower lip. Emma groaned. Shrugging off her fleeting subjugation to the dominant bosom, the blonde rose up proudly and encircled the brunette's bottom. Drawing Kate towards her, she bumped the soft breasts deliberately into her face, relishing the shudder of their satin warmth, then slowly kissed them. Kissed, then licked, every square millimetre of their softness. At Emma's belly, Kate's dark bush prickled deliciously. Emma swept her belly from side to side. Soon her skin had captured a smear of Kate's weeping scald.

They collapsed down into the satin, wriggling and writhing, each frantic in their desire. Naked and impassioned, they were well matched. Perfectly poised in the equilibrium of their lust. Palms caressed thighs, then hands cupped and squeezed submissive buttocks. Clefts were stretched to the limit of their sweet ache. Wet fingertips scrabbled at seething slits. Briefly, Emma rode Kate's breasts with her squashed cheeks, burying the bosom beneath her hot bottom, screaming as a nipple pierced her sphincter's wet heat. Briefly, Kate rode Emma, bringing her stinging slit to the blonde's tongue.

They rolled apart, bosom unpeeling from bosom, their pubic nests parting with a soft crackle. Panting, they held hands. It was suddenly understood. Unspoken, but understood. They had reached a sexual impasse. Drowning helplessly in their delicious desire, they both wanted to dominate and be dominated. Each yearning to own and be owned by the other.

Kate, an accomplished spanker, the natural dominant, was now softened and gentled by Emma's sweet affection and sharp desire.

Emma, emboldened after tasting the sharp fruits of dispensing discipline, no longer meekly submissive in those sharp desires.

Their hands gripped tightly. Sexual knowledge flowed from skin to skin, from vein to vein, from pulse to echoing pulse.

In silence, each sought the other. Entwining, the blonde brought her mouth to the brunette's slit. Embracing, the brunette buried her lips into the blonde's wet heat. Cradling each other's head between clamped thighs, they rocked and moaned. Soon the silence of their bed was broken only by the soft sucking and lapping sounds as both surrendered in the primal, mutual flesh-kiss perfected by Lesbos and her bond-maidens so many centuries before.

Marion Aylott-Inche was escorted down to Felicity Flint's study at nine-fifteen the following morning. The Head had breakfasted lightly.

'My only appetite is for her pain,' she had remarked, refusing the proffered plateful of bacon and eggs in the refectory.

The gym mistress was scheduled to depart at noon. All the arrangements had been attended to – the packing completed, the hire car ordered. To depart at noon. To leave Laments in disgrace, denied a penny's compensation. At noon, the gym mistress would face her uncertain future far away from Laments, but for the rest of the morning, Marion was the Head's, to be punished as Felicity Flint pleased.

Kate and Emma bundled the gym mistress into the study. Marion, strong and dangerous, shrugged their gripping hands away and glared at them.

'I wish to speak with you, Flint. There is the matter of my severance settlement to discuss before I leave. I've discovered a penalty clause in my contract –'

'The only matter to settle, Aylott-Inche, before I throw you out, is the penalty I propose to make you pay.'

Marion paled visibly. Rallying, she protested hotly. 'I deserve to be rewarded for all I have done here at Laments!'

'You shall certainly be fully rewarded,' the Head murmured suavely, rising from her desk and unfastening the cuff of her shirt-blouse. 'On that question, the trustees have made their views perfectly plain.' The Head tightened her rolled sleeve above her elbow and unpicked her gold watch from her wrist. 'You are, in their opinion, entitled to no financial package whatsoever.'

232

'How dare they!' Marion spluttered furiously.

'But I find myself agreeing with you,' Felicity Flint purred.

Marion, perceiving a change of mind, tossed her head back. 'Of course you do. I should be fully rewarded. I'm due at least –'

'I have done my calculations, and believe me, you are going to get everything due to you. I promise.'

Unaware of the delicious irony, Marion smiled smugly and turned to depart in triumph.

'Stop,' the Head barked.

Marion paused at the study door.

'Get back here and strip. Strip down and give me your bare bottom, bitch. I promised you full settlement and by God full settlement is exactly what my cane is going to give you.'

Emma and Kate both advanced, bearing down on the powerful gym mistress. Marion squared her shoulders.

'Don't forget the video tape, Miss Aylott-Inche. How instructive it would prove to any recruitment agencies seeking to fill vacancies for the post of gym mistress.'

'You wouldn't!'

'Consider carefully before you call my bluff. I believe the cards are all in my hand.'

And Marion knew she had a busted flush. Her pale complexion, hopeless gaze and drooping head betrayed her empty hand.

Kate and Emma unceremoniously stripped the gym mistress. She struggled half-heartedly, more in a squall of rage than real resistance. She was easily overwhelmed despite her lithe, agile strength. Proudly, they presented her, head bowed in her nakedness and shame, to the stern gaze of Dr Flint.

The Head casually nodded to her desk, instructing Marion to approach it. Marion refused, her shrill voice protesting angrily as she tried in vain to conceal her nipples and pubic nest from Dr Flint's searching eyes.

'I believe I told you to approach the desk and bend over, did I not? Hmm? Very well then. Across the desk,

Aylott-Inche. And be quick about it. I haven't got all day. Only –' the Head lowered her voice to a curdling whisper '– all morning.'

The gym mistress trod the carpet in mounting dread. Her toes whitened as she gripped the pile fiercely, 'Across the desk, at once. I am going to make sure that you taste the pain you have been inflicting on the innocent. Oh, yes, Aylott-Inche. It is time for you to be repaid in full. In your own coinage.'

'I was only –'

'Abusing the position of trust you enjoyed. Intimate instruction is the method here at Laments. Not your brutal bullying. That's it, down across the desk. Feet wider, if you will. Give me your bottom for my bamboo.'

The gym mistress meekly complied, bending face down across the polished surface of the desk.

'Gagged?' Kate enquired politely.

'I'll have her raw. Better to hear her squeal. Instant evidence of pain – Litmus test for any punisher. The cries of the punished, along with their reddening stripes.'

'The girls?' Emma wondered.

'Mme Puton has been instructed to take them all for a good long walk. They should have achieved the perimeter wall by now. From there, no doubt the market day bus will pick them up and take them into town,' the Head predicted omnisciently. 'There, Mme Puton will purchase nylon stockings, lipsticks and goodness knows what wickedness. I gave her fifty pounds to do so. A little treat. Especially tonight, when she will be called upon to help them dress and apply make-up.'

Emma grinned.

'There is no one here to be disturbed by her howling under my lash,' Dr Flint murmured. 'Except ourselves, of course.'

The desk creaked softly under Marion's weight. Pinning her outstretched arms into the desktop, Emma and Kate battled to trap and control the nude's splayed legs at each ankle, locking Marion into the punishment position.

'In natural justice, to be sure, both of you should be allowed to whip the bitch,' Dr Flint conceded. 'I know how much both of you have suffered at her hands. Indeed, what lengths you went to and what sacrifices you both made to save Laments. From her. For me. But –' her voice rose sharply '– as Head of Laments it is as much my duty as my desire to personally administer her punishment.'

Kate and Emma bowed to the Head's decision.

'You will remain, as my loyal deputies, to observe that full justice is done. And I trust the experience will be a pleasurable one for you both.'

'Deputies?' they whispered excitedly.

'No, I did not say that, exactly.'

Kate and Emma blushed in confusion.

'I said, and I meant, loyal deputies. She –' the Head tapped the bare bottom of her former bursar and bullying gym mistress '– was a deputy. But not, I now learn, a loyal one.'

'But I'm not sure –' Emma murmured.

'You have both more than proved your worth, and will make excellent deputies. Laments is lucky, as am I, to have you, Emma. And of course, you, Kate.'

They thanked the Head and kissed above the bare buttocks below.

'My first decision as re-instated Head.' Dr Flint nodded judiciously, extracting her cane unhurriedly from the fumed oak chest of drawers. 'And it was a decision that gave me a great deal of pleasure. As will the second decision I took. The decision to punish this bitch.'

Despite their dominant stance above her bending nakedness, Marion wriggled and writhed. 'Hold her hard,' the Head warned.

Kate and Emma glanced across their jerking captive. Intuitively, they both reached down, sliding their hands to meet at Marion's proud bush. As their hands became fists, tugging firmly, Marion became rigid – rigidly obedient as her pubic coils and outer labia were painfully yanked.

Swishing her bamboo cane twice, the Head sliced it down through the air. The thin whistle's cruel note brought Marion up a fraction on her scrabbling toes despite the firm control at her pubic delta. Emma and Kate tightened their grip on her nest, stretching the tugged flesh-lips sharply. Their action rendered their victim utterly immobile. Marion was now bare bottomed, bending and helpless before the bamboo.

The Head turned, cane raised, and briskly saluted the tennis amazons gazing down from the study wall. Dr Flint returned to address her former deputy's buttocks, bringing the quivering tip of her cane down to the bulging cheeks. Their smoothness tightened at the cane's dominant tap-tap-tap against their curves.

Marion cursed, struggling desperately.

The gym mistress grunted as she slumped back down into the desk, her hot breath clouding its polished sheen. The cane caressed the outer curves of her upturned cheeks, indenting their swell as Dr Flint exerted a little pressure. The gym mistress clenched her buttocks – prompting her punisher to snarl with displeasure.

Felicity Flint, standing directly behind the bending nude, stepped back in order to level the tip of her whippy wood at the upper vanishing point of the tightly creased cleft. Twisting the cane, and driving it inwards, she forced the cleft to widen imperceptibly before slowly dragging the cane down to trace the dark divide between the swollen cheeks.

'Relax your buttocks, bitch. I want them big and soft; so that they soak up every stinging stroke.'

Marion attempted to tread the air with her left foot. Kate squeezed her fist tightly, instantly returning her victim rigidly into the prescribed position for pain.

'Big and soft, bitch. I'm waiting.'

Emma gazed down and saw the buttocks unclench, loosen and joggle slightly as the gym mistress sullenly obeyed the Head's stern command.

The clock on the wall showed eight minutes to ten. The cane sliced down seven times by the time it showed a minute past the hour – about a stroke a minute, Emma calculated. A slow, searching punishment. And such control of pace. Such self-possession in Dr Flint. Such a display of supreme and absolute assurance. Such total domination.

Swish, slice. Swish, swipe.

There came a gasp of exertion from the punisher – as if she were serving an ace across the net. The shrill whisper of the venomous cane was like a ball whizzing through the singing air. The dull grunt of the bare-bottomed gym mistress was like the groan of the beaten player after a punishing set.

Swish, swipe. Swish, slice.

10.23 a.m. Already, some thirty strokes had whipped down to stripe and sear the defenceless cheeks.

Marion Aylott-Inche's screams grew louder, more lurid. Unpocketing a tennis ball, the Head forced it in between the snarling, stretched lips of the squealing gym mistress.

Swish, whomp. The hypnotic hiss-lash of the cane as it swiped the jerking buttocks viciously sucked Emma down into a deliciously mesmeric trance. Glancing down briefly just in time to see the cane bequeath yet another crimson stripe to the bluish-purple weals, Emma shivered. Such a whipping was almost inconceivable. And yet it was happening. Here and now. Her hands were filled with the struggling flesh of the naked woman being caned. Her eyes and ears were filled with evidence of Marion's dark sorrow. Her nipples were hardened by it. Emma's cleft ached sweetly from it. Her slit seethed.

Swish, swipe. Swish, swipe. Five minutes to eleven. Dr Flint paused, dragged her skirt up over her hips and thumbed her *broderie Anglais* knickers down. The lace strained between her bronzed thighs.

11.24 a.m. Shit – that's how many strokes? But Emma had lost track. It had all become almost too much for her spinning brain to bear. Almost. Eighty-five strokes, a tiny voice whispered with goblin-glee into her conscious mind. Eighty-five. Emma started to come. Oh, shit, no! Not now. She glanced across at Kate. The dark eyes told their own story, boldly confessing all. Kate had orgasmed at the seventy-third stroke.

Dr Flint, allowing the cool morning air to play at her hot slit, quietly placed the cane down upon the desk top. Four and a half deliberate inches from Marion's tear-drowned eyes. Extracting the tennis ball from the punished nude's mouth, the Head held it up. Emma and Kate shuddered. It had almost been bitten clean through.

'Agony made visible. Another little trophy from the great game,' Dr Flint whispered, turning the wet, shredded ball around in her fingers. Stepping up to the bamboo-savaged buttocks, she casually – contemptuously – dried her wetness on their hot curves. Dragging up her lace knickers and smoothing down her skirt, she stretched across to pluck up her cane.

'I am going for a little walk in the herb garden, my dears,' she said softly. 'I want her out of here and well away from Laments by noon. Sharp. Until then, my dears, she is yours.'

Silently returning the chewed tennis ball and bamboo cane to the top drawer in the fumed oak chest, the Head returned to the desk with a wickedly ribbed red rubber dildo and two dimpled table-tennis bats.

Emma thumbed the tiny pinpricks of hard rubber on the surface of her bat. In a sudden shaft of late morning sunlight, the tip of the ten-inch dildo sparkled.

'I trust, my dears,' the Head whispered, 'that you will use your twenty-eight minutes imaginatively. Yes, by all means, be imaginative,' she counselled, 'but above all, be brutal.'

Two days later, Dr Flint intercepted Emma as she was bringing her money-management tutorial to a satisfactory conclusion.

'Something I want you to see.'

More timetable changes? Making total tennis an all-embracing project was proving something of a challenge. A rewarding challenge, but tricky. To date, Mme Puton had only managed to get her class to chant out '*Quinze-L'Amour*'.

'This way,' the Head chivvied, barely able to conceal her pleasure.

What on earth? New designs for pert, tight-fitting uniforms? Letters of application for the three tennis-coach posts recently advertised?

Laments had been humming. With the sudden departure of so many staff, departures yet to be replaced, Dr Flint, Emma, Kate and Mme Puton had been working hard to maintain good order and discipline. The pupils had been wonderful throughout the turmoil but Laments was Laments and bottoms had to be bared and beaten.

'Keep your eyes closed until I say so,' Felicity Flint warned. Emma felt the gravel scrunch under feet.

'There.'

Emma squealed when she opened her eyes and saw the low, sleek lines of The Beast glinting in the sunlight.

'Tracked her down eventually. Told the trustees we needed transport, being off the beaten track. They don't know a handcart from a hatchback. Pleased?'

Emma skipped around The Beast twice before rejoining the Head and, hugging her affectionately, kissing Felicity Flint full on the mouth.

'Goodness,' Dr Flint gurgled, 'no need for that. Not here, not now. Later, perhaps,' she murmured. 'Pop along to my study this evening after supper,' she suggested in a conspiratorial whisper, 'and we can plan some summer picnics. Perhaps a spin, next Sunday?'

'I can't seem to make sense of this spread sheet,' Ann Cordery said, approaching Emma's desk after class.

Emma looked up, her throat tightening. The pulse at her temple quickened.

'Can you explain?' the girl pleaded, furrowing her pretty forehead deliciously.

Emma calculated quickly. Not the figures on the spread sheet. Her chances of avoiding detection. Kate had a suspicion about Emma's hots for the Cordery girl. But, Emma remembered, Kate was busy conducting the three new tennis coaches around the grounds. And Mme Puton was still with the Head, deciding on which uniform was going to bear the recently devised Laments logo: a sheaf of canes, above the legend *Ameliorement par la douleur*. The departure from the more traditional Latin had been justified by the exactness of the French phrase.

'Will you?'

Ann Cordery nestled closer to the desk, willingly accepting Emma's hand up her short pleated skirt. The fabric danced at Emma's knuckles. Nestling closer, Ann Cordery eagerly accepted Emma's controlling palm beneath her tiny skirt, thrusting her tightly cottoned-pantied cheeks into the dominant caress of her beautiful tutor.

'I – I –' Ann stuttered, bowing her reddening face in shame.

'Something distracted you, perhaps?'

'Yes.'

'You were playing with yourself?'

'Mmm.'

'And what were you thinking about as you played with pussy?'

'You,' Ann Cordery confessed simply. 'I thought of you. Spanking me. You haven't done so. Yet.'

'We can't have you being distracted from your prep, can we?' Emma whispered, taloning the captive buttock's softness. 'Across my knee. Panties down, if you please.'

It was the end of the first week of March. Yellow daffodils were sprouting on the edge of the dense copse. Inside the dark spinney, vixens barked at night to attract a mate.

Kate and Felicity Flint were strolling arm in arm down the darkened corridor. At the open door of the junior dorm, they heard smothered squeals.

'Who is on dorm patrol tonight?' the Head enquired.

'Emma,' Kate whispered.

'Settling in well, isn't she? Between us, we've made her a mistress Laments can be proud of.'

Inside the junior dorm, Bubble and Squeak, caught by Emma tying up a little redhead with the new regulation pearl grey tights, were trembling by their beds. Around the darkened dorm, all the other girls were peeping over their duvets as Emma methodically rolled up the grey tights before restoring them to their rightful place.

Sitting on the bed, she beckoned Bubble forward and, skilfully grappling the wriggling nude, spread her competently across her lap.

240

The staccato of ringing spanks brought a shrill response from the punished schoolgirl as her soft bottom reddened and bounced.

At the door, Kate placed her lips at Dr Flint's ear.

'I do believe Bubble's just squeaked.'

Four minutes later, after the second spanking came to its sharp conclusion, Dr Flint peeped through the open door into the dorm. In the pool of yellow light from the bedside bulb, she spotted the shine of the darkening stain on Emma's nylon-stockinged thighs. Pressing her lips to Kate's ear, she gurgled triumphantly, 'And I do believe Squeak has just bubbled.'

Nexus

NEXUS NEW BOOKS

To be published in June

DRAWN TO DISCIPLINE
Tara Black
£5.99

Student Judith Wilson lands a job at the Nemesis Archive, an institution dedicated to the documentation of errant female desire, under the imperious Samantha James. Unable to accept correction at the hands of the Director, she is forced to resign. But one manuscript in particular has awoken her guilty fascination with corporal punishment, and leads her to its author and her obscure Rigorist Order in Brittany. The discipline practised there brings Judith's assertive sexuality into a class of its own, and she returns to the Archive to bring her wayward former co-workers to heel.

ISBN 0 352 33626 9

SLAVE REVELATIONS
Jennifer Jane Pope
£5.99

The third book in Jennifer Jane Pope's *Slave* series continues the story of the bizarre pony-carting institution hidden from prying eyes on a remote Scottish island. Those who seek to investigate befall some curious fates: Tommy is now Tammy and Alex is – well, still not at all happy with pony-girl slavery. And who or what has given the pony-girls their genetically re-engineered pain thresholds?

ISBN 0 352 33627 7

PLEASURE ISLAND
Aran Ashe
£5.99

The beautiful Anya, betrothed to the prince of Lidir, has set sail for his kingdom. On the way, her ship is beset by pirates. Captured and put into chains, Anya is subjected to a harsh shipboard regime of punishment and cruel pleasures at the hands of the captain and his crew. When landfall is made on a mysterious island populated by dark-eyed amazons, Anya plots her escape, unaware of the fate that awaits anyone who dares to venture ashore. A Nexus Classic.

ISBN 0 352 33628 5

To be published in July

PENNY PIECES
Penny Birch
£5.99

Penny Pieces is a collection of Penny Birch's tales of corporal punishment, public humiliation and perverted pleasures from nettling to knicker-wetting. But this time Penny lets her characters do the talking. Here she brings you *their* stories: there's Naomi, for instance, the all-girl wrestler; or Paulette, the pretty make-up artist who's angling for a spanking. Not least, of course, there's Penny herself. Whether finding novel uses for a climbing harness, stuck in a pillory, or sploshing around in mud, Penny's still the cheekiest minx of them all.

ISBN 0 352 33631 5

PLEASURE TOY
Aishling Morgan
£5.99

Set in an alternate world of gothic eroticism, *Pleasure Toy* follows the fortunes of the city state of Suza, led by the flagellant but fair Lord Comus and his Ladyship, the beautiful Tian-Sha. When a slaver, Savarin, appears in their midst, Comus and his ursine retainer, Arsag, force him to flee, leaving behind the collection of bizarre beasts he had captured. Their integration into Suzan life creates new and exciting possibilities for such a pleasure-loving society. But Suza has not heard the last of the slaver, and its inhabitants soon find that Savarin's kiss is more punishing than they had thought.

ISBN 0 352 33634 X

LETTERS TO CHLOE
Stefan Gerrard
£5.99

The letters were found in a locked briefcase in a London mansion. Shocking and explicit, they are all addressed to the same mysterious woman: Chloe. It is clear that the relationship between the writer and Chloe is no ordinary one. The letters describe a liaison governed by power; a liaison which transforms an innocent young woman into a powerful sexual enigma. Each letter pushes Chloe a little nearer to the limits of sexual role-play, testing her obedience, her willingness to explore ever more extreme taboos until, as events reach their climax, the question must be asked: who is really in control? A Nexus Classic.

ISBN 0 352 33632 3

If you would like more information about Nexus titles, please visit our website at www.nexus-books.co.uk, or send a stamped addressed envelope to:

Nexus, Thames Wharf Studios,
Rainville Road, London W6 9HA

BLACK LACE NEW BOOKS

To be published in June

STRICTLY CONFIDENTIAL
Alison Tyler
£5.99

Carolyn Winters is a smooth-talking disc jockey at a hip LA radio station. Although known for her sexy banter over the airwaves, she leads a reclusive life. Carolyn grows dependent on living vicariously through her flirtatious roommate Dahlia, eavesdropping and then covertly watching as her roommate's sexual behaviour becomes more and more bizarre. But Carolyn's life is thrown into chaos when Dahlia is murdered, and she must overcome her fears – and possibly admit to her own voyeuristic pleasures – in order to bring the killer to justice.

ISBN 0 352 33624 2

SUMMER FEVER
Alison Ricci
£5.99

Lara McIntyre has lusted after artist Jake Fitzgerald for almost two decades. As a warm, dazzling summer unfolds, she makes a journey back to the student house where they first met, determined to satisfy her physical craving somehow. And then, ensconced in the old beach house once more, she discovers her true sexual self. Playing with costume, cosmetics, blatant exhibitionism and the inspiration of a younger lover, the hot frenzied season builds to a peak – but not without complications.

ISBN 0 352 33625 0

CONTINUUM
Portia Da Costa
£5.99

When Joanna Darrell agrees to take a break from an office job that has begun to bore her, she takes her first step into a new continuum of strange experiences. She is introduced to people whose way of life revolves around the giving and receiving of enjoyable punishment, and she becomes intrigued enough to experiment. Drawn in by a chain of coincidences, like Alice in a decadent wonderland, she enters a parallel world of perversity and unusual pleasure. A Black Lace Special Reprint.

ISBN 0 352 33620 8

To be published in July

SYMPHONY X
Jasmine Stone
£5.99

Katie is a viola player running away from her cheating husband and humdrum life. The tour of Symphony Xevertes not only takes her to Europe but also to the realm of deep sexual satisfaction. She is joined by a dominatrix diva and a bass singer whose voice is so low he's known as the Human Vibrator. After distractions like these, how will Katie be able to maintain her wild life and allow herself to fall in love again?

ISBN 0 352 33629 3

OPENING ACTS
Suki Cunningham
£5.99

When London actress Holly Parker arrives in a remote Cornish village to begin rehearsing a new play, everyone there – from her landlord to her theatre director – seems to have an earthier attitude towards sex. Brought to a state of constant sexual arousal and confusion, Holly seeks guidance in the form of local therapist, Joshua Delaney. He is the one man who can't touch her – but he is the only one she truly desires. Will she be able to use her new-found sense of sexual adventure to seduce him?

ISBN 0 352 33630 7

THE SEVEN-YEAR LIST
Zoe le Verdier
£5.99

Julia is an ambitious young photographer. In two weeks' time she is due to marry her trustworthy but dull fiancé. Then an invitation to a college reunion arrives. Julia remembers that seven years ago herself and her classmates made a list of their goals and ambitions. Old rivalries, jealousies and flirtations are picked up where they were left off and sexual tensions run high. Soon Julia finds herself caught between two men but neither of them are her fiancé. How will she explain herself to her friends? And what decisions will she make? A Black Lace Special Reprint.

ISBN 0 352 33254 9

NEXUS BACKLIST

This information is correct at time of printing. For up-to-date information, please visit our website at www.nexus-books.co.uk

All books are priced at £5.99 unless another price is given.

Nexus books with a contemporary setting

ACCIDENTS WILL HAPPEN	Lucy Golden ISBN 0 352 33596 3	☐
ANGEL	Lindsay Gordon ISBN 0 352 33590 4	☐
THE BLACK MASQUE	Lisette Ashton ISBN 0 352 33372 3	☐
THE BLACK WIDOW	Lisette Ashton ISBN 0 352 33338 3	☐
THE BOND	Lindsay Gordon ISBN 0 352 33480 0	☐
BROUGHT TO HEEL	Arabella Knight ISBN 0 352 33508 4	☐
CANDY IN CAPTIVITY	Arabella Knight ISBN 0 352 33495 9	☐
CAPTIVES OF THE PRIVATE HOUSE	Esme Ombreux ISBN 0 352 33619 6	☐
DANCE OF SUBMISSION	Lisette Ashton ISBN 0 352 33450 9	☐
DARK DELIGHTS	Maria del Rey ISBN 0 352 33276 X	☐
DARK DESIRES	Maria del Rey ISBN 0 352 33072 4	☐
DISCIPLES OF SHAME	Stephanie Calvin ISBN 0 352 33343 X	☐
DISCIPLINE OF THE PRIVATE HOUSE	Esme Ombreux ISBN 0 352 33459 2	☐

DISCIPLINED SKIN	Wendy Swanscombe ISBN 0 352 33541 6	☐
DISPLAYS OF EXPERIENCE	Lucy Golden ISBN 0 352 33505 X	☐
AN EDUCATION IN THE PRIVATE HOUSE	Esme Ombreux ISBN 0 352 33525 4	☐
EMMA'S SECRET DOMINATION	Hilary James ISBN 0 352 33226 3	☐
GISELLE	Jean Aveline ISBN 0 352 33440 1	☐
GROOMING LUCY	Yvonne Marshall ISBN 0 352 33529 7	☐
HEART OF DESIRE	Maria del Rey ISBN 0 352 32900 9	☐
HIS MISTRESS'S VOICE	G. C. Scott ISBN 0 352 33425 8	☐
HOUSE RULES	G. C. Scott ISBN 0 352 33441 X	☐
IN FOR A PENNY	Penny Birch ISBN 0 352 33449 5	☐
LESSONS IN OBEDIENCE	Lucy Golden ISBN 0 352 33550 5	☐
NURSES ENSLAVED	Yolanda Celbridge ISBN 0 352 33601 3	☐
ONE WEEK IN THE PRIVATE HOUSE	Esme Ombreux ISBN 0 352 32788 X	☐
THE ORDER	Nadine Somers ISBN 0 352 33460 6	☐
THE PALACE OF EROS	Delver Maddingley ISBN 0 352 32921 1	☐
PEEPING AT PAMELA	Yolanda Celbridge ISBN 0 352 33538 6	☐
PLAYTHING	Penny Birch ISBN 0 352 33493 2	☐
THE PLEASURE CHAMBER	Brigitte Markham ISBN 0 352 33371 5	☐
POLICE LADIES	Yolanda Celbridge ISBN 0 352 33489 4	☐
SANDRA'S NEW SCHOOL	Yolanda Celbridge ISBN 0 352 33454 1	☐

SKIN SLAVE	Yolanda Celbridge	☐
	ISBN 0 352 33507 6	
THE SLAVE AUCTION	Lisette Ashton	☐
	ISBN 0 352 33481 9	
SLAVE EXODUS	Jennifer Jane Pope	☐
	ISBN 0 352 33551 3	
SLAVE GENESIS	Jennifer Jane Pope	☐
	ISBN 0 352 33503 3	
SLAVE SENTENCE	Lisette Ashton	☐
	ISBN 0 352 33494 0	
SOLDIER GIRLS	Yolanda Celbridge	☐
	ISBN 0 352 33586 6	
THE SUBMISSION GALLERY	Lindsay Gordon	☐
	ISBN 0 352 33370 7	
SURRENDER	Laura Bowen	☐
	ISBN 0 352 33524 6	
TAKING PAINS TO PLEASE	Arabella Knight	☐
	ISBN 0 352 33369 3	
TIE AND TEASE	Penny Birch	☐
	ISBN 0 352 33591 2	
TIGHT WHITE COTTON	Penny Birch	☐
	ISBN 0 352 33537 8	
THE TORTURE CHAMBER	Lisette Ashton	☐
	ISBN 0 352 33530 0	
THE TRAINING OF FALLEN ANGELS	Kendal Grahame	☐
	ISBN 0 352 33224 7	
THE YOUNG WIFE	Stephanie Calvin	☐
	ISBN 0 352 33502 5	
WHIPPING BOY	G. C. Scott	☐
	ISBN 0 352 33595 5	

Nexus books with Ancient and Fantasy settings

CAPTIVE	Aishling Morgan	☐
	ISBN 0 352 33585 8	
THE CASTLE OF MALDONA	Yolanda Celbridge	☐
	ISBN 0 352 33149 6	
DEEP BLUE	Aishling Morgan	☐
	ISBN 0 352 33600 5	
THE FOREST OF BONDAGE	Aran Ashe	☐
	ISBN 0 352 32803 7	
MAIDEN	Aishling Morgan	☐

	ISBN 0 352 33466 5	☐
NYMPHS OF DIONYSUS £4.99	Susan Tinoff ISBN 0 352 33150 X	
THE SLAVE OF LIDIR	Aran Ashe ISBN 0 352 33504 1	☐
TIGER, TIGER	Aishling Morgan ISBN 0 352 33455 X	☐
THE WARRIOR QUEEN	Kendal Grahame ISBN 0 352 33294 8	☐

Edwardian, Victorian and older erotica

BEATRICE	Anonymous ISBN 0 352 31326 9	☐
CONFESSION OF AN ENGLISH SLAVE	Yolanda Celbridge ISBN 0 352 33433 9	☐
DEVON CREAM	Aishling Morgan ISBN 0 352 33488 6	☐
THE GOVERNESS AT ST AGATHA'S	Yolanda Celbridge ISBN 0 352 32986 6	☐
PURITY	Aishling Morgan ISBN 0 352 33510 6	☐
THE TRAINING OF AN ENGLISH GENTLEMAN	Yolanda Celbridge ISBN 0 352 33348 0	☐

Samplers and collections

NEW EROTICA 4	Various ISBN 0 352 33290 5	☐
NEW EROTICA 5	Various ISBN 0 352 33540 8	☐
EROTICON 1	Various ISBN 0 352 33593 9	☐
EROTICON 2	Various ISBN 0 352 33594 7	☐
EROTICON 3	Various ISBN 0 352 33597 1	☐
EROTICON 4	Various ISBN 0 352 33602 1	☐

Nexus Classics

A new imprint dedicated to putting the finest works of erotic fiction back in print.

AGONY AUNT	G.C. Scott	☐
	ISBN 0 352 33353 7	
BOUND TO SERVE	Amanda Ware	☐
	ISBN 0 352 33457 6	
BOUND TO SUBMIT	Amanda Ware	☐
	ISBN 0 352 33451 7	
CHOOSING LOVERS FOR JUSTINE	Aran Ashe	☐
	ISBN 0 352 33351 0	
DIFFERENT STROKES	Sarah Veitch	☐
	ISBN 0 352 33531 9	
EDEN UNVEILED	Maria del Rey	☐
	ISBN 0 352 33542 4	
THE HANDMAIDENS	Aran Ashe	☐
	ISBN 0 352 33282 4	
HIS MISTRESS'S VOICE	G. C. Scott	☐
	ISBN 0 352 33425 8	
THE IMAGE	Jean de Berg	☐
	ISBN 0 352 33350 2	
THE INSTITUTE	Maria del Rey	☐
	ISBN 0 352 33352 9	
LINGERING LESSONS	Sarah Veitch	☐
	ISBN 0 352 33539 4	
A MATTER OF POSSESSION	G. C. Scott	☐
	ISBN 0 352 33468 1	
OBSESSION	Maria del Rey	☐
	ISBN 0 352 33375 8	
THE PLEASURE PRINCIPLE	Maria del Rey	☐
	ISBN 0 352 33482 7	
SERVING TIME	Sarah Veitch	☐
	ISBN 0 352 33509 2	
SISTERHOOD OF THE INSTITUTE	Maria del Rey	☐
	ISBN 0 352 33456 8	
THE TRAINING GROUNDS	Sarah Veitch	☐
	ISBN 0 352 33526 2	
UNDERWORLD	Maria del Rey	☐
	ISBN 0 352 33552 1	

------ ✂ -----------------------------

Please send me the books I have ticked above.

Name   ....

Address   ....

            ....

            ....

            .... Post code ....

Send to: Cash Sales, Nexus Books, Thames Wharf Studios, Rainville Road, London W6 9HA

US customers: for prices and details of how to order books for delivery by mail, call 1-800-805-1083.

Please enclose a cheque or postal order, made payable to **Nexus Books Ltd**, to the value of the books you have ordered plus postage and packing costs as follows:
   UK and BFPO – £1.00 for the first book, 50p for each subsequent book.
   Overseas (including Republic of Ireland) – £2.00 for the first book, £1.00 for each subsequent book.

If you would prefer to pay by VISA, ACCESS/MASTER-CARD, AMEX, DINERS CLUB, AMEX or SWITCH, please write your card number and expiry date here:

....

Please allow up to 28 days for delivery.

Signature ....

------ ✂ -----------------------------